THE
WONDERS
OF
DOCTOR
BENT

PAUL CRAWFORD

CRANTHORPE
—MILLNER—
PUBLISHERS

Copyright © Paul Crawford (2025)

The right of Paul Crawford to be identified as author of this work has been asserted by them in accordance with section 77 and 78 of the Copyright, Designs and Patents Act 1988.

All rights reserved. No part of this publication may be reproduced, stored in a retrieval system, or transmitted in any form or by any means, electronic, mechanical, photocopying, recording, or otherwise, without the prior permission of the publishers.

Any person who commits any unauthorised act in relation to this publication may be liable to criminal prosecution and civil claims for damages.

This book is a work of fiction. Names, characters, places and incidents are either products of the author's imagination or are used fictitiously. Any resemblance to actual events or locales or persons, living or dead, is entirely coincidental.

First published by Cranthorpe Millner Publishers (2025)

Printed and bound in the UK through Xpedient Book Print

ISBN 978-1-80378-265-2 (Paperback)

www.cranthorpemillner.com

Cranthorpe Millner Publishers

PRAISE FOR
THE WONDERS OF DOCTOR BENT

"Crawford is a master storyteller. Be prepared to be taken on a thrilling adventure that delves into the very essence of what makes us human..." – Professor Ahmed Hankir, Consultant Psychiatrist, author of *The Breakthrough*

"A brilliantly written thriller exploring the dire consequences of adverse childhood experiences, trauma, loss, grief and depression." – Gene Beresin MD, Professor of Psychiatry at Harvard Medical School

"A celebration of the resilience of the human spirit, Crawford's moving storytelling and vivid characters take the reader on an emotional journey of grief, loss, and love." – Thomas Curran, leading psychologist and author of *The Perfection Trap*

"A wonderful, wry and smart story." – Steve Schlozman MD, author of *The Zombie Autopsies*

"A beautifully written and engaging psychological thriller that will keep you thinking long after the final page." – Dr David Crepaz-Keay FRSPH, Mental Health Foundation

"Loved the book! An engaging and entertaining novel, offering a vividly realised version of life in the contemporary English midlands." – James Moran, Professor of Modern English Literature and Drama at The University of Nottingham

"Well-crafted and intriguing... an insightful novel portraying human fragility and weakness." – Ronnie Brown, author of the *Restless Souls* trilogy

"Enjoyably riveting... a subtle education on the jeopardy of mental illness, daily life in a forensic hospital, the hidden skills of mental health workers, and hearteningly, the power of an individual and a community to anchor and support." – Gaye Poole, author of *Edges of Me*

"A hair of the dog that bit us."

John Heywood, *Proverbes* (1546)

PROLOGUE

The yellow grass came into focus through a bank of mist. Above the fringes of white stood a blurred structure with indistinct material hanging at regular intervals. As the camera zoomed in, it looked like a swing, the kind found in any public park. The frame had no chains or seats. Just single bolts of some kind attached to the skulls of three corpses: two male and one female. All were naked except for khaki shorts. The men were slim and frail with hollowed abdomens. The woman was smaller, her exposed breasts like drips of candle wax. All wore boots on their feet. In fact, there were six different kinds on the three pairs of feet. The camera captured each immaculately polished piece of footwear secured by laces, hooks or Velcro. The bodies hung still, erect, arms at their sides in the breezeless air. All was quiet and nothing stirred for some time except the odd rabbit, invisible creatures in last year's leaves, or crows punctuating the sky. Then there was the sound of an engine and everything changed.

1

Jason knelt beside his twin brother's tombstone. He read the epitaph etched in the marble, shaking his head at "Aged 35". The whole thing seemed unreal. This was the first death in his family. Except his father, of course, but that never counted. He had hardly known or loved him. Jason had been close to Will, calling him Umbie because his black hair fell away from his head like an umbrella. It was an umbrella that he wished had stayed open but now lay closed beneath the heaped and settling soil. Umbie, who meant the most to Jason apart from his wife, Poppy, was now in the smallest of spaces, stinking, invisible.

The brothers had been close. They had gone to the same Catholic boarding school, Saint Ergonwald's, and were inseparable. There, Jason followed Umbie about like a barely detached shadow, bedding in the same dormitory, sitting next to him in class and often wearing the same expression, although they were not identical twins. Such was the intimacy of their joined childhood that the two brothers seemed to know what each other was thinking and feeling.

It was raining again with a gusting wind that threatened to unbutton Jason's coat. He felt the urge to fall prostrate, become soft and defeated. Yet he did not move. He refused to yield. He refused to cry. Instead, he settled for the illusion of tears brought by the rain gathering around his eyes and spilling down his cheeks. He watched the silver beads rolling from his black overcoat onto the coppery spikes of grass.

Jason pretended Umbie was walking around the gravestone

saying, "Look! Look! I am not dead. It was all a game." He wanted to see twigs snap under his brother's feet and the grass crease where he trod. As the squall diminished, Jason shook his head, dislodging a few droplets that had pooled together in the dent of his skull, sending them into the last, resilient hairs above his ears. He thought of the funeral, remembering how slippery the grass had been and how by pure luck the priest had not joined Umbie. Father O'Connell had stumbled towards the oblong hole. Instinctively, one of the altar boys had grabbed his cassock and changed his fate. It was rather funny, but laughter remained imprisoned for the day.

Jason bowed his head and vowed not to mourn, believing it would weaken the acid of revenge. He crouched down, checked the desire for grief and, screwing his fingers into a ball, hit his brother's newly installed tombstone. His fist thumped rhythmically, making splashes. *I must be hard. I must bring about a second death*, he told himself. His eyes, like the mottling found in old books or slightly cloudy vinegar, widened and darkened at the thought. Jason imagined bringing Umbie's killer to his knees and mercilessly beating him to a pulp. He wanted to hear a sickening slash of muscle and the crack of marrow exposed. With these thoughts, he grew increasingly agitated, standing up and pacing about, his coat unfolding, his hand brushing water from his face. The rain had stopped now and the sun burst through. He sniffed and swallowed to halt the tears forming in the corners of his eyes. He threw his body one way and then the other, trying to shake himself hard and dry. He looked anywhere but at his brother's name on the headstone.

Just as he began to get a grip on his feelings, he heard the jolting report of a gun firing, clattering in the air. Jason cast around looking for the source of the explosion and finally caught sight of a figure at the far side of the cemetery, holding a smoking shotgun. It was Danny the gravedigger. From a grey, swirling flock in the darkening sky, a single pigeon fell to the earth. The rest peeled off and headed in an erratic wave, changing direction every few seconds. The rumour was true after all: the gravedigger really did shoot racing pigeons. As Jason watched, Danny appeared to break the gun as if it were a small, dark branch. Then, the gravedigger walked on between the plots before finally stooping down where the bird had fallen. Jason watched him and sensed that later that day Danny would brag about his marksmanship to the other gravediggers who kept their corner of The Sow's Ear. Jason's thoughts about the needless killing turned suddenly to the shotgun itself. *Now that is something I would like to get my hands on*, he thought. He would be shooting more than pigeons if he got the chance. Thinking about how he might acquire the weapon, he moved away from where his brother lay deep and still, and strode out through the gate into Barnabus Lane.

The lane curved down towards the railway line dividing Ardinweald in two. From the corner Jason approached, the old station ran eastward along the valley. It had closed years before when Jason was still at Saint Ergonwald's. The only trains that ran the line now carried radioactive waste to dumping grounds west of Ardinweald, skirting the city of Nottingham, before heading south towards Templeford. They ran at night, in the early hours, at high speed.

When finally he reached The Sow's Ear, Jason considered going in for a drink and hesitated on the pavement. As he did so, one of the younger gravediggers walked past him, left his spade outside against the wall and entered the bar. There was a noticeable rise in the conversation and then the sound cut off. Jason thought about drowning his sorrows. Perhaps he could find out more about the shotgun, although he was sure that Danny kept it in the old cemetery lodge. He decided there would be plenty of time to get information about the weapon and he had downed enough beer since his brother's death. Therefore, he passed on, the anticipated phantom tang of hops fading on his tongue. With a final look at the oldest pub in Ardinweald with its warped supports and buckled thatch, he crossed the lane, his wet coat hanging heavily on his back, his trousers uncomfortably damp, the pink-red sun unreal beneath the blackening cloud.

When Jason got home, Detective Inspector Mosby was waiting for him. The detective had striking looks for all the wrong reasons. Jason found it difficult not to stare at the ugly birthmark that spread across his cheek and down his neck like a butterfly with a wing missing. Inspector Mosby nodded as Jason approached. Already, Jason began reading his face as he might one of the numerous literary works stacked in his study. He noted the slightly closed, wincing eyes and the way his teeth repeatedly combed his lower lip. It was clear that there had been little progress in solving the murder case. No one had come forward in the weeks since the death of his brother. No further clues. No DNA match. Jason shook his head. He sensed the killer was getting away. Yet he was determined to bring him to justice.

'No news for me, then?' Jason diagnosed, taking out his keys and letting himself and the detective into the house.

'No, nothing as yet, I'm afraid.'

'Come through to the kitchen.'

Mosby followed Jason down the hallway to the rear of the spacious house.

'Drink?'

'Not for me, thanks.'

Jason switched on the kettle anyway and sat back against the washing machine. Inspector Mosby perched awkwardly on the rickety kitchen stool. They looked at each other for a few moments. Then Jason started up.

'I'll find him myself, you know,' he vowed. 'Not only find him, but leave no trace of him.' Here, Jason was already having fantasies about how he might dispose of the body. Yet, for all his bravado, he was unsure as to how he would find the killer in the first place.

'Now,' Mosby grunted, fiddling with his wedding ring, 'the law is the law, Dr Hemp, and the law decides who is guilty and punishes them.'

Jason barely listened, transposing a set of scales onto the detective's glasses.

'It's been a terrible business,' Mosby continued, 'and I'll be deaf to your threats, of course, but we really are doing our best. You know how it is.'

'No, I don't know! What the hell are your men doing?'

The outburst surprised the detective. The criticism stung him. He nudged his rimless glasses back up his nose and jutted out his chin. A hefty silence followed during which both men averted their eyes. Jason looked out of the window. Inspector Mosby took out a pad from his pocket and scribbled something. As the pen bled its symbols in neat, meticulous lines, the sun divided the tabletop and made him shield his eyes. Jason saw how dirty his collar was.

†

Jason kicked the mulch of last year's leaves gathered around the cemetery gates. He was back visiting his brother's tomb, feeling no one understood the depth of his grief, not even his wife. He stopped for a moment and looked at the rows of gravestones dipping away into the valley. The place was deserted and eerie, yet the atmosphere did not bother him. Jason was comfortable with the dead and continued along the gravel path, gazing down at Ardinweald's sunlit roofs, birdsong filtering into his hairy ears. Out beyond the valley, he could just make out the spire of Saint Ergonwald's, like a witch's finger on the horizon.

Pulling his collar up to block the cold morning wind, Jason ambled past yet another wire basket stuffed with rotting flowers. The gravel crunched beneath his leather-soled shoes.

He wondered when Professor Porter at the School of English would pester him to return from compassionate leave. These days, he considered the university a factory processing students like chickens and, most ironically, an anti-intellectual place. His colleagues had been supportive over Umbie's death, yet he knew they did not expect him to mourn indefinitely. The students needed their tutorials, but he still had to submit a monograph for the latest research assessment exercise and curriculum meetings loomed. Yet for the time being, he could not begin to consider returning to work. On those days that he did manage to get out of bed, he would spend most of his time obsessively scraping the internet for information about his brother's death.

Jason breathed deeply and pressed on, turning towards Umbie's grave, a low sun lighting his face and obscuring his view. As he approached the plot, he saw a figure standing beside it. It was his mother. She stood over the grave, her peach-skinned cheeks daubed with powder, her bony, meatless body robed in a coat she had bought from Oxfam. All her life she had given everything for her two boys, trying to keep the worst of their father from them, with his homemade beer and fondness for beatings. She lifted her head and managed a fragile smile.

'Hello, son,' she greeted him as he stepped over a discarded tin urn and drew close.

'Hi, Mum,' he said, kissing her on the cheek and putting an arm around her shoulders.

They stood, staring down at the now-familiar patch of earth. For several minutes, they said nothing. Then Mrs Hemp broke the silence.

'I can't believe he's dead, Jason.'

'Nor can I,' he said, giving her shoulder a further squeeze.

'He talks to me all the time,' she admitted. 'And I've seen him. Last night he stood at the end of my bed as real as you are now. He told me he was at peace.'

Jason shook his head pitifully. He looked sideways at her gentle, milky-blue eyes, loosening cheeks and mock fur gathered round her neck. On the lids of her eyes, the powder had come away, revealing shiny skin, as if newly hatched.

'He told me not to worry,' she whispered, her lips turning inwards and silvery beads catching in her sparse eyelashes. 'He's gone to a better place.'

Jason doubted that very much and stared at his mother's trembling lips. His eyes bulged with tears. Sensing the numbness of stone and the mockery of the sun, he asked his brother to help him find the killer, to point from beyond the grave. Yet Jason knew there would be no transmission. Only phantom comments would fill his head. His brother's tongue lay shrivelled and silent beneath his feet. With that awareness, Jason wiped his nose across his knuckles and blinked away the water gathering on his eyelids.

'I bought these,' his mother said quietly, crouching down and placing a delicate spray of gladiolus on her son's grave. She closed her eyes in prayer.

Jason shoved his hands into his pockets and shivered as she lost her composure once more. Her thin lips wobbled and her head shook. Powder broke away from her face. Her fine hair caught in the wind.

'My son!' she squealed, her fingers digging into her cheek, her eyes flinching. 'My baby!'

At that, she went into a fitful, frenzied dance, her handkerchief waving at the end of her manic fingertips, her pale-pink gums on show, revealing the join of her false teeth. Jason embraced her, gathering her to him, squeezing the diminutive cage of her body.

'How could they do this?' she screamed.

Jason said nothing. He tightened the grip of his big arm across her small, frail shoulders. 'Come on, now,' he said. 'It's all right. It's

OK.'

'He will not be alone, Jason,' Mrs Hemp insisted, wheezing asthmatically, beginning to blubber again. 'He'll have company. He won't be alone.'

'Of course not,' Jason comforted his mother, drawing her away from the tombstone.

Jason imagined Umbie suffering the ghostly presence of their father. The idea of his twin brother sharing an afterlife with the old drunk made him shudder. For some reason, Umbie had always come off worst in their father's rages fuelled by barely fermented, cloudy, homemade beer. "You'll never amount to anything," their father would slur, beating the eldest of the twins. "You were in such a rush to get into the world that you left your brain behind for your brother to pick up!" Umbie suffered from this nitpicking throughout his earliest years, losing the will to study his books. He had to endure the contrast with Jason who buckled down and gained the highest grades at Saint Ergonwald's. Yet he did not hold this against him. Years later, at Jason's doctoral graduation party, Umbie hugged his brother. "I am proud of you," he told him. "You are the brains of the family! As for me, from our childhood to this age, I have nothing to write home about." At that point, their red-faced father was slapping Jason on the back and announcing to anyone who would listen, "Here's my son, *Doctor* Hemp!"

Jason shook his head to dislodge his father's voice and guided his mother along the path, her body heaving with every sob. The branches of the trees curling above them flailed the vast sky, quite blind to the emotion below. A crow flew past nonchalantly, its jelly eyes aiming for one of the many wire bins. Jason watched it settle, quiver and shit on the crushed, rotting flowers. Gripping the collar of his dark coat, he dipped his big, balding head and guided his mother through the cemetery gates and down the winding driveway. When they reached the corner of Barnabus Lane, his mother pulled her arm free and adjusted the knot of her lace scarf.

'I want to be on my own,' she said, blowing her nose into her large, ever-present white handkerchief.

'I'll walk you home.'

'No,' she insisted. 'I can manage. Just leave me now, Jason. I'll be fine.' To reinforce her words, she began to walk at quite a pace, her heels scratching at the paving stones.

Jason stood perfectly still, watching her slim body shrink as she moved further and further away. She stumbled, corrected herself and disappeared out of view.

Jason turned and walked back along the driveway into the cemetery. He fought back tears, but could not prevent a shriek of agony from leaving his mouth. He wanted to destroy, break or crush something with his bare, raw hands and bite with his teeth. Yet there was nothing except air to chastise. His fists thrashed out madly. He wanted to screw his fingers into the trees around him, rip at the bark, crack his fingernails and bleed. Unseen, he wrestled with his thoughts, his teeth clamping, his head pounding.

Exhausted, Jason came back to Umbie's grave. He stared for a long time at it and then threw himself down on the grass. With his cheekbone resting against the white oblong of stone, he howled like a child.

'Umbie! You can't be dead!' he cried. Tears trickled down his cheek and dripped onto the stone, the image of his twin floating like a balloon at the back of his skull. 'Umbie!' He gazed at the blurred whiteness of stone, his heart tight, his mind scraped out.

After a while, he sat up, rubbing the hollows of his eyes, and looked around the cemetery. It was intensely quiet. No wind brushed at the wintry soil. Clouds had drifted like snow and blocked the sun. Two magpies clapped themselves into the sky above the observatory ruins, their stiff, papery tails fanning the already cool air. When he finally stood up, Jason caught sight of a raven hopping from one newly turned mound to another. He picked up a handful of green ornamental stones from a nearby grave and hurled them at the bird. It rose briefly into the air, showing its diamond-shaped tail and gurgling *kronk-kronk-kronk* before settling further away.

2

A whoosh of fire spread out across the ceiling like an upside-down orange sea. Umbie panicked, his heart crunching. All around him, the flames rolled and consumed. The air was dying. The roof was warping. His tongue was slipping into the back of his throat like a lizard trying to escape the heat. He had to think fast. A sudden wind of flame blew him through the air like a doll. He landed heavily at the main stairwell of the southernmost wing of the old hospital. It was ridiculous. He had few choices. If he ran down the stairs, he would burn to a crisp before he reached the bottom. His brain fizzed. He felt his flesh begin to cook. If he jumped down the well with his weak knees, he might break a leg or worse. It was not such a big drop and he would have a good chance of surviving it. If he stayed where he was, he faced certain death. He had no choice. He jumped, thrashing the air, and hit the stone-tiled floor.

The fall removed what little air stirred in his lungs, but he was alive at least. Choking, gasping, spewing, he rolled over, looking up at a burning, stairwell. He shook his head. *Keep cool. Think. Plan. Move.* That was what he did.

Umbie knew Pastures Hospital intimately. As a young man, he had worked there as a porter. He knew everything behind its red brick and white stone. He knew there were eighteen miles of telephone wire and thirty-five miles of gas, water and oxygen pipes. All of the twenty-seven-foot-wide pavilions stood on end would run for one mile. The staircases, altogether, rose higher than Blackpool Tower. Umbie could walk the old hospital in his dreams, down to the last converted sluice, to the wing where the electrical marvels of X-ray had once been, to the wrinkling blue paint of the now derelict WRVS hut. In his memory, he could still smell the disinfectant, the polish and the sweat of Pastures. It had pressed its olfactory thumbprint into his mind. He knew all the hidden spaces, especially the grid of underground tunnels running beneath the buildings, through which he and the other porters delivered food baskets to the wards, broken equipment to the workshops or the dead to the mortuary to spare the fears of other patients.

In its heyday, a generous horseshoe of woods and fields had surrounded Pastures. It was its own closed, little world. While many of the porters, domestics, caterers and clerical and administrative staff travelled to work by bus or train from various quarters of the city, the majority of nurses and doctors remained on-site, with a prefabricated social club, The Whistleblower, at the centre of their universe. It had been Umbie's favourite watering hole in his happier, portering days.

Now all that seemed a long time ago as he pulled his smoking body across the tiles towards the dark green door, the scorching fire goading his bruised muscles and jolted bones. At least his knees had held up in the fall, although his head had taken a bump. He kicked out like a frog with his bare feet, slipping and sliding, stars popping in his eyes. As he reached the door, his head became a whirligig and his extended hand doubled in his disrupted vision. His outstretched fingers gripped the brass knob and turned with such desperate hope that when it opened with the tiniest creak, the animal of his body threw itself through and down the cold, stone steps into pitch darkness. For once, the darkness held no fear. The darkness was pure joy.

Umbie lay quietly on his side for some time, drawing short breaths and attempting to get his thoughts together. This was difficult and his ears were full of rumbling sounds and sudden crashes. *Think*, he told himself. *Think your way forward*. Yet it was hard to think. When he did, his flimsy thoughts kept going back to the fire. It had been so sudden and fierce and surely inspired by some kind of accelerant. He suspected arson and that he was the target. After all, they had warned him what would happen if he ever crossed them. Well, he had certainly done that.

'Shit!' he cried out. 'Shit! Shit! Shit!' His knees throbbed with pain now that the adrenaline had begun to subside. All around him the rushing and hissing of air continued.

He lay on the cold ground, flexing his legs to test the damage of the fall and looked up through a panel of thick glass cobbles that brought dregs of light down into the tunnel from ground level. Umbie studied his cut and bruised hand. He could only see the vaguest edges of his flesh. His trousers felt wet with either blood or sweat. He turned on his side to inspect his legs, but could not distinguish colour. The rationed light left everything black.

There was the sound of an explosion of glass above. Then another, moments later. Umbie tried to comfort himself. He had survived the fire and the fall. The gang members who had tried to kill him had probably left by now, satisfied with a job well done. He set his head back down on the floor and looked up at the few cobbles of poor light. For now, he was safe here in the tunnel. Yet he knew that would all change once he got back above ground. He would have to lie low somewhere and keep out of sight for as long as possible. Curling his body and with his eyes wide to trace objects in the gloom, he conjured up a mental plan of the old hospital and visualised the grid of tunnels. He was in the main artery leading to the old workshops. All he had to do was make his way to one of the other staircases. As he moved forward, his mind jolted back to the night at The Sow's Ear when he had made a fateful decision.

†

It was a night filled with the sound of dominoes falling. Umbie had sat nearest the door as always. It had become a habit. He knew that if trouble broke out, he could easily make good his escape. He kept his hand of dotted bricks shielded from view as the other members of the gang slammed theirs down hard onto the table in a hypnotic rhythm. He counted the dots and began to work out the best odds. He looked around the cupped hands and the little pile of full and broken matchsticks that stood for money. It was a nice pot if he could win it. He concentrated and studied the blocks in his hand closely before slamming one down. As he quickly looked at his hand before focusing on the wider game, an argument blew up at the bar. Pike, a drunken punter, was having it out with Tom, the youngest of the gouty owner Frank's sons. Tom looked a pushover, but everyone knew he had one of the strongest kinds of defence.

'I have a knife in my pocket, so you'll serve me first!' the man shouted at him, to which Tom replied coolly, 'See that man there? He has a gun, so I'll serve him first!'

The bar erupted in laughter and the punter sucked in his face.

Unlike the other gang members playing dominoes, Umbie had a day job. He did not depend exclusively on the money that came from their criminal enterprise. Even better, he had worked out how to manipulate the gang to his benefit and bring in some serious cash. He smiled as he thought about the swindle that had already started to lift him out of the painful mediocrity of his life. Within weeks, he had managed to pay off the remaining mortgage on his small studio apartment at the new Pastures development. The con worked like a dream. As he read the dots on the blocks in his hand, he nodded confidently before smacking one down again on the table. A final six and blank finished the game and he quickly counted the matchsticks, taking note of what everyone owed him.

As the rest of the gang threw their remaining slabs into the middle of the table to go again, Umbie felt invincible. He was getting a much bigger slice of the cake than any one of them, and why not? He was the one taking the greatest risk. He was right at the business end of their illegal activity, exposed and likely to go away for a very long time if things ever got out. He gave this some thought as the matchsticks began to pile up again. His mind was not in the game now. He was thinking about how the gang would respond if they found out about the deception. He looked into the eyes of each member, assessing the risk and noting the level of threat each of them posed. They all thought Umbie was merely calculating the dots in their hands. Instead, he was having a good look inside, scrutinising the emptiness of their souls.

†

It had been a huge fire and Umbie wondered if it had killed anyone. He shivered with the thought. During his time working as a porter at the hospital, he had seen the damage that fire did to people who set themselves alight. How jolly they were without nerve endings. They would smile and joke as the water left their bodies and infection set in. It was a terrible thing to see. Soon afterwards, Umbie had the job of pushing them on a shrouded trolley through the network of tunnels to the mortuary.

As a siren wowed the air, he imagined the casualties from the fire. He shook his head. This was all because he had become greedy and double-crossed the gang. He knew there were families with children in the residential block. He had met some of them in the communal areas: the kid with the braces on his teeth and the little girl battling gravity on her oversized bicycle.

'Fucking hell!' he cursed.

Why did I do it? Why did I go and stick my head in the hornet's nest? Did I expect not to get stung? Now they were clearly onto him. He thought about all the consequences of his decision, stumbling along, a hand on the wall of the tunnel to steady himself.

Umbie suddenly wished he could go back to that simpler time of portering, of a less-than-satisfactory, uneventful life. He recalled wearing a plain magenta uniform and moving up and down the bleak hospital corridor, the longest in England, the spine of activity in Pastures. He had walked so many times under its first archway with the hospital's motto: *nunquam claudimus*. Sometimes the patients he pushed in wheelchairs would ask what it meant and Umbie delighted in applying his rudimentary Latin from his time at Saint Ergonwald's—trying to indicate that he was more than a simple porter. "It means we never close," he would tell them, which brought a puzzled "Uh?", "Oh!" or "24/7, right?". Umbie had his own rather morbid interpretation and had the habit of quietly murmuring, "Yes, we bloody do!" each time he passed under the gold-leafed words.

Portering was exhausting work. "Walk, walk, walk the corridor," he would complain to his brother Jason. "That's all I do." He hardly stopped. He was a faultless signpost to those lost within the walls of the hospital. In the rare moments of rest between moving patients or trolleys, he would hold back his shoulders and press his right foot firmly into the ground. It was how he liked to stand, his foot planted like a root, immovable. It was a foot of power, but also weakness. It was a foot of fear and pity. It was a sign of need as if what he had become would be lost if he lifted that foot of his. If he lifted it, he would weaken and surely, slowly decline and overturn the hospital maxim.

He had promised himself that one day he would amount to more than a porter. He would step out of the shadow of his older twin brother. All he needed was the right ladder to come along and he would climb it like a monkey. No sooner would his hand reach a higher rung than the other would overtake it and reach higher still. Up and up he would go, all the time seeking the approval his dead father could not provide, until his feet looked certain to beat his hands to the top. He would be more like Jason. He would be visible. He would be valued. He would be—*loved*.

Yet, for all his drive and ambition, there was still little to show off all these years later. He had moved from portering at the hospital to a job as a care assistant in a nursing home. It paid better, but he hated the work. Every day was the same: washing the stink from the fusty bodies of the residents, shaving the old men and feeding many of them so excruciatingly slowly with mashed-up food. He tired of holding plastic beakers to their rice paper lips and sitting on the arm of a chair watching endless daytime TV, listening to the babble, passing time, waiting, waiting, waiting for the shift to end. The successful life he dreamed about eluded him. Even when a ladder had finally presented itself in the swindle, the perfect crime, what then? Well, he knew the answer now. That ladder had turned into one hell of a snake.

†

The fire was raging at Pastures. A section of the roof collapsed and part of the recently constructed walls broke away. In the heat and confusion, firefighters raced to control the flames as ambulance crew and paramedics worked to revive some of the residents, especially a mother and young daughter who had inhaled the thick, acrid smoke. People were standing around with bonfire faces, as the police tried to get them to move away from the inferno. Jason was pushing through the crowd, pulling at shoulders, apologising as he squeezed through. He had heard about the fire. Now he saw and felt it.

'Hey, has anyone seen my brother?' he was shouting. 'My brother lives here!' He raced past a young boy coughing liquid smoke from his lungs and caught hold of a firefighter. 'Where's my brother? Have you seen him? He lives on the first floor. Will Hemp.'

The fire officer shook his head impatiently and waved him away.

There was another explosion that sent glass, bricks and slates raining down onto the service road.

'Get back!' demanded a police officer. 'Move away!'

Red sparks in the dying light swept over Jason's head. 'My brother's still in there!' he shouted, dancing round firefighters and their hosepipe. 'Umbie!'

He watched in desperation as the firefighters directed a jet of water at the broken windows of his brother's flat.

'Do something!'

The next explosion of glass sent Jason sprawling in the rubble. When he got up, he had a clear sensation that Umbie had gone, that he was no more. Paralysed by this thought, he stood up, trembling, with a gormless expression as a light drizzle slanted across the scene like blips on an old movie.

Down in the darkness, Umbie rested, savouring the cool air in his lungs. He guessed that his few possessions would now be fine ash rising in a plume over Sherwood Forest. Above his head, he could hear people shouting and the sound of heavy machinery. Now he focused on getting out of the network of tunnels. He was thirsty. The blood had dried on his skin and the pounding inside his skull had eased a little. He considered his options, squinting with the burden of thought into the darkness. There was another stairway further along the tunnel. However, they had so much trouble with tramps bedding down in the tunnels that the Residents Association had insisted on locking it. He would need to turn off to the left and try a different route.

Grimacing, Umbie hauled himself along. It was cold underground, especially with just a shirt on his back. Now and again, he heard the sound of water he knew came from the firefighting above ground. *You are a survivor! Visualise where you need to be. Push forward. Live.* Things could have been so much worse. He could so easily have broken his neck in the fall.

Umbie passed beneath another oblong of cobbled glass and feet moving across it. He calculated that he was where the service road branched off through the residential complex. In the glow of the fire, people were rushing back and forth and Umbie thought he caught sight of his brother standing for a moment on the transparent cobbles. It was difficult to say from that angle and through the glass. Umbie did not shout out. He knew that his voice would not carry. As he stared upward, a fat section of hosepipe slipped into view. A boot was kicking it into place. He thought he heard a man crying, 'Get back! Get back!' and then the pavement light filled with black rubber soles, churning up a thick, smearing mud.

Umbie turned once more to the task of moving forward, his knees seizing up. As the scraps of firelight filtered down, he felt anxious. He began to fear the tunnel had collapsed further along, trapping him. His heart pounded at the thought and he gasped for breath. He moved with more urgency, suddenly aware that the temperature had fallen noticeably. He might freeze to death in the tunnel. It was so bitterly cold outside.

He could only move slowly, gingerly, his knees heavy and swollen. His muscles had little spring to them and his hot, dry mouth was busily sucking for air as he travelled in small steps. Eventually, he found another stairway and managed to lever his body up each of the eight stone steps to the small platform running to the door. He reached for the large metal knob, turning it slowly, closing his eyes in hope, and pulled back.

'Please be open,' he muttered. There was no movement. 'Fucking hell,' he cried, shivering now, gloomy thoughts seeping into his mind.

He felt a deep and sudden chill grip his body, a terrible sinking of his bowels. His breathing was rapid and shallow, scooping for air.

He tried the door again, twisting the knob as far as it would go and yanking it backwards. There was no movement at first, but with several panicky attempts, it opened suddenly and he welcomed the cold draught of air that hit him. Quickly and despite the pain, he climbed out of the place, opposing, dark kidney shapes of his bare wet feet left on each step. Now he was on open ground and exposed. He looked anxiously around him and up at the clouds rushing by. Fear took hold of him again. *Were the assailants out here?* Perhaps they were still around, waiting to finish the job. Umbie hunkered down, keeping low, scanning the crowd of onlookers, police and firefighters, picking what looked like the smoothest path for his naked feet. He doubted that his attackers would try anything with so many police around. Before he could think another thought, a hand grabbed his shoulder and spun him around. Umbie's heart froze, cancelling its beats. He waited for the cold knuckle of a gun at his head or a paper-cut sensation across his neck. He fell to the ground, curling up protectively into a ball of flesh, eyes closing, expecting the end.

'Umbie!'

It was Jason. Umbie gingerly opened an eye and looked up into his brother's face, stretched taut, blackened by smoke.

'Fucking hell,' Umbie gasped, 'I thought you were *them*?'

'Them?' his brother asked. 'Who are you talking about?'

Umbie let his words fold away and accepted his brother's hand, pulling him to his feet. His knees creaked. He groaned and grimaced as Jason ushered him away from the building and the broken glass. Umbie kept his head down, but his eyes scoured for threat. He did not notice the figures standing further back in a pool of darkness with only the briefest glint of polished metal to give one of them away.

3

'Now, let's see,' said Inspector Mosby. 'I have here one of your previous statements.' He glanced into Jason's computer-blazed eyes. 'Shall I read it out?'

Jason shrugged his wide shoulders and began thinking about work again. He had been avoiding going into the School of English for weeks now and had a course on sixteenth-century Renaissance literature to deliver next semester. Yet he had too much on his mind. Somebody else would have to cover that module, he decided, watching Mosby flick through the thin pages of his black notebook. Jason picked at his nails, drawing dirt out and brushing it away to the floor. Irritated, he waited for the detective inspector to begin reading.

'Here we are,' Mosby said with a chirpy, annoying voice. 'Your statement runs as follows: "After the fire at Pastures, my brother came to live with us. He seemed very nervous and did not go out much. My wife and I thought that he might have developed some kind of post-traumatic disorder. He seemed preoccupied. He did not see a GP or anything. After a few weeks, he became more relaxed and we decided to go out for a drink at The Half Moon. On our return at about eleven thirty, the attack started in the subway. It all happened very quickly. A gang of three men came out of nowhere. They punched me to the ground. I tried to see their faces, but it was dark and I could not make them out. One of the assailants had a knife. I saw it flashing. He had Umbie by the throat. I got up and tried to stop him by pulling at his hair, but the others shoved and kicked me against the wall. When the gang ran off, I saw what they had done to my brother.

He was dead. His wallet lay empty on the ground next to him."'

Inspector Mosby licked his fingers and turned the page without looking up. Jason wiped his nose with a dry, crumbling piece of tissue.

The detective was shaking his head, closing the little book in a slow, dispirited way. Jason said nothing. He chewed his lip and gazed down at the floor.

'Unfortunately, it's not a great deal to go on,' added Mosby.

'No,' agreed Jason. 'But the hair I pulled from the man's head will help, surely? The man *is* the hair. Well, that's what you said.'

There was a protracted silence.

'Yes, if he's on our national database.'

The news was just what Jason did not want to hear. He had placed a great deal of hope in the science of DNA profiling. After the murder, he read about this and knew its power and reach. Now, he began shaking his head and drawing his lips inwards in dismay.

'Well, that's just great, isn't it?' he said finally.

'I agree it is very disappointing for all concerned, Dr Hemp. Sometimes new cases come onto the database. And if we do find a suspect, we can see if there's a match.'

Mosby wore his best conciliatory expression.

'If you find a suspect,' Jason muttered.

†

Jason sat in a hot bath, trying hard to relax. He always enjoyed a good soak and he needed as much comfort as possible just now. He did not believe Inspector Mosby would find his brother's killer. Whoever attacked Umbie was slipping through the fingers of justice as easily as bathwater. Jason looked at his body angling down towards the plughole and thought of his brother lying in his coffin. The satin enamel of the tub matched the silk of the wooden box's interior. Jason shuddered at the thought as his toe touched the cold tap and an icy trickle of water sped across his foot. He took refuge in the hot water, sinking himself deeper, knees higher, the bubbles catching his rounded chin. Slowly, the foam fizzed away as his big ribcage lifted free like an island, his heart beating tiny ripples into the water. Closing his eyes, Jason breathed steadily, moistly, sighing deeply. Yet his calm was soon broken.

Jason experienced another dream-like flashback of his brother's death. It was such that the swirl and buckle of snowflakes, blown about like little white flies, replaced the steaming water. It took a while for the shocking assault to subside and for Jason to regain composure. He panted, trying to stay calm, to quieten his beating heart. He had these sudden flashbacks or dream states regularly since the murder. They came during the day and at night, intruding without invitation, bringing his body close to exhaustion.

This time, the flashback provoked a random quote in his mind. It was from his PhD on the dramatist John Heywood: *"A hair of the dog that bit us."* The phrase literally struck him and made the flesh on his neck and head crawl. For with it came an idea—the most peculiar idea Jason had in his whole life—something irrational and superstitious, yet deliciously compelling. Still breathing heavily, he lay back down in the cooling bathwater and considered it. It was a crazy, weird thing to do, yet Jason suddenly felt that anything, however bizarre, was better than nothing—even something as ridiculous as what he now considered. After all, Inspector Mosby and his team had failed to track down Umbie's killer. DNA testing had found no one on the police database. Whoever killed Umbie was a clean skin. It looked increasingly likely that he would get away with it. The justice system had let him down and Jason pictured the attacker free and untouchable. That was an unbearable thought. The more he mulled this over, the more his strange idea grew on him. It was something rooted in a Catholic past. Although he rarely reflected on matters of faith or even his biblical studies, he now found a little relief in the possibility of bridging the spiritual world and summoning unseen forces into play. It would put things at a sacramental, magical level.

Despite the best efforts of Jason's neatly carved, rational brain struggling to accept the notion, part of him—a remnant—found it irresistible. He thought about what had sprung to mind some more before reaching down past his shiny knees to pull the plug. *A hair of the dog that bit us*, he repeated in his head several times over. It was as if his thesis had more to offer than tenure at the university. His mind had suddenly blown off the dust from the tome that no one else read and found a brilliant, dark kernel of an idea. Pleased with himself, impatient now to put the idea into play, he found and tugged the little chain at the end of the bath. Yet, when he brought his hand back, it hesitated at the scar just below his left knee. He fingered the soft, thin tissue and his mind wandered.

†

Saturday was a free day at Saint Ergonwald's, a day when the boys shut their books—something Jason struggled to do—and let their socks corrugate. Unlike the other boarders or dayboys, Umbie and Jason could not travel home. It was not that it was too far. It was just that their father insisted on them staying there. He did not want them around except for the odd holy day. He was far too busy with his scrap metal business, collecting the tote for the local parish church and brewing his homemade beer. It was enough, from his point of view, to have the twins back for holidays. If they did attempt an unscheduled visit, he would more than likely take off his belt to them. He judged them with the buckle and a limited mind. Both brothers had grown used to the situation. They accepted being part of an alternative, institutional family. The staff at Saint Ergonwald's could be strict about things like attending chapel and submitting homework on time, but otherwise, they were friendly and kind.

If nothing else, the threat of their father's beer-affected mood and having to witness their mother cowed all the time, kept the twins away.

With the weather so bright and warm, the brothers chose to visit Round Hill about five miles from the school and a similar distance from Ardinweald. On top of the hill stood an old locust tree with a rope from its thickest branch. The view from there was spectacular. On a clear day, the twins could see for miles all around. It was a waterless island. Jason brought along the packed lunch that the school cook had made up for the few resident boys who had not been able to go home. In the brown paper bag, he carried cheese-and-pickle sandwiches, overripe tomatoes, bruised apples and oatmeal biscuits. In addition to these, Umbie had purchased a large glass bottle of lemonade from the nearby corner shop. Full of the enthusiasm a morning can bring, they trod the five miles to their favourite haunt, dust kicking up from their shoes, hoping no one had commandeered the tree. Of course, it was *their* tree. They had not planted it, but the rope was theirs and that was enough for ownership.

They scanned for intruders as they climbed and when they reached the top of the hill, it appeared that they had the place to themselves. Umbie and Jason inspected the fissured bark of the old locust tree and gave the rayon rope a proprietorial tug. The sun was high now and burning their necks, prickling through their white school shirts. Umbie was the first to swing out on the rope, looking up into the leaves creasing and shimmering in the full air.

Jason sat in the deep shadow of the tree and opened the brown bag, pulling out a slightly curled cheese-and-pickle sandwich.

'Want one?' he asked, gesturing to his brother.

'Not just now,' answered Umbie, swinging out into the hot, gassy light; the branch creaking as he took his pendulum journey from horizon to horizon.

'This is the life!' shouted Jason, mashing his food.

'You can see Nottingham today,' Umbie cried out, flying in an arc, blowing dust from the ground. His cool-blue eyes looked past the blurring rope and beyond the Ministry of Defence's land that stretched for miles, mostly hidden by dense woodland and out as far as the eye could see. 'It's so clear!' he added, his black hair trailing.

Jason was hardly listening, his eyes closed, savouring the pickle taste. He opened them again and looked around him. In that moment he wished for nothing more. Seated in the hood of shade provided by the tree, he savoured the peaceful, natural sounds of the birds, and gazed out on the brightly lit countryside. It was an idyllic scene apart from the stumps of felled trees penned off behind a partly collapsed set of railings.

Jason took up the lemonade bottle and opened it. There was a delightful fizz and froth of gas that reminded him of the annual family holiday to Scarborough, where they would stay for a week at The Royal Hotel. His father would bring along two crates of bottled homemade beer, complete with labels. While their parents kept to the balcony overhanging the cliffs, Jason and Umbie would take the old lift down to the beach with just enough money to buy pop and cones of chips. Now and then, their mother escaped the balcony and joined them, purchasing sticks of rock or silly hats. They would spend most of the holiday near the harbour hunting in the rock pools, something their father intermittently witnessed through the powerful, black binoculars that he brought to accompany his daytime supping.

As Jason gulped a mouthful of the sweet lemonade, Umbie came down from the rope. He was hungry now and his hands were sore from holding on. He sat down next to Jason, massaging life back into his fingers.

'Boy, it's hot,' he said, his blood-red face cooling in the shadow. 'It's got to be the hottest so far. This is better than doing Latin!'

Jason just raised his eyebrows. He enjoyed Latin almost as much as Greek or the original Aramaic that the visiting canon taught when covering the New Testament. He even loved the Bible, or rather, all the different versions of it. He had read most of these, not as religious texts, but simply as works of literature. His passion was not religion. He studied theological tracts as one might read the works of William Shakespeare or Charles Dickens. He read everything he could put his hands on. While the other boys enjoyed sport, fighting or other pastimes, he tucked himself away in the generous school library. He assiduously collected words and phrases, adding them to a series of little notebooks. Now, polishing off an oatmeal biscuit and prompted by his brother's disparagement of education, he reached into his pocket and took out a thin volume of *Sir Gawain and the Green Knight* that he had stashed in his trouser pocket. He had barely started the first paragraph when Umbie snatched it from him.

'Give it a rest,' he told him. 'We haven't come all this way to read books. You can do that back at school. That's all you do, for God's sake!'

For a second or two, Jason looked set for an argument, the afterimage of beloved text fading on his retina. Yet he relented, accepting his brother's need for company.

'Yeah, you're right,' he said, standing up and taking hold of the rope. He examined its helter-skelter twine before lifting his feet and swinging out into the light.

†

As Jason's reverie continued and the bath emptied, a white van pulled up outside. It moved slowly forward, away from the streetlight. The rest of the road was deserted. This was one of the better districts of Nottingham and nothing stirred. Only the rain ruffled the silence. It hissed and pooled on the damaged roof of the vehicle. Inside the cabin sat a huge man, smoking. The glow from his cigarette swelled through the wet, dark windscreen. The fag moved up and down slowly, rhythmically, as he listened to the phone pressed to the side of his skull. He wore a thick black sweatshirt. His face hid beneath a dipped dark blue sports cap. His head appeared small in comparison to his expansive, muscular frame. When briefly revealed, the driver's nose did not seem to achieve full genetic length. It fell short and turned upward in the manner of a fruit bat.

'Yes,' he said to the air in front of him, holding the tiny phone in his wide, coarse palm. 'I understand.'

He drew again on the cigarette and blew upward, building his own private fog within the cabin. He inhaled fast, impatiently, only pausing for a while as he listened more carefully. Then, with a shake of his head, he doused the nub of it in the tray, sending flakes of ash over the black butt of a Walther PKK pistol next to his thigh. He had decorated the gun with his nickname in silver enamel paint: "Dazzler". He slid it back under the passenger seat.

'No, whatever they want,' he said gnomically. 'Yes, I'm OK with it. Tell me if they change their mind. I always deliver on time.'

He put down the phone, engaged the engine and moved away, the wheels temporarily scarring the wet surface.

Fifty yards away, Jason was still enjoying his memories, with the last of the bathwater running away.

†

'Whee!' Jason cried, enjoying the blow of wind to his face.

It was a slit of happiness, his head rolling back, his heart pumping strongly. He closed his eyes. What a feeling! The hot sun turned the inside of his eyelids a translucent red. He opened them again and saw the lush green leaves twitching. Jason had missed the old locust tree. He missed the rhythm of the swinging rope, its arc and the creaking branch. He swung back and forth, the grass rolling out beyond the stumps of trees to the horizon. As he flew, his brain returned to books and quotes:

> "*Calm was the day, and through the trembling air*
> *Sweet breathing Zephyrus did softly play.*"

Just as the words of Edmund Spenser intruded, Jason saw something that punctured them and made them flat in comparison—for what he saw had a much deeper root inside of him—something that commanded attention. The rope swung back, held for an instant and took him forward once more. In his excitement, his head pounding suddenly with blood, he willed a better view, putting as much force into his swing as possible, driving himself closer to the canopy of the old tree. Then he saw it again!

Jason strained his eyes to absorb for a second time the spectacle of pink-white, shimmering flesh. His mind crackled as he tried to set down a memory of what lay beyond the tips of the long grass: the tail of a spine, an asterisk, and a scribble of dark hair. Then gravity's backswing removed the exquisite, fleeting image. Jason threw his body forward with more force, giving it everything he had, escaping the glue of the earth, rising higher and higher. His heart burst now. He could make out the lines and play of anatomy. He fought with the rope to swing further from the dull ground, higher still, craning his neck.

'What are you doing?' asked Umbie, suspicious about Jason's urgent, manic swinging.

'Shush! Be quiet, will you?' Jason pleaded, stretching, his head refusing to yield to the backswing.

At this furthest point of voyeurism, his fingers suddenly lost their grip and he fell heavily and poorly. He rolled onto the grass, but an iron railing pierced his leg just beneath the kneecap. As Jason wailed, spittle trailing from his open, anguished mouth, the lovers he had spied quickly gathered their clothes and ran off in a panic.

Umbie was quickly at his brother's side. The rusty spike dislodged with a light, sucking sound and Jason wrapped his fingers over the gaping hole. He writhed in pain, his tears flowing as easily as the blood onto the rubbery grass. When he wiped his leg clean, however, the cavity just filled again.

'What on earth were you playing at?' Umbie cried.

'Oh, God!' Jason gasped, breathing madly, moaning, twisting and clasping his knee.

'You'll be all right. Just calm down,' his brother told him.

'Shit, the bleeding won't stop!'

Umbie took off one of his long socks and tied it around his brother's knee. Then he lifted Jason into his arms, strong out of fear, and carried him over the grass and down the path. He was very heavy, yet the blood seeping through the makeshift bandage spurred him on.

'I'm going to die!' Jason cried. He had forgotten all about the lovers panicked into their clothes.

'Don't be daft!' Umbie told him, struggling along. 'It's only a scratch.'

Umbie carried him down from the hill, his legs buckling, weaving along the path to the main road. It was a long walk to the nearest houses. Jason clung to his twin, leaving snot and tears in the crook of his neck and a trail of blood along the pavement. Umbie was breathing hard now, once or twice staggering into the gutter before correcting himself. He struggled to keep a grip on his brother's clammy body, as the pair of them embraced as closely as they had when they shared the same womb.

†

The water formed a whirlpool at the plughole, gurgling and sucking rudely at Jason's heel. He felt the weight returning to his body as the tub drained. Looking at the hairs between his legs, glistening in the stark light from the unshaded bulb, he savoured again his memory of Round Hill. With the flow of water dragging between his buttocks, he touched the scar below his knee and gave a long, deep sigh. He suddenly felt a pang of guilt that he had not returned the favour and saved his brother's life. The feeling overwhelmed him. He pinched his tearful eyes, shaking his cooling head, regretting that he only grabbed the assailant's hair. In the days after the killing, a local reporter questioned his response to the attack. Jason's reply sounded weak, like a half-hearted effort to defend his twin brother. The report blamed the brothers for being out at night in a notoriously bad area of the city. Worse still, another journalist underlined that the attack happened in an area blighted by cuckooing. The message was clear: the brothers were up to no good and did not deserve public sympathy.

When the bath finally emptied, Jason heaved himself out, slipping a little on the black-stippled floor. He took a fresh white towel from the rail and began to dry himself, the soft fabric comforting him at first, but then slowly turning damp, cold and loveless.

Hanging the towel untidily over the rail, he dressed quickly, squeezing his feet into worn tartan slippers. Then he tripped the light and went downstairs into the sitting room, where a copy of his navy-blue bound thesis kept the door open. Poppy had put it there as a statement of her contempt for higher education. After all, she had to work long shifts at the laundry to support him during the doctorate and they had nearly broken up over it. At first, Jason had protested at seeing his *magnum opus* used in this way, sometimes returning it to the bookcase only for Poppy to put it back on the floor. Now he stooped down and picked it up yet again, examining the gold-leafed coat of arms of the University of Sheffield on the front, his name along the spine. He opened it, read the title, *The Affective Impact of Proverbs*, and then the abstract and first few lines before placing it back against the bottom of the door and stepping around Juju lying nearby.

It was very dark outside. All Jason could see were the yellow lights of the other houses. It was almost time to fetch Poppy. He kicked his slippers at Juju, making him roll over and run for cover under the heavy table. There he lay quietly, nervously, orange flames flickering in his slit eyes. Jason glanced at the clock. Poppy hated him being late. She was the manager of the laundry at the local general hospital and expected him to be as punctual as her workers. Without further ado, Jason took out his phone and thumbed a text to let her know he was on his way. Then he changed into his shoes and left the house.

4

It was a smell of flannel left too long in basins or cabbage water. The laundry was all this and more. There was the distinct and pungent odour of incontinence and detergent. Jason walked alongside the conveyor belt that transported dirty linen towards two enormous washing machines. The noise was deafening. As the linen tumbled on, men and women in protective gear sorted it into categories, untangling soiled knickers from towels from vests from sheets, casting each down a different chute.

Jason walked towards the end of the laundry and up the wooden stairs to Poppy's office. Behind him, palls of steam lifted from awkward-looking machines and pipes that ran everywhere. At the top of the stairs, he watched as large sacks of washing ran on hooks along rails towards the rear of the building. Then Jason turned and pushed at the door of Poppy's office.

Poppy did not see Jason. She was busy banging her fist on the table and jabbing her finger at the reddening, round-shouldered supervisor. Her thick lips vibrated angrily, her arms remonstrating. Her dull, green eyes, like bread mould, shifted and challenged. The man backed down, hung his head low and bit his tongue. He averted his gaze and quickly left the office twiddling a pen in his hands. Jason stepped aside to let him pass. Poppy looked at her husband, lifted her head to the grimy, damp ceiling and sighed.

'Dave just ruined a whole washing cycle!' she complained.

'How come?' Jason asked sympathetically, perching on the edge of the cluttered desk.

'He didn't check the temperature! He was running it cold. You can't kill the bugs like that!'

Jason nodded in agreement. 'Of course not,' he said, thinking of deadly spores lurking in the filaments of hospital sheets. It did not bear thinking about. 'As Leacock wrote, "*the general idea in any first-class laundry is to see—*"'

'Please, Jason, the hospital board are breathing down my neck with their effectiveness and efficiency crap. The last thing I need is one of your quotes!'

'It was only a short one.'

'Well, leave it shorter still, there's a love.'

Jason could not help but finish the quote in his own head: "*... that no shirt or collar ever comes back twice.*"

The laundry was hot and humid. Already, beads of sweat formed on Jason's wide brow and upper lip and he had no choice other than to unbutton his overcoat and run his fingers back over his pate. He looked fed up. Poppy reached over and took hold of his hands in a rare expression of intimacy.

'Did Inspector Mosby call?' she asked him.

'He came,' he said miserably, drawing away, uncomfortable with his hands held so closely. 'Except the whole thing's useless. No one has come forward. I got the impression that Mosby suspects Umbie was involved in something. You know, as if he were a criminal!'

'Umbie? Ridiculous.'

'Well, that's what he implied. He never knew him. Umbie would not hurt a fly. He wasn't up to anything funny or illicit.'

'Of course, he wasn't. What did the inspector suspect he might be involved in?'

'He never said.'

'I don't know,' Poppy sighed. 'It doesn't sound very promising, does it? Anyway, never mind all that for now. How are things at the university? Have you been in today?'

'No, I can't face it.' Jason was shaking his head, distracted. He did not want to think about going back to work, lecturing students, debating literary theory or marking the next batch of essays. He had to focus on the real, hard business of what had so recently happened. He had to come to terms with it and find out who killed his twin brother.

'Well, I think it will be good to get back as soon as you can,' said Poppy.

'Yes, I know, but I'm not ready. I want something done.'

'It is still early, Jason. The police will get a breakthrough.'

Jason shook his head. 'I don't think they'll catch the murderer,' he mumbled, his head sagging.

Poppy was behind him now. She stroked the wisps of hair behind his ears and kissed his cheek. Again, Jason moved away. Just now, he found compassion painful.

'Umbie was a blank, I kept telling Inspector Mosby. I know I'll have to find the killer myself.'

Poppy said nothing.

'Mosby asked me if I could remember anything strange that Umbie had said. I told him the only thing I could think of, but he was not impressed. He stormed off just like that.'

Poppy shook her head sadly. 'Well, it sounds like he is as frustrated as you. Just look at you,' she said, stroking the stubble on his chin. 'You're exhausted. You smell nice, though!'

Jason moved his head back and smiled weakly with a puff of air down his nose. 'I had a bath.'

'Wow, that's a good sign! You could do with a shave too!'

'Sure.'

Poppy tidied her own dark hair and started to get her stuff ready to head home. In the main body of the laundry, the men and women continued to dip their hands into the stream of dirty linen. Jason gazed through the small, grubby window at the big pressing machines that folded the sheets. He saw the huge cylinder that revolved, drying clothes with its fierce, burning air.

'I'll find the killer,' Jason vowed, his expression resolute, his eyebrows knit. 'I'll get him.'

Poppy's chin dropped to her chest in despair. Her thick, tough lips quivered slightly, but she just grabbed her bag and started to head out of the office. 'Jason, leave it to the police, love. Come on, let's go!' she said.

'I'll track down and kill the bastard,' he persisted.

Poppy sighed heavily again, not knowing how to respond to her husband's obsession. His whole voice and manner changed with these threats.

On the laundry floor, the men and women went silently about their work. Poppy waved to Dave, the supervisor, reprogramming the temperature levels.

'The police know best,' Poppy insisted. 'It's their job, now leave them to it. You will put yourself at risk if you get involved. Umbie wouldn't want that.'

†

An old Land Rover burst through the long grass that had grown over the deserted track two miles south of the Ministry of Defence and screeched to a halt just yards from the standing figures of Umbie and fellow gambler, fabled loan shark and owner of a hairdressing salon, Jim Ryan. Foul exhaust smoke pumped into the air from the idling vehicle. Ryan stepped to one side, his nostrils closing, running his hand over his ironically bald, sweating head and then down over his spiky chin and a black T-shirt. Despite being small, he had a calm, fearless expression. His thin eyebrows set to poker mode. The only thing that suggested an undercurrent of anxiety was the way he kept slowly turning a monogrammed ring on his finger.

Umbie stood back a little. After all, Ryan was in charge.

Three men, all in fatigues, got out of the vehicle, but only one moved forward in a business-like way. He was much taller than the rest, with short, ruffled copper hair and tan gloves.

'Jim.'

'Gerry.'

'Right, let's not fuck about,' Gerry said in a clipped, tidy accent, yet with something regional lurking in the vowels. He pointed at the van behind Umbie and Ryan. 'Let's see what you have.'

Ryan nodded and went with him, opening the van door and letting him peer inside. Gerry inspected what lay there before directing his colleagues to transfer the large bag to their vehicle. They stowed it away beneath a heavy canvas sheet.

'OK,' said Gerry, his body erect, chin elevated. 'So how are we fixed for two more?'

Ryan looked to Umbie for an answer and Umbie in turn faced Gerry, who stared at him coldly, keeping closed, tight lips.

'Should be all right,' Umbie said with a few increasingly confident nods. 'When do you need them?'

'ASAP,' Gerry said, laying the tip of his tongue on his bottom lip.

'Right, OK,' said Ryan.

At that, Gerry took a wad of banknotes from his jacket pocket and handed them over to Ryan.

'No fuckups, yeah?'

'No.'

'Only,' he said, suddenly serious again in the blink of an eye, 'we don't want complications, do we?'

'Not at all,' Ryan agreed.

'Is Dazzler still on it?'

'Yes.'

'Good. I like to know we have a mop and bucket just in case,' Gerry told him, making eye contact with Umbie as if suspecting him of weakness, that if anybody was going to screw things up it would be him.

Ryan read it. 'Don't worry about this fella,' he said. 'He's sound.'

'Storage?' Gerry asked matter-of-factly.

Ryan acknowledged Umbie with a little sideways nod of his head. 'All sorted.'

Gerry seemed unimpressed, but left it there. 'Call me, yeah?' Then he joined the other men in the Land Rover and drove away down the overgrown track.

Ryan and Umbie watched the vehicle and trail of exhaust disappear from view before heading back to the van.

In the cab, Ryan unfolded the bundle of banknotes and counted out Umbie's share. 'Not bad, huh?'

'No,' Umbie agreed.

'Make sure you keep the others on board, OK? It looks like this is going to be a nice little earner. When can you get the next ones?'

'Hard to say,' Umbie said with a shrug. 'I just need to choose carefully.'

'Fair enough,' said Ryan. 'Give me a call when you're ready.'

†

'Now remind me,' said Inspector Mosby. 'What exactly were you doing in that part of the city?'

'As I told you before, we were just on our way back from The Half Moon,' repeated Jason. 'It's where we both liked to hang out. It is a rough area, but that is where you find the best real ale in this city. Look, why do you keep asking *me* questions? You should be out there interviewing suspects! If your men were any good, we would have the man who killed my brother by now. He must be local, probably a druggie?'

'We don't know that,' argued the detective, straightening up and sitting down again. 'He could be from anywhere.'

'Who,' said Jason firmly, 'would stab my brother in the eye? He was nobody. He did nothing. He hurt no one. He was a blank.'

Inspector Mosby scratched the parting in his short, grey hair. 'Well, someone thought differently. Someone did not like him. There is a death. A motive is to be found.'

'But they emptied his wallet. It was probably a mugging, right. To feed a habit or whatever?'

'Well, perhaps, yet sometimes it is made to look that way, you know, to set us off on the wrong track. I think your brother might have been involved in something. After all, they killed him and not you.'

'Involved? What do you mean? My brother was no criminal, if that is what you mean. Look, as I said, he was a blank! He was a care assistant at a nursing home, for God's sake! You know, serving up slop and cleaning false teeth!'

5

Jason paced back and forth in his study. He had tried to answer the slew of emails that had come through over the last week, from disgruntled doctoral students feeling abandoned or colleagues requesting he attend various curriculum or research meetings. At first, he replied in neutral, polite language, yet soon found himself responding in terse ways. Eventually, he turned to simply jabbing the delete button. Now he was crying from deep inside, white flume gathering at the corners of his mouth. As his mouth opened, a thick string of saliva ran between his lips. He was alone upstairs. Poppy was downstairs.

He took a bath to distract himself from his gloomy thoughts, however, his poor mood and tearfulness continued. He moved about, stepping past the columns of books along the landing. He was quick for such a large man. It was as if he were trying to catch reality out, moving so briskly to leave his old selves in the past, in the sweep and blur of his movements. His teeth glinted and the fine hairs on his now almost-naked body shone. He headed into the bedroom and lay down on the bed in a stupor, with a towel wrapped around his waist, staring at nothing.

Jason knew it was cold, but could not rise or get under the duvet. He lay there shivering away, lips slowly tinged with blue. Downstairs, Poppy sat next to the fire with Juju lying across her lap, the television burbling on. Outside, the sky had cleared and an icy blackness took hold of Ardinweald.

Jason shuddered again and breathed out candyfloss air. His eyes stared upward as a spasm of trembling washed over him. Goose pimples peaked as his skin stretched taut and his teeth gently chattered. He was thinking about his wife and Umbie, and whether things would have turned out differently had they stayed together. Umbie had fallen first for Poppy's jaw-breaking looks, perfect calves and wonderful smile that crunched her thickly lashed eyes. Poppy's mother did all she could to split them up by lacing her daughter's meals with heavy doses of garlic. It worked. After the initial flourish, Umbie lost interest and moved on. Yet Mrs Wragg barely had time to rejoice before the younger-by-five-minutes twin took over. Jason's sense of smell was blunter and his commitment fiercer. Umbie gave his blessing, thinking they were probably a better match. He was right. As the second Hemp to hold out flowers and draw the elastic around Poppy's hips, Jason knew he would marry her.

As he lay in a cool stupor, a quote from Defoe's *The Character of the Late Dr S. Annesley* entered his mind:

"The best of men cannot suspend their fate:
The good die early, and the bad die late."

†

'Yeah, OK, Pops. Just give me a minute,' said Jason.

His wife had a great move. As he lay on his back, she twisted her knuckles into his breastbone.

'Shit!' he cried, throwing himself sideways. 'I wish you wouldn't do that!'

'And I wish I had a husband first thing in the morning. Do you know what time it is? You have a meeting with your head of school. You can't keep putting him off.'

Jason turned on his side and groaned, but knew Poppy was right. Several months had now passed by since Umbie's death and the university work had piled up. He had been going back in for short visits in what Occupational Health called a phased return. He felt nauseous each time he went in, avoiding colleagues in the corridor and quickly hiding in his office hoping no one would disturb him. The idea of sitting in the staff room drinking coffee with them made him anxious. Yet it got him out of the house and from under Poppy's feet.

His brief visits to the university also afforded Jason the time to investigate his brother's finances and collate as much information as possible surrounding his death. This was partly to settle matters with the family solicitor, not least some debts. The solicitor had managed to clear these with the sale of Umbie's flat at Pastures. Unbeknownst to Jason, his brother had made a big overpayment to clear the mortgage for the property. How he had managed that on his salary at the care home remained a mystery. Yet, apart from the financial side of things, Jason extended his amateur sleuthing to learn as much as possible about the places and people that Umbie knew. He even had a map of the city attached to his office noteboard with lots of coloured pins for all the locations his brother frequented. Several of these places Jason had deduced from Inspector Mosby's questions about his brother's various whereabouts on the days and weeks leading up to the attack.

Jason kept all this detective work in his office to hoodwink Poppy. He did not want her to know that he was taking on the failing investigation. His phased return to the university gave him the opportunity to do this. Even if colleagues interrupted him, Jason knew he would simply look like a scholar, pursuing his latest research project. Now, lying in bed, he decided not to wait for more prompting from his wife. He would meet with the head of school, Professor Porter, and continue his own personal mission to find Umbie's killer. He knew that Porter wanted him back in the saddle, as it were. Jason would need to fight shy of recovery to avoid increasing amounts of teaching. For the time being, he could not face the lecture hall.

'Well?' pursued his wife.

'Yes, all right,' Jason gave in, massaging his brow.

The news that he was going into the university pleased Poppy so much that she began singing quietly to herself as she went downstairs.

Jason remained on his side, staring blankly ahead, trying to summon the energy to get up. It was a slow resurrection. He took a quick shower, with the jet at its hottest and fiercest, hurting the back of his neck. Then he dressed and shaved, tucking in the collar of his fresh, white shirt. The blunt razor tugged painfully. He held his nose out of the way, wincing, as he dragged it over his lip. Finally, he attached bits of toilet paper where the skin bled and went downstairs.

Poppy was still in a good mood when Jason sat down at the kitchen table. The radio was on and she was singing along while preparing a simple breakfast for him of pink grapefruit, toast and marmalade. It was a rare treat. Normally, Jason and Poppy took breakfast separately at different times.

'More toast?' she asked, dropping a mug of tea in front of him.

'No, that should be fine,' he said, starting to feel more positive about the day ahead. 'Do you need a lift to the laundry?'

'No, you're OK, I'll get the bus. Just pick me up at the usual time.'

'Are you sure, Pops?'

'Yes, thanks. How are you getting into the university?'

'I think I'll walk. I need the exercise.'

'Good idea,' Poppy told him, putting on her coat and picking up her bag. 'Right then, I'm off.' She bent over and kissed him on the top of his head. 'Have a good day.'

'You, too,' he said through a mouthful of toast and marmalade.

After Poppy left, Jason quickly gathered the things he needed: a pen, a black notebook and a small digital camera. He shoved them into the hip pockets of his coat. Then he checked he had his keys, phone and wallet before leaving the house and heading to where

Ardinweald merged with the more troubled fringe of Nottingham. It was an area known for gun crime and sex work, never mind cuckooing, and where the popular real-ale pub, The Half Moon, stood.

†

It was a good thirty-minute walk to The Half Moon and as Jason got closer, his skin prickled with fear. He scrutinised every face he saw, curling his right fist ready to defend himself and once or twice taking the precaution of crossing to the other side of the road. Now and again, at key points in the journey towards the spot where Umbie fell, Jason took out his camera and filmed around him, trying to be as discreet as possible, before continuing on his journey. He had walked this route many times since Umbie's death. Yet he had decided that getting it all on video might help his analysis. He was looking for something that might prove useful to his enquiry. A small detail, anything. *Was this the way the killer came? Did the gang come from the Meadows? St Ann's? Basford?*

Jason pondered all this as he walked downhill towards The Half Moon, which sat back from the road. It was a small, unexceptional, whitewashed building with a poorly painted board of an owl passing a blank fat white crescent. Yet what the pub lacked in character it more than made up in its legendary range of real ales. The pub was a favourite haunt of the Hemp brothers despite it lying in a crime-ridden district. Until Umbie's death, Jason had barely considered the risks of the neighbourhood, partly because of his imposing body. Now and again, Poppy had warned of the tough streets and alleys. "It's not some no-go area of the US, for God's sake!" he had told her. Now he felt very different.

He walked quickly past The Half Moon and down to the bleak, concrete roundabout near the murder spot. There, on the other side of the road, was the slope leading to the fateful subway that took pedestrians under the busy traffic. Jason stopped again and turned the camera to video mode while keeping an eye on people and assessing whether they were a threat to him, limiting his filming to a few minutes before setting off for the petrol station on the far side of the roundabout. He kept checking over his shoulder as he went even though it was daylight.

The petrol station was empty except for one car and its driver watching the pump display. At the rear of the forecourt was a small shop, heavily protected with security shutters and CCTV. Someone had taped a notice on the kiosk window stating, "PAY FOR FULE FIRST". Jason felt uplifted when he saw the number of cameras pointing in all directions. He wondered whether they had captured Umbie's murderer coming out of the nearby subway or perhaps even visiting the tiny shop beforehand to buy cigarettes. He imagined that Inspector Mosby and his team had already checked, but it did no harm to enquire.

Jason moved quickly across the greasy, oil-spattered tarmac and into the little building. A buzzer sounded and the cashier quickly sized him up from behind a toughened glass screen. Jason smiled in an attempt to disarm him and then purchased a couple of out-of-date chocolate bars to symbolise that he was just a customer and not concealing a weapon. Another car came onto the forecourt and the cashier took down the registration number before prodding a button to switch on the pump. Jason pushed the bars of chocolate forward.

'Any petrol?' asked the cashier, wiping his fingers over his bright red hoodie.

'No, just these.'

The cashier put them through the scanner.

Jason waved his card at the contactless reader and then hesitated before turning away. 'Is the manager in?'

The young man frowned and sucked his teeth. 'What do you

want him for?' he asked.

'I just need to speak to him about the CCTV cameras. It's important.'

'Well, he's not here.'

Jason looked out from the kiosk at the quiet forecourt. 'OK, er, when does he come in?'

'I don't know. He just visits when he wants to.'

'Right, thanks. That's a big help.'

Jason turned away, but just before he exited, the cashier called out to him and beckoned with his fingers.

'Hey,' he said, appearing to soften his manner and tone. 'Why are you interested in the cameras?'

Jason looked at the young man's eyes and the cluster of freckles across his cheeks. 'I'm trying to find my brother's killer. I was hoping the cameras on the forecourt might have captured him on video.'

'Your brother was the one stabbed in the subway, yeah?'

'That's right.'

'I'm sorry, man. That was a terrible thing to happen. I mean, sorry I was sharp and that.'

'It's OK.'

'But listen, you are wasting your time, right, with the CCTV.'

Jason shook his head and grimaced. 'Go on,' he insisted impatiently.

'There are no recordings.'

'None?'

The cashier shook his head. 'No,' he told Jason. 'The cameras are all fake. They're just empty boxes.'

6

Professor Porter shouted for his secretary through the half-closed office door. The light ticking of her computer keyboard stopped. There came the noise of the printer and then finally a little suppressed scream of frustration. After a further delay, Valerie walked into Porter's office, clearly not in the best of moods, but forcing herself to breathe deeply and join her fine, delicate hands together to signal a willingness to serve.

'Ah, Val, Jason and I would love one of your specials.'

'Yes, of course.' She turned to Jason. 'Milk? Sugar?'

'Just milk please,' he told her, noting her irritation with the summons.

'And a few biscuits please,' Professor Porter added, oblivious to his secretary's lips tightening inwards.

Professor Porter sat away from his desk, near a wall of books. He was six feet five with a much-ridiculed stoop from years of book reading and desk work. He filled one of the bright modern occasional chairs in what was an otherwise gloomy office. Jason stared at his senior colleague's large, age-mottled hands and then at his pink and blue striped socks flashing confidence despite his otherwise dull, scholarly attire of jacket and corduroys. Professor Porter crossed his arms and stared intently at his junior colleague for a long time. The bell in the clock tower sounded high above the courtyard and students crossed the quad to get to their various lectures. Jason felt guilty. He had neglected his work. Now he looked into his superior's dark, inscrutable eyes and grew uncomfortable. *What is he thinking?*

'So, how's the phased return going?' Professor Porter opened the meeting, uncrossing his arms and rubbing his brow.

'Er, OK,' Jason hesitated.

'Well, it has not been easy for you, Jason. Do you feel you have enough support? The university takes mental health very seriously. There is counselling if you need it.'

'No, I think I can manage, thank you.'

Professor Porter lifted and joined his big hands in front of his nose as if praying for tact. He remained silent for longer than comfortable. Jason had grown used to his colleague's tactic of winkling staff out of their defensive shells. Yet Jason said nothing until the silence became unbearable and Professor Porter continued.

'So, you are back one day a week or two half days, is that correct?'

'Yes,' answered Jason.

'And how do you feel about increasing this a little? Let's say to two or three days a week?'

Jason looked out into the now empty white quad. It was clean, almost clinically so, like an operating theatre. From this side of the Dyson Building, there was little greenery. Out of sight lay the splendid lake and woodlands that mirrored the city's more traditional, long-established university. In fact, the lake was not the only similarity. Nottingham East University, or NEU for short, had cloned much of the older institution's architecture, although on a more modest scale. NEU hoped that visually associating their recently developed institution with the city's more prestigious university would attract overseas students. Such marketing piracy proved successful. Despite the inferior quality of the build, the website images for both universities appeared remarkably similar and won NEU valuable students from China, India and Nigeria.

'The thing is,' continued Professor Porter, 'we are thin on the ground right now. We have two colleagues on maternity leave. You may recall that Professor Littlewood is off on long-term sick. Anyway, the upshot is we don't really know if he will make it.'

'Oh no, I am sorry to hear that,' said Jason. He really liked the renowned Hardy scholar.

'Not good,' Professor Porter concluded, unfolding his arms and running his hands up and down his thighs. 'The big you-know-what,' he said quietly.

As Jason looked at his senior colleague, framed by the window as a living portrait, he wondered whether he still aimed to be vice-chancellor and move into the plush executive suite of offices on the other side of the quad. He was an Oxonian after all, had brought in more than his fair share of external research money and knew how to handle disputes between university departments. Yet, the more entrepreneurial professors considered his kind of leadership old hat.

'So,' Professor Porter pursued. 'What about two days a week?'

Jason took and held a deep breath, looking at his colleague's puffed-out, questioning lips. He knew he had to appear to get on with his life. He sensed that if he showed willingness, he could buy more time. He could do a string of lectures and disappear again on the pretext of working from home.

'Yes,' he told him.

Professor Porter's mouth drew into a business smile. 'That's excellent!'

Just then, Valerie entered the office backwards, still out of sorts, setting a tray of drinks in the middle of Professor Porter's desk. She left, closing the door noisily. Jason watched Professor Porter get up and pour the tea, his fingers moving listlessly. The tea looked intentionally stewed and tasted bitter. Jason took several malted biscuits to soften the blow.

Professor Porter slurped away, and did not speak for a while. In the silence, Jason browsed the books on the shelves next to him. Unsurprisingly, nearly all the volumes were on Viking literature.

'So,' asked Professor Porter, setting down his cup, 'how is the investigation going?'

For a cold moment, Jason thought he was referring to the sleuthing he had been conducting during work time in his office along the corridor. He swallowed heavily, but quickly determined that the head of school's question was general in nature.

'Not very well,' he admitted. 'It has all gone quiet.'

Professor Porter grimaced and seemed to study the motes of book dust in the air in front of him. 'Now look, Jason, if you can't manage the two days just let me know. I'm sure colleagues will understand.'

Jason knew the fake compassion game and went through the motions. 'No, I'll be fine. I'll be in tomorrow.'

With that, Jason placed his cup on the desk and the meeting closed with meandering salutations.

Back in the corridor, Jason sighed with relief and took out his phone to update Poppy. With his eyes down and thumbing a few kisses on the screen, he nearly collided with someone he quickly assumed to be a mature student.

'Sorry,' he apologised, barely looking up.

'That's OK,' said Dazzler, moving to one side and turning studiously to a board of timetables, a pen to his lips and books under his arm.

†

There was something different about the laundry. It was darker than usual and the air bristled with a yellowish storm light. Only a few of the fluorescent tubes were on and the laundry workers seemed preoccupied and sullen. The men and women picking at the endless stream of fouled linen with rubber-gloved hands barely acknowledged him. They usually nodded or waved. He studied their sweaty faces and saw how they averted their eyes. Something was clearly the matter. Perhaps his wife had just balled them out for something. He smiled tentatively in their direction and crossed the floor, holding his nose to the stench, moving alongside the whirring conveyor belt, cutting through the steam that escaped countless silver pipes. He felt suddenly grateful to have such a flexible, clean job at the university. He did not have to process the spillage and bodily smears of sick patients. His mood had improved after settling things with Professor Porter and there was almost a spring to his step as he climbed the wooden stairs to Poppy's office.

He pushed open the door to find Poppy with her head dipped low, clasping a mug of coffee, silent.

'What's up?' he asked. 'The crew out there all look a bit glum. Did Dave run it cold again?'

Slowly, his wife's head lifted from the coffee, and she stared at him in silence.

'Hey, I know that look! I went into work. Didn't you get my text?'

Poppy turned the mug in her hands and pulled a serious face.

Jason frowned and walked cautiously over to her desk. 'You need to do something about the lighting out there. It's a bit gloomy.'

'Gloomy?' Poppy laughed in a short, abrupt way, shaking her head.

Jason saw her strange, disturbed gaze. He looked awkwardly at her pale, drawn face. He could now see that her eyelids and nose were red from crying.

'The lights will soon be out for good,' she said in a monotone. Her lips opened and closed in exaggerated circles, her tongue shifting back and forth across her top teeth.

Jason held the back of his neck, not knowing what to think or say. He had not seen his wife quite like this before. 'I don't follow you,' he mumbled finally.

'The laundry,' muttered Poppy, picking up her coffee and staring deeply into it. 'They're closing us down.'

'What? No!'

'We're for the chop,' she told him, her green eyes oily again, catching the lights of her office.

Jason was dumbfounded. He looked disbelievingly at the ceiling and then down at his wife. He swallowed hard and shook his head.

'When?' His eyes moved all over the place as if he were tracking a fly.

'I don't know! Soon,' Poppy sobbed, her head resting now on folded arms, her spine heaving and falling.

Jason moved round and sat on the desk, gently reaching over, and stroking her head. Poppy drew sharp little breaths, crying hoarsely as her husband whispered soothing words in her ear and caressed the hair from her cheek. She straightened up and covered her face with a hand. Jason drew a strand of wet hair from her swollen, trembling lips and bent forward to kiss her forehead.

'What am I to do?' she asked jerkily. 'First Umbie, now this!'

Jason's hand moved over her back in slow, circular movements. 'We'll think of something. There must be other laundries,' he said gently.

'It's hard,' she sobbed. 'After all these years.'

'I know,' comforted Jason.

'The contract's going to that huge laundry on the other side of the city. I knew this would happen once they closed Pastures down and turned it into luxury flats. They centralise everything these days, cutting costs.'

Poppy panted heavily and began crying again. The appearance of Jason had released all the emotion that had built up inside her during the long shift. Now her face was like crumpled paper. There was pain and loss of pride.

'When was all this decided?'

'They told me officially this morning,' sniffed Poppy, her eyes inflamed.

'Officially? So, you knew this was going to happen?' Jason

pinched his lips into a beak.

'I knew it was a possibility. I kept quiet. You had enough to worry about, what with Umbie. I thought,' she said biting the corner of her lip, 'they might change their minds.'

'Hmm,' managed Jason.

Poppy closed her eyes. Jason watched her scratching the desk with her nails. He could see how devastating the news had been. His wife liked to be busy, engaged and at the heart of things. A fever of resentment ran through his veins.

'How can they treat you like this?' he burst out angrily. His chin thrust out and his muscles hardened. He began pacing the office.

Poppy looked out of the observation window at the rumbling conveyor belt below. She looked at the line of workers and worried about them. They had families to feed and kids to clothe. She imagined them all having to attend the local food bank in the coming weeks and months.

'All those years I put in,' she complained. 'All the sweat and tears. How will we manage?'

'Let's go home,' suggested Jason, disturbed at seeing Poppy so undone. 'My salary will just about cover the mortgage and everything. Something else will turn up. Perhaps there will be vacancies at the laundry taking the contract?' Jason offered his hand, and she took it. 'Come on,' he said, easing her onto her feet and bringing her coat. 'Let's go.'

He was shaking his head as he led her out of the dim office. How could the world be so punishing? Umbie was dead. Poppy was losing her steady job. He saw how her eyes grew blurred and distant.

'You'll get another position.'

'Will I?' she whispered, the skin of her face trembling.

'Somewhere. With all your experience.'

'No one will touch me.'

'Don't say that!' snapped Jason.

'It's true. I waste money. That is what the hospital estates told me! Wasting money in the NHS is like committing murder.'

'Murder?' Jason frowned. 'Wasting money is nothing like murder.'

7

A robin landed like a flame on the headless angel. It looked dispassionately at Jason sitting on his brother's tombstone holding a spray of white carnations bought from the vendor at the cemetery gates. Jason did not look up. Twisting sideways, his eyes squinting at the grooved epitaph, he began thinking again about Poppy and her redundancy. She was not coping very well with it, lying in bed until noon and not bothering to make up her face or sort her hair. On top of this, the increased workload at the university gave additional pressure. At a time when he wanted to make progress with his enquiry into Umbie's death, he found an overwhelming number of tasks crammed into the two days a week he agreed with Professor Porter. He had been delivering poorly prepared lectures one after the other without his usual game show host persona. The students had queued at his office door waiting to consult him about their assignments. The intense workload made him rue being a popular tutor. Blazed and defeated, with stacks of unmarked essays and exam scripts preventing the free movement of his swivel chair, he saw one student after the other. He hid his grief at all times, putting on his jolly voice, which sounded increasingly bogus. Now, in the quietness of the cemetery and with his brother underground, he tried to push the university and the laundry out of his mind.

It was Sunday and the early morning wind had vanished and left thick clouds hanging stubbornly over Ardinweald. Jason set the flowers for his brother to one side and undid his overcoat, freeing the material from under his buttocks and letting it ruck behind him.

The sudden movements disturbed the robin standing nearby. It flew away like a spark and left Jason alone with his thoughts. He drew up his knees and looked between the gaps of headstones littering the cemetery.

Down past the water tap, Danny the gravedigger was busy as usual. His small figure bent then straightened as he shovelled heaps of reddish soil into an invisible hole. He was like a machine, his white sleeves rolled up. Jason studied from afar the often-ridiculed burier of Ardinweald's dead. It was a job for life, Jason mused, unlike Poppy's at the laundry. Every day came new diggings, the laying of artificial grass around the edges of an oblong hole and coiled straps for the descent set in place. Afterwards, Danny would fill in the newly inhabited graves as he did now. Jason looked down at Umbie's tombstone, patting the finished roof of the gravedigger's labours before removing the wilted gladiolus that his mother had placed in the little urn. He quickly emptied out the soured water and folded the stalks of the dead flowers. With an old man's sigh, Jason got back to his feet to visit the standpipe for fresh water. As he headed off across the gently sloping land, his movement on the gravel path merged with the sound of feet on crisp, powdery snow, and his consciousness shifted, building its way into the recent past, a dream-world winter with Umbie in it.

†

There was Umbie now, gobbing phlegm into the gutter and laughing, grabbing Jason's shoulder, squeezing it heartily, warmly. He let go and they separated, drifting away, but soon drew close once more and collided, weaving along the tightrope of a pavement, sliding on the snow that lay thickly on the flagstones. They were the last to leave The Half Moon to make their way back across town. The sodium lights above picked out the fall of snow. Now and then, a taxi ran past in the dark slush, but otherwise, the streets were wintry quiet.

'Steady! Steady!' shouted Umbie, tripping over his own feet, skidding into the snow-caked bushes adorning a section of wasteland and almost causing his poor knees to relapse. He was laughing hysterically. 'I'm totally rat-arsed!' he said, struggling across the slippery pavement.

'So am I,' admitted Jason, trying to focus his eyes, the hoppy ale still on his tongue, lacing his breath.

On the way to the subway that led beneath the large, ill-lit roundabout, Umbie opened his fly and pissed yellow into the crisp, deepening snow.

'That'll melt anything,' he said proudly. 'Better than salt.'

Jason walked on a short distance, lifting his face, and enjoying the rare play of snowflakes on his skin. Opening his mouth, he let them swirl inside and dissolve. Then he heard his brother shouting and turned.

'What did you say?'

'We ought to build a snowman!'

'Yeah, right.'

Jason savoured the fresh cold air and slowly carried on towards the subway. Umbie caught up, kicking snow at his brother, and pelting him with a powdery ball of the stuff. It shattered on Jason's thick, balding head.

'You little bastard!' he cried, quickly returning the favour with his own crumbling snowball.

It clipped Umbie's ear. More followed until eventually the twins fell into each other's arms in a part-wrestling, part-affectionate tangle. Behind them, a security light came on briefly, lighting up three men walking towards them in a determined, resolute fashion.

Jason and Umbie continued down beneath the roundabout patting each other's backs and laughing from their bellies.

'God, I'm knackered!' wheezed Jason, stopping to catch his

breath.

'More exercise,' advised his brother. 'Typical bloody lecturer. You'll explode at your desk one of these days!'

What a strange choice of words, thought Jason, but his brother was right, he had every chance to keel over from his sedentary labour. If his life were to flash before him, it would mostly include endless frames of his hands on a keyboard.

The brothers stumbled into the narrow, wet, slippery tunnel opening.

Jason yawned, looking forward to his bed, and listened to the echo of their twinned feet as they moved through the short section of subway.

As they reached the end and just before stepping back into the heavy snowfall, the small gang of men that had followed them clambered down the steep verge. Jason's hand reached out across Umbie's chest.

'Watch out!' he warned, anxiously peering through the veil of white.

Before he knew what was happening, fists pounded into him. Something flashed through the air like an icicle in the blur of arms and knuckles. Under the thick, swirling sky, Jason somehow managed to keep on his feet, pulling and grabbing, trying to avoid the glinting knife. He caught hold of the assailant and held tight, briefly. Then came a punch just above his ear followed by the full poke of a boot between his legs. Keeling over, gasping for breath, holding his testicles with one hand, Jason slumped back against the damp low wall of the verge.

It took a while for Jason to get his bearings. He rubbed and shook his head clear and got back to his feet, feeling nauseous. The gang had left the way they had come, a chain of muddy prints in the snow. All went suddenly quiet except for his laboured breathing. Then he heard a weak mewling followed by an unearthly gasp from the other side of the tunnel entrance. When Jason finally managed to step forward, he knew it must be his brother. He lay curled up in the snow, a halo of red around his head. Jason stumbled over to where he lay. Umbie was face down. There was no movement or sound from him. He was as still as a dead bird. Jason shook him and rolled him over onto his back, seeing the knife's entry point. He turned away vomiting an evening of ale close to the body.

Umbie's right eye was a mush of blood and jelly. His mouth was wide open and his tongue a lifeless rag. His undamaged eye was open, glassy, fixed. This image ballooned and shrank in Jason's mind. The adrenaline removed the pain from the blows he had sustained. It was all he could do to lift his phone up to his battered face. As he did so, he saw a clump of hair fall in slow, fantastic motion from his unfurled palm. It dropped to the snow. He stepped over it and knelt down next to his older twin, calling for an ambulance. He hoped to see steam rise suddenly from his resurrected mouth, but there was none. He felt his neck and thrust his hand down onto his still ribcage, before starting fruitless yet dutiful CPR.

When the ambulance crew arrived, Jason had been pumping his brother's dead heart for fifteen minutes.

Next to his lifeless body was the wallet Jason had bought him, open and empty. All his cards and cash had gone. He folded it like a treasured gift and put it in his pocket. Then, with the ambulance crew starting to shake their heads in defeat, Jason saw the large clump of hair nearly covered by snowfall. He gathered it up and shoved it into his coat pocket. When the police finally arrived in force, he breathlessly explained what had happened. Then he handed over Umbie's empty wallet, thinking it might hold DNA evidence.

'The gang emptied it,' he told them.

Similarly, he reached into his pocket to hand over the hair wrenched from the knifeman's head. As he removed it, Jason stealthily divided it with his fingers, returning part of the dark trophy to the safety of his coat pocket, to ensure vital evidence did not go missing. After all, there were so many stories of criminal or inattentive police officers.

'I pulled this from the attacker's head,' he told them, holding out his hand. 'I didn't see his face. Just run a DNA check and you should have your man!' Then he pointed out the snow-coated footprints of the gang.

†

In a fugue state, Jason found himself at the standpipe with the urn in his hands and water overflowing onto his feet and the bottom of his trousers. He quickly switched off the tap and went back down the path to the grave. The boundary between sleep and wakefulness had blurred again, leaving him disorientated and somewhat dissociated from everything around him. It was an unsettling feeling and he wondered not for the first time whether he was starting to lose his mind. When he finished arranging the carnations as tidily as possible at Umbie's grave he stood back, raised his chin, and vowed to hunt down his brother's killer. Nearby, Danny the gravedigger stopped digging and took a cigarette from his mouth. He looked on impassively for a few moments before popping the fag back onto his lip and carrying on with his digging.

With all that had happened with Poppy at the laundry and starting back to work at the university, Jason had not yet revisited the idea he had for the remnant of the killer's hair he kept back and stored safely in an old tobacco tin. Now, with the flashback of the assault, the magical idea of what to do with the surplus evidence returned. With his logical mind partly unravelled by the play of grief, Jason smiled darkly. *A hair of the dog that bit us*, he mouthed silently. It might work, he decided, relishing the clot of syllables. It was no sillier than other kinds of religious bunkum. Anything was worth a shot. After all, his recent detective work had yielded nothing but useless CCTV cameras. The police investigation had faltered. Even the gang's footprints melted away before the forensic crime unit could attend the scene.

Barely aware of his surroundings, Jason closed his eyes, his yellowed teeth clamped together, planning what to do with the hair. All the early years of Catholic ritual and liturgy combined in his imagination. He steadied himself with a hand on the headless angel in the adjacent burial plot before heading off along the gravel path towards the black gates, his coat opening and buckling in the wind of his movement. At the flower stall, he blanked the vendor offering a respectful smile. Jason was in his own world, brow furled and flushed with intent.

†

Poppy retired early to her bed in the spare bedroom, which had the best Wi-Fi signal. She liked to read for a while or browse the internet and since Umbie's death, could avoid Jason's alcohol-fuelled snoring and nightmare awakenings. With the laundry closing, she found comfort in this routine, and Jason relished the freedom of late nights watching rubbish TV. Yet, as he sat watching the News 24 channel with Juju at his feet, he had other ideas. He sat quietly until Poppy's electric toothbrush died, the bathroom light clicked off and the floorboards resumed their silence. Then he left the television burbling away and went into the kitchen and put the kettle on, creating the familiar soundscape that cloaked leaving the house through the back door.

Outside, the air smelled sweetly of freshly mown grass. Earlier in the day, Mr Norris had cut his prized lawn with his infernal petrol mower. Now Jason kept an eye out for his nosey neighbour, moving quickly along the garden path to the small pond where Poppy kept her kitsch family of garden gnomes. With a paranoid look over his shoulder, checking the eye line to his neighbour, Jason lifted up the largest one, complete with a lineless fishing rod, and rooted around. Soon enough, his fingers found the old tobacco tin in which he had placed the killer's hair and set off back to the house, meeting Juju who now prowled on top of the fence.

Once inside, Jason examined the tin lid, wiping away fragments of dirt, keeping an ear out for Poppy stirring. He checked the clock in the living room, turned up the television volume a shade and headed back into the kitchen. When he opened the tin with a kind of reverence, he found the remnant of dry, brown hair from the murderer's head. It lay like a tiny, boneless animal on its side. For some time, Jason stared at the clump of hair, poked at its strands and tried to extrapolate from the hair to a man.

Then, reaching up to the shelves near the fridge, he pulled down Poppy's cookery books, one by one. He quickly studied each in turn, setting aside the Italian, Chinese and Indian volumes and focusing on traditional, English cuisine. There were several promising, food-smeared titles: *Tea Time Favourites*, *Farmhouse Kitchen* and *Queen's Desserts*. Eventually, he found one without a cover or spine, marked simply *Good Old-Fashioned Cooking* and opened it.

The poorly bound pages threatened to detach themselves as he searched eagerly through sponges, cupcakes, wedding cakes and so on. Smoothing out a folded page, he found the kind of recipe he was looking for: Seville Cake.

With the television burbling away about a Russian incursion into Finnish waters, Jason collected bowls of various shapes, sizes and colours, and as many of the necessary items to bake the cake. Now and again, he stepped into the hallway to listen out for Poppy. There was no movement, and the kitchen and spare bedroom were at opposite ends of the building. Jason got back to work, measuring each quantity of the basic ingredients in a tatty plastic jug. Strictly speaking, he did not follow the recipe at all. For a start, he had no brandy, oranges or spice. Yet this did not matter. Jason had found sufficient items hidden away: flour, caster sugar, baking powder, butter, eggs and a heap of dusty sultanas. He had also unearthed a slightly warped wooden spoon, shallow cake tin and a wad of greaseproof paper.

Jason's fingers danced over each item, his mind whirring, his teeth clicking together. He messed about with the bowls in front of him, trying to bring some order to them. Trembling slightly, his head damp with sweat, he took the smallest of the tins and daubed it with a knob of butter before preparing the greaseproof paper. A deep negativity enlivened him in a strange way. With his gut tight, he concentrated on what he was doing. This was no ordinary culinary adventure. He was baking a cake to invoke unseen powers, forces or influences to help track down the killer. It was an act intimately rooted in the religion of his youth. It would be a cake that was more than its ingredients. It would become a sacrament of revenge.

He patted the thin, grey paper inside the cake tin, his eyes burning, his teeth scraping his tongue. Putting the tin to one side, he began to cream the sugar and butter in the huge, white bowl. When he finished doing this, he stirred in handfuls of flour and a sprinkling of baking powder. *That is how it should be*, he told himself, *rushed, imperfect, urgent*. He smashed three eggs against the chipped edge of the bowl, savouring the violence, not caring if bits of shell fell into the mixture. Then he stirred fiercely with the wooden spoon, his eyes wide, keenly focused. Finally, he added the old sultanas well past their sell-by-date, tucked away at the back of one of the cupboards. When he finished his preparations, Jason wiped his brow and rubbed his hands on a clean tea towel. Now there was only one vital ingredient missing.

Slapping flour dust from his worn, blue corduroy trousers, he smiled darkly as he gathered the hair from the old tobacco tin.

He examined the bulbs at the end of the plucked hair, imagining a missing patch on the murderer's scalp. Then he sprinkled it like sundried herbs onto the wet and glossy cake mixture. Round and round, he whipped the gloopy substance until his elbow ached. Finally, wiping flour from his fingers, Jason poured the mixture into the cake tin and put it in the oven.

Then he sat down at the kitchen table, his face dripping with sweat, his head prickled by the heat. He felt suddenly exhausted. He reached around and took a couple of beers from the fridge, opened them and gulped them down one after the other. His mind was racing and his eyes darted in all directions with the shifting thoughts. So many ideas came into his head that he lost sense of time passing. First a quarter-hour, then a half-hour and soon an hour slipped by as the air filled with the comforting smell of hot cake, and his mind continued to wander until he fell asleep.

†

Outside, Dazzler had been watching Jason going in and out of the side door to the kitchen and busy cooking. He had a good view of the property from the position he took up on the quiet, dark road. He studied the house in detail, watching Juju prowl. He noted the nocturnal movements and behaviours of neighbours. As he drew on his cigarette, he marvelled at how much people gave away about themselves without even knowing. From this and previous stakeouts, he could predict the sequence of lights going on and off in the different buildings. He could see that when Jason remained downstairs, the light to his wife's bedroom turned off between 22:00 and 22:10. He noted when the neighbours went in and out. He could guess which residents had prostate trouble from toilet lights coming on in the middle of the night. Spying through the opera glasses that he bought at a car boot sale, Dazzler gathered the key information he needed.

Satisfied with his surveillance of Jason's home as well as his earlier stakeout of the university, and with little other social movement to speak of, Dazzler was more than ready should he get the call.

He decided to head off, putting down the opera glasses and ringing in for the night.

'All the prep is done,' he said, 'in case you need a delivery. I will await your order.'

The voice at the other end was brusque, to the point. 'Anything we should worry about?'

'No, nothing,' answered Dazzler. Then he paused and spoke again. 'I don't think the customer is going to be a problem.'

'Good,' the voice came back. 'You can head back to the warehouse.'

†

Jason awoke with a jolt to the smell of burnt cake. It was a foul, sickly odour, and he suddenly realised where he was and what he had been doing. He jumped up, nearly knocking over the empty beer bottles, and raced to the oven, grabbing a tea towel on the way, silver sparks tracing across his eyes. As he opened the door, smoke poured out into the kitchen, making it difficult to see inside the cooker.

'Shit!' he hissed, reaching in blindly and burning his fingers.

He waved them cool, cursed some more and tried again. After a couple of attempts, he managed to retrieve the tin and examine the glossy, black surface of the cremated cake. It was nothing like the illustration in the old cookery book. He tipped it out onto a spare plate. It was hard and rocked from side to side before becoming still. Then Jason opened the window and back door, fanning away the smoke and allowing fresh air to circulate into the kitchen. As well as her keen eyes and ears, Poppy had a good nose and Jason did not want an argument with her.

He quickly wrapped the hot cake in silver foil and left the house for the garage. It was his cluttered man cave and full of things that Poppy had no interest in: garden equipment, tools, leftover wall tiles, rusting bikes, a dartboard, ladders, boxes of yellowing journal papers and book notes. Kicking a path through various bags of unwanted clothes that never made it to charity shops, Jason reached up to the shelves of paint and varnish. He made space there for the cake, hiding it behind a stiff wallpaper brush.

Sitting down for a moment on an overturned bucket and catching his breath, Jason looked around at the general chaos. The place needed clearing out. It was as bad as his office at the university. He looked up at where he had squirrelled away the cake and found comfort in his burnt creation. It was such a bizarre thing to make. It was irrational. Yet, already, Jason grew emboldened by this private, culinary effort. Huddled in the dark garage, he felt like some kind of shaman or medieval priest summoning unearthly, magical powers. Jason found succour in the idea that this sacramental act might bring the invisible, impalpable world of spirits into play. For once, he dropped his secular view and called on forces unseen, unknown and beyond science or words to break through. *The murderer is out there. I am on his tail.* He was thinking about all this when he caught sight of the luminous dial of his watch and noted it was getting very late.

Back inside, he found Poppy in the kitchen, unimpressed by the mess, opening a window to clear the air.

'What are you playing at?' she shouted. 'Since when have you been interested in cooking at this time of night?'

8

The next morning, Jason left for work, carrying yet another batch of marked essays under his arm. He drove to the campus in his old, blue Volvo estate and parked in his usual space overlooking the lake. Once there, he sat in his seat for twenty minutes before gaining sufficient motivation to walk the short distance to the Dyson Building. It was the slowest walk ever. As he crept forward, he felt empty of everything except the determination to find Umbie's murderer. The idea of work continued to nauseate him. It was all about the mortgage now and maintaining a half-decent pension given the loss of Poppy's job. He was on his way to forty and still a jobbing lecturer with only one proper book, a remaindered first novel and eleven journal papers to his name.

There had been a time when his little office on the ground floor was a hive of activity, with a stream of postgraduates keen for supervision. This early enthusiasm for academic life soon dwindled. Besides, gaining promotion was all about attracting external monies from research councils—something he was hopeless at doing. For, at heart, Jason was just a teacher.

When he entered the Dyson Building, he did his best to avoid colleagues, moving quickly along the mustard-coloured corridor, packed with noticeboards, posters for conferences and a display cabinet holding the faculty's latest publications. His only academic book, *Reading Emotion in the Renaissance*, looked tired compared to the rest, now relegated to the lowest shelf. When it first came out and had prominence, he used to stop and proudly inspect it, admiring the attractively designed cover. Now it was a reminder that he was out of date, lagging behind sparkier colleagues; that he was not part of the hyper-productive, bean-counting world of NEU.

He opened the door to his office as quickly and quietly as the batch of essays allowed. Then he picked his way between piles of sprawled documents to sit at the desk by the window. Newspaper cuttings and reports about his brother's death, digital photographs of the murder scene and a street map of Nottingham adorned the large space between the bookcases and the door. Yellow highlighter outlined the boundary of the city and district of Ardinweald. The map marked with different coloured pins detailing all the various known locations that his brother had visited in the month leading up to his death remained unchanged. The route the brothers had taken to and from The Half Moon on the night of the attack stood out in red.

Jason fired up his computer, but did not feel motivated to attend to his work emails or finalise a mark sheet for the essays now stacked in front of him on the desk. Instead, he wanted to revisit and decipher all the details surrounding his brother's death. To spur him on, he unpinned the print of a grainy photograph of his dead brother macabrely released online and stared at it for several minutes. Then he began to scan all the information stuck to the wall.

A knock on the office door interrupted Jason's review. At first, he remained silent. It was his favourite trick. He had even taken to locking his door from the inside in case anyone tried the handle. Whoever stood on the other side knew he was resident because second and then third knocks followed. Jason quickly opened one of the marked essays.

'Yes?' he said loudly, irritated.

The door to his office opened and Dazzler entered backwards, carrying a brush and black bin liner.

'Sorry,' he said. 'I'll be as quick as I can.'

Dazzler emptied the paper bin under the desk, added a new liner and quickly licked the floor with the wide brush, observing the cuttings and photographs on the wall. He noted the piles of documents sprawled out across the office. In his large, impeccable rubber-soled boots, he picked his way across the room, inspecting the general mess.

Jason barely acknowledged his presence. He had grown used to the intrusion of cleaners, although normally they came towards the end of the day.

'That'll do, now,' he told him. 'Please close the door after you.'

Dazzler hesitated, trying to assimilate as much information as he could while acting nonchalantly.

Irritated, Jason looked more closely at the stocky figure. 'Don't I know you?' he asked, frowning. He thought he had seen him before.

'No, I don't think so. I'm new,' Dazzler explained.

'For a moment I had you down as one of our mature students. Anyway, please let me get on with my work, thank you. I know it is a mess in here, but it is *my* mess, and I will sort it.'

Dazzler nodded. 'Yes, of course.'

After he left, Jason breathed a sigh of relief that was to be short-lived. No sooner had Dazzler vacated the room than his phone rang.

His heart sank. It was Inspector Mosby.

'Hello, Dr Hemp,' he said, sounding in a buoyant mood. 'Is this a good time to call? Can you speak?'

Jason was keen to hear news, the phone pressed to his ear. 'Yes, it's fine, go on,' he told him, immediately impatient.

'I'll be as brief as possible.'

'OK.'

'Well, we have made some progress with the case.'

Jason drew a sharp breath and his heart started pounding, wondering if this was the breakthrough news he had been waiting so long for. He suffered the detective's dramatic pause, picturing him chewing the temple tips of his glasses, the unfortunate birthmark partly masked by his hand.

'Have you arrested someone?' he asked.

There was a longer silence before the inspector spoke.

'Not quite.'

Jason felt himself slide back into cynical mode. 'You're going to arrest someone?'

'No.'

'You're—'

'Please, Dr Hemp, I wanted to let you know that we're onto something. We have a *major* new lead.'

A tingling sensation ran up Jason's spine and neck. Despite doubts about the police investigation, he wanted to hear good news. He wanted to be optimistic. His mouth opened and his tongue slid out over his lip as if to taste the air.

'What sort of lead?' he asked finally.

'Well, I can't say too much at the moment,' Mosby told him, 'but I think it's safe to say we have opened up a new and very promising line of enquiry.'

Jason grimaced, unconvinced. 'You *are* onto something?'

'Yes.'

'You know *who* did it?' he persisted.

'Not exactly. However, we think it is a significant development. I cannot be more specific at this stage. I just wanted you to know.'

The early promise of the news vanished now and Jason dipped his head, poking his tongue into the back of his teeth. 'So, you don't know who killed my brother, but you have a lead?'

'Yes.'

Jason was shaking his head, his usual pessimism returning. He heard an exasperated puff of air from the other end of the line.

'It's a start,' the inspector insisted.

'Yeah, and probably a false one,' Jason despaired.

'Look, all this is going to take time,' Mosby persevered. 'Please be realistic. We're picking up intelligence, asking questions, going through things with a fine—'

'Tooth comb?'

'Yes.'

Jason had heard enough. Everything sounded woolly. He stood up at his desk, frustrated and angry. He began pacing back and forth across the office, stepping around the piles of unmarked essays. He ran his fingers through the little hair remaining over his ears before speaking his mind.

'And how many men have you got on this?' he asked.

'Look, we are using all the resources at our disposal. We have to tread carefully.'

Jason slapped his forehead in a fit of anguish and exasperation. 'You're going to mess up! I know it!'

'Dr Hemp, please! I can understand how you feel, but these things aren't simple.'

'They are simple from my perspective. Find the killer. Find him quickly,' said Jason, kicking at one of the piles of essays, sending them across the newly brushed floor.

Feelings of revenge swirled in his mind in dark, icy waves. Once again, he sensed the police were incapable of bringing justice. It would be for him to avenge his brother's death. Only he could seek out and destroy Umbie's killer. He was unsure whether he could achieve this, by magic or otherwise, but he knew he would have to try. As he thought it through, his mind swirled back to fragments of his brotherly life.

†

The bishop's visit to Saint Ergonwald's on the Feast of Corpus Christi presented too good an opportunity for brothers Hemp with their history of tomfoolery. The bishop came with his flowing purple cassock and the Gospels on his tongue. He came to extol, to shine, to lift hearts and finally to indulge in the festive meal that followed the celebration of mass. It was always a fabulous meal. Everyone knew that there was nothing like the bishop's visit for improving the quality of the meat or indeed puddings for that matter. On such occasions, the cook prepared the traditional fare of Leper's Leg—a scabby pastry filled with a bloody mess of berries, coated in thick custard that the boys lovingly referred to as pus. "Pass the pus," they would say.

Yet, while the rest of the students attended mass in the chapel, the twins hid in one of the sour and stinking cubicles in the *Lavatorium* before stealing away to find the bishop's chamber, where he stayed during his visits, compelled to play a trick on him. The pranksters carried an old football, a honey stocking and a ginger wig they found behind the stage in the old Northcote Building.

'I'm not sure this is a good idea,' warned Umbie.

'Shush!' insisted Jason, pricking his ears, creeping across the polished floor.

They tiptoed along the corridor that led to the guest quarters, hugging its wood-panelled wall, trying to turn feet into cotton. Ancient furniture stood beneath shadowy paintings of past rectors of the college. Nervously, Jason and Umbie hesitated outside the target room. An old grandfather clock chimed and set their nerves on edge, so they quickly opened the door and went inside. It was an enormous space and much bigger than they expected, with a high ceiling and tall, arched windows. A baroque bed floated like an ornate barge on a red luxurious carpet. Even the oak wardrobe was colossal. Jason and Umbie listened attentively, standing before the huge dress mirror, their lungs heaving and their hearts juddering.

'I hope we don't get caught,' whispered Umbie, laying the football on the bed and slowly, methodically shrouding it with the stocking.

'Just get on with it,' insisted Jason, rifling through the deep drawer at the base of the wardrobe and taking out some blankets and other linen. 'We can use these,' he said, throwing them onto the bed. 'And here's the wig!' He cast it to his brother.

Umbie pushed his black hair from his eyes and peeled back the eiderdown quilt to reveal a creaseless silk sheet. He attached the wig to the flesh-coloured football and placed it on the pillow, while Jason rolled up blankets into makeshift limbs. With spare linen plumped up to form ribs and a hip, the dummy took shape. At first, the rough anatomy looked unconvincing, but with the quilt drawn back over it, the structure came to uncanny, spooky life. With the tousled wig visible, Jason and Umbie smiled broadly, admiring the deception. With that, the pranksters made good their escape, hurrying back along the corridor and downstairs, sniggering and thumping each other.

Back in the main cloister, the twins hid again in the *Lavatorium* until mass ended, and they were able to mingle in with the crowd of boys heading for the *Refectorium*. As they did so, they caught the enquiring looks of classmates. Umbie and Jason proudly raised thumbs or winked as they filed through with everyone else into the dining area and took their seats at the table. Midst the clatter of dishes and cutlery as the prefects set the tables, the brothers kept their own counsel. The rest of the boys laughed and talked in animated fashion, waiting for the rector and bishop to join them, salivating over the food that lay in silver dishes before their eyes.

After a long delay, there was still no sign of the eminent guest or the rector. They were unusually late. Everyone wondered what had happened to them, including the procurator, who fidgeted with his especially long fingers and kept vigil at the door. The chatter grew and expectant stomachs whirred. It was some time before the rector eventually entered the refectory, accompanied by the bishop whose face looked as flushed as the Leper's Leg now steaming on a trolley. The boys sat up straight and looked mystified at the football and stocking swinging from the rector's fist. They fell silent as he raised the ball into the air like John the Baptist's head, parading the thing all the way down the hall to the high table.

'The bishop,' he said, 'was most distressed at finding a body in his bed.'

Jason and Umbie grew deeply quiet. They lowered their heads as the rector passed by. Just as they breathed a sigh of relief, he doubled-back and clamped his hands on both their shoulders. His tight grip made the brothers jolt upright. As their hearts raced, the rector set his round, silvered head between theirs and whispered in a strong Lancashire accent,

'Eeh, lads, no Leper's Leg for you!'

9

As Jason got out of the Volvo and walked across the laundry car park, he felt for his wife. Poppy had spent years working her way up to management level and he knew that the loss of the job would hit her hard. Worse still, by the look of things, the process of dismantling the building and its contents was already well underway. Several skips, full to the brim, stood at the main entrance and Jason failed to detect the usual rhythm of noise coming from the place. The washing tubs, presses and drying cylinders were all silent. As he put his head against one of the dusty windows, he could see that even the large conveyor belt where the workers sorted out the linen was at a standstill. The place looked forlorn as men in luminous yellow overalls, like foul, upright locusts, removed fixtures and fittings, devouring everything in sight. It seemed indecent to do all this while Poppy was still there. He shook his head sadly and wondered if she would adjust. All this would surely dent his wife's fast-ebbing pride.

When Jason moved inside, he felt the drop in temperature. The place had always been hot and humid. Now it felt alien and unwelcoming, although far less smelly. Some of the men were breaking up the larger clothes presses while others wrenched sheet metal from the industrial dryer. This produced a monstrous, almost human whining, as if the machine were objecting to its fate. More bits came away and clattered to the damp, musty concrete. Jason inspected the demolition team's animated faces, their rubbery necks and glistening teeth. They seemed to be enjoying their work and he imagined a ball and chain would soon rip the heart out of the building.

Jason crossed the main floor, carving his way through a mist of dust, trying to avoid eye contact with the men. He was so angry he felt like knocking into them as he passed by. The workers sensed his aggression and quickly stepped out of his path. After all, he was not a small man. Even so, Jason nearly caught one of the younger ones with his shoulder as he bore down on Poppy's office. Then he jogged up the wooden stairs to the platform at the top. With a quick valedictory inspection of the dark, geometric patches on the floor where some of the machines had once stood, he opened the office door.

Poppy looked up from her desk and cracked the weakest, flimsiest smile, utter defeat written across her face. Mountains of papers, bills, statements and memos shrouded the desk, and a generation of envelopes and files littered the floor all around her. Some of the documents had old stamps on them. Jason surveyed his wife's former territory, his eyes falling on stripped cabinets, shabby boxes, old redundant mechanical and electric typewriters, and a mop and a bucket. He turned swiftly and thumped the doorjamb with the heel of his hand. The dull thud echoed out into the emptying heart of the building.

'God, I can't bear to look!' he said. 'It's unbelievable! They are not hanging about, are they?'

Poppy began to cry more deeply, then primitively, from the gut and thread of her being. She started to pull the drawers from her desk, turning them upside down. All manner of things bounced across the floorboards. Not satisfied with this blind, tearful rage, Poppy swiped everything from her desk and sent it skittering before Jason's feet. As always, Jason froze in the face of such an emotional outburst. He looked on, scratching his balding, desolate head, swallowing drily. Finally, Poppy relented, crouching in a strange, apelike manner beside her desk, her head bobbing on a wave of tears. Then Jason crossed the paper-strewn floorboards, a biro cracking under his foot, and bent down to wrap his wife in his arms, brushing his lips back and forth over her jerking head.

'Come on,' he comforted. 'Let's get out of here.'

Poppy did not move for some time. Eventually, she caught Jason's eyes and rose unsteadily to her feet. He embraced her, pulling her head into his chest and stroking it. Then slowly, he guided her out of the office, down the steps and across the main floor of the laundry. They both winced with each blow of hammers on metal. The men in their luminous overalls did not stop or stare. They simply got on with demolition.

Outside, Jason escorted Poppy to the car, his big arm wrapped around her shoulder. He opened the passenger door, tenderly feeding her into the front passenger seat. Then he walked round to the driver's side, swearing under his breath and taking a final look at the condemned building before driving away at high speed, the wheels skidding on the oily ground between the amputated barriers. Jason did not slow down. He hit the main carriageway with the suspension creaking and tyres squealing. He was so angry at how the hospital authorities had treated his wife. Primed for rage now, he tailgated a car going slowly in the fast lane, cursing, flashing his lights and blasting his horn.

'Slow down!' Poppy told him, despite her otherwise torpid state.

'OK, Pops,' he relented, easing off the accelerator and allowing the Volvo to fall back.

When they got home, Juju was waiting for them on the drive. He moved to one side as Jason steered the car onto the gravel. As they got out, Juju came forward and presented a dead sparrow that he had caught. A bloody feather protruded from between his sharp, perfect teeth.

'I wish he'd leave the birds alone,' Poppy complained, walking up to the front door.

'It's just nature,' replied Jason in a tired, subdued voice, resigned to material reality and thinking about his brother's corpse lying in the ground. He stopped and addressed Juju. 'You know, don't you, boy?'

The cat looked through him with a gaze of unknowing.

'You know we're just meat puppets, right? That's all we are.'

†

Jason sat close to the gas fire in the front room of his mother's house, watching the flames buckle, straighten and lick the artificial lumps of coal. Poppy sat opposite, silent, her eyes downcast and vacant, her hands like dead fish in her lap. Jason looked briefly, anxiously at her pale cheeks and then at his mother standing with her back to him at the window. It was the same window that he had pressed his face to all those years ago to spy Umbie and Poppy in their first, short-lived clinch. Now the watery light of the table lamp outlined Mrs Hemp's peachy, soft face. Her small, curving back shuddered and fell still.

'You'll have to pull together,' she advised, almost whispered. 'You and Poppy need each other more than ever now. Jason? Do you understand?'

'Perfectly,' he mumbled restlessly, charmed as always by the unravelling, evaporating snakes of fire.

'Umbie's looking over us now. He's still with us,' his mother intoned in her dreamy, recalcitrant Catholic way. 'I visited him this morning and felt his presence.'

Jason picked his fingernails and gazed at the collection of religious statues that kept vigil in the room, from the two-foot plastic figure of the Sacred Heart of Jesus on top of the old radiogram to the collection of luminous holy water bottles from Lourdes in the shape of the Virgin Mary on the mantelpiece. There was no escape from these watchful icons. As a boy, Jason had suffered pangs of guilt in their presence, especially before the Holy Child of Prague carefully positioned above his bed and Our Lady of Fatima to police the toilet. Jason had lost count of the many times that they had clouded the joy of his body.

After a long silence, Mrs Hemp spoke again. 'Poppy says you've been acting rather strangely.'

Jason looked up sharply, nettled that Poppy had been reporting to his mother on the state of his mind. Suddenly, he felt alienated and isolated in the shrine of statues. He stared angrily at his wife.

'She says you're mad for revenge!' Mrs Hemp continued.

Jason was fuming now.

'Now that is wrong, Jason. That won't help anyone.'

Jason went over to the fire and picked up the redundant poker. He jabbed the fake coals into a better position, allowing the gas-fuelled flames to gather more fully. Then he placed the poker back in its brass holder and sat back down. He put his head in his hands and sighed deeply.

'We have to turn the other cheek,' his mother insisted, moving away from the window and sitting down next to the old needlework stool—a perch the twins had fought over on wintry evenings away from Saint Ergonwald's. 'We have to learn to forgive.' Yet forgiveness was hard, even for Mrs Hemp, and she began to cry quietly, noiselessly, searching the pockets of her cardigan for a handkerchief.

After a long silence, Jason spoke up again. 'I was closest to Umbie and understood him more than anyone,' he said in a sullen mood. 'He had no friends except me. He was my twin brother. He was, no, *is* part of me. You can't turn the cheek of a dead man, so I won't be turning mine.'

'Such fine words!' mocked Poppy. 'You're not at work now.'

Jason blanked her. 'All I want,' he said looking at the poker in its holder, 'is the man who did it.'

'The police will find him. It's not your business,' his mother warned tearfully. 'They'll get a lead, you'll see.'

Jason laughed coarsely.

'Why are you laughing?'

'They have one already,' he told her.

'You didn't say,' complained Poppy, before Mrs Hemp could respond. 'Well, there you go. They are onto something. So, leave it to them and stop thinking about revenge. It will not do you any good. Listen to your mum.'

Jason's face turned sour. 'You obviously have more faith in the police than I do,' he said.

Now Mrs Hemp was rubbing her arthritic knuckles in frustration, the bowls of her eyes still moist. 'They know best, Jason.'

He was shaking his head now. 'I could do a better job,' he told her.

This brought contemptuous laughter from Poppy and Mrs Hemp rubbed her bumpy hands even harder, distressed by her son's comments.

'Jason, please,' his mother implored. 'You must look after one another now, especially with Poppy losing her job. Please, you should stop any silly thoughts of revenge. Focus on your work at the university, otherwise, things could turn out even worse for both of you!'

For a moment, Jason seemed to back down. He squeezed his lips together and gazed at the dark circles around his wife's eyes. His head started to nod.

'You are right,' he said. He held Poppy's limp, leaden hands and began to stroke them.

'We all have so much to bear,' Mrs Hemp added hopefully.

Jason nodded, looking around, surrounded on all sides by plastic heaven. 'Yes,' he said staring hard into the eyes of the Sacred Heart of Jesus. 'You are right about that.'

†

Jason moved through the black gates of the cemetery, his long coat open, carrying a small parcel under his arm. His eyes darted about and his feet kicked up the gravel as he took long, determined strides past the big, dark crucifix. He had no time to mark the flight of a brambling that skirted the hedgerows. He had no time to acknowledge Danny the gravedigger who lifted his spade in greeting. Jason hurried on past the water tap, the bright sun on his sweat-filmed face. The rest of the cemetery was quiet. The sound of chopped earth resumed as the gravedigger continued to dig a new hole next to a magnificent tomb set over one of Ardinweald's richest and now stillest families.

When Jason reached Umbie's tombstone, he quickly sat down, out of sight, took the package from his coat pocket and began to open it. The foil glittered in the sharp sunlight. Carefully, Jason peeled it back, revealing the burnt lump of cake he had cooked and stored in the garage. He stared at it, transfixed, his eyes as wide as saucers. He began stroking its black, shiny surface with great reverence. With each caress, the smile on his face transformed into a grin. He lifted the cake gently from the foil, dry crumbs and shrivelled currants falling away onto his lap and the cold tombstone. Jason's body trembled now. He licked his lips and set the lump of cake to one side. Then, with his eyes darkening in the shadow cast by the headstone, he spoke to his brother.

'This is a sacrament of revenge,' he said. 'It will lead me to your killer.'

Jason checked over his shoulder that nobody was standing nearby in the observatory ruins or coming through the wall of beech trees. There was only the gravedigger and he was down a hole, the sound of his shovelling interrupting the gentle birdsong. Happy in his isolation, Jason took a knife from his coat pocket and began to chop the shrunken, gritty cake into little segments. As he did so, he hummed intermittently, as if he now had an appetite. When he finished, he cleaned the knife between his thumb and finger and placed it on the tombstone. The cake was in six wedges.

Then, like old Father O'Connell, the fuddled chaplain at Saint Ergonwald's who had kindly officiated at Umbie's funeral, Jason held his hands over the cake to consecrate it. His fingers shook as he entertained scruples about what he was doing, yet he remained determined to perform his own twisted liturgy. In a parody of the chaplain and with the rubric of the Catholic Mass still deeply ingrained, he raised the cake in his hands and mumbled quietly,

'Blessed are you, Lord, God of all creation. Through your goodness, we have this cake to offer, which earth has given and human hands have made. It will become for us the—' Here Jason paused to consider the phrasing, but could not find the words.

Now Jason looked around again, feeling conspicuous in his bizarre ritual, quickly stuffing each slice of the small cake, one after the other, into his mouth. As he ate, moiling saliva, his eyes closed in a kind of ecstasy. His jaw chomped and he breathed noisily through his nose, swallowing down each bolus. Now and then, he felt the hairs from the murderer's head catch like the finest kipper bones, making him retch a little. Yet, he persevered and drove the cake down his throat. Only after working up a good deal of spittle was he able to eat the last segment.

'Lead me to him,' he chanted quietly as he put the silver foil and knife back into his coat pocket and brushed ant-like crumbs from the white marble.

No sooner had he made this incantation and with the cake barely in his stomach than the sacrament seemed to work its magic, filling his mind with an idea of how to find the killer. The strategy surprised him. He slapped his forehead several times in admonition for not thinking of this before. How could he overlook something quite so direct, so obvious? He laughed briefly like a failed ignition and shook his head, the tip of his tongue searching for fragments of hair caught like floss between his teeth. He badly needed a drink now, so he set off for the water tap. He turned it on and stuck his head under it. The steady stream broke around his chin and splashed generously onto the gravel. He took a mouthful, only stopping when a nasty tang intruded. He grimaced and spat the water out. Then he saw the little sign: "NOT POTABLE" and shrugged, closing the faucet. Despite the foul taste, at least the water had done the trick of wetting his mouth.

As he turned away, the gravel crunching under his feet, Jason believed he could harness the spirit world. He thought about good-luck charms, voodoo dolls, black cats, chicken wishbones, blowing out candles, kissing dice, knocking wood, throwing salt over the shoulder, the number thirteen, breaking mirrors, not walking under ladders, avoiding cracks in pavements and not opening umbrellas in the house. He saw Father O'Connell lifting and eating the Body of Christ. Of course, all this sat uncomfortably with Jason's life as a university lecturer, a man of learning. Yet, the mental habits of his Catholic past had returned in his grief and desperation. He had reached out to a nonsensical force to guide him to Umbie's killer. More suited to medieval times, to seasons of history and culture when priests hid in holes and superstition reigned, he had fallen back into old thinking. By the time Jason left the cemetery, passing through its iron gates, he had convinced himself that his actions were no less foolish than any other spiritual fetish. He was just like anyone else indulging in the absurd and grappling with unjustified beliefs.

10

It was a cold, windy day, and Jason stood in the middle of the pavement on Ardinweald High Street, watching heads of shoppers floating by: shaven, unshaven, pale, ruddy, mouse-skulled, native or foreign. Not one hat did he see. Admittedly, he had only been observing for a matter of minutes, but even so, Jason felt disappointed. Sitting down on the low wall fronting the parish church, he figured things out in his hot, tightening mind. It seemed logical that Umbie's killer would be wearing a hat of some kind. After all, how else would he hide a tear in his scalp? Jason had checked online and found that ripped-out hair follicles can take months to recover, if at all. It was likely that the killer still had a patch of hair missing. Looking around, hats were definitely not in fashion. Even after half an hour of studying Ardonian heads, Jason saw only three flat caps worn by old men, and teenagers with hoodie-covered baseball caps. Disappointed, he got up and crossed the road, mingling with the crowds, wanting to extend his search. He was as convinced as ever that the killer must be a local man.

All along High Street, Jason moved in and out of shops, keeping his eyes peeled. There was little headwear to draw his attention. In the busiest part of Ardinweald, between the baker and the library, he only saw two elderly sisters with woolly hats leaving a charity shop and a child with a cotton bonnet. He found the same pattern in the market square where people gathered around the fountain. For quite some time, Jason just stood watching the jet of water spurting at the threatening clouds above, letting people move around him. Then he got back on with his mission and continued down High Street that doglegged through the older part of Ardinweald, with its traditional Victorian fronts, towards Nottingham Road and the less prosperous side of the city.

On this stretch was a music shop, an estate agent, several banks, a number of boutiques and McCartie's, the butcher's, with its pigs in the window, rabbits and pheasants at the door, and sawdust everywhere, even on the pavement. Jason stopped briefly outside and stared at the bright red meat. Mrs McCartie was leaning over neatly arranged trays, scooping the best mince into a thin, white bag while her husband worked at the butcher's block to the rear of the shop.

Jason was tempted to go inside and buy some lamb chops for later. He never bought produce from the small outlets in Ardinweald, preferring his local supermarket, but after weeks of eating convenient tinned or frozen food, he liked the idea of some fresh meat. However, even the small queue of customers put him off. Besides, he had his task at hand so moved away from the window. As he did so, he saw the bobbing reflection of a woodland boonie hat—the kind worn by military personnel. It belonged to a powerful-looking man with a thick neck who wore a black T-shirt, army trousers and boots. Tattoos adorned his muscular, toned arms and he walked knuckles forward. Jason hesitated, suddenly anxious about a possible confrontation. The man looked like trouble, the kind of person with blood on his hands. Despite his nervousness, Jason set off after him, eventually finding the nerve to step in his path, holding up a shaking hand.

'Excuse me,' he said as politely as he could manage, but at a pitch that betrayed his fear.

The man stopped with his hands twitching and with lips pushed out in an aggressive, questioning way. 'Yeah? What do you want?'

Jason pulled at his ear nervously, unable to gain eye contact, knowing that he could be standing in front of Umbie's killer. 'I wonder if, er,' he struggled. 'I could look at your head?'

'Fuck off! You're joking, right?' said the man, tucking the back of his T-shirt into his trousers and puffing up his chest.

'No.'

The man frowned heavily at Jason and then unexpectedly boomed with laughter. The noise sent Jason backwards, knocking into another pedestrian. He gave an apology, feeling totally awkward and ridiculous, turning this way and that on the pavement, in part to see whether he was now isolated and at the mercy of the strongly built man.

'You want to see *my* head?' grunted the man tapping his brow and fending Jason off with the palm of his hand. 'I think you should ask someone to look at yours!'

Jason suddenly felt humiliated at his amateurish quest and having drawn the curiosity of other people on the street, did not know what to do for the best. He watched as the man sauntered away, cursing. For all Jason knew, the man with the boonie was Umbie's killer. However, in a comedic gesture, the man turned back towards him, lifted his hat and pointed at his head in a mocking gesture. His short brown, crew cut was neat and unblemished.

'You nutter!' the man told him, turning away, with his middle finger in the air.

Jason walked quickly in the opposite direction, towards the city and much nearer to where Umbie had fallen. He decided he would go to one of Nottingham's biggest and most popular shopping malls. The volume of shoppers would give him more chance to locate his brother's killer. He also realised that asking to see people's heads would not work. It was too off-the-wall. He would have to take a risk and simply knock off or remove people's headwear should he spot a likely candidate. With the consecrated pieces of cake in his belly and mind, Jason knew he had to act. Umbie's killer would not come to him. Only he could bring justice. His reputation was at stake, of course, but what was that compared to the monstrosity of Umbie's death? He began to invest more in the sacrament he had taken, willing it along with an increased mix of blind belief and hope. If he sent hats flying, he could quickly say sorry, as if it were an accident. Then he would have just enough time to check the person's scalp and, if needed or threatened, run away into the crowd.

Jason was delighted that it had started to rain by the time he arrived at the mall. The change in weather would bring people together inside for his inspection. With grim determination, he strode through the pillared entrance, looking up briefly at the ribbed arches, glass canopy and elegant café balcony before turning his attention to the wide variety of heads. He walked slowly past the little boutiques, breathless, his eyes scanning back and forth. Now and again, shoppers took a dislike to his intense staring and curled their lips at him, tutting and drawing in their chins. As wave after wave of them broke around him, Jason sensed there was a good chance of finding his quarry.

Eventually, he spotted a man with a dirty black fedora and his heart and skin froze over. The man looked just as hard-faced as the man with the boonie outside McCartie's, but not so powerfully built. He also looked sharp, with his hat tilted back from his face. He had a vape dangling from his lip and walked at people, forcing them to step aside. Jason hesitated slightly, looking around, opening and closing his twitching hands before setting off after him, weaving around the other shoppers. Within a minute or so, he was bearing down on his target and chopping the hat from his head. It flipped backwards onto the floor. Kicked by passing feet, the hat came to rest several feet away. As the man searched for it and picked it up, Jason quickly scanned the man's compressed hair.

He was not Umbie's killer. Jason could see clearly that his hair was the wrong colour. It was also intact. While the man dusted off the fedora and plonked it back on his head, looking around for his assailant, Jason had already turned on his heel and disappeared. By dodging and hunching low, he hid in the crowd. It was as if he were back in a scrum on Saint Ergonwald's rugby field. He only slowed down and rose to his normal height when he felt confident that the man was not carving his way after him.

Despite the adrenaline rush, Jason felt less energised by his mission now. It seemed rather pathetic and futile. Puffing and panting, he felt miserable that he had traded in his dignity in this way, yet such a feeling did not stop him from examining heads as he made his way through the mall. He began coaching himself that nothing was too ridiculous if it led to him finding the murderer. For that, he vowed to sacrifice everything.

As he moved past the elaborate, famous public mechanical clock, he caught sight of three young men.

They looked intimidating, their faces heavily shadowed and obscured in damp hoodies. Jason quickly shifted his position, appearing to take an interest in a store window display, but tracking them in the reflection. All of the young men kept their hoods up, attracting Jason's suspicion. They all wore the same dark grey clothing and training shoes. He watched as they loitered by the clock, forming a circle. They looked very shifty, constantly checking around them. Each carried a little bag, the kind used by drug suppliers in the city.

Jason saw how one of the group kept looking up, appearing to scan for CCTV cameras, his features briefly visible. Jason noted a frond of dark brown hair dividing his brow and the kind of gaunt, scrawny face that he associated with drug addiction. Indeed, the other members of what Jason now viewed as a gang kept tapping each other, sometimes fist to fist or in a sly way that suggested they might be transferring illicit substances between them. They looked like the kind of people that broke into homes or mugged people. After all, drug addicts always needed money, and Umbie's attackers had emptied his wallet. With some concern that the man with the fedora might double back and collar him, and having decided upon his target, Jason made his move.

He walked quickly and directly at the group, keeping his head down as if he were some middle-aged punk in a rush to leave the mall. Then he pounced. He was fast and skilful, belying his years. His hands pulled back each of the young men's hoods, and his eager eyes began to inspect the integrity of their hair. As he studied them, he saw how their heads twisted and ducked. Then before Jason knew what was happening, he felt a crack on his nose and hit the floor, blood gushing everywhere. It all happened in a blur. One of the young men had head-butted him.

Soon enough, Jason found himself looking up at security guards from the mall, mouthing into their walkie-talkies. His eyes filled with silver sparks. The man with the fedora was there, standing next to the three young men.

'Yes, we caught him on camera, don't worry,' said one of the guards, reaching down and grabbing Jason under the arms. 'Right, on your feet,' he added, tugging at him.

Jason's heels scrambled in his own blood as he straightened up, wincing. He squeezed the bridge of his nose to stem the bleed.

'What the fuck was that about?' asked one of the grim-faced youths he had assaulted.

Jason swallowed drily and opened his mouth to say something. Yet his tongue was like wire wool and merely garbled.

At that point, two police officers arrived. Jason was pleased to see that they immediately began quizzing the gang members, taking their details. All the hoods were off now and they looked far less menacing. Jason felt relieved that things were going the right way. After all, the one who smashed his beak would surely face charges.

'Thanks, lads,' said the male officer. 'We'll be in touch if we need a statement.'

Jason frowned heavily, astonished that the police were engaging in a bit of banter with the hoodies. The taller of the youths twirled an index finger at his right temple. After a short time, the gang drifted freely away into the mall crowd.

'Hey! Hey!' shouted Jason, coming round now, trying to get after them, aware that he had lost the chance to examine their heads properly before being floored, but the male officer held him firmly by the collar of his coat. 'Look what they've done,' Jason complained, pointing to his bloody nose. 'Don't just stand there! Arrest them!'

The officer shook his head lightly, completely unmoved.

'Did you get them on CCTV?' Jason appealed to the security guard.

The female officer turned to the man with the fedora and spoke to him briefly. When she finished, she came back to Jason and got him to take out his wallet, checking his ID. She passed a driving licence to her collegue and then addressed Jason directly, slipping handcuffs over his wrists.

'I am arresting you on suspicion of assault, you do not have to say anything, but it may harm your defence if you do not mention when questioned something you later rely on in court. Anything you do say may be given in evidence.'

'What? I am not going anywhere with you,' Jason said, struggling to get away.

However, the officers converged and the cuffs suddenly tightened. Jason complained that his wrists hurt, but the police ignored him, handling him through the curious onlookers out onto the rain-drenched street and into the waiting van.

†

Poppy sat in Inspector Mosby's sparse office dabbing her eyes with a paper handkerchief, her hair like a mop, her lower lip quivering. A bubble of saliva formed as she opened her sour, musty mouth. She stared bleakly through the barred windows into an unkempt, sodden yard, worrying for Jason, for herself, for his mother. There had never been such shame as now. She croaked into the handkerchief, filling it with hot tears, smudging it with lipstick, covering her mortified, shrunken face. Inspector Mosby sat opposite on a hard chair, bending forward, zipping his fingers together under his nose.

'I understand what Jason's been through. It has been a difficult time for him. Did he tell you that we are closing in on your brother-in-law's killer?'

Poppy was not really listening. Waves of tears fell copiously onto her shrouded fingers. Inspector Mosby looked at her wild, tousled hair and then at his own highly polished shoes. After a few moments, he stood up and crossed the room to the barred window, his face softening in the remains of the storm light, his birthmark becoming less obvious. He looked up at the dark clouds, pressed together like oily sardines.

Poppy stared at the long weeds that had made their way up to the bottom of the window. 'Where is he? Can I see him?'

'He's in the next room.'

'I can't work it out,' she snivelled. 'What is he up to? It's not like him.'

'His behaviour is certainly strange,' admitted the inspector.

'Why would he knock hats off people's heads?'

'I have no idea, Mrs Hemp. Perhaps he is still in a kind of grief shock. It does happen.'

For a moment, Poppy sat quiet and thoughtless as if she were the handkerchief, crumpled and wet in her hand. A sudden break in the thick clouds allowed a burst of sunlight through the bars of the window, casting stripes across the grey floor. Mosby looked at how they slanted towards the doorway and over Poppy, her face deleted. Then the light faded once more.

'It'll get round the town, the university, everywhere. He will be a laughing stock. I am so afraid. I fear he is going to do something even worse. I can't bear it!' confessed Poppy.

'Try to stay calm,' urged the detective.

Poppy drew a deep breath.

'That's right, that's better, now then.'

Poppy blew hard and long into another handkerchief until her tears dried and her shoulders became still. She was in a corner of her mind without edges. In the resurgent sunlight, a stripe of light moved back slowly over her face. Her hand opened, and the handkerchief fell to the floor. At that point, the desk sergeant entered the room with two cups of tea and placed them on the table.

'Have you called Dr Bent?' Mosby asked him.

'Yes, sir.'

'And?'

'He's on his way.'

'Good. Let me know when he arrives.'

When the desk sergeant left the room, Mosby slid one of the cups in front of Poppy.

'There's a tea,' he said gently.

She thanked him and took the cup into her shaking hands. Inspector Mosby waited for her to settle a little before continuing.

'How's he been lately?'

Poppy looked up. 'He's been weird,' she said.

'Weird?'

Poppy set her cup back down on the table and, picking up the handkerchief again, blew her nose. 'He's been wandering the garden at night and even baking cakes in the early hours of the morning.'

'Sleepwalking?'

'No, I don't think so, but he is just not right,' moaned Poppy with flustered breath, wagging her head from side to side, quite agitated, starting to lose control of her emotions again. 'He's obsessed with finding Umbie's killer. All he wants is revenge. It's all he thinks about.' Poppy breathed rapidly, looking as if she would progress into a panic attack.

'Now, Mrs Hemp, please. Try to keep calm,' Mosby sensitively advised her, coming round the table and placing a hand on her shoulder.

'I've lost my job. I have lost everything! Umbie is dead and Jason's—'

Mosby sat back down again. 'Things will turn out OK. You'll see.'

Now Poppy was shaking her head dramatically. 'No, they won't!'

Mosby stood up and walked across the stripes that brightened and then faded suddenly as the late sun moved behind yet another bank of cloud.

Poppy looked up, her lips full, vulnerable, her breathing still affected. 'I think my husband's going mad,' she confessed.

She blinked her thick, smudged eyelids. The stripes grew bold again.

11

Even consultant psychiatrists get depressed and Dr Bent felt bummed out as he travelled down on his motorbike to attend court. The usual bursts of speed he put the Harley through had not cleared his head this time. His mood was resolutely low and he knew that it was likely to get worse rather than better. As he pulled up outside the intimidating red brick building, he created quite a stir among passersby. For Dr Bent was definitely singular and followed his name: refractory. His ancestors came from land with bent grass, rushes or reeds. He wore black leathers and was fully six feet two inches of gothic ornament. When he took off his helmet, his curious detachable hair extension uncoiled down his back. He did not acknowledge the questioning eyes or murmurings of the public. He slowly, methodically tidied his striking black Lycra vest and leggings with beringed fingers. He fiddled with the multiple silver piercings in his ears. Then he headed for the court entrance with his usual stomp.

The court security guards pulled faces at each other as Dr Bent removed all the metal from his person, just as he did at Foston Hall, the largest and most forbidding high-security hospital where he was now Medical Director after a stellar rise through the clinical ranks. Fortunately, this morning, at court, he had remembered to leave his more private set of bodily adornments on the bedside table at his apartment, a short walk from the high perimeter fence of the hospital. Now, he handed over his helmet and goggles for safe storage and placed the jewellery from his fingers and ears, heavy spike-adorned motorbike boots, skull-buckle belt, hair extension and jacket in the tray. One of the guards asked him to lift his inked arms and waved a paddle wand around him, frowning at the fruity bike odour of his armpits. Then Dr Bent walked through nonchalantly in his bare feet to gather his stuff.

As soon as he cleared security, and with his boots back on, Dr Bent stomped off to find Court Number Three, moving past various barristers carrying documents. They moved in their wigs, gowns, wing collars or collarets like peculiar turkeys, sporting two white bands that hung from their necks. Dr Bent's dark attire almost blended with theirs. He found their subdued gobbling rather odd, stopping and starting with an economy of sound. A few of them noted Dr Bent with cursory and stereotypical assessments before returning to their conversations. He proceeded to the correct door, gave his name to the attendant and slipped into the public gallery. He felt he had entered a house of worship, taking the last free space on the first of two rows of benches. It irked him. He was not a spiritual person. He had witnessed far too many traumas in his lifetime and listened to countless religious delusions. Unfortunately, Foston Hall housed many candidates for Messiahs or Satans. It was a hospital for patients with mental health problems exhibiting high-risk behaviour such as violence or sexual offending. It catered for those who posed a grave and immediate risk to the public.

Dr Bent sat quietly, his head bowed in contemplation; hands clasped together, wet with sweat. His forehead also leaked, even though it was not a hot day. People behind him muttered about the leathery smell from the stranger in the gothic clothes. They winced in distaste at the tail of hair falling from the back of his skull, the strange bits of coloured fabric tied into it and the monochrome, Celtic tattoos on his upper arms. They studied the silver hoops that distended his earlobes. This scrutiny went on for some time while Dr Bent rocked a little, disturbed by his reflections. His head bowed lower with the pain of his thoughts. The knuckles of his strong hands blanched with the increased pressure of clasping. He tried to calm himself by picking at his fingernails that held traces of bike dirt and oil.

Finally, the bailiff of Court Number Three called for everyone to rise for the session led by Honourable Judge Masterson. Everyone, including Dr Bent, rose dutifully, postured as for a funeral. In a way, it was just that. Judge Masterson used the pause to raise a respectful tension in the air before entering briskly in his red robe and stern wig, taking barely any time at all to sit behind his bench, perfunctorily adjusting the black microphone. With only his upper chest, head and arms visible, he stared directly to the rear of the courtroom and the high-walled, glass dock like an oversized fish tank in which the defendant appeared standing with a powerful-looking guard. Dr Bent summoned up the courage to lift his head and peer into the dock. The man in his eighties had thin white hair, a slightly flattened nose and expressionless eyes hunkered down behind a prominent brow. He was steadying himself with one hand on a wooden rail. The court was quiet. In noose-like silence, Dr Bent waited, his heart beating rapidly now. He knew the man was a psychopath, a narcissist. All his years of training had made that blatantly clear.

Above and behind the judge hung the royal coat of arms. Below, an extended pit held a stenographer and advocates for the plaintiff and defendant. The jury box stood empty. The defendant had eventually pleaded guilty after the case had been elevated to the crown court by magistrates. The sentencing was for the judge alone.

His Honour Judge Masterson spoke quietly and seriously as he gave his finding. Everyone remained in place behind respective benches. Dr Bent's body swayed nervously in the pause for emphasis offered by the judge before providing an account of his determination. The seriousness of the crimes was set out. Judge Masterson explained the tariff for each criminal offence. There would be leniency for pleading guilty, he told the court, stating that this was the *one and only good thing* the defendant had done. He had also factored in the age of the defendant. This legal calculation continued for some time before Judge Masterson leant forward on his forearms and joined his hands. Lifting his head and looking directly into the eyes of the old man in the dock, he announced a very long sentence.

The defendant did not flicker. His face remained as still as the royal coat of arms above the head of Judge Masterson. Dr Bent looked into the glass dock at the shrunken figure. He saw now that the man had a walking stick and was talking to the guard looming over him. He had taken off his court headphones and placed them on the shelf beneath the wall of glass. Then he stood up and with stick in hand headed briskly and without any sign of pain towards the door leading back into the courtroom. It was now clear to Dr Bent that the man had been faking frailty. The stick was a sympathy prop that had failed. The guard shook his head mockingly and quickly took hold of the old man's elbow, guiding him in the opposite direction toward the door leading down to the cells and the awaiting prison van. The old man appeared puzzled and asked the guard something. The guard did not respond except to feed him through the doorway and out of the public realm. *That man looks remarkably like my father*, thought Dr Bent.

†

Foston Hall lay dark and forbidding in beautiful countryside. On approach from the higher ground to the south, racing downhill as fast as the Harley and the road surface allowed, Dr Bent could see for miles. Yet he knew that at Foston Hall, from the flatness of its security and high fences, there was a restricted view of the surrounding, stunning land. The four hundred mostly male patients had little access to the open air, with limited, circular tarmacadam paths in each controlled section. On his appointment as Medical

Director, one of the first things he did was to set up a committee for improving the environment for all those unfortunate enough to have ended up inside the high-security hospital, including over two thousand staff. Dr Bent retained a deep empathy for those patients in the facility who had done things beyond their control, terrible things. They had ended up with indeterminate sentences for following command hallucinations to kill loved ones or members of the public. His empathy for many of the other patients was more circumspect, not least those with dangerous personality disorders who walked the line between illness and standing trial for their crimes: serial killers, kidnappers of royalty, child killers and clinicians wielding the power of God over life and death. Either way, he believed that leaving patients to go stir-crazy in their confinement was a danger for everyone.

As he flew along, his jacket inflating in the icy air of his speed, Dr Bent tried to shake off the courtroom and the defendant performing disability. The defence team had tried to place him on the autism spectrum with Aspergers. They insisted on a lower bar of personal responsibility, stressing a lack of awareness of the consequences of his actions. Fortunately, the judge did not buy it, concluding that the defendant had the capacity and used it in despicable ways. The judge had him in his crosshairs, saw him for what he was, a cruel narcissist, and passed the right verdict and sentence. Now the convicted offender would be on his way in a white prison van to Stafford Prison. Dr Bent did not feel triumphant or happy about this, just relieved. The Lodger, as he called him, had gone down.

The high speed and buffeting from the wind were as turbulent as the dark thoughts inside Dr Bent's skull. As his body took hits of air and dips in the tarmac, his mind careered again through all that had happened. Foston Hall and the comfort of his apartment could not come soon enough. He accelerated along a straight section of country lane without thought of the sheep or cows that sometimes escaped their fields. His goggles pressed into his cheekbones, his arms stiffened and tears pooled. The Harley gave all it had. Dr Bent opened the throttle fully. He wanted to blow away the cobwebs of his grief and loss. He wanted the air to cut through his brain, a helmet-shaped mousse of fat and protein, perform a lobotomy and erase all those bad thoughts. When a tractor started to emerge from a field, he nearly got his wish, missing its baling spikes by a whisker.

At the next bend in the road, closing in on Foston Hall, Dr Bent dropped his speed, sobered by the flash of the tractor's long metal spikes and gory end. Although he wanted to die on a daily basis, he did not wish to die *like that*.

†

In the year before the court case, Dr Bent had struggled with depression to the point that Dr Tim Sargent, a senior colleague and friend at Foston Hall, persuaded him to try psychoanalysis. Dr Sargent had noted his poor concentration, more dishevelled appearance and fruitier than usual body odour and with kind honesty told him so. At first, Dr Bent felt reluctant to try it. He did not rate the therapy. It had little evidence supporting it. It was in decline. Yet his colleague gently nudged him that it might work, that he should open the box of childhood and look inside if his mood were to improve. Dr Bent knew he required a more predictable mental state if he was going to take on the big responsibility of running the biggest high-security hospital in England when the current medical director retired at the end of the year. He knew he had to do something to get himself in contention. His depression had become intractable. He struggled to sleep and had frequent suicidal thoughts. The usual medications did not work. Discreet online cognitive behaviour therapy and a host of other mind lifts did nothing.

Eventually, Dr Bent agreed with his friend and decided to try the couch. Yet as one of the most published consultant forensic psychiatrists in the country, with highly cited research papers in *The Lancet* and other chief journals, he felt ashamed. He kept hearing in his head the words *doctor heal thyself* and knew he had failed miserably in lifting his own mood. He had long suspected something awful had happened in the distant past and that his brain had erased or buried the memory to protect him. He knew there were some hard, calcified traumas locked deep in his skull. Although Dr Bent felt reluctant to poke around to find out exactly what had happened, he conceded to his friend's sound advice. If he wanted that final promotion to the helm, he needed to pull himself back from the brink. He had to get himself to a better place. Dr Sargent had suggested out-of-town therapy where Dr Bent could retain his anonymity and protect his stellar reputation and trajectory. Dr Bent looked at the options and chose a facility affording a decent bike ride.

†

On his first visit to the John Connolly Hospital in Manchester, a converted Victorian mansion near the city centre, Dr Bent found himself waiting beneath a huge, off-white marble fireplace. He studied its bluish veins, similar to his own marmoreal hands that gleamed a little now with sweat. He looked around him and up above the hearth at the shadow of where an impressive picture had once hung and felt exposed and vulnerable. He did not like the role reversal of this: the doctor had become the client. Now he was dependent on someone else's expertise—Dr Gluck—a mystery interlocutor. *Perhaps she will be the executioner of my childhood*, thought Dr Bent. He felt entirely bogus despite his foreboding that something had happened to him many years ago—literally, a gut feeling. He had only familiar, good memories of a decent upbringing. The Bents had been hardworking, generous and salt of the earth folk.

The place was empty but for one other client, an underfed young man leafing through old magazines, tapping his foot. In what was once a palatial dining hall, the wooden floor amplified the repetitive sound. Irritated by it, Dr Bent stood up and began stomping back and forth in front of the rigid hearth, his beringed fingers clasped behind his back. This did the trick. As he paced, his clomping resonated through the space. He annihilated the noise of the other client. As he moved, leaning forward from the waist in his characteristic manner, Dr Bent considered walking out and merely reporting to his colleague that he had attended psychoanalysis. Yet he knew that Tim was hawkish and would pursue the truth with his dark, languorous eyes.

After some time, gently and quietly, Dr Gluck appeared, crossing the space and introducing herself without physical contact of any kind, palming Dr Bent towards the stairs. He followed her up two flights and down a narrow passageway to a small unprepossessing room with a single chair and bare mattress bed. Dr Bent froze immediately, disconcerted to find himself in a bedroom *not* a bedroom—something other.

Dr Gluck was German, trained in the US, and kept her bobbed head at a curious angle. Dr Bent traced her jawline and wondered if there had been bone or tooth damage, a neck injury or some other trauma to her head. He observed that something about her face jarred. She looked like she was holding a sweet interminably behind the dash of her mouth.

'Do make yourself comfortable on the bed,' she announced in a calm, measured way.

The pillow lay at the wrong end of the bed that was *not* a bed. There was no wall behind or corner to shelter in. There was no cocoon, refuge or protection. Dr Bent felt exposed. He interpreted the scene as a stress test for trust and dithered.

'Yes, please, lie down,' Dr Gluck encouraged him. 'There's no need to take off your boots.'

Dr Bent rehearsed his approach before bringing his hairpiece around over his chest, sitting down and then swinging his biker feet to the end of the mattress. His spike-adorned boots rested on a fresh sheet of blue paper that had been set out to protect the fabric. As he lay there with crossed arms, Dr Gluck took the little chair and placed this behind the pillow-end. She was going to be the missing wall. Dr Bent felt as if he were at the dentist for an extraction or the hairdresser having his hair cut back. He wondered how Dr Gluck would operate in the bloodless fashion of their related albeit different professions. At the same time, he began struggling with memories of the only time in his life that he received a full body massage. He had been a student in Amsterdam. It had proved the opposite of relaxing, his abdomen turning to ice, like a washboard to a silky touch.

As Dr Bent tried to calm himself, head tilted forward with a view of nothing but his feet and the oversized roll of blue paper next to the bed, Dr Gluck's disembodied voice took centre stage.

'Please, try to relax,' she said with cool empathy. 'What brought you here today?'

Dr Bent shifted anxiously on the mattress, suddenly aware of an aura of negative pressure behind him. He experienced the bodiless voice of Dr Gluck as some kind of extraction device, a vacuum to draw out the truth, to pull at the lid of the black box in the middle of his memories. It was as stark and unnerving as that. It felt unnatural.

'A colleague suggested I try this,' he answered factually.

'Someone at Foston Hall?'

He paused. 'Yes.'

'So,' she pursued, then fell entirely silent for a long period.

This tiny word burrowed into the crown of Dr Bent's head. He waited for more words, but none came. *So*. His eyes moved around looking for something in his immediate field of vision to focus on and distract himself with, yet there was nothing: an empty room, a roll of blue paper, blank magnolia walls, a white ceiling and a window to nowhere. He wondered if Dr Gluck had quietly got up and left the room. He could not hear her breathing. She had become the invisible, non-judgemental listener. He could say anything. He could lift the rock set over his childhood and see what lay underneath. Yet would he be able to do that? The brain that was not his own kept things hidden and his mouth firmly shut. His mind whirred with all kinds of thoughts, images and desolations. This search for an entry point to the past went on for a long time. Now and then, he became aware he was mumbling away in a natural trance. Yet, in his head, everything was quiet. Eventually, the spell broke with the voice of Dr Gluck simply stating that the session had ended and she would see him on the same day at the same time the following week.

Dr Bent sat up as if woken by something in the dead of night. Had he spoken? Was the mumbling intelligible? Did he lose awareness? Had she hypnotised him? He thanked her without really knowing what service she had provided. Now visible at his side, with her lips still pinched together and no further communication, Dr Gluck gestured towards the door. Dr Bent spun off the bed and adjusted his tail of hair. He wanted to say something meaningful, yet did not form the words. Instead, he gave a weak but sincere thank you and left the room. Back out on the little corridor, he walked away slowly in a daze and without his usual stomp. This was the first time he had personally experienced psychoanalysis. Dr Gluck was clearly a Freudian and the bed, a more utilitarian substitute for a couch, had worked its magic. He had begun to free associate as he lay there. His mind had started to unfurl. He had begun to loosen the joints between his conscious and unconscious state.

†

Dr Bent shifted uncomfortably on the bed that was *not* a bed. He was anxious and hot, pickled in the silence of Dr Gluck. He feared speaking to her except in a neutral, edited way. His scalp tingled with her invisible presence. The opportunity and threat of free association of ideas lay between them. He began thinking about the ride over through Matlock where he had stopped briefly to inspect other motorbikes parked up alongside the Derwent. His mind drifted, recollecting the winding roads of the Peak District, looping through Eyam, the village that fell victim to the bubonic plague. He had read about its history and had always wished to see it for himself. He found himself talking about it.

'I came through Eyam on the way here today,' he told Dr Gluck. 'I don't know if you have ever been there?'

No response.

'During the plague, the villagers quarantined themselves to avoid catastrophy elsewhere. They set up a *cordon sanitaire*. Nobody came out. Nobody went in. The fleas kept jumping and doing their worst. About a third of the villagers succumbed and died.'

As if the fleas were present in the room, Dr Bent brushed at his tight black vest and continued talking about pandemics and the importance of social distancing. Dr Gluck did not respond. She maintained her therapeutic vigil, avoiding conversational cues and comforts, only her breathing and the fine friction of her pen audible as she made notes. Dr Bent lifted his blue eyes to their furthermost to glimpse the therapist behind his sweating head, but she sat out of range.

At that point, Dr Bent fell into a long and deep reflection with his hands joined across his chest and staring up at the blank ceiling. He felt at a complete loss. He felt ridiculous just talking randomly. He questioned the efficacy of psychoanalysis. It had all seemed reasonable during his training. He had put the technique away in his doctor's bag as one of several tools of the mind trade. Down the years, he had referred several of his patients for this remedy. Yet now the shine and grandeur of Sigmund Freud disappeared. On the couch for the first time, he doubted the whole enterprise. As he remained unsure, shaking his head and pursing his lips, his breathing gradually changed. The steady, quiet rhythm became a faster, nasal draw and then a burst of sighing.

All this time, Dr Gluck sat with a straight back behind him, her notes on her crossed knee, pen hanging over her notepad, head tilted to one side in rapt attention. Whatever lay buried in his childhood, bolted down, radioactive within a sarcophagus, would leak out. The position and response of Dr Bent's body had already spoken loudly. It was just that he did not know this yet.

Finally, Dr Bent surfaced in a jerking paroxysm, his eyes dilating; darkening.

'Raspberries!' he cried out.

12

Dr Bent sat at his desk and stared at the blank paper in front of him. He had always found it easier to write up case notes by hand. The laptop remained like a closed, silver clam to one side. Yet on that particular morning, he struggled to get words down. His hand hovered endlessly over the paper. His writing arm felt heavier than usual as if subject to a strange and powerful gravity. He persevered and wrote a little more then stopped. He put the pen down and sighed, massaging his head and neck. He despaired that he had ridden all the way to Dr Gluck in Manchester to find nothing but raspberries in his brain. Outside, an alarm sounded from Redwood Block. Dr Bent did not stir or flinch. These noises were a familiar soundscape. Foston Hall could sound at times like a monstrous bear pit. Each block had its unique alarm tone and sequence. Redwood gave off a *beep-beep-beep*. Cedar, where the most infamous inmates who had committed the most appalling crimes lived, *beep-boop-beep*. Pine signalled *woop-woop-woop*. Finally, Oak sounded *woop-boop-woop*. In a major threat such as fire, the continuous bell rang out, and then everyone moved to emergency station points for direct instruction on action.

The *beep-beep-beep* from Redwood intruded on Dr Bent's writing. He lifted and put down his pen several times as the ink in the well of his skull dried up. Instead, he picked up the sharp ceremonial katara he had bought while attending a conference in India. He used it to open letters (mostly medical or court reports) and the odd parcel. Although a stabbing blade, its edges were extremely sharp. He stared at the image of the Hindu God, Hanuman, like a little dancing monkey, engraved near the hilt, turning it over in his hands. He then lifted the blade to his neck and rehearsed what he would do if his depression continued unabated. This was not the first time he had toyed with a final surgery. In the early hours of the morning, in his dark blue velvet dressing gown, he often stumbled like a dementia sufferer through the dark of his apartment to take up the dagger and deliberate alone on *the* final solution. He tutored survival. He battled to resist the temptation. He cried and even growled at these times in the struggle to put the knife down and return to his bed.

†

'How's it going?' asked Dr Tim Sargent, joining Dr Bent in the far corner of the staff canteen at Foston Hall. No one else was around.

Dr Bent looked up from the large black filter coffee he supped. He appeared brighter. His face had a bit of colour and his eyes were lively.

'Well, I am not sure to be honest, Tim,' he said. 'I've never been a big fan of Freud, as you know. But let's say it is proving interesting.'

'Interesting? OK. That's a start.' Dr Sargent stirred a little milk into his tea and nodded gently, encouragingly, his eyes steady, unyielding.

'Yes, interesting,' confirmed Dr Bent before taking another draught of his coffee, holding it up in front of his chin.

Dr Sargent could see that Dr Bent's coffee mug had turned into a residual piece of armour, so he changed the topic. 'Still enjoying the bike? It's a good run over to Manchester.'

Dr Bent smiled, happy to change the subject. 'Now, that's the best therapy! Perhaps you should get one, Tim. Midlife crisis and all that?'

Dr Sargent automatically reached up and fingered the rondel of scalp showing through the back of his mud-brown hair. He tried to forget about it when looking in the bathroom mirror every morning and night, brushing his teeth with the best rotary brush money could buy. From the front, his face, dark eyes and athletic frame looked youthful after half a century of gravity and the stress hormone cortisol doing untold damage to his telomeres. Yet now and then, a random photograph or mirror combination would confirm his truant hair.

'I've often thought of buying one,' he admitted bringing his hand back down to his cup and fidgeting with the teaspoon. 'Harleys are fantastic! But it would look a bit odd if we both rode the same model!'

'Not at all! Get a different colour!'

'Maybe I will do just that,' he said with a smile, showing his perfect teeth.

'Now,' said Dr Bent suddenly in a no-nonsense, business mode. 'What do you think about my applying for one of those healthy environment large programme grants? I have written a draft. Can you look over it?'

'Yes, sure, no problem. This is for the raised ground, right?'

'Yes, and for a few additional features. Might as well go big! Upgrade some of our other facilities at the same time.' As if to underline his confidence, he downed the rest of his coffee.

'Of course, why not? Do you think they will cough up? It will certainly improve your chances of becoming Medical Director.'

'I will give the funders every reason to unlock the purse strings,' Dr Bent told him.

'How much are you going for?'

Dr Bent lent forward conspiratorially even though the old canteen was deserted and whispered in his ear.

Dr Sargent caught the scent of improved hygiene. 'Bloody hell!' he cried, knocking the green institutional teacup flying, stunned by Dr Bent's ambition. 'You're joking right?'

'Nope! I am not messing around, Tim! Go big or go home, as

they say.'

'Well, that *is* big!' agreed Dr Sargent mopping up the dregs of tea in the saucer. 'If you land that, well, well, that's a game changer! Plus, a new café and—'

Dr Bent cracked his fingers, getting ready for the afternoon's clinical rounds. 'Indeed.'

†

'I'm frightened to speak to you,' Dr Bent admitted during his next session with Dr Gluck. 'I am afraid you will make me a prisoner of your notes. That you will misunderstand what I say to you.' He paused. 'I would be trapped there, a grotesque fictional character. Future readers, clinicians, would end up treating and judging a fiction instead of me.' Dr Bent could just have easily been saying this about his own patients and the copious notes he made about their statements and behaviour.

Unusually, Dr Gluck spoke. 'It is hard sharing thoughts with others. Are you afraid to speak of things that have happened to you?'

'Well, just trying to think what might have happened is hard enough,' admitted Dr Bent, comforted that Dr Gluck had relented from her psychoanalytic purity. 'It is not always easy to separate fuzzy memories and reality.'

'Yes, of course,' she encouraged.

Dr Bent relaxed a little now. He stopped clasping tightly his moist hands, twiddling his rings and took a full breath. Dr Gluck seemed genuinely concerned about him.

'I don't know what you want to hear,' he said eventually.

'Well,' she started, 'we need to explore what is driving your depression. Getting to the bottom of this may help you move forward.'

'Yes, I know that,' he whispered, more to himself than to her.

'Good. Then we might be able to change your situation.'

'My job is very important to me,' Dr Bent confessed. 'I don't want adverse reports. That is why I worry that anything I say may be used against me.'

Dr Gluck nodded. 'Do you think that likely?'

'Yes, I do.'

Dr Gluck sighed gently, giving his slightly paranoid comments some thought. 'Would it help if I told you I have my own code for key or sensitive information? As I informed you in the appointment letter, unless you mention something with serious ethical and legal implications, I will not share information with anyone else. The content of these sessions will remain inscrutable.'

'Thank you,' said Dr Bent, reassured. It was what he expected, but he struggled to trust even fellow clinicians.

'You said that your job is very important to you. Can you say a little more about this?'

At this point, Dr Gluck chose to stop the conversation and lay down more silence like a poultice, yet Dr Bent did not immediately unfurl his thoughts and unlock his memories. It was a while before he spoke again.

'The other day I walked around the hospital. I did not quite grasp how big the place is. It is a world in itself, an island. Actually, Foston Hall is more like a prison ship, you know. The patients are prisoners. It is the kind of place you might get cabin fever. In fact, I had a touch of this after working there for only a couple of months. I could go freely from the main campus to the staff accommodation block outside the security fences but, nevertheless, I often felt imprisoned during my shifts.'

He paused and stared at nothing for a while before starting up again.

'I don't think this is relevant to my depression, yet empathy is a dangerous thing. I think I am far too empathic for my own good. I mean, I even feel sad leaving a soap behind in a hotel room.'

Once again, he stopped for a moment, frowning a little.

'Even though the patients at Foston have done or intended to do a lot of bad things, really awful stuff, I feel sorry for many of them, especially those with schizophrenia. What did they do to deserve the kind of life behind security fences?'

The faint scratch of Dr Gluck's pen interpolated briefly.

'They are confined there in redbrick blocks. The grounds are depressing. I mean truly *depressing*. There are black security gates between each sector of the campus and all the buildings have those airlock double doors. The whole institution is set in a slight bowl or dip in the otherwise flat landscape. Even if they go outside, the patients cannot see much of the surrounding countryside. It is like this!' Dr Bent pointed an oil-embroidered finger at the shallow crater of his Lycra-covered belly button. 'All they see is a gently rising locality of car parks and uninspiring grass.'

Dr Gluck maintained her silence and Dr Bent's thoughts meandered. Now, he was back in the garden of his childhood home. It was a garden without grass, just a dirt patch divided by a concrete path, surrounded by a picket fence. It had rained and leaves sticky with dew had fallen from the two huge lime trees at the far end. Dr Bent was holding a leaf in his hands, staring at luminous green aphids moving along its veins. His little shirt was open and he could see his own belly. He poked at it with his adhesive fingers.

'As a child, I thought I had been operated on,' he spoke with force and resolve, jolting Dr Gluck and her pen into action. 'I asked my parents how I came by the faint scar in a vertical line down my stomach. They told me, quite rightly, that the mark was little more than a stretch mark. To confirm my error, my mother raised her blouse to show her own collection of these. I was happy and reassured, yet still mystified by the mark dividing my belly. I blamed the lodger who was staying in our house. I blamed him, but did not know why.'

Dr Gluck's pen whispered through the air. The afternoon light dimmed with passing clouds across the otherwise vacant window.

'I guess I was about six or seven at the time. No, six. I was six.' Dr Bent went quiet for some time, his eyes closed now, his face flickering, guttering. 'The lodger would arrive at our house in the evenings, but I would never see him leave in the mornings. He rode a red moped or what my father called a *pop pop*. Everything was different with him around. The lights were dimmer. The dark nights lasted longer. He rarely spoke, if at all. He was big like my father. They both smoked pipes and had thick necks with prominent throat apples. They could have been brothers for all I knew. I can still smell the tobacco. Now and then, I would break up an oblong piece of the stuff into strings of fibre for my father. I would thumb these directly into his pipe.'

Dr Gluck coughed lightly.

Dr Bent continued. 'I tried not to be in the yard when the lodger came back through the old gate, pushing his *pop pop* over the step and resting it near the dustbins. I tried to keep off the long-tiled hallway to avoid the path to his room. He would lumber along it with his coat over his shoulder like gigantic, folded wings. He became a kind of mystery birdman or oversized bat hiding away downstairs in the cold middle room of our house, with its linoleum floor and old radiogram. I would hear him moving about or switching radio channels to full volume. At night, I would make a cocoon out of my bedding. Sometimes, the bedroom door would open and I would shut my eyes. First, I would smell his soured breath. Then I would hear him inspecting things in the room. The Sing-a-Song-of-Sixpence top would start spinning. I would hear the lodger adjusting the little wall clock with the painted face of a black boy, pulling at the chains and metal pinecones. The boy's eyes would then move from side to side with every tick and tock.'

†

Dr Bent occupied his usual table in the far corner of the old canteen, away from junior colleagues who remained in their own bubble of gossip. He was polishing off a plate of cheese pizza and chips. Unlike most of his colleagues, he preferred large amounts of carbohydrates to vegetables and fruit. The latter gave him gas. As a dietary *postscriptum*, a ginger cake and custard stood cooling to one side.

'Mind if I join you?' asked Dr Tim Sargent, setting down his plate of salmon and mixed salad.

'No, please do,' said Dr Bent, noting the file tucked under his colleague's arm. 'Ah, is that what I think it is?' he asked in his usual radio voice, taking a gulp of his coffee.

'Yes, just a few tweaks,' Dr Sargent told him, handing over the revised draft of a grant application. 'I didn't go through the figures. I guess you will leave that to John in finance?'

Dr Bent opened the file and quickly scanned the documents, noting the red pencil marks. 'I want to get this off as soon as possible.'

'That's good. What is the turnaround? When will you find out if you are successful?'

'I am not sure, Tim,' answered Dr Bent, popping the last rim of pizza crust into his mouth and pulling the ginger cake and custard into view. 'But I guess the money has to be disbursed before the end of the tax year.'

Dr Sargent nodded and tucked into his luminously coloured salad. 'Well,' he said with a rogue piece of lettuce escaping his mouth, 'if you pull this off, it really will be something to crow about!'

†

'My mother was warm and cuddly,' confided Dr Bent. 'She had large—' He paused and sighed deeply before continuing. 'She made hearty stews, hash with thick gravy and the best crispy fries. My father was an inventor. I would watch him build his prototypes, smoke lifting from his yellow pipe as steadily as the burn from his soldering iron. He could make anything, *absolutely anything* he put his mind to: a radio, an eternal motion machine, a telescope. His first telescope used a shaving mirror and could only pick up our neighbour Pat's blurry undergarments on the washing line. Yet he persevered, and soon, with more adjustments, we were spying craters on the moon. He was the best father I could ever want or imagine. He never went to university, but everyone called him *professor*. He read books on space, algebra and hypnotherapy. He was a good cook and I loved to sit and watch him burn the hair from pig's trotters for supper. He would wash them under the tap and let me hold the cold flesh so I could study their structure like an anatomy student. He explained how the pressure cooker worked. He took time to show me the release valve that spun and whistled out hot pork. He even bought me a Mamod engine to try my own experiments with steam. This was my entry point into the Sciences.'

Dr Bent entered a reverie of all these moments.

'My father was a carpenter by trade, but had the skills of a joiner. I would go with him to get supplies from Ansell's, our local dealer. I loved the smell of the freshly cut wood spurting from their saws. Back home, he would make simple furniture or frames to mould concrete flagstones. He taught me how to shape dovetail joints by bashing a chisel with the heel of my hand, turn a hand drill and whet a knife.'

Yet just as quickly as Dr Bent reflected on these happy times, his mind wandered off and his face grew tense again. With a faraway gaze, he stared through the ceiling.

'I had frequent nightmares as a kid,' he said, half turning his head towards Dr Gluck. 'Mostly these ended with bats chasing me. Then I would wake up as soggy as a wet autumn leaf and race into the main bedroom where my parents slept. I would jump on top of them and my father would tuck me under his soapy arm. I would smell the soldering iron smoke in his hair, feel safe and fall back to sleep. If I was not at school or in church, I took to the larder and the little cool space under the stairs to read a book. I was always reading as a kid. I felt safe there, away from the lodger.'

Dr Bent had begun to swallow air nervously.

'The door was just big enough for me to crawl inside with a torch. I would hide for hours. Sometimes, I would hear the lodger through the wall of the living room, speaking to my mother and father. Sometimes they argued. I did not know why. Mostly, they spoke in a hushed tone. Now and again, the lodger would enter the larder to remove his coat from the line of hooks and I would be as still as a mouse in my den. As soon as he had left the house, I would move from the tiny cellar and larder, out through the living room and kitchen into the outbuildings that housed my father's tools or the garden where I liked to dig holes to Australia. These felt safe places.'

'It was during the lodger's time that my mother entered Birchwood Hospital. At the time, my father told me that she had a problem with her *nerves*. I did not know what this meant or what the asylum would do to help her. I barely knew where it was located at the time. Yet I did not worry. My father was strong. He knew how to cook. We would frequently eat pig's trotters with all kinds of vegetables. He encouraged me to focus on other things apart from my mother. He made a go-kart with discarded pram wheels and gave me a pair of his old boxing gloves to beat a sack of grass cuttings he tied to the picket fence. From time to time, he would come out to demonstrate how to protect what he called my little glass chin. This reassured me and gave me confidence that I could defend myself if the lodger kept coming into my bedroom.'

Dr Gluck's pen scratched away. She studied Dr Bent's recumbent body like a living hieroglyph.

'Years later, at college, I wondered what had happened back then. To me, to my mother. I asked my father many times, but he just repeated that she had bad *nerves*. The lodger had long gone, yet I suspected that whatever had happened, it involved him in some way. Who was he? Why was I so afraid of him? My father told me they needed the money from renting out the room. There had been a downturn in the economy and many folk were out of work, including my father. Carpenters were two-a-penny and even when he quickly trained up as an electrician, work eluded him. I knew something bad had happened back then. Long after my mother came out of the asylum, she did not like to answer my questions or concerns. She flinched when I told her that I thought the lodger might have done something bad to me, coming into my bedroom at night and going through my stuff. I asked her straight one day what she knew. I challenged her. "What happened to send you into the asylum?" I asked. "Come on, tell me!" However, she just dropped her head and answered, "I will *never* be able to tell you."'

In the silence that followed, Dr Gluck divined Dr Bent's agitated face before taking a few additional notes and lifting her pen.

'We will have to stop there,' she announced. 'We have reached the end of the session.'

13

When the grant decision letter finally arrived at his accommodation at Foston Hall, Dr Bent hesitated in opening it. He had put in a lot of work in making the case for substantial changes to the hospital. He had sent through multiple forms and supporting documents complete with provisional architectural and landscaping designs. Everything he proposed, from ground movements to lighting, had to be set out in granular detail. Supported by a large team, it had proved a mammoth task and one that Dr Bent did not wish to repeat. With some trepidation, he ran a finger over the embossed letters of the grant-awarding body on the envelope and unfolded the single, high-quality paper announcement contained inside. He quickly scanned the text for the telling phrases: "We regret to inform you—"; "We received many applications—"; "Unfortunately on this occasion—". With none of these in sight, he read the text at a normal rate, his jaw dropping as the millions of pounds appeared in bold font. It was short, but very sweet.

†

Dr Bent knew that the trick of survival was to stand up, put one foot in front of the other and do the little things in life, like shaving. His little thing was changing the display of rings on his fingers. He moved them around. The plain, thick silver band on his left thumb went over to the right one. The silver tourmaline ring on his right hand swopped middle fingers. Finally, he transferred the pewter serpent ring from his left to his right hand, completing the temporary renovation.

On reflection, Dr Bent felt that psychoanalysis had been going well. Dr Gluck's wall of silence had driven him back into his childhood and he had begun to see that the lodger was not someone you could easily forget. The therapy had not yet dismissed the black dog of depression, but he felt it might do that, in time. He just needed to work out the connection between the lodger and raspberries. This association flummoxed him. Yet, that morning, he had things to do. He did not have the luxury to identify past trauma.

He picked up the diary from his desk and ran his finger down the listed assessments, consultations and meetings at Foston Hall. He smiled as he realised that the whole morning had been set aside for the project based on his latest book, *The New Asylum*, a radical approach to treating the "criminally insane". It had generated a lot of controversy, yet crucially found substantial funding. He breathed deeply with satisfaction that he would be making such a difference to Foston Hall. Despite the hospital's long and established reputation, he had managed to convince the funding body that things should change. He pleaded the case for an architecture of hope to mitigate its prisonlike environment.

Fortunately, with a left-leaning government in office, Dr Bent's suggestions had met with support. The millions of pounds that appeared in bold on the grant decision letter had transferred into Foston Hall's accounts and, after several weeks of additional clarifications, a workforce of architects, engineers and builders took over the hospital's main car park. Dr Bent had expected the development to get into the media and cause a heated debate. He imagined the press accusing him of trying to turn Foston Hall into a holiday camp, making things far "too easy" for "murdering scum" and psychopaths. At such moments, Dr Bent envisaged protests at the gates of Foston Hall. He imagined passionately defending his remaking of a peaceful, safe place where people with profound mental disabilities could recover something from their damaged and limited lives. He rehearsed statements about how the inmates were patients, victims of their own minds and deserving of sympathy.

In the end, no such media storm occurred, and tons of aggregates started to pile up alongside the high-security hospital ready to form the newly proposed landscaping within its grounds. A pop-up construction village appeared, with various container-style accommodations and offices, all kinds of earthmovers, equipment and tools. Everything sat outside the high perimeter fence. Hospital Security allowed nothing to enter the institution without first checking it had been included in the inventory. They checked the identities of the workforce and their tools, scanning them through to the construction site. At the end of the working day, Hospital Security accounted for all items going in or out, large or small. They reminded the temporary workforce of the dangers of tools going missing in a hospital housing some of the country's most violent offenders.

Now, as Dr Bent left his accommodation block and crossed the pop-up community, he waved happily left and right as he stomped through. He stopped as he passed a JCB, inspecting its anatomy in the same way he looked over motorbikes, including his Harley. It was the way his father had studied and fixed up bangers—old Sunbeams, Zephyrs and Anglias—all those years ago. For a moment, Dr Bent felt the urge to crawl under the JCB and inspect it more closely. Yet key decisions needed making at the *new asylum* meeting, so with a valedictory pat of the yellow-coated metal, Dr Bent continued his forthright walk round to the main entrance of the hospital.

In reception, he greeted the staff and moved through security, taking off his ear jewellery, rings, hair extension, belt and boots, collecting them from the end of the scanner and placing them in his personal locker. He put on his standard-issue black shoes and entered the double airlock door to the inner main courtyard of the hospital. Already he could see the construction workers milling about on the large area of blank, unused land at the far side of the site. It was about the area of two football fields. Several huge piles of grey aggregate lay on the surface like ancient burial mounds, ready for distribution to afford the planned elevation.

As usual, the *new asylum* meeting was in the old boardroom as this gave the best view over the construction site. The room was dark, with paintings of previous medical directors hung on the oak panelling. Dr Bent looked at them and wondered how his less mainstream image would sit among these should the tradition continue. With the medical director's chair now vacant and with a massive grant under his direction, he sensed it would not be long before he took up the role.

The kitchen staff had already placed tea, coffee and a bowl of mini-pack biscuits at the end of the large oak table. Dr Bent rifled through it to find his favourite ones and poured himself a black coffee. He was soon joined by Yvonne Cooper, Director of Estates; John Carr, Director of Finance; Saif Ali Khan, Director of Human Resources; Bethany Wall, the Senior Occupational Therapist; and Dr Alice Wang, a newly appointed psychologist representing the clinical staff. Dr Bent checked the clock at the far end and took his seat under the fireplace as always, looking out of the large windows. Debbie Moss, Director of Patient Involvement, entered at the last minute, grabbed a coffee and biscuit and took her seat with the others. Dr Bent waited for the chitchat to die down.

'Well,' he said, gesturing out of the window. 'This is really happening! They are not messing about! By all accounts, they should be finished with the main groundwork within a few weeks! How do we stand financially?'

'Yes, all good,' John answered flicking through the spreadsheets he always had with him. 'We just have one or two things outstanding.'

'Such as?' Dr Bent asked.

'The artists,' John said, adjusting his rimless glasses and scrutinising the printouts. 'We need to decide which designs we want to go with. Payment for materials has to be upfront.'

At this point, Yvonne spoke up, as usual with her steel pen raised into the air. 'We need to think about personal safety when making our decision,' she advised. 'I am all for sculpture, however, we do need to be careful. The three candidates are all very good, but some of the designs are more appropriate than others.'

'OK, well, let's go through each one,' suggested Dr Bent.

Already Saif Ali was busy flicking through the designs in the meeting pack while nibbling a biscuit. 'They all look great to me,' he said.

'Well, they may all look fine,' answered Yvonne, wishing to mark her authority in estates. 'Still, the first two might not gain approval.'

Everyone looked more closely at the designs in question.

'Both of these,' she insisted, 'could be used to self-harm. The rounded edges here could cause serious blunt injuries to the head.' She held the designs up. 'Or again, arms could be pushed through here and here,' she said indicating the hazards.

The committee examined the designs and had to admit that she had a point.

'Well,' said Dr Bent, 'I agree with Yvonne on this. The third design is more *practical*. It says here that it is made of a strong but flexible material. It has more curves and undulations. Everything with the other two is so straight, you know, box-like. We have enough ninety-degree geometry in this place. I also like the fact that these sculptures double up as seating. That fits the brief. What do people think?'

'Yes,' Saif Ali conceded, nodding with his lips puckered. 'I can go with that. The design looks good.'

'Yeah, more natural,' agreed John. 'Also, more competitively priced.'

Yvonne smiled with a little shake of her head. John never saw past pound signs.

'OK, Yvonne?' asked Dr Bent.

'Yes, number three looks right. It's certainly going to make Foston look more like a campus than a high-security hospital.'

'Absolutely! That was the vision. How can we rehabilitate patients who cannot see more than a hundred yards of countryside? How can they reflect? How can they find meaning and hope?'

'This is so exciting,' said Dr Wang who had listened in deferential silence up until this point.

'Do you know what the staff are starting to call the project?' asked Saif Ali.

'I have no idea,' said Dr Bent.

Saif Ali adopted a pregnant pause before Bethany Wall interrupted him, spoiling his line.

'The *wonders* of Dr Bent,' she chirped.

†

Dr Bent's heart thumped heavily and he gasped for breath. His ringed fingers were rubbing his abdomen as if he were searching for the vertical stretch mark that had troubled him as a child or trying to smooth away the dip of his belly button. His movements were frenzied now as he writhed on the bed that was *not* a bed. He panted as if he had just finished a run or achieved a ton up along a winding country lane. His eyes stretched as he looked around the fake bedroom. The ceiling was blank again. The window gave nothing but a grey sky. The blue roll of paper stood inert. Only his feet twitched with the pumping blood of revelation. He listened to the scratching sound of Dr Gluck's pen. She was writing copiously. Now Dr Bent's hands slowed their movements across his belly. His breathing gradually deepened. He swallowed the air around him and started to sigh.

'Did I speak?' he asked finally.

'Yes,' confirmed Dr Gluck gently.

'I told you?'

Dr Gluck remained silent, leaving Dr Bent unsure whether or not he had blurted out what now cohered under the dome of his skull.

'The lodger,' he repeated. 'He used to blow raspberries on my stomach.'

'Yes,' confirmed Dr Gluck. 'You told me this. Please go on.'

Now Dr Gluck fell silent once more and watched as Dr Bent turned on his side and drew his knees up to his chest in defence. He thought about the lodger blowing raspberries and remembered the initial fun of this. It had made him squeal with laughter and anxiety at the same time. It placed him between joy and fear. Yet now darker memories began to loosen from their lockdown. As his mind unfolded, Dr Bent began to experience the lodger's visits to his room as a child. He watched the scene gain colour and definition, making his breathing quicken. His hands began to blanch as they wrapped around his black leather knees and pulled inwards. It was as if he were trying to become as small as possible, like a tiny comma, and disappear from the flickering screen of his memory. His lungs began to heave as he felt the sensation of the raspberry blow.

He experienced again how he froze and pretended to sleep, but then succumbed to the funny sound and sensations creeping down his abdomen. He opened his eyes and saw the head of the lodger where it should not be. He could smell his sour breath and tried to push him away, his own delight contradicting the strangeness of it all, the spinning top on the cupboard still turning. The lodger continued to lift and drop his head, then stopped suddenly and became still. When finally, the lodger raised his head in slow motion, the face was that of his father.

†

'My dad!' howled Dr Bent squeezing himself further into a ball and crying in sheer grief, his mouth opening wide, almost growling with the realisation of what his mother knew, but could never tell him.

She had known and done nothing! That was why she ended up in Birchwood Hospital! The vague and fuzzy memories had gathered in their shameful details.

'Fuck, fuck, fuck,' he cursed. He rarely swore, yet now found only expletives would convey what he felt. 'What the fuck? Oh my God, no, no!' he cried, twisting and turning from side to side.

Not my father? Surely, I must be mistaken, he thought. Yet, however much he tried to envisage the lodger's face and force it back onto the skull in his lap, like a strange, living sporran, the features of his father returned.

'Fucking hell!' he blurted. 'It wasn't the lodger after all! He was just a mask for my father!'

What followed was interminable groaning, the kind that comes with deep trauma. It was several minutes before this sound tailed into silence.

Dr Bent remained quiet and still for a very long time, well beyond the end of the therapy session. Dr Gluck did not interrupt his comatose state, ringing down to reception to cancel her next appointment. She kept still, her pen poised over the therapy notes. She regarded Dr Bent with the cool empathy of her profession.

Eventually, he slowly unfurled himself, bleary-eyed, getting his bearings. He stared into the middle distance for several seconds. Then in a sudden frenzy of disgust, he began wiping his stomach before realising it was dry. He sat up unlocked from the past on the bed that was not a bed.

Dr Gluck scribbled "UR" in her notes for unconscious reconstruction, "D" for dissociation and "L-F" for the doppelganger lodger-father. Then she put her pen and file to one side in a symbolic gesture of closure. Yet closure would take much longer for Dr Bent who stared ahead newly woken, grimly reborn, and facing the unspeakable death of trust.

14

Jason sat in an interview room, cotton wool packed into his nostrils to stem the blood, feeling subdued and lost. He looked up at Dr Bent who sat across from him, disbelieving anyone quite so shabby could be a doctor or even the psychiatrist on call to assess people brought into custody. Jason examined the silver rings in the doctor's ears and on his fingers. He saw how Dr Bent's hands had caught dirt or oil, and marvelled at the brightly coloured rags in the long rat-tail of hair that he had pulled forward over his chest as he sat down. Jason wondered whether the weight of it drew the last of his hair further back from his brow. Even more incongruous for his profession were the gothic boots adorned with silver spikes. The platforms of these boots were at least three inches deep—as if built for the time when sewage filled the street.

Initially, Jason felt somewhat afraid of the strange-looking man with his black silk vest and various monochrome tattoos on his upper arms. Yet, as soon as Dr Bent started speaking, Jason appreciated his mellifluous, radio voice. It was not stuffy and received pronunciation. It was not quite the Queen's English, but free of regional grit. This educated voice countered Jason's first impressions and he started to feel guilty that he had dismissed the doctor on appearance alone. *Don't judge a book by its cover*, he reminded himself. He started to relax and trust him; the tone of his voice underlining years of study. Perhaps Dr Bent would understand his mission to find his brother's killer.

Jason answered the psychiatrist's preliminary, general questions about his social background and health in a factual, honest way.

Then Dr Bent clearly wanted to focus on events surrounding his arrest.

'Can you tell me a little more about what happened today?' he asked gently, crossing his legs and joining his beringed fingers.

Dabbing and twitching his sore nose, Jason studied the white scar on Bent's left cheek. It was like a small piece of torn paper in the shape of Africa. He lowered his eyes to inspect the incongruous, leather boots. Then Jason tried to give his answer as faithfully as possible.

'I don't know what I'm doing,' he admitted in an expiring voice, feeling crushed and vulnerable. His head glistened with sweat.

Jason's lips twisted one way and then the other. His feet tapped the floor. His heart wheeled and palpitated. Once again, he saw the mocking, scoffing faces of the hoodies and felt the stinging of his bruised flesh. Then there was the embarrassment and humiliation of ending up in handcuffs. He wondered where Poppy was. He wanted to be with her as surely as a baby needs a teat. Yet he knew that she would be angry with him. He lifted his eyes to the bland ceiling.

After several moments of silence, the psychiatrist spoke again. 'You don't know or can't say?'

'It's hard to put into words.'

'Can you try?' Dr Bent asked very courteously, switching the rings on his fingers. 'It would be helpful to know what you have been going through. I imagine many people are concerned about you?'

'Well, I guess my wife, for sure,' Jason said with a heavy sigh, watching the psychiatrist now twiddling the silver tunnel that decorated his left earlobe.

He also noted how Dr Bent rarely made eye contact. It was as if he were painfully shy, introverted, autistic or depressed even. His eyes kept flicking away at just the point when their pupils were destined to meet. It was as if he did not wish to intrude in any obvious way or allow access to his own dark soul.

'Look,' said Jason, 'I was out searching for my brother's killer.

It is that simple. I got myself into a scuffle and, well, you can see for yourself.' He pointed at his nose.

'Uh-huh, OK,' Dr Bent said quietly. 'Inspector Mosby gave me a quick overview of the circumstances surrounding your brother's death. I can only imagine how difficult this must be for you and your family.'

'It's been awful,' admitted Jason.

'Yes, of course.'

At that point, Dr Bent maintained a lengthy yet attentive silence, rather than subject Jason to further questions. After a while, Jason opened up.

'All I want is to find whoever did it,' he told him. 'It's all I can think of at the moment.'

'Right, OK,' prompted the psychiatrist.

'I had a clump of the murderer's hair, you see. I pulled it from his head during the attack.'

Dr Bent was taking notes again. 'Go on.'

'Well, I went out looking for the guy. I can only think he is a local. I decided that he would be attempting to cover over the missing patch. That's why I went round knocking people's hats from their heads.'

Dr Bent held his chin and frowned slightly. 'Sounds logical,' he reflected. 'Can I just go back to something you said a moment ago?'

'Yes.'

'You said you *had* a clump of the murderer's hair. What did you mean by that?'

Jason drew his head backwards and narrowed his eyes, impressed at how carefully the psychiatrist had been listening to him.

'Let's say I got rid of it.' Jason could see from Dr Bent's tilted head and lips pulled to the side that he did not buy the answer. 'OK, I ate it, or rather some of it. You see, I gave most of the stuff to Inspector Mosby for DNA testing.'

'But you ate the rest?'

'Yes, in a cake. I baked a cake and ate it.'

'I see.' Again, Dr Bent applied the silence.

'As a sacrament of revenge,' Jason finally admitted. 'I know, I know,' he added, holding up his hands. 'You think I'm mad. It is a crazy thing to do, and I am talking to the right person now, huh? You see, I lost faith in the police getting anywhere with their investigation. I thought, well, I might as well call on the spirit world. I thought it was worth a shot. I ate the hair like the people eating Jesus every Sunday! I took *the hair of the dog that bit us.*'

As Jason dried up, feeling overwrought, he sensed that the psychiatrist did not seem particularly surprised. After another pause, Dr Bent continued along a slightly different track.

'I gather you are still off work at the moment?'

'That's right,' answered Jason.

'OK. And would you say you are coping generally?'

'Honestly?'

'Yes.'

'To tell you the truth, I'm not on top of things. My wife has probably told you that anyway. What happened to my brother is eating me up inside.'

'Do you feel you need help with this?'

'What do you mean, like counselling?'

'Yes.'

'I don't think so.'

'Talking about your loss may help, Jason. If you don't want to see anyone in person, you can even get help online these days.'

'No, you're all right. I want to manage things in my own way, if that's OK?'

Dr Bent smiled warmly. 'If you do feel you need help, ring this number.' He reached forward and handed Jason a card. 'You can call it anytime day or night. Someone will always be on the other end of the phone.'

With that, Dr Bent closed his notes and stood up. He stepped

'Strictly speaking, this man is not mentally ill. He has insight and, at this point, he is not a danger to himself or the public. Certainly, I have no intention of applying a section of the Mental Health Act if that is what you mean?' He paused briefly before continuing. 'Let's see how things go. His behaviour is a little odd, but it is still early days. He is clearly very deeply affected by what happened to his brother.'

Mosby clasped the back of his neck and scratched his head at this comment. The idea that Dr Bent found Jason strange was ironic given the psychiatrist's gothic clothes, boots, earrings and rings. It was hard to believe that the man standing in front of him was one of the country's leading psychiatrists.

'It is not uncommon for people to have peculiar ideas or beliefs after someone close has died,' Dr Bent continued in a whisper. 'People can experience hallucinations and become depressed when they lose someone close. And, of course, it was his *twin* brother.'

Mosby was not convinced, but kept his counsel.

'The man is grieving,' insisted Dr Bent in his calm, measured voice. 'We all grieve differently. I agree that the level of his reaction is a cause for concern. Sometimes people go into an angry phase, yet it should resolve. At this point, I think we can only offer him our support. The last thing he needs is an appearance before magistrates.'

'This won't go to court,' Mosby confirmed. 'No one is pressing charges.'

'Excellent. Anyway, look, I've got to get back to the hospital.'

Dr Bent adjusted the oatmeal, padlocked army kitbag, said goodbye to Inspector Mosby and turned to leave. As he did so, the inspector continued to observe him, still bemused as to how the psychiatrist had become so powerful. After all, Dr Bent was the Medical Director of Foston Hall, the high-security hospital, and responsible for the court-diversion scheme based at Ardinweald Mental Health NHS Foundation Trust.

With Dr Bent gone, the inspector turned his attention to Jason, who awaited his fate. He walked back along the corridor and entered forward and offered his hand. Jason gathered himself and stood. He took the doctor's lightly gripping hand, suddenly aware of the distinctive body odour of the psychiatrist.

'As I said,' Dr Bent repeated. 'Just ring that number if you decide you want some *earthly* help, OK? And in the meantime, I will write to your GP to let her know that I've seen you.'

'Thanks,' said Jason, struck by the doctor's relaxed, kind manner. He genuinely seemed to care.

'All the best with sorting things here. Hopefully, they won't detain you for too long,' Dr Bent signed off, opening the door, unnaturally tall in his boots, slinging the grubby kitbag holding his medical files over his shoulder.

†

Inspector Mosby was resting back on the corridor wall, waiting to speak with Dr Bent as soon as he left the interview room. He jerked upright as the doctor came out of the interview room.

'How did you get on?' he asked.

Dr Bent ushered the detective inspector away from the door and spoke very quietly to avoid sharing any information about Jason more widely.

'Well, he is obviously deeply upset at his brother's death,' he said, his voice dropping even further as a few police officers moved along the corridor.

Mosby scratched his birthmark. 'Do you think he could be a danger to himself or others?'

'Mmm, right, well, so far he's only got himself into a bit of a scrape.'

'Yes,' said the detective, 'but I'm worried about what he might do in future. He seems determined to avenge his brother's death. Do you not think the guy's out of control, delusional or something?'

'Well, let's not overreact,' answered Dr Bent as equably as possible.

the interview room.

As he entered, Jason looked up, slowly, dejectedly.

The inspector rested his large hands on the back of the chair the psychiatrist had sat in, bearing down until his fingers blanched.

'OK,' he said. 'Let's get you home. We are just issuing you with a caution today.'

It took a while for Jason to take in what he said. Then his mouth fell open a little with obvious relief and slowly turned into a nervous, grateful smile.

'So, I don't have to go to court?' he asked.

'That's right,' the inspector told him.

'Thank you so much, Inspector Mosby! I am sorry to have caused all this trouble. I am really sorry.'

The detective was pleased to hear Jason's profuse apology, not least because he had been so critical of his policing skills. Now he escorted him to the duty sergeant's desk to pick up his belongings, standing by while he gathered his coat, wallet, watch, keys and a handful of loose change. Jason was all fingers and thumbs collecting his stuff. Several coins dropped to the floor and Inspector Mosby watched as Jason's wife came from the waiting area to help pick them up. She was glaring at her wayward husband with tight lips, but eventually softened when he presented the kind of cowed expression of someone just diagnosed with cancer. The inspector overheard Jason informing his wife that he had only received a caution and would not be going to court. The relief was obvious with Poppy mouthing *thank you* to Inspector Mosby, taking Jason's elbow and nudging him to the exit.

Once Jason and Poppy had left the building, the duty sergeant spoke up.

'He's one of my daughter's lecturers.'

15

The next day Jason was back at the university. His nose had lost the cotton bungs, but he could not hide the yellow-tinged bruising spreading out beneath his eyes. Poppy had insisted he went to work. He sat in his office, ill at ease, indecisive, holding his freshly shaven chin that was blotchy and speckled with blood. He did not feel like marking the latest pile of essays next to his desk. He did not want to prepare his lectures. He did not even feel the energy to continue his amateur detective work. The shame of his arrest burnt fiercely. Mostly, he was ashamed of putting Poppy through the mill so soon after losing her job. He had failed miserably to find Umbie's killer and gazed out of the office window at the students passing by, his nose tingling.

As he looked out, his mind drifted back to the events the day before that seemed so ridiculous now. He recalled the man with the boonie hat mocking him. He saw the fedora rolling across the ground and the three youths in their grey hoodies loitering near the public clock. He rubbed his damaged nose at this point and accepted that he deserved the hit. Knocking off hats was mad behaviour, he decided. It was as if he had regressed to his childhood. It had also brought his first consultation with a psychiatrist. The memory of Dr Bent and his physical appearance stood sharply in his mind, as did his peculiar scent.

Jason felt pathetic, incapable of carving his own fate, powerless to avenge the bones of Umbie. *What do I know about tracking murderers?* He regretted his idiotic, clownish behaviour. He shook his head heavily. *As if eating a cake could help. A grown man*, he chided, *eating cakes and cuffing hats from heads!* He began to shake with frustration.

When he looked over at the meticulous sleuthing on the notice board in his office, he knew he had to get back to the rational side of business. If he was going to find Umbie's killer, he needed to stay cool and data-driven. Knocking off hats and pulling down hoods was part of an irrational side to grief. He had let his head go loose with all the magic and mystery of an old, dead faith. *Eating a cake as a sacrament of revenge, for goodness' sake!* To have any chance of success in his private investigation, he needed to remain calm and stay focused. Yet he felt a long way from composure. His emotions roiled with the humiliation from the day before. He was seething and wound up. Even now as he checked the time ahead of his first lecture of the day, his hands balled into fists, the blood blanching from the skin.

Jason quickly turned his attention to the shelf on the far side of the office where he kept his slightly yellowing lecture notes. He dug through them until he found what he needed: Robert Southwell Notes#2 and the corresponding volume of verse from the bookcase. Although he used PowerPoint for his lectures, he still liked to have his notes just in case he lost track of his thoughts. He rarely consulted them these days, after so many presentations, but he felt reassured by their presence at the lectern.

Now, with a quick glance at the clock, he headed out of the office and down the main corridor, towards the lecture hall. He crossed paths with fellow scholar Paddy Kilkenny coming back from there.

'Good to see you back,' he said after clearing phlegm from his throat. Now his own teaching load would get a bit lighter. 'Are you doing the next session?'

'Yes,' said Jason examining Paddy's teeth. They protruded like a boxer's gum shield. 'What are the students like?'

'A bit quiet, you know. You have to dig a bit. My God, what

happened to your nose?'

'Someone head-butted me,' Jason said, yet quickly moved away, not wishing to stop and chat.

'Ah, you're joking! When did that happen?'

'Sorry, Paddy, I need to get into the hall.'

'Catch you later then,' Paddy told him with a shrug, lifting a valedictory hand, but Jason had already slipped through the double doors. 'OK, whatever,' mumbled Paddy, sticking the key in his office door.

Yet Jason did not escape the building before Professor Porter stuck his head out of his office and asked him inside.

'Please sit down,' he told him.

'I have a lecture,' Jason said, pulling up a chair.

'I know. Still, they can wait five minutes,' he said staring at Jason's nose.

Jason avoided eye contact with the head of school, feeling particularly sheepish about his injury and the events surrounding it.

Professor Porter was clearly uncomfortable, now fiddling with his garish pink tie. Jason watched him, trying to decipher what was going on behind those rheumy eyes.

'I'll get straight to the point,' Porter announced finally, pressing his fingers into a steeple beneath his nose. 'I heard what happened at the weekend.'

Jason lowered his gaze and chewed his lip, pulling nervously at the wilder-than-usual hair over his ears.

'I don't know everything,' Porter explained. 'But I am very concerned that you are bringing the university into disrepute.'

'What do you know?' asked Jason, on the defensive and starting to bristle.

'That you were in a fight and that the police were involved.'

'OK,' said Jason, his voice rising. 'So, there was a fight. How exactly is this any business of the university? Are you at all concerned that I may have been attacked?'

Jason could see that Professor Porter felt shocked by the sharp manner in which he spoke. It was quite unlike him. He watched as Porter gulped a mouthful of air and held onto his tie.

'Well, now this is rather out of character,' he blustered, his spine perpendicular to the world below. 'Do you need more time off?'

'No, I don't. I just want people to keep their noses out of my business,' Jason complained, rather ironically in the circumstances. 'Now, if you don't mind, I've got a lecture to give.'

With that, Jason got up and left.

†

The students had already gathered outside the auditorium when Jason arrived. They stood in little groups or alone, holding all kinds of bags, folders and books. He moved through them, guarding his bruised nose with his hand. The students knew all about the injury, and the hum of gossip intensified, accompanied by elbow nudges and eye signals. Jason felt acutely self-conscious as he entered the lecture hall, brushing his hair over his ears. As the students filed in behind him and took to the benches more quietly than expected, he avoided eye contact with them and nervously began to set out his lecture notes in the right order. When he finished signing into the lectern and uploading the set of slides, he perched on the edge of the desk at the front of the auditorium and waited for any stragglers, keeping an eye on his watch, steadying his nerves.

Outside, the mist had lifted and a sharp, blustery wind had started to nudge the trees lining that side of the building. Jason was grateful for the distraction of looking out from the rather stale-smelling auditorium as the seats filled up. He watched the branches flail and lose small, fragile twigs with each gust. Then he took his usual few deep breaths, massaging his cheeks a little with the heels of his hands. It was how he always prepared himself before speaking in public. It prevented the judder to the voice that less-experienced public speakers often suffered when beginning a lecture.

After a quick check that everyone had found seats, Jason stood up. With a few preparatory coughs, he picked up a bookmarked volume and began reading Robert Southwell's *The Burning Babe*:

"'As I in hoary winter's night stood shivering in the snow,
Surpris'd I was with sudden heat which made my heart to glow...'"

There was some giggling at the back of the room. Jason closed the book onto his forefinger. He was not happy. It was enough returning to the university to teach, but after the fraught meeting with Professor Porter, his nerves were on edge, and he took a dim view of this kind of silliness. He was just not in the mood for it.

'I fail to see anything funny in the poem,' he said, keeping a straight, challenging face. 'Come on, why are you laughing?' he insisted, staring into the gloom of blurred heads until the noise ceased. When it did, he opened the book again and read on in a louder voice, *"'As though his floods should quench his flames, which with his tears...'"*

There was more laughter and Jason closed the book again, saving his place. He was exasperated now and noted several students who were unable to shake off their fit of giggling. He addressed them specifically with a volley of questions about the poem. Each question went unanswered in silence. He responded with a long, deliberate closing of his eyes and dipped his head to his chest, before rearing up.

'Have you lost your tongues this morning?' he asked throatily. 'Or should I assume that none of you has read the text?'

Now all the students maintained and deepened a strange, rebellious silence. Jason shot piercing looks here and there, trying to bully them into some sort of comment, but there was nothing coming back. The audience was effectively dying on him, and he did not have the animation or humour to bring it back to life. He had never lost control of a lecture hall in all his years of teaching. Yet now, seeing some of the students smirking and looking down at him as if he were a creature for experiment, Jason felt his gut drop and a feeling of panic washed over him.

'What's so funny?' he asked, disturbed and frustrated. He paraded up the steps on one side of the auditorium, and then the other, like some manic game show host.

Yet the silence continued as Jason's heart rate increased. His breathing grew heavy with the fear of failure. He glared at Bradley and Doherty, two students renowned for acting the fool. He suspected they were behind the antics of this particular cohort. They hid their eyes and certainly looked guilty about something. Jason felt like cracking their heads together. He racked his brain for a way of regaining control of the class. Normally, he achieved ascendancy and authority. However, he had lost a great deal of confidence since Umbie's death. He had felt increasingly vulnerable to stress and knew that students could be merciless if they smelled the blood of a tutor.

Jason sensed the usual respect for his elevated status beginning to wilt. Now students openly broke their silence and began chatting amongst themselves, giggling loudly and ignoring him entirely. They seemed to be enjoying their newfound power over him.

'OK, OK,' he said trying to appear unaffected by the disruption, acting more laid back, yet pacing in front of the lectern. 'Share the joke, come on,' he coaxed. 'You've had your bit of fun.'

Once more, the students turned resolutely, lawlessly quiet. Perhaps they were embarrassed. Jason was confused. He decided to turn their silence into a positive signal.

'Right, that's better. Shall we—'

At that point, Jason became aware of something scribbled on the wipe board in the corner of his eye. He did not inspect it on entering the auditorium. When he turned to look, his mouth dropped open in astonishment and further still in shame. Students had drawn various kinds of hats. There was a ten-gallon version, a 1970s wide brim and others that defied description, even a Robin Hood. The doodles were clearly in more than one hand, and someone had written "THE MAD HATTER" above them.

The book Jason held fell to the floor.

He spun around now to face the students, glaring at them, covering his mouth to prevent a series of expletives from issuing forth. He felt his legs desert him. Numb and wobbling, he staggered back towards the lectern. He looked out at the audience bewildered and gormless. The students avoided eye contact. Even Bradley and Doherty hid their heads.

Tears welled up in Jason's eyes and he was blinking rapidly. He held on to the lectern now, his ears buzzing, heart palpitating, throat cramping. He wiped his mouth with the flat of his hand and stared at the wall of students in front of him. Sobbing sounds, choking sounds, swelled in the funnel of Jason's neck. He hid his face in his hands for a second time. When he looked up again, he saw that many of the students looked uncomfortable witnessing his fragility.

'Who did it?' shrieked Jason suddenly at the top of his voice, his face hot and wet.

Everyone in the auditorium froze with the loudness of his appeal. Jason's spittle fell like chalk dust. He cried out even louder.

'Who did this?' he yelled.

No one answered. The students sat stiffly in their rows as Jason cast around, trying to land his eyes on the insensitive artists. He had no success amongst the dipped heads.

Jason started pounding on the lectern and asked a third time to flush the student out. Then a few students, breaking ranks, started to remonstrate with Bradley and Doherty, calling them idiots.

He now had confirmation of who exactly thought it funny to make such humiliating drawings and flew towards them, leaping up the left side of the auditorium as students drew back lest he strike out. Within seconds, he caught hold of Bradley and threw him crashing down onto the steps while Doherty managed to vault athletically each row of seats and out of reach. Nothing like this had ever happened before and the rest of the students began pouring out of the lecture hall, afraid Jason might extend his assault.

Jason felt the anger surging through him, pressing for release. He picked up students' files and water bottles and hurled them this way and that. If the auditorium seats had been loose, he would have thrown those too.

Only slowly, Jason relented and staggered back along an empty row to see Bradley lying with his white face tilted back over a step. He was unconscious and his arm looked broken, at an odd angle to the rest of his sprawled body. Jason stood over him, motionless, his hands at his side, lip trembling. Sweat poured down his bluish, damaged nose.

'Quick, someone call an ambulance!' one of the students instructed, bending over Bradley's still body.

Soon enough, there were shouts along the corridor outside and eventually the sound of heavier feet approaching. Jason was looking around for sight of Doherty, but he had long escaped.

'The little bastard! Where is he?' he screamed, saliva dribbling from his lip as he headed back down to the front of the hall, kicking the book of Southey's poetry out of his path.

The book spun and came to rest at the feet of one of three heavily built university security guards.

16

On waking, all that Jason could remember was a large, red brick building with two towers at the front. He tried to picture them in more detail, sifting through a confused, distorted memory. Sluggishly, he probed his disorientated brain and recalled a pyramid. *That was it: a pyramid!* A pyramid of grey slates capped each tower. *What day was it?* It was light, and he was lying on a bed in the bay of a dormitory. *How long have I been here? Where am I?* All his brain could drum up was a stone archway. He had seen it before, but could not place it. Jason sat up, frightened and anxious, and swung his legs over the side of the bed. His bare feet touched the cold floor. Out through the narrow window, he could see a playing field surrounded by trees and a high brick wall.

Jason stood up and moved unsteadily and drowsily out of the little bay, his mouth like sandpaper, his nose blocked, his vision blurred. In the aisle, it dawned on him that he was wearing pyjamas. They were not his own but a ghastly, salmon pink with words printed on them. He tried to focus his eyes tightly enough to read what they said, clawing at the loose trouser bottoms. The words appeared in blue, within a stretched diamond. Slowly he read, "PROPERTY OF BIRCHWOOD HOSPITAL, ARDINWEALD MENTAL HEALTH NHS FOUNDATION TRUST". His chin fell. He smiled nervously, ashamed, shaking his head, blowing air through his wide nostrils. He looked out of a window on the other side of the dormitory and saw the old gatehouse and familiar street, confirming he was exactly where his pyjamas stated he was.

Jason staggered down the aisle of the dormitory, his brain full of thorns. He could only manage to move sluggishly past other bays of beds. There, partly hidden by curtains, one or two patients slept cocooned in their blankets. Jason headed towards a buff door at the far end. He looked at himself in its round, thick safety glass. He saw the skipping ropes beneath his eyes. *Where is Poppy? Does she know I am here?* Up above, a camera with a little red light whirred and moved, staring directly down at him. He walked along a short corridor to the stairs, his movements slow. Another camera on the stairwell picked him up and turned to follow his every step. He felt disabled, barely able to shuffle forwards. The stairwell was darker than the corridor and forced him to take his time, grasping the round, wooden handrail that ran along the wall with both hands. It took several minutes to descend a single flight. The process exhausted him. By the time he reached the turning point, he was sweating and breathing heavily. He wondered what was wrong with him. He felt faint, but wanted to find out more about his situation.

He remembered Bradley falling back onto the lecture hall steps. Then he recalled the security guards racing towards him. He ranted and raved as they tried pinning him to the floor. Then the police took over, putting a spit bag over his head even though he did not think he was gobbing at anybody. They had taken him somewhere clinical, possibly the Accident & Emergency Unit, where he had his trousers pulled down and was turned on his side. He thought they were going to rape him, and he writhed about for all he was worth, trying to get free. They looked like male nurses or doctors. "We are going to give you something to help you, Dr Hemp," one of them said just before he felt a needle in his right buttock. The sting of it made him clench and tense up his body. The voice came again, "Try and relax, Dr Hemp. It won't hurt so much." Then nothing.

Now, as Jason moved slowly down the stairs, he came upon another patient and drew back, alarmed, wondering who he was and what he wanted. The man was wearing a rainbow-coloured jumper and unfashionably flared trousers that came halfway up his shins. He poked Jason in the belly and burst out laughing.

'Got a ciggy? Ciggy? Got one?' he cried.

'What?' asked Jason helplessly, gripping the handrail.

'Ciggy! Ciggy! Go on, give us one!'

Jason managed to decipher his words. 'I haven't got any! I don't smoke!' he told him.

'Woooh!' lamented the man like a siren, his bad teeth overhanging his lip.

Jason grimaced, feeling repulsed, his path blocked. 'OK,' he said. 'Let me get past.'

'Harg!' bellowed the man, pushing something into Jason's palm before leaving him alone with groin-stretching leaps up the stairs.

Jason heard the camera track the man before returning to follow his own slow progress to the ground floor. He was dripping with sweat and panting heavily. He shook his dizzy, clouded head, trying to clear it, screwing up his eyes. When he opened them again, he stared into his palm at what the patient had donated. It was a large brown button. *What was all that about?* Yet he did not give the matter further thought and discarded it. He paused for a while, nervously picking at his teeth with a fingernail, trying to figure out what he should do next. *How can I get out of this place?* He moved down into a more brightly lit section of the corridor. Then he found his way, accompanied by another camera, into a large day room.

Immediately, Jason winced at the babble of sound coming from a television secured high on one wall. Several male patients sat on uncomfortable-looking maroon chairs bolted into the beige floor, their heads fixed on the screen, expressionless. Others were mithering, slumped or fast asleep catching flies. No one was smoking, but the smell pervaded the room. Most of the people in the room looked exhausted and isolated. There was very little sign of activity and certainly no joy. It was a workshop for generalised boredom. Two young men in cheap-looking grey suits and open-necked white shirts stood back against one wall, vigilant yet relaxed. Jason suspected they were the nursing staff. He looked at them steadily. They did not return his gaze.

Jason stood in the middle of the room, bemused and trying to come to terms with his situation. He edged forward, looking around at the uninspiring framed artwork on the walls. At the far end stood a battered ping-pong table, with its net drooping lifelessly, and a useless, dented ball on the floor. Jason did not know what to do or where to go. He swallowed drily, blinked absently and ran his fingers over his chest and belly. After a few moments of indecision, he stumbled onward, holding onto his loose pyjama bottoms and observing the inmates. An overweight man caught his eye, his hands twitching, his head arched backwards. He was wearing a stained white T-shirt, jogging pants and trainers. His fingernails were long and ridged. His mouth was half-open and his furred tongue rested on his bottom lip as if he were about to receive Holy Communion. Nearby, another patient slouched forward in his chair, turning his fingers around a roll-your-own cigarette. He flicked his bloodshot eyes briefly at Jason, but did not greet him.

Suddenly, Jason felt a firm hand placed on his shoulder from behind just like the rector of Saint Ergonwald's all those years ago. Jason spun around slowly.

'Welcome to Birchwood,' a man said, smiling warmly. He was Malaysian, with bright teeth and a trimmed beard. He also wore a grey suit, but one with superior thread. The lapel badge read "Mr Singh, Charge Nurse".

He was stockier than the other nursing staff.

'You're showing your bits,' he told him.

Jason let his fist unfurl and grimace soften. He looked down and closed the slash in his donated jim-jams.

'What am I doing here?' Jason complained. 'What's going on?'

'I'll explain when you get dressed,' said Mr Singh in a reassuring voice. 'You're probably a bit confused. Try not to worry. I am the nurse in charge of this unit and I will be coordinating your care. My office is just through those doors to the right. One of the nursing assistants will take you back upstairs and show you to your locker. Hopefully, your family can bring a change of clothes later today.'

Jason thought about what had happened at the university. He shook his head and looked straight into Mr Singh's eyes. 'I'm not mad!' he said, holding his throat, his heart beginning to wobble. He felt stripped down and reduced. His life was going haywire.

'Nobody said you were,' replied Mr Singh in a relaxed, friendly voice. 'But obviously, things got too much for you, right? At the university? You were in quite a state when they brought you here. They had no choice other than to give you a little inj—'

'Yes, I know all about that.'

Mr Singh waved over the slimmer of the two nursing assistants. 'This is Dan,' he said, introducing his colleague. 'If you go back upstairs with him, he will help you get dressed.'

'I can dress myself!' Jason objected.

'Even better,' said Mr Singh with a pat on Jason's arm. 'Then we will have a cup of tea, OK?'

Jason dearly wanted a drink. His throat, mouth and tongue were very dry. Mr Singh smiled to close the conversation and left for his office, glancing briefly at the other patients. Jason hesitated, fingering his brow, trying to make sense of everything. Dan was saying something to him, but his mind was elsewhere. Any dignity or pride he had now fell away. He looked down at his bare feet and felt sick that he had ended up in the local bin. Mr Singh and Dan seemed friendly. *Can I trust them? Am I going to get another injection at some point?*

'Right, let's get you into your clothes,' Dan nudged.

Jason staggered along, the nursing assistant lightly holding onto his elbow, steadying him as he moved back through the day room and its televisual soundscape. Soon enough, they were mounting the flight of stairs.

At the side of Jason's allocated bed, Dan opened a small locker. Inside he found a plastic carrier bag with the clothes Jason had worn the day before. He unfolded a pair of crumpled, slightly torn blue corduroys they had yanked free to inject him. Nursing staff had removed the leather belt. That was now under lock and key in the main storeroom. Jason's blue shirt looked far from fresh, with heavy tidemarks around the pits. His socks had disappeared, and his underpants were slightly soiled but passable. Jason's black shoes stood at the bottom of the locker. Dan set the items out on the bed and the footwear on the floor nearby, then moved away to allow Jason some privacy to change. Jason had no toiletries to mitigate the stale clothing. He dressed slowly, still sluggish from whatever chemical they injected the night before. Buttoning up his trousers, Jason slipped his feet into his cold, black shoes and went to tie them, yet the laces had gone.

'You will get those back later,' Dan explained. 'So take extra care going down the stairs.'

Jason looked out of the window into the much-reduced hospital grounds. He could not believe what was happening to him. *What will the university do? Will I lose my job or face a court case for assault?* He had become overwrought since his brother's death, but saw that as perfectly normal. As he wondered what his family or friends would make of him now, among the mentally ill of Ardinweald, his thoughts turned to his wife, Poppy. He wanted to see her. He wanted to be back home in a familiar setting. He could only hope that they would discharge him from the hospital as soon as possible. *I do not have schizophrenia or manic depression. Mental hospitals are surely for people with these conditions.* Determined to discuss his situation, he turned and headed off back downstairs.

'I am going to see Mr Singh,' Jason informed Dan in a calm, steady voice.

'Sure,' answered Dan, following him, 'his office is off the main foyer.'

Back in the day room, with Dan pointing the way through the beech-coloured doors, Jason walked nervously past the other patients, trying not to catch their eyes. He ran his fingers through the bushed hair above his ears, smelling his own body odour wafting up from the dank shirt and the cool air wrapping around his bare ankles. It seemed as if he had changed from lecturer to tramp overnight. He lifted his chin and tried to throw off any air of being an inmate as he went looking for Mr Singh, passing the manic patient he had met on the stairs earlier. The man breezed through carrying a pair of ping-pong bats and asking one patient after another for a game. They all refused. This time, he ignored Jason completely, beginning to semaphore invisible aircraft.

Jason pressed on through the double doors at the end of the day room and out into a large, impressive foyer furnished with plants and pleasant coffee tables complete with Birchwood Hospital's glossy newsletters.

He saw Mr Singh, out of his office, confronting a young man.

'What do you think this is then?' he spoke loudly, pushing a spliff under the man's nostrils. 'That's not Golden Virginia, is it?'

'Yeah, it is,' the man said, his hands upturned.

'Look here,' said Mr Singh. 'I can smell cannabis a mile off.' The charge nurse sniffed the air as if to prove his point, letting his finger drop from the patient's red face to his chest. 'Last warning,' he said tapping it. 'If I catch you smoking this stuff again, you will be discharged and back sleeping in a cardboard box. I do not want that to happen. And I don't think you do either.'

At that point, Jason saw an opportunity just to walk out of the building and avoid any discussion with Mr Singh. He sneaked past, hugging the clean, pastel-pink wall. He managed to reach the main doors and look briefly through one of the porthole windows at a path and poorly maintained grass border when the charge nurse spotted him.

'And where do you think you're going?'

'I'm out of here,' Jason announced, pulling at his shirt as if to indicate that tidy clothes meant a tidy mind.

'Ah,' Mr Singh said, quickly moving alongside him. 'I think we better have a little chat.'

Jason's hand rested on the door handle. 'Well, I would rather get off. My wife will be wondering where I am.'

'She knows you are here,' Mr Singh informed him. 'She phoned last night, but you were still heavily sedated.'

'Did she?'

'Yes.'

'Well, I'm all right now. I will get off home. It is not as if I am mad. I am not hearing voices or anything like that. I'm a university lecturer, respectable, you know, professional.'

The charge nurse listened attentively, scratching the hairs on his chin, gazing at Jason with serious, half-closed eyes.

'I don't know why they brought me here,' Jason continued. 'So, OK, I blew my top, but what's so strange about that? We all get hot under the collar sometimes, especially when under pressure. You can see I'm *compos mentis*.' He paused for a few seconds. 'There now,' he said. 'I've explained myself. If you don't mind, I'll be getting along.'

'It's not quite that simple,' stated Mr Singh, rolling a biro between his fingers.

'How do you mean?'

Mr Singh guided Jason away from the doors. 'Please, come into my office for a minute.'

He ushered Jason inside a small room with a very high ceiling and a wipe board like those used at the university.

The charge nurse sat at his desk and typed a password into the computer to bring up Jason's notes.

'Sit down, sit down,' he said affably.

Jason sat down on the edge of the chair ready for a quick escape.

Mr Singh clocked this and smiled, trying hard to put him at his ease. 'Look, I'm sorry about what happened to your brother. I read about it in the papers, of course. It must be a hard thing to deal with.'

Jason frowned, unsure whether Mr Singh really cared or whether he was just going through the motions. 'Yes, it is.'

At this point, the charge nurse gestured through the glass partition. Soon enough, a young man with a streak of dyed pink hair and a diamond stud in the crease of his nose popped his head round the door.

'Charlie, can you make a tea for us?' asked Mr Singh.

The young man nodded and sauntered off.

'Is he a nurse?' Jason asked.

Mr Singh chuckled. 'A student nurse,' he replied, twiddling the silver registration badge pinned to his lapel. 'But if you think he's a bit different, wait till you see Dr Bent, the consultant.'

Immediately, silver rings, monochrome tattoos, gothic boots and that slightly rancid odour filled Jason's mind. 'I've already had the pleasure,' he said, looking out along the side of the building.

'Ah, yes, of course, at the police station,' said Mr Singh, scrolling down the computer screen. 'All part of the new court-diversion scheme.'

'Sorry?' asked Jason.

'It is one of Dr Bent's ideas. He believes that too many people with mental illnesses end up before the courts. He started this new initiative of diverting such people to mental health services at the earliest opportunity. He is quite a character. He creates a stir wherever he goes. He is famous, of course, after all the changes he has made at Foston Hall.'

'The high-security hospital?'

'Yes, that's right. What did you make of him?'

'He seemed all right,' Jason admitted.

Mr Singh was nodding. 'Yes, he is a sound guy. Now, where were we? Ah, yes. Let me just get this up on the screen.' The charge nurse double-clicked his mouse. 'There we are. If you look here,' he said, turning the monitor round for Jason to see, 'you came in on a 136 of the Mental Health Act and you are now on an emergency section.'

'Emergency section?' cried Jason, alarmed.

'For your safety.'

'I'm not mentally ill!' Jason pleaded. 'I'm not a danger to anyone. I want to speak with Dr Bent. Can I please see him?'

Mr Singh held up his hands and gestured for Jason to calm down. 'He will be coming to see you.'

'When? Look, I want this sorted so I can get on my way.'

'I understand that,' the charge nurse tried to mollify him. 'These days we want people to return home as soon as possible, if they have one of course. But you will probably need to stay here for a short while.'

'You're joking, right? You cannot keep me here!' Jason challenged, standing up to his full, just short-of-imposing height. 'I don't have to stay. You can't force me.'

'I'm afraid,' said the charge nurse firmly, 'that we have the power to keep you on the unit until Dr Bent advises otherwise. If you do manage to leave, the police will be notified and you'll be returned to us.'

Jason started to panic now. He could feel his heart pounding and his breathing quickened. 'And what if I don't cooperate? What then? You'll give me another injection, right?'

'Look,' said Mr Singh, trying to ease the tension that had built up between them. 'Dr Bent will be along shortly and you can talk everything through with him.'

Jason's lips were quivering now.

At that point, Charlie popped his pink-streaked head around the door. 'Tea?'

'Yes, come in,' Mr Singh beckoned.

Charlie set the tray of mugs on one of the empty chairs and left. Mr Singh followed him into the corridor briefly and gave instructions out of Jason's earshot. Charlie nodded and went on his way.

When Mr Singh returned to his swivel chair, he handed one of the mugs of tea to Jason. It had lots of milk added to reduce the chance of scalding incidents.

'Sugar?'

'Four spoons, please.'

Mr Singh raised his dark eyebrows, yet spooned the granules in without saying anything. Jason's hands were shaking so much he spilt some of the warm tea onto his lap.

'If you remain calm, it will be better for you,' the charge nurse advised him. 'They had little choice but to inject you the other day. You were in a very agitated state. They only use rapid tranquillization like that as a last resort. In fact, where possible, we like to treat people in their own homes.'

Jason showed his surprise. 'Well, I'm fine now. I don't need to be here.'

'That's good,' encouraged Mr Singh, 'and you can discuss this with Dr Bent when he does his rounds. He will want to get you home as soon as possible. Let us see how things go. OK?'

'It doesn't sound like I've got much choice,' complained Jason, noting a stocky nurse he had not seen before standing by the exit, head shaved and a roll of flesh at his tight collar. With his dark grey suit, he could have been mistaken for a nightclub bouncer.

'As far as we are concerned, you have been brought here for your own safety,' said Mr Singh equably, leaning back in his chair.

Jason shifted his weight off the buttock that was still sore from the needle. 'Poppy will be sick with worry,' he groaned.

'If you bear with me,' said the charge nurse, 'I'll read your rights under the Mental Health Act.'

Jason looked at the computer screen, his eyes glazed and blurred like worn, scuffed marbles. 'I have some then?' he mumbled.

17

Back in the large, gloomy day room, Jason sat next to one of the windows and gazed out onto the playing field where local youths chased a football across wet, marshy turf, occasionally driving it over the line between crooked, vandalised goalposts. He was not particularly interested in football. He had always preferred watching rugby or cricket. Yet it was something to do as boredom quickly set in like *rigor mortis*. There was nothing duller than waiting around in hospital. Now and again, Jason's eyes drooped towards sleep. Several times, he nodded off for a few moments only to jerk awake to see purplish clouds moving in an endless shoal across the sky and the footballers coming together or dispersing before his eyes.

In the chair to one side, a sallow-faced man leaned forward, his arm supporting his head like a pillar, his eyes staring into the middle distance. He seemed out of it. He did not blink or look up. Jason observed his greasy, matted hair and iron-filing chin. The man lifted his eyes eventually, feeling the pull of Jason's gaze. As they contemplated sharing a few words, the brightly dressed patient Jason had met earlier interrupted them.

'Do you have any money?' he cried, pulling his trousers further up his legs, fidgeting. 'I only need a pound. Do you?'

'No,' Jason answered, not looking up.

The patient raced away to the far side of the room to ask someone else.

'Manic,' diagnosed the man opposite, stirred from his inner darkness.

'Oh, right,' said Jason frowning.

'They don't stop. On the go all the time. He will probably have a heart attack if he keeps it up. Might be a blessing, though?'

Jason nodded and watched as the patient's monotonous speech and eyes fell away again. He seemed prone to withdraw. Now Jason felt like talking.

'What are you in for?' he asked, pretty sure it must be depression.

'I tried to kill myself,' the man said matter-of-factly, raising his head with some effort. He drew back the sleeves of his shirt, revealing bandaged wrists. 'I got it wrong again. I think it is better if you cut downward instead of across. That way you can—'

'Yeah, OK,' Jason dissuaded him, feeling slightly nauseous. 'I'd rather not know.'

'Yes, of course. I'm sorry.'

Jason shook his head and studied the expressionless man. He noted the heavy dandruff dusting his dark shoulders. He seemed such a sad, lifeless figure, a living ghost. Yet his clothes indicated a successful past. The blue-striped shirt was stylish and his brown laceless shoes were clearly expensive.

'I used to run a business,' the man disclosed with a deadpan expression.

'What happened?'

Here he paused and pouted his lips before speaking. 'I found out the business owned me and when it went to the wall, I lost everything: my house, wife and the kids. Molly is only five. Daniel is seven. It broke my heart.'

'I'm sorry,' whispered Jason sympathetically.

'So am I,' the patient said, sucking at his cheeks. 'It was my third attempt to finish things. Next time, I will take more tablets and cut—'

'Let's not go there,' pleaded Jason.

'Sorry,' the man told him.

After a few minutes, Jason repaired the conversation. 'I don't know what to say,' he admitted.

'No, I suppose you don't. Who does? This last time I did it here on the ward, but they found me.'

'Well, I hope you feel better soon,' Jason told him.

However, the man did not answer. In fact, he had withdrawn back into himself, closing his eyes although he was not asleep.

Jason shook his head again and looked out at the football pitch and surrounding buildings. The match had ended and the players had gone home, and nothing moved except for a stray dog that headed towards the few trees that remained in the grounds. Now Jason turned over in his mind all that had happened at the university. His decline had been humiliating, to say the least, and he cursed Umbie's killer for bringing him to this low point. The murderer had taken more than his brother's life. He had destroyed Jason's reputation as well. All those years of respectable and dignified existence would count for nothing. His slate was now far from clean.

It seemed likely that he would lose his job. His medical notes would hang around his neck. He would be a laughingstock in Ardinweald—a village nutter. In a way, he could not fall any further. He was already at the bottom.

Jason sat quite still, looking into the middle distance, wondering when Poppy would visit him, what would happen next and the extent of Bradley's injuries. Yet the more he thought about it, the more he sensed that the incident at the university had brought him to a nadir, where he had nothing to lose now by going the whole hog and killing Umbie's murderer, if he could only find him. He settled into this idea, musing about his whereabouts. As Jason scoured his imagination for a way to track him down, a food trolley came noisily through the double doors at the end of the ward. The smell perked him up. He had not eaten since breakfast the day before and felt suddenly ravenous.

Jason joined the other patients at the tables in the cramped dining area and waited as Charlie and a care assistant handed out trays of food. They were friendly and considerate, checking dietary preferences marked on chits and taking the time to deal with any queries or complaints. Eventually, it was Jason's turn.

'What would you like?' Charlie asked.

'What is there?'

'Chicken nuggets, beef casserole or pasta bake.'

'Er, I'll have the casserole, please.'

Charlie handed him a tray. 'There you go.'

With the casserole, mash and peas in front of him, Jason felt a bit brighter. He acknowledged one or two of the other patients and tucked in. The food was better than he expected, although he struggled to adapt to the lightness of the foam plate and plastic cutlery. The knife was flimsy, and the fork had webbed feet that made it difficult to spear anything. He assumed that this was all part of risk management in a hospital like this. Yet, despite the utensils, he quickly cleared his plate and sat quietly waiting for dessert—a choice of rice pudding, strawberry mousse or a piece of fresh fruit. He chose the rice and set about the plastic bowl with barely a pause for breath, wolfing it down. Then he leant back in his chair, a blob of the stuff hanging from his chin. Charlie was smiling at him.

'Did you enjoy that?'

'Not bad,' Jason had to admit.

'That's what we like to hear.'

Just then, the double doors opened again and a tall, thin man with long, wild, grey hair and a weak chin entered. He looked smart yet casual, in a black jacket and jeans. He spoke briefly and deferentially to Charlie and the care assistant.

'Oh, watch out! Here he comes,' warned one of the patients sitting across from Jason.

'Who is he?' Jason asked.

'He used to be a patient, but now he runs the Service Users Council.'

'What's that?'

'It's where patients—sorry, service users—can have their say, you know. Say what you do not like, etcetera. They—'

The chair of the council cut short his explanation. 'Good afternoon, gentlemen,' he boomed. 'We are just about to start our meeting, so if you can make your way through. We are in the green room today. That's right, come along!'

Jason raised his eyebrows, finding the chivvying tone of the ex-patient somewhat ironic.

A few of the patients got up from their tables, guarding their stomachs for indigestion and reluctantly headed to the green room.

'That's it! Stand up for your rights! Get your voice heard! Sir?'

Jason realised he was being addressed. 'No, thank you,' Jason told him. 'I'll give that a miss. It's not for me.'

'Not for you? That's not the attitude!'

Jason looked straight into the man's eyes. 'It is *my* attitude, thank you. Now, I'd be grateful if you would leave me alone.'

'Well, OK, but—'

Charlie noted the change in tone and intervened. 'If he doesn't want to go then that's up to him.'

'Yes, OK, *student* nurse.'

'I'm just expressing my rights,' Jason added with a grimace more than a smile.

The man backed away, a little defeated, and focused on a different group of patients, shepherding them out of the day room.

†

Later that evening, as darkness closed in, Jason felt lonely and depressed. He barely knew anyone on the ward, nor did he want to, and certainly not by attending the Service Users Council. Apart from the relief offered by the football match, he had spent the afternoon either snoozing or watching patients talk to themselves, stare into space, roll their tongues, jabber to the voices in their heads or gawp at the television. The man with rainbow clothing had not stopped all this time, moving through the day room like a tornado, disturbing everyone and winding them up. Now and again, the nurses had to intervene to keep the peace.

The bright lights in the day room and sparse furniture did not help Jason's mood. Nor did the cheap, dry sandwiches presented as an evening meal. Everything added up to nothing. He sat alone, as far away from others as possible, trying to ignore the television. He did not want to talk to anyone and was in no mood for fools, even if they had serious mental health problems. Wiping his eyes and sniffing, Jason looked across the deserted playing field, the sodium lamps in the street softening the dark trees along the perimeter. He felt very tense and tucked his fingers into fists. It was a warning sign to those who had eyes to see. With his lips pressed tightly together and breathing through his nose, he stared vacantly ahead, mulling over all that had happened to him and waiting for visiting time.

He stayed like this as the minutes turned to hours and visiting time began. It was only then that he emerged from his mental bubble, his fingers slowly unfurling, and turned to face the opposite set of windows, looking out for Poppy. He wondered if she would visit. He began to doubt she would, watching for movement under the dark stone archway at the end of the access road. A few people trickled into the grounds. Yet, as Jason noted with mounting anxiety, they all turned out to be the visitors of other patients or members of staff coming on duty. It was not until much later that a small figure appeared, lit intermittently by the pools of streetlight that graced the access road. Jason's breathing eased as he recognised Poppy's particular gait. He smiled, with effort and mixed emotion. He wanted to see his wife, yet he did not want her to see him. He bowed his head as she got closer to the building, feeling awkward and self-conscious, and his pride more than dented.

When eventually Charlie showed Poppy through to the day room, she looked extremely nervous, crossing the floor carefully, keeping an eye out on other patients and their visitors. She seemed to be assessing Jason's mental state as she approached him.

'I'm all right, Pops,' he told her, as Charlie moved away to lean on the windowsill, keeping up his general observations.

Jason stood and tried to kiss his wife's cheek, but only managed the slightest contact as she pulled away. Poppy did not want to be touched. She was upset and angry about what had happened.

'I brought a change of clothes, toothbrush, that sort of stuff. I gather razors are carefully controlled,' she told him. She handed over a full plastic bag.

'You shouldn't have come,' he said, averting his eyes. 'Not here. Not to this place.'

'I had to,' argued Poppy. 'Who else is going to visit you? Your mother is at her wit's end.'

'How are you?'

'How do you think I am?' she snapped. 'Just look at me! I saw the GP this morning. He's put me on Valium again!'

'I'm sorry. I know I've messed up big time,' Jason apologised, his head as heavy as a wet sponge.

'What's happening to us, Jason? I never thought I would see my husband end up in a, in a—' Yet Poppy could not voice the words.

'I'm not mad, Pops,' he said looking deeply into her dull-green eyes.

However, the fear of madness hung over his wife like a buzzing electric pylon. She twisted her wedding ring round and round her finger.

'You don't think I'm mad, do you?' he asked.

Jason could see how Poppy hid her eyes from him. She hunched over, drawing her wedding ring painfully back and forth over her knuckle.

'I brought you some grapes,' she said, wanting to change the subject and rummaging in the plastic bag for them. She handed them over before taking out her purse and giving him a twenty-pound note. 'For papers and things,' she told him. 'I think they have a little shop on the grounds here.'

Jason merely nodded, irritated by his wife's presence, but grateful at the same time. He watched as she delved into the plastic bag once more.

'And here are your pyjamas,' she said, passing them to him.

Jason was glad to see these. There was nothing worse than wearing stamped, institutional nightwear. He held onto his familiar claret pyjamas as if they were defining him as sane, civilised.

'How's the student? Bradley?' he asked, lowering his eyes and pinching his nose.

There was a long delay.

'He suffered a concussion and a broken arm, but he's OK. They kept him in hospital overnight just in case.'

'That's good,' he said. 'Will it go to court?'

'I don't know,' said Poppy. 'Let's wait and see.'

'Well, the university will probably sack me after this,' he mumbled, sucking in his cheeks.

Poppy was shaking her head. 'Why did you do it, Jason?'

He looked down at the floor. 'I don't know. I just blew up. The students knew about my arrest, and Bradley and his sidekick, Doherty—right clowns, the pair of them—always winding up the tutors—drew hats all over the wipe board.'

'And that's it?' asked Poppy disbelievingly. 'So, you go and assault one of them?'

'I didn't mean to—' Jason could see that Poppy was angry. 'There was more to it than that,' he tried to explain.

Poppy had her *it-better-be-good* look.

'I was already wound up,' he told her. 'Professor Porter had me in his office for a ticking off about my arrest, and the students started playing up while I was doing the lecture. Then I saw what they drew on the board, you know? With the words "Mad Hatter", and—'

'You saw red?'

'Yes.'

For a moment it struck Jason that what the students had done was no worse than the numerous and occasionally cruel pranks he and Umbie had carried out at Saint Ergonwald's.

'How did they know about the arrest?' Poppy asked, trying to keep herself calm.

'I've a fair idea, but it doesn't matter now. I guess plenty of people are tapping their heads when my name is mentioned.'

His wife ignored his self-pity and changed the subject. 'Have you seen a doctor yet?'

Jason raised his eyebrows. 'This is the NHS, right? What do you think?'

'The nurse said something about a ward round tomorrow?'

They sat down with little privacy.

'All I know is that I'm on some sort of section of the Mental Health Act. They want to assess me. Or so they say.'

'Have you had another injection?'

'No.'

Poppy breathed out long and hard. 'Well, that's something,' she conceded.

'I suppose so, but I don't know why they have to keep me here. Things just got on top of me. That is all. I'm not mad,' he insisted, twirling his finger at his head. 'I didn't think they could do this sort of thing. I cannot leave the ward, you know. I feel like a prisoner, a criminal. The patients in here have more than pigeons in the loft! It's pretty scary!'

Poppy bit her lip and peered anxiously into his eyes. 'Everything was fine until Umbie's death,' she mumbled.

'Look, all will be fine again,' Jason tried to comfort her. 'It's just a matter of time. I could be out by Thursday. Then, believe me, I'll settle things.'

'What do you mean?'

Jason held up his hand, closing down the conversation. 'It's OK.'

'No, come on! What do you mean?'

'I'll just sort things, right?'

'No, it's not all right. What are you planning to do?'

Jason sighed deeply and writhed about in his seat. 'Nothing,' he told her.

Poppy squinted as if that would help her to discern what was going on in his head. Jason went quiet, rubbed his eyes, and ruffled the hair over his right ear.

'Look, Pops,' he said, 'I know you think I'm losing it. I can see from the way you keep looking at me. But I know who I am.'

The phrase suddenly struck him. It was like the opening line of one of John Clare's poems, *I Am!*, from when he was at Northampton Asylum:

"I am—yet what I am, none cares or knows;
My friends forsake me like a memory lost."

Jason felt a similar profound isolation and grunted to fend off the tears. *At least I have Poppy for support*, he told himself. *She has not deserted me.* Yet his wife was in despair over him, flopping back in the chair, wondering what had happened to her husband. Here he was in the local mental hospital, having assaulted one of his students, and, if that was not bad enough, he was now mumbling to himself.

Jason was oblivious to her frustration, looking away, inscrutable. His eyes were moist and fixed. Poppy made small talk with the odd barb of criticism. Soon enough, visiting time ended and Jason headed off for his locker, carrying the plastic bag of home comforts and necessities.

18

That night, Jason lay on his bed eating the last of the dusty, seeded grapes, staring at the dark, indistinct shapes and shadows of the dormitory. His tongue searched for the little jellied pips as he listened to the intermittent farting, burping and rustling of bed linen. He heard the groans and sighs of the lonely and the outcast, and spat a seed from his mouth, appalled by the unpredictable human zoo around him. He feared someone attacking him as he slept. Even though the unit had night cameras and the nurses walked regular rounds of the building, he did not feel safe. He drew his blanket protectively to his chin and brought his feet away from the unknown, threatening bottom of the bed. If he could have built a boma, he would have done so.

Jason sat in the darkness, crushing the grapes in his mouth one after the other. The cool, sweet juice burst down his throat, easing the dryness that had plagued him all day, no doubt caused by the injection and reduced fluids. Now and again, he rejected the slightly bitter skin into the palm of his hand and flicked it into the air, not caring where it landed. When he had consumed the whole bunch, he lay back, unable to sleep and alert to every sound, sweating freely onto his pillow, which was as comfortless as a sack of pebbles.

It was in the long, early hours that Jason decided he must escape from the ward despite being on a section and regardless of the wishes of his wife or Dr Bent. He needed to track down Umbie's killer—the cause of continued misery and upset, the bringer of woes. He would find him if it was the last thing he did. He thought again about the hoodies in the arcade. Was one of them the killer? They had looked the part. Yet Jason had been frustrated in his enquiry. If only he had been able to check his scalp properly. If only the police had kept out of it. Perhaps he would get a second chance, by catching the suspect on his own and getting a closer look. However, now another idea came to him. It was something he had neglected and should have done ages ago. He thought about this as he tried to get to sleep, patting his stomach, willing the sacrament on.

†

The next morning Jason was up early. The hangover effect of the sedation had worn off completely now, and he knew he had to act. He did not trust Mr Singh. Nor did he trust the doctors, even the benign and celebrated Dr Bent. More than that, he did not trust the Mental Health Act. There was no way he was going to stay around for further injections or pills. He had spent much of the night planning his exit. Yet before he could escape, he had to find a way to leave the hospital unobserved.

While the other patients breakfasted, Jason reconnoitred the corridors and all the fire doors. He saw that the nursing staff were getting ready to do the medication round. This would give him the advantage. At the one end of the building next to the toilets, the fire door gave the best access to the hospital driveway. He knew that this part of the city could get very busy, and it would be easy to hide in a crowd once outside. If he were quick, he calculated, he would get clear long before the staff on the unit had a chance to respond.

As an argument broke out about tablets, Jason seized the opportunity and ran for the fire door, breaking the tube of glass that secured it. As he pushed it open, a squealing alarm sounded that sent him pelting away from the building. Quickly, without looking back, he slipped off his laceless shoes, thrust them into the black bin liner with his dirty clothes and ran across the grass barefoot towards the main gate. There was no one on the grounds to stop him, and besides, he was ready to use force if necessary. He calculated that by the time the staff located the breach, he would be gone. He would not return home, as that would be the first place they would come searching for him. Instead, he would stay at a cheap guesthouse on the far side of Ardinweald. He would take as much cash out on his cards in one withdrawal to avoid further tracking from his purchases. On a burst of adrenaline, he fled the place, struggling to keep his trousers up for lack of a belt.

Jason's eyes fogged up as he sped away onto the access road. At first, he moved fast, athletically even, homing in on the archway that Poppy had moved under the day before. By the time he reached it, he was puffing and panting. The rain did not help, driving into his hot face. As he ran, one hand holding up his trousers, he turned to look back, stretching his eyelids, half expecting to see nurses giving chase. There was no one. Just in case, he put on another late burst of speed that sent him under the archway and out onto the street. His eagerness to escape and the wet surface almost sent him under a bus, with passengers turning their heads to look at him through the filthy windows. The vehicle eased quietly away, with a burst of electric power. He took out his laceless shoes and put them on.

Catching his breath, Jason headed off in the direction of Ardinweald, his eyebrows and sideburns gathering beads of sweat. He felt homeless. He looked homeless. As he went, he forced people out of his way in an eagerness to put some distance between himself and the hospital. The light rain peppered his head and caught in the bowls of his ears. As he ran, his lungs burned and water dripped off the tip of his nose. His muscles ached with unfamiliar exertion, but he kept going, away from the city, expecting heavy hands to fall suddenly on his shoulders at any moment.

On he went, his feet jolted by the weight of his body, weaving slightly, stopping only to take out his daily maximum at a cashpoint, not even bothering to hide his face from the microscopic camera. Eventually, he reached the southern end of Ardinweald Park, pushing forward, his jowls rising and falling, his heart drumming his ribs. When Jason reached the park, he came to a faltering halt, letting go of his trousers and grabbing onto the arrow-topped railings to take huge gulps of air. He thought he might be having a heart attack. Bent over and with his legs like jelly, he threw up the contents of his stomach—mostly grapes from the night before—before suffering a volley of unproductive retching. He cursed his unfit body. It was the body of a lecturer, and he regretted the fact that his typing fingers were the most exercised parts of his anatomy. A full three minutes passed before he could straighten up, grab onto his trousers and contemplate how best to resume his journey. He knew he had no time to lose. If they had not done so already, it would not be long before the hospital reported him missing to the police, and he was determined to make his visit to Umbie's place of work and avoid them, perhaps indefinitely.

Jason knew he had to get off the main road. One way or another he had to travel without notice. The park and railway line were his best options. He quickly squeezed through a gap in the railings by collapsing his ribcage a little. On the other side, it was slippery and sodden from the night's rainfall and Jason twisted his ankle painfully as he came out of the bushes onto the open grass. He hopped and balanced on one leg, cursing. When the pain finally eased, he hobbled away, hugging the line of bushes. Puddles of water broke under his feet and grew still again as he progressed out of view of the road. He felt vulnerable, hunted. A few Ardonians walked their dogs, yanking leads, relaxing them and tugging once more. One dog dipped its bottom to the long grass, leaving a gift for the local footballers and children visiting the park.

Within ten minutes, Jason reached the northernmost tip of the recreation ground that met the railway embankment. At this far end, many of the railings were missing and he easily ducked through before picking his way up the uneven slope, following a path trampled through blackberry. Once on top, he could see the cemetery on the other side of the valley, its stones like white flowers at this distance. The Sow's Ear stood partly obscured by a hood of trees.

Jason stood still at the side of the track, looking down at the oil-spattered beams and then along the silvery rails that tapered into the horizon. As he did so, he remembered the train journey to Saint Ergonwald's with Umbie. The journey was a metaphor for their escape from their father. The twins would ride at the end of a carriage with their heads out of a window, hair blown away from their faces. Despite their father, life was simpler then. Now Jason felt everything had grown complex, serious and grim. He moved beside the track and with a kick of his best foot, set off eastward.

To his left, Jason could see the untidy backs of the shops along High Street and the rubbish that accumulated in neglected spaces. On his right, beneath the cemetery, the park continued to broaden, with more grassland where the pigeon fanciers released their birds. As he struggled over the stones towards the far end of Marlborough Road, he tripped, corrected himself and stepped onto the railway line itself, moving from beam to beam, unafraid of trains. Nothing came down this stretch of track in the daytime. Before long, he arrived at another fence, partly dismantled by vandals who had kicked out numerous slats of wood. Jason went through the hole and stood for a while, resting against an old wall, getting his breath back. Slowly he recovered, buttoning his shirt where it had come undone and trying to stroke his trousers clean. He badly needed to change. He headed off to find a bed for the night.

19

Jason woke from a poor night on a lumpy bed at one of Ardinweald's worst lodging houses. He had provided a false name and paid in cash. He knew there was little chance of being found there, at least for now. He felt bad about not telling Poppy his plans. After a quick shower and changing into the clothes she had brought him, he headed downstairs and tucked into a miserable English breakfast. There were only a few other guests in the cramped, grim dining room. They looked like casual labourers. As he left, he made a bit of small talk with the owner and pawed the few dog-eared novels and tourist leaflets at the desk. He took one of the leaflets with him as he sauntered out, studying it as if about to fill his day with visiting a ruined abbey despite the rain that had now started to fall. Once out of sight, he stuffed the leaflet into his coat pocket and walked as quickly as possible away from the main road towards Umbie's workplace on the other side of Ardinweald. On the way, he bought fresh shoelaces.

After nearly an hour, Jason found himself standing outside the nursing home with its Victorian porch and cherry trees in the garden. The black script on the faded white and damaged sign read: "Sain artha's Nursing Ho"—Umbie's workplace. Jason had visited it once or twice some years before, but this time he came to find clues to his brother's death. *It was worth a try. Perhaps the staff here know something. Did Umbie get into an argument with anybody? What did he talk about at work? Did he leave anything behind in his locker?* As Jason crossed the road with his hands in defensive fists, he kept an eye out for police. He was sure that the hospital had notified them of his absconsion and would consider him a potential danger to himself or others.

Walking unsteadily, feeling alienated from the ground beneath him and anxious that the police might escort him back to the hospital at any moment, he studied the sprawling nursing home with its various extensions. He paused for a second or two before pushing the gate open and walking up the path. He prayed that the visit might provide some pieces of the puzzle to finding out exactly who killed his brother. After all, it had begun to dawn on Jason that the possibility of catching up with Umbie's killer was fading as each day passed. He knew that already the trail was going cold.

Beneath the porch and out of view and the rain, Jason breathed a sigh of relief and rang the bell. He could not tell if it made a sound. As he waited, he held his nose under his armpit and sniffed. The hot shower and change of clothes that morning had worked. Despite a makeshift night in the guesthouse, he was half-presentable.

After quite a wait, the matron, Mrs Honeybourne, finally opened the door. At first, she frowned heavily, but then opened up her face.

'Oh, hello, Dr Hemp, how nice to see you!'

Jason offered a large, coarse hand that wrapped around her cool, damp fingers.

'Sorry,' she said. 'Alcohol gel. I have just been, anyway—'

'No worries,' answered Jason. 'Could I have a brief word?' Jason looked steadily at her forehead, escaping her finely lidded eyes.

'Yes, of course! Please, come in.'

'Thanks,' he said, allowing Mrs Honeybourne to guide him into the broad, spacious entrance hall.

For a moment, he felt old, infirm and needing care. The matron did not seem unduly concerned by his clearly rumpled and now damp clothes. She probably had his sartorial disarray as down to sheer grief.

'How good to see you,' she said with her counselling voice. 'I often think of Umbie. We were all very shocked by what happened. Well, we still *are*, of course. The funeral was very special. It is so important to have a good send-off. I found your eulogy deeply moving.' She paused for breath and continued. 'You gave a lovely quote at the end. What was it again?'

Jason struggled to gather the form of words. 'Sorry, no, it's gone.'

'It's OK, don't worry. Everything must be difficult for you just now.'

Jason coughed weakly and nodded, his heart filled with pure, obsessive revenge—nothing more, nothing less.

'Please come on through,' she told him. 'It's been a while since you visited us. Is it two years now?'

'Longer, I think,' Jason corrected her.

'Gosh, doesn't time fly. Well, we're a much bigger place now,' she said proudly. 'We've extended into another wing. In fact, we are now the largest nursing home in Ardinweald!'

Jason pretended to be impressed. However, the strong background odour of urine told him differently. The olfactory landscape kept him grounded and intent on business.

'I need to speak with you about my brother,' he said, explaining his visit.

Mrs Honeybourne took him through the main day room. 'Yes, of course. Let us go into my office. You probably recognise a few of our residents,' she said, casting her hand around the gaggle of old men and women, a few of whom nodded and murmured on Jason's entry. 'Look, everyone,' announced the matron. 'I've brought a nice young man to see you all.'

'Oh, yes,' said two or three of them. Most of the men were dozing, barely lifting their eyelids before they drooped again.

'This is Dr Hemp. He has visited us before, but most of you will remember his brother, Umbie.'

A number of the female residents muttered or sighed. Others

seemed to scrape at their memories for the word "Umbie", then tutted and shut down. Jason smiled awkwardly and stared at the nearest woman, who was intent on spearing a ball of pink wool with her knitting needles.

'We have some new residents, of course,' rambled Mrs Honeybourne. 'Faces do change.'

There was no response.

Mrs Honeybourne laughed softly, her face crinkling lightly as she drew Jason across a patterned carpet that covered up all kinds of stains.

'Hello,' said one woman, rather delayed, her mind labouring to compute Jason's presence. She appeared quite ancient, with hair sprouting from her semolina upper lip and her back curling down towards the ground. 'How nice! Are you the doctor?' she asked throatily, looking up, a large-print romance unopened in her lap. 'I need to see you about my water tablets. You see, I've been—'

'He's not a *real* doctor,' interrupted Mrs Honeybourne.

'What do you mean he's not a *real* one?'

Jason bit his tongue and went along with the script. 'I'm a doctor of literature,' he explained.

There was a long deciphering.

'Oh,' she said finally.

One of the other residents took over.

'He's a nice-looking man, though, isn't he?' said a woman struggling to keep hold of her teacup and saucer.

'I'm afraid,' explained Mrs Honeybourne, chuckling, 'our ladies do enjoy the company of men. They adored Umbie, of course.'

'We like the ones with a bit of life left in them,' said the woman knitting patches for a quilt and nodding at the sleeping male residents.

Jason scratched his ear and smiled, ill at ease in his crumpled shirt, turning his attention to the long, well-established garden with its giant cedar rising up from the immaculate lawn. It was the first time he had really noticed it. He cocked his head to one side and peered at the green needles and egg-shaped cones. It must have stood there for centuries, he decided. With the old tree and surrounded by people at various stages of dementia or frailty, he thought about the passage of time and his own decline. Hung above a turntable with its stack of vinyl records was a board giving the day, date, and weather in big black letters. "SUNNY" it read. Jason shook his head sadly. *Shoot me*, he thought before catching sight of a large picture of a minor royal opening the nursing home. *Shoot me twice*, he reconsidered.

It was at this point that he heard someone whispering intently to his left. A woman with long, dirty fingernails was slumped in a wheelchair and obviously struggling to speak. She caught Jason's eye as if with a fishhook.

'He was wonderful,' she said. 'He really was. Nothing was too much for your brother.' The resident turned her eyes to Mrs Honeybourne and continued. 'Do you remember how he cared for Harry when he was dying? Poor Harry—he had no one, you see—no one in the whole world. He had a little tattoo of an anchor on one of his knuckles. I liked him. I think he was a gunner on a ship in the last war. He was always stroking it. Umbie was very good with him. He was good with Betty and John too. He really looked after the lonely ones, you see. Those that had no family to look out for them. Your brother was quite wonderful.'

'Yes, he was,' agreed the matron.

As another resident joined the delayed appraisal of his brother, Jason felt proud of his twin's legacy as a first-class carer. He imagined Harry and the other residents were in the best possible hands.

†

Harry had been one of the strongest residents at Saint Martha's Nursing Home. He had been a champion boxer, winning featherweight titles in the Navy Championships. The craft of pugilism led to his dementia. His care notes told of a gentle, loving husband who would not see anyone go short, often giving away his silverware to keep friends and their families afloat in depressed years. Then, with time, came increased memory problems. He turned violent with frustration and confusion. He struck everyone and everything, still very capable of landing blows on chins. After lashing out too many times, his wife placed him in the care of Mrs Honeybourne and her team. Over the years, Harry's aggression subsided, and the remnant of his ravaged mind grew calm again. He even outlived his devoted wife.

It was late in the progression of that horrible disease that Umbie found Harry lying on his back, fists up by his chin and elbows welded to his ribs, as if keeping up his guard for a final assault. Although Umbie tried to straighten out the arms, it was impossible, and he had to leave the resident mirroring the figure of a boxer on his one remaining, tarnished silver trophy that stood on the windowsill.

Umbie had seen a lot of death in his time at the nursing home. He knew the procedure. He opened the window to let the air freshen, but also to offer an exit for the released spirit of Harry, and notified Mrs Honeybourne who, in turn, asked Dr White to visit and confirm the death. In the meantime, with the ring of muscles that had once preserved Harry's dignity open, Umbie cleaned up and prepared his body for inspection. He rolled up the dirty sheet Harry was lying on, placed a new one underneath and shifted his remarkably light corpse back and forth. Soon enough, the body was lying on clean bedding with an incontinence pad between its legs and shrouded by a crisply ironed sheet. Then, closing the window and drawing the curtains, Umbie left what remained of Harry in his utter and final isolation and went off for a cup of tea.

Later that afternoon, Dr White looked in, drew back the sheet and made his perfunctory examination. He signed the official forms required to release the body to the undertakers and left Umbie to continue his ministrations. Mrs Honeybourne relied increasingly on the ever-faithful Umbie to make all the necessary arrangements for the removal of the body. As Harry had no remaining family, his transfer and cremation fell under the city council's pauper arrangements, and Umbie made various calls such that, within a few hours, two men, dressed in black suits, white shirts and black ties arrived at the rear of the building. Umbie escorted them discreetly through to Harry's room, avoiding the other residents. Once there, Harry's body was lifted into a temporary wooden coffin and wheeled to the only lift in the building. The men had to tilt the coffin upright to get in. As they did so, Harry's corpse shifted forward and they heard what must have been the head bump against the wood as if in protest. As the lift descended, the respectful silence and demeanour of Umbie and the undertakers continued. Umbie guided the men along a corridor, out of view of the other residents, into the dark blue van parked outside.

20

Apart from a few weeks with Saint John's Ambulance in his youth, Jason had done little to match his brother's caring life. True, he was good with the students when they brought their problems to him, but he knew that his twin had progressed to a different level. He was devoted to the community's elders. He had stood with them in the shadow of death. He had not left them alone at the end.

'Let's go and have our chat,' suggested Mrs Honeybourne, straightening her cardigan. 'I'll just ask the cook to make a drink. Tea? Coffee?'

'Tea would be nice, thank you, with just a spot of milk and—'

'Sugar?'

'Yes, please. Four spoons.'

Mrs Honeybourne raised her eyebrows at the amount. 'Too much sugar's not good for you, you know,' she told him before heading over to the kitchen's serving hatch and shouting through for drinks.

Jason held his chin, trying to think of all the questions he could ask the matron about his brother.

Mrs Honeybourne quickly returned from the hatch and guided Jason down a narrow, dark corridor and into a fusty, cramped office. There was an old commode there, boxes of large disposable nappies stacked by a desk, and two plastic chairs.

Jason sat down.

'Now, how can we help you?' she asked warmly.

Jason rubbed his lips together, unsure what to say. After a long moment, he found his tongue. 'I just wanted to find out more about my brother, that's all.'

Mrs Honeybourne looked surprised. What could she or her staff tell Jason that he did not already know? 'I'm not quite sure what you mean.'

Now Jason struggled when he spoke. 'Well, er, I am trying to piece things together, you know, from the murder. I had hoped you might be able to tell me something.'

Mrs Honeybourne smiled. 'What do you want to know?'

'I am not sure really,' he confessed. 'I just want to—'

Mrs Honeybourne waited politely. It was some time before Jason spoke again.

'Did he get into arguments with anybody?' he asked finally.

'Not that I know of,' she answered, a little puzzled by his line of questioning, as the cook entered with the hot drinks.

Jason was grateful for the cup of sweet, scalding tea. He was suddenly thirsty after the morning's salty breakfast.

'No? OK. Could you tell me what he liked to talk about while he was at work? Any information would help.'

After a long pause, Mrs Honeybourne said, 'I don't wish to disappoint you, but I knew very little about your brother, nothing more really than what our ladies out there told you. He was a wonderful carer, yet he was a quiet man. He kept his cards close to his chest.' Mrs Honeybourne took a long sip of her sugarless tea, keeping her eyes on Jason's unshaven face.

'No, you're right,' he admitted. 'He led a simple life, but that's just it. Why would anyone want to murder him? I am trying to come to terms with his death, and I want to draw close to him again now he has gone. I thought you or your staff might help fill in some of the gaps. You see, sometimes I feel I hardly knew him. And if I did not know him, then—' He suddenly felt cold, panicked and afflicted by an overwhelming sense that he did not know anyone at all.

What does that mean? What does that make me? He battled to set his thoughts in a different groove.

'Did my brother have a locker for his clothes?' he asked. 'Only, I wondered if he might have left stuff behind.'

'No, I'm afraid not,' answered Mrs Honeybourne, frowning heavily, the way she did when she first answered the door to him. 'I understand you must be under considerable stress,' Mrs Honeybourne told him in her most sensitive, sympathetic voice. 'I just wish I had something more to tell you.'

'I'd be grateful for anything at the moment,' Jason said in a defeated tone.

Mrs Honeybourne's eyes watered. She blinked her fleshy eyelids and extended her heart to Jason, wanting to ease his grief. 'Umbie was a lovely man. Nothing was ever too much for him. He never moaned. He was always cheerful,' she said, pulling in her lips, struggling to pad out her knowledge of him. 'It'll be hard to find someone to replace him.'

Mrs Honeybourne's apparent sincerity affected Jason. A lump came to his throat. The matron continued building up a picture of his kind, dead brother.

'He was quiet, as I said. Yet he was popular. But he seemed to think a lot, you know, have things on his mind.'

'Popular?' questioned Jason, leaning forward in his chair. 'In what way was he popular?'

'With the residents,' said Mrs Honeybourne. 'And staff.'

'Ah, I thought you meant outside of the home.' Jason gazed into the slowly cooling tea in his cup.

'Well, that as well,' said the matron. 'He wasn't short of friends, was he?'

'He wasn't?'

'No. He seemed to have quite a few.'

'Did he?' This was news to Jason.

'Yes,' she said, looking into the air, casting her eyes to the left.

Jason uncrossed his legs and sat forward again. 'What kind of friends?'

'Well, I assume they were his friends. Male friends, you know,' she clarified. 'There was often someone waiting for him after work or leaving him a message.'

'Now you're just trying to comfort me,' Jason insisted, holding his balding head.

As far as he was concerned, Umbie had very few friends. He was quite the loner. There was only Jason and a few ale drinkers in his social circle. Umbie had given up his football mates a long time ago.

Mrs Honeybourne's cup fell away from her lips and Jason could see that she was puzzled. He felt suddenly uncomfortable, an outsider to his brother's life.

'I was—' Jason did not go on. He looked at Mrs Honeybourne without seeing her. His face went noticeably grey, and his eyes flicked this way and that, agitated and restless.

'I assure you, Dr Hemp,' she said, 'Umbie did have friends and they visited him from time to time.'

'But he never let on to me. Are you sure?' His voice quivered.

'Absolutely,' she answered, afraid of the stormy light that filled Jason's eyes.

'Friends, you say?'

'Yes. There was one man in particular—'

Jason leaned forward again, putting down the cup, his hands spreading out across the desk, his fingertips almost touching those of Mrs Honeybourne. She quickly withdrew them.

'Who?' he asked eagerly, standing up now, with quick, strange, jerking movements.

He paced back and forth across the office carpet. The cups rocked in their saucers with his movements on the loose floorboards. He grew more and more flustered. He felt bitter that Umbie had secret friends. *Why didn't I know about them? What else had my brother hidden from me? I had always thought we were so close and knew everything about each other.*

'I think his name was Ryan.'

'Ryan? Ryan?' Jason stopped in his tracks and stared at Mrs Honeybourne. 'That name rings a bell,' he admitted, sitting back down again, leaning forward, his hands clasped together.

Then it dawned on him who it might be.

'Jim Ryan?'

'He owns that fancy barbershop on York Road,' she added.

'Headquarters.'

'Yes.'

'He visited Umbie?'

'Numerous times,' affirmed Mrs Honeybourne.

'This is all new to me,' Jason complained irritably, taking another gulp of tea.

He had heard about Jim Ryan from a colleague at the university who had run up debts and turned for help from the barber-cum-loan shark. He got himself into a right state about paying him back. Had the same happened to Umbie? Jason's mind raced with the new information. Suddenly, his brother's death slotted into the frame. He imagined Jim Ryan sending heavies around to get his money back. *Was the attack in the subway the conclusion of failed payments?* The thought seized hold of Jason and already he began planning his route to visit the barber and find out. His agitation grew with all these thoughts until his whole body trembled for action. He stood up quickly, putting down the teacup on the desk.

'I have to go,' he told Mrs Honeybourne suddenly, moving around the spare commode to the door.

'Yes, of course, I—'

Jason was not engaging now. He had one idea in his mind. It set off all the wiring under his skull.

Mrs Honeybourne could do nothing but follow Jason's eager steps through the lounge to the front of the building, ignoring a request for the toilet from one of the residents.

Soon enough, Jason was outside again, with only a hand in the air as a vague goodbye, leaving Mrs Honeybourne holding her chin. He walked quickly, slipping on the wet tarmac, checking that the coast was clear and keeping his head down. The rain had given over. A sharp, cold, bullying wind took its place. His teeth ached between his biting, anxious jaw, and his stomach filled with the gas of fried breakfast.

He hurried along Marlborough Road, leaning into the rising slope with his hands swinging, touching the flaps of his coat. A gusting wind opposed him. He set his nose like a flint against it, walking as quickly as he could, mumbling under his breath and staring at Ardinweald Parish Church, which rose black above High Street. On he went, his shoes scuffing the ground, passing an old man creeping along as slow as a slug. As Jason overtook him, he kept an eye out for CCTV and the police. He turned down a winding alley at the back of the shops and kept out of view, looping back to High Street further along, nearer to his chosen destination, Headquarters.

All the time, Jason was thinking about Jim Ryan. *Surely, he was no friend to Umbie.* Jason had never seen them together at The Half Moon or anywhere else for that matter. He guessed that the connection was all about money. Now he needed to find out what he had to say about his brother. *Did he owe Ryan money? Did Ryan send out enforcers to punish him for not paying him back?*

With his teeth beginning to weld together, Jason slapped his frustrated, puzzled brow with the heel of his hand. It seemed as if Umbie had led a double life, a shadow life. If this was true, it meant he was a liar. It meant that Jason's core belief in their closeness would fall apart. He felt the cold touch of panic again as he thought of his brother as a stranger, yet managed to hold it back.

High Street was busy with people walking past shops, checking their profiles and the goods that pressed for their attention. Jason looked up and noticed the little black dome cameras keeping watch on the public. He dipped his head, but knew it would not be long before the police identified him.

Further along, the main carriageway led south to the General Hospital laundry where Poppy had worked for so many years. As he approached Headquarters, he wondered whether his wife was cursing him for absconding. He wanted to let her know he was OK, but felt driven to use what little time he might have before being picked up to find out more about the events leading to Umbie's murder. Time was running out. He had to move fast to solve the riddle. The last thing he needed was to be stuck away in a mental hospital for weeks on end, with the killer's tracks cooling by the day.

Jason hurried on past the various boutiques and a ramshackle taxi shed with its poorly constructed mast rising high into the chopping air. Just beyond the fish-and-chip shop and down past estate agents, solicitors, a balti house, newsagents and McCartie's, on the corner of York Road, stood Headquarters.

Without dropping his pace and quite oblivious now to the dull pain that returned to his sprained ankle, Jason headed for the barbershop's distinctive, traditional red-and-white pole. He did not want anything to delay his meeting with Ryan. Jason had questions stacked up in his mind. He felt convinced he would know if the barber was behind Umbie's death. *It will be as easy as applying litmus paper. I will detect the acid. I will feel the burn.* Yet he also dreaded exactly what he might learn about his brother.

Jason hesitated before crossing the road to Headquarters. He wondered how Jim Ryan might respond to the many questions he had for him. *Perhaps he won't be alone and he'll set thugs onto me, kicking me out the back of the shop among the wheelie bins with a squeezed neck and another bloody nose. Perhaps worse.* Jason gulped with the thoughts, looking at various Ardonians behind the large window, their heads tilted back in basins or subjected to fast-moving scissors. Although the building was down at heel, with poor lighting, it was popular. In fact, it was the most frequented barbershop in the area, with Jim Ryan only employing young, beautiful women. The local men came in droves, waiting in turn to mount one of several red leather chairs that stood on their chrome bases. They came for the head massage as much as the cut. They came to ramble on about football, parties or holidays, as a girl of their dreams combed back and snipped their hair, and ran the electric shearer up and down their reddened necks, causing them to gasp in sheer ecstasy.

Plucking up courage, Jason quickly stuffed a loose shirttail into his clean trousers. Then, with a nervous look up at yet another black camera dome, he set off across the road.

A screech of brakes halted his journey.

Jason froze, flinching, waiting for the crumpling impact. Nothing came. He opened his eyes again slowly, peering sideways into the windscreen of the vehicle. It could not have been worse. He thought of running, but the muscles in his legs felt heavy and his ankle had grown swollen and sore, competing with the pain in his right buttock and the dull ache of his still bruised nose. He considered all possibilities, yet these quickly ran aground as his slightly blurred vision settled on the unmistakable birthmark of Inspector Mosby glowering behind the steering wheel.

21

The pyramid-topped towers of Birchwood Hospital came into view, poking at yet more dark clouds that moved in from the northwest. Jason stared at the sky through the side window of Inspector Mosby's police car, his breath condensing, forming an oval of mist on its surface. It was dark for noon, and there was the strange kind of bristling light that augured further stormy weather. Mosby had hardly spoken to Jason during the journey, merely glancing into the mirror now and then. As they turned through the arched entrance to the hospital, the silence continued. There was little to discuss. Jason knew how his words would count for little. This was the price for having anything to do with the world of psychiatry. He was now one of the incomprehensible. He was a mind refugee.

Mosby drove fast over the barely visible speed bumps set down on the access road, and around to the new admissions block. Jason saw a little more of the hospital on the way: a number of modern, bungalow-style units, surrounded by cheap, bright fencing, and an old building, possibly a chapel or recreation hall. Jason stared at the remnant of the old asylum until the car turned towards the ward he had escaped from the day before. He could see the same set of patients in their chairs and Mr Singh doling out tablets ahead of lunch. As the car jerked to a halt, a good storm looked ready to break the deadly monotony.

Jason felt he was in a dream, dissociated from reality. The respectable Dr Hemp, lecturer, was arriving back at the mental hospital. In a fugue state, he did not hear the passenger door unlock and it took a while for him to perceive the sound of Inspector Mosby tapping impatiently on the roof of the vehicle. Jason squeezed himself out and straightened up, looking at the building in front of him. As Mosby brought him to the main black doors with porthole windows, he felt his body grow heavy and defeated. The lassitude made him slump forwards when the detective's custodial hand guided him inside, past Mr Singh's office with the wipe board of patients' names. Jason saw "AWOL" written in red marker next to his name.

Inspector Mosby walked Jason through into the day room and presented him to Mr Singh who quickly closed and locked the drug trolley.

'Just in time for some lunch,' he told Jason in a friendly, welcoming tone, palming him to an empty chair. Charlie was on duty and Mr Singh indicated with a nod of his head that he should attend to Jason and keep an eye on him.

'We ran into each other—literally,' explained Inspector Mosby. 'See if you can keep him on the ward this time, guys?' With that, he turned to leave.

Yet not before Mr Singh came back at him. 'You do your job and we'll do ours. This is not a forensic unit, you know. We are not running a prison.' He then escorted the detective off the unit.

As if willed by Mr Singh himself, torrential rain drenched Inspector Mosby on leaving the building, turning his white shirt translucent.

Mr Singh peered through one of the porthole windows, watching him gradually disappear into the bad weather. Then he went back into his office and rubbed out the "AWOL" next to Jason's name.

'Welcome back,' he muttered to no one. He knew he would have to keep Jason under closer observation, at least until Dr Bent reviewed the case.

He looked at the live camera coverage, satisfied that Charlie had a close eye on the returned patient.

On the ward, Jason ate little of the tuna sandwich on offer. The fried breakfast at the lodging house was still working its way through. As he pushed the plate of food to one side and drank a cup of tea, he gave more thought to the information from Mrs Honeybourne. Now he had a vital lead on whoever killed Umbie. Soon enough, Jason knew he would get his chance to interrogate Jim Ryan. He was in his sights and Jason could take his time to learn more about him. *Ryan was not going anywhere. Headquarters was no hiding place.* As Jason finished his tea, he knew he was onto something. He could feel it in his bones.

Jason looked over at Charlie sitting opposite at an angle, with an assumed nonchalance to cloak his observation.

'When will I get out of here?' Jason asked him.

'That depends on your behaviour,' he said, picking at his nails.

'I'm not mad,' repeated Jason firmly. 'I can't believe this place can take normal, sane citizens off the street and bang them up. I want to see the doctor!'

'Dr Bent.'

'Yes, Dr Bent. Can you please ask him to come and see me?'

Now Mr Singh was back in the dining area and answered him. 'Not a problem,' he said. 'I have already informed him of your return and he will be along this afternoon. In the meantime, please relax as much as you can and remain on the ward. If you run off again it will not help your case, you know?'

Jason took a long breath. 'Right, OK,' he said with a sniff. 'When does that section run out?'

Mr Singh caressed his beard. 'Well it very much depends on Dr Bent's review so let's wait for that,' he answered.

Jason drew his lips together and nodded. All being well, Dr Bent would discharge him and he could get on with his investigation. Once released Jason decided he would go straight over to Headquarters to interrogate Jim Ryan. It would be a long afternoon, but Jason knew he just needed to keep his nose clean and speak to Dr Bent coherently and calmly so as not to give cause for further detainment.

†

That afternoon, Jason spent much of the time dozing off when not reflecting on what Mrs Honeybourne had told him or resenting the close observation of Charlie who continued to be preoccupied with his nails. Little else happened between the other nurses and patients. The television was on, providing a kind of medication that left everyone inert. Jason's thoughts turned to Jim Ryan again. He wondered about the relationship the hairdresser had forged with Umbie. *Loan sharks kept victims, not friends.* Jason anticipated being back in his office at the university, pinning a photograph of Ryan on his wall of evidence, beginning to tie things together. Of course, he was not sure whether the university would allow him back there anytime soon, but he would cross that bridge when he came to it. For now, he drew comfort from visualising new data for his amateur enquiry.

Outside, the rain persisted, whipping its way across the deserted playing field. Jason looked past the beads of water tracking down the glass, twinkling beneath the ward's fluorescent lights as he imagined walking into Headquarters the next day and confronting Ryan. If he was not involved in Umbie's death, he might know who was. Whatever the facts, Jason sensed that his own amateurish net was closing in on the killer. He sighed heavily and looked over at Charlie who maintained his vigil, arms crossed, perched in his favourite haunt on the windowsill beneath the television. The patients remained in suspended animation, slouched in their chairs, heads tilted backwards to watch the succession of dull afternoon programmes. They sat through house auctions, life in the countryside and the latest innovation in de-carbonising the planet. At the far end of the day room, the hands on the large unadorned ward clock progressed infinitesimally to the hour of Dr Bent's visit. Everything would hinge on the psychiatrist's assessment and decision. Until then, Jason had to bear shadowing from Charlie, even to the toilet, and the numbing boredom of hospital life.

Whenever Jason got up, Charlie matched his every movement. Now and again, while waiting for Dr Bent's arrival, Jason entertained himself by taking long strolls through the unit—upstairs to his bed space and back again—just to move Charlie around, like a puppet on strings.

'Now who has the power?' Jason muttered under his breath.

Yet this satisfaction was short-lived when Jason realised he needed to evacuate his bowels. There, behind a cubicle door that did not lock, he had no choice but to unload his greasy English breakfast to an audience of one: Charlie. For someone who had always taken the trouble to maintain the anonymity of his turds, Jason found this particularly humiliating. The stench he produced underlined the shame he felt and drew a stark response from the student nurse.

'Bloody hell, have you been eating babies' nappies?' he complained.

With that, Jason returned to the day room.

†

Jason woke from a slumber in his chair on the ward to the slightly unpleasant, fruity odour of Dr Bent who was standing over him, dressed in black. The pheromones intruded and roused Jason who widened his sleep-crusted eyes and slowly sat upright, stretching his way back into reality. Barely awake, he stared at Dr Bent's thick, studded, rubber-soled leather boots, silky black trousers and thick belt. He lifted his eyes to the equally black vest topped with dark hairs on a pale, milky chest. With a stifled yawn and wakeful shiver in his spine, Jason finally looked at the consultant psychiatrist's calm face and the large, silver rings that trained gaping holes in his ears.

'Oh, hello, Jason,' said Dr Bent in his familiar radio voice. 'How are we getting along?'

Dr Bent was smiling warmly and holding out his beringed hand. As he did so, his long hair extension swished around his shoulder into full view. It was like an old bell rope and Jason studied its amalgam of matted hair and ribbons. Fairy-tale images of Rapunzel came to mind as he tried to stifle another yawn. He saw the psychiatrist as a male version of this character but, perhaps, a rather depressed one. For, despite Jason's own problems, he diagnosed in the psychiatrist an undertow of melancholy. Was it the way he dipped his head or tended to stoop? Was it the all-too-brief eye contact? Whatever it was, Jason sensed Dr Bent was in as much need of help as anyone else in the hospital.

Jason took the consultant psychiatrist's dry hand and shook it before settling back into his chair, yawning once more and rubbing his left eye.

Dr Bent struggled to suppress a yawn himself, his mouth opening halfway to reveal numerous fillings. He said something, but Jason was still half-asleep, massaging his stubbly chin, brushing what little hair remained behind his ears. All Jason caught then was the last of the doctor's words.

'I can see you are tired.' Dr Bent sat down on one of the chairs, as always avoiding direct or sustained eye contact.

Jason furrowed his brow, trying to focus his attention. He wanted to get off the ward. He wanted to check out Jim Ryan. The thought was like smelling salts and he became suddenly alert and aware that he needed to be on his best behaviour with the doctor. After all, Dr Bent would make the decision about his discharge from the unit.

Dr Bent looked askance at Jason, dipping his head forward, his hands shoved between his shiny black knees. The sight of the psychiatrist amused Jason. He was an object of fascination. He began counting the doctor's ear piercings, finding twelve in all. He suspected that there were more hidden from view elsewhere on his body. When the psychiatrist removed his leather jacket, Jason studied the monochrome patterns adorning his triceps and biceps.

'So, how do you feel?' Dr Bent asked gently.

Jason felt he might ask the same question, yet hesitated and looked dismally at Dr Bent's inquisitive, relaxed face.

'Let's say pissed off. I think it is over the top sticking me in here,' Jason told him.

The psychiatrist nodded his head, listening attentively. 'Well, OK, but you posed a danger to yourself and others, Jason. We felt you needed to be admitted to hospital, for your own safety as much as anything.'

'But I don't need *your* kind of help.'

Dr Bent did not answer. He sat quietly, nodding, still avoiding Jason's eyes.

'I'd like to go home,' Jason pressed.

Dr Bent smiled sympathetically. 'Well, we don't want to keep you here longer than necessary. I'd like to send you home at the earliest opportunity.'

'You would?'

'Yes, of course. If you can bear with us a day or so, please. We need to carry out a few routine tests—blood, urine, that sort of thing—and assess your needs generally. Look, can I suggest that we go somewhere a little more private to talk? I'd like to get your perspective on what happened at the university the other day.'

Although Jason was unhappy about being on the ward, he sensed that Dr Bent really was concerned about him and wanted to help.

'OK,' he said after a few moments of silence, 'but I don't want the nurses standing over me.'

'Sure, no problem,' said Dr Bent. He turned and told Charlie he would take Jason on his own to one of the side rooms.

Jason followed the psychiatrist through two sets of double doors to the other side of the building where the décor was much nicer, in pastel shades with carpeted floors and individual rooms. Jason could see from the names and designations on the doors that this wing of the building was for the psychologists, psychotherapists and psychiatrists. It smelled fresher, and the noise level dropped substantially.

'This will do,' Dr Bent said, showing Jason into a good-sized room. It had decent natural light, two comfortable sitting chairs and a square coffee table complete with a box of tissues. 'Please, take a seat.'

Jason noted how the psychiatrist was careful to take the chair nearest the door. He guessed he had learned to position himself defensively in case patients turned violent. Jason could not blame him for taking precautions, given his recent outbursts of temper. He watched as Dr Bent adjusted his position to best advantage an escape.

'Now, Jason, we're here to help you,' opened the psychiatrist, sitting with his head bowed but eyes indirectly watchful, his fingers joined across his slight paunch. His long legs, uncrossed, splayed out. 'You've got yourself into a bit of a scrape a couple of times now, and this suggests you are not coping with things.'

Jason said nothing. He looked at a white tissue peeping out from the lips of the box on the coffee table and at the unframed pre-Raphaelite print on the wall opposite.

'Can you tell me in your own words what happened at the university? What were you *feeling*?' As he spoke, Dr Bent made only brief, carefully judged eye contact from under the shelf of his brow, affording engagement but not intruding. He faced Jason at an angle.

In the prolonged silence that followed, the psychiatrist did not make a noise or gesture. He sat in repose, and Jason thought he looked peculiarly feminine despite his size. More than that, he looked sad.

Not the sad look of someone bereaved, working through a divorce or denied access to his children. It was something less obvious, difficult to identify—something inside, but caught in the crinkling around his eyes, the way his lips puckered and the deeply lined brow that deformed the little scar on his cheek.

Jason felt for the first time since being in the hospital that this was someone he could talk to, someone who might understand. Mr Singh and the nurses were friendly enough and did not seem to delight in authority, yet they came across as going through the motions. Dr Bent had a deeper, richer, palpable emotional depth. He conveyed he cared whether he did or not. Jason sensed he could trust him a little.

'What was I feeling?' Jason repeated.

'Yes,' encouraged Dr Bent.

Jason composed himself, tugged at his clothes and dabbed his sweat-coated head. He pressed his back into the chair, wiped his brow with one of the tissues and breathed awkwardly in silence. Dr Bent was looking at him in such a composed, non-judgmental way that he sensed he did not have to lie. Jason felt a pull, an attraction to confess his interior world to the psychiatrist. He felt magnetically drawn to disclose the architecture of his mind.

'I felt like killing everyone,' Jason said finally.

As soon as he said these words, it was as if someone else had spoken. He immediately wanted to take them back. The tone of his voice was darker, rougher than his usual educated regional accent. The stark confession shocked Jason but not the psychiatrist who remained still, listening, with only the slow rolling back and forth of his lips indicating that the lights were on inside.

Now Jason was concerned that his words would be written down in his medical notes and come back to haunt him in the future. He heard a barrister with a rising voice turning to the jury for effect: "Didn't you inform Dr Bent that—" Realising the power of language and its ability to condemn people to life in prison, Jason backtracked, keen to establish the context of his comment.

'Please don't write that in your notes,' he said anxiously, rubbing his left eye with the knuckle of his forefinger. 'Not as I spoke it in that stark way. I was being metaphorical. I just felt terribly angry at everything, at everyone. I just want to kill one person. I WANT AN END TO MY GRIEF!'

Dr Bent was nodding gently despite Jason's raised voice. 'Jason, please say what you want without fear. I have a policy of showing my reports to patients if they wish to see them. I encourage rejoinders to my own interpretations. You will have an opportunity to write your own comments in the medical notes should I fail to capture the spirit of your words. Now, could you say a little more about your desire for revenge?'

†

'What do you mean you can't come?' Jason whined.

'I don't feel I can face it,' explained Poppy on the ward landline.

'But I need you.'

It went quiet at the other end.

'Pops? Hello?'

'I'm still here,' she said. 'I'm not feeling too good. I am tired and angry. I did not sleep a wink last night, and then I had the police around here this morning looking for you. I've had to double up on my tablets just to get through the day.'

'I am so sorry, Pops, really I am. I promise I will not run off again. I promise.'

There was no answer. A pickling kind of silence that Poppy used to good effect during their arguments ensued. It gave a clear signal that Jason would have to work very hard to gain her favour. He tried being as upbeat as possible.

'Dr Bent wants to discharge me as soon as possible,' he told her.

'I could be home tomorrow or the next day. He even took me off special observation. I hated that.'

Silence.

'He says what happened is part of a grief reaction made worse by the fact that Umbie was my twin brother and twins share a unique, deep bond.'

More silence.

'He is going to refer me to a psychologist to explore ways of dealing with my anger over Umbie's death. Although, he did warn me that it could be quite a wait. He diagnosed that my grief is overwhelming. He said it was the kind that comes without holidays.'

'What about medication? Are they giving you anything?' Poppy asked after another long pause.

'No.'

'No?' Poppy sounded surprised, yet she was genuinely pleased. 'That's good,' she told him. 'So, behave yourself now, please. I want you back home.'

'OK, Pops. I promise.'

'Look,' she relented. 'I'll see you tomorrow if they don't discharge you first. OK? I will bring your electric razor and a change of clothes. Do you need anything else?'

'Not that I can think of,' he said in a flat, monotone voice.

Then the natural cycle of conversation tailed off into longer silences before Jason decided to close it down.

'Right, I will get off then,' he told her as a profound emptiness opened up inside of him.

He stared for several seconds at the handset and jabbed it dead. He felt scooped out and dispirited. The homely voice of Poppy contrasted sharply with the stark institutional ward. With his head bowed down, he ambled back into the main area. He sat as far away as possible from the burbling television and patients bathing in its shimmering light.

Nearby, one of the patients pinned his eyes to the ceiling, his

'What?' Mr Singh snapped. He was clearly irritated. 'I am on my break!'

'I think someone might be about to hang themselves!'

'Shit!' cried the charge nurse, quickly dumping the newspaper and checking the camera coverage. He could see nothing salient. 'Where?'

'He ran upstairs,' Jason told him as Mr Singh raced out of the office, calling for backup from Charlie and one of the agency nurses, who had been fixing a drink in the small kitchen area.

As they tore through the day room, the other patients barely looked round. They had become used to these noisy interruptions. Jason brought up the rear, fearful of what they might find.

The nurses raced past the toilets and up the stairs to the dormitory, divided by partitions. They inspected each bay in turn. Jason followed them, expecting to hear choking sounds coming from the paranoid patient. The silence suggested they were too late.

'Stay back!' ordered the charge nurse, his hand stretched out in warning, hearing movement behind one of the partitions.

Mr Singh, the nurses and finally Jason saw the man, who had wrapped himself in wires, on his bed pleasuring himself, trying to prove his fertility on a wave of asphyxiation, adjusting the flex around his neck. Jason stared at the man in disbelief, wondering what other surprises this dumping ground for the unhinged might hold. His heart was still pounding at the thought of the hanging, and he felt like giving the man a good beating. The man was obviously deranged and provoking him could prove disastrous. The nurses simply unwound the wire from his neck as if this were a common ritual, disconfirming the presence of lasers.

fine, white hands at his side. Jason was wary of him. He learned from one of the other patients that this scrawny-necked fellow had recently had a spell in the intensive care unit after attacking one of the nurses. The patient seemed particularly restless and paranoid, looking around quickly to catch sight of whoever he believed to be a threat. Jason avoided eye contact and simply studied the hospital grounds as if something there particularly fascinated him. Suddenly, the man jumped up, pulled out a bundle of coloured wires that he had squirrelled away in one of his pockets and started dropping his trousers. Next, his pants came down and he began to wrap the wires around his testicles.

'Get that fucking laser out of here!' he shouted, looking around at everyone. 'I am not going to let you bastards make me impotent!'

Jason sat up bolt upright now, ready to escape if needed. For a moment, he felt like Dr Bent, carefully sitting by the exit. He felt shocked and vulnerable at the sight of the man in such obvious free fall. He had never seen anyone in full-blown paranoid psychosis. Now that madness was close up, right in front of him, he despaired.

The man cried out again. 'You can't kill my sperm!'

Jason marvelled at the multi-coloured wiring around the man's testicles.

'Try firing through this shit!' the man shouted triumphantly, pulling up his pants and trousers, distracting the other patients from the television. Then he proceeded to draw a thicker, white flex from his other pocket and wrap it in extinguishing loops around his neck before running out of the day room, his face already puce for lack of oxygen.

Jason stood up now, watching as the patient headed for the stairs. The nurses had all left the day room temporarily, so Jason ran to the office. He found Mr Singh with his feet up on his desk, the veil of tabloid blocking his view of the cameras.

Jason burst in, making the charge nurse jump. 'Quick!' he gasp 'Quick!'

22

Foston Hall was one of the largest high-security hospitals in the country and previously the home of the Vaughan family until the 1930s when the building fell into a parlous state. The health authority bought the pile in 1950 and since then, the eighteenth-century building accreted two new wings and a series of individual, specialist units within its large, fenced grounds. To one side of the original building stood a modern reception area with security check-in. On the other side of the locked doors stood various facilities one might expect in such an institution, including a staff canteen, gym and multifaith chapel. These and other facilities Dr Bent upgraded on his appointment in charge, striving for the right balance between a prison and a sanctuary. His *wonders*, as staff and inmates called them, extended to a new swimming pool, library, auditorium, café and elevated parkland within the grounds to afford uninterrupted views of the surrounding countryside beyond the grim double-security fence that encircled the hospital. It was all part of his vision of what he called *the new asylum*.

However, Dr Bent could not see this enriching idyll from the medical director's apartment on the staff estate where he awoke. He stared at the light coming through the window, feeling heavy, lethargic and sinking into the mattress. His mouth was squashed open, and his dull eyes looked out into a blurry middle distance as he summoned the energy to move, to rise from his bed. It was never easy. Depression was just that: a pressing down. Most days he battled the inertia, the retarding nature of his illness. It was worst in the morning, as if during the night the happy chemicals had congealed in some deep recess of his brain. What he needed was a mug of thick, black coffee, but just getting out of bed was a struggle. He lay there looking at nothing, working some movement into his muscles. Seconds passed, then minutes, and almost an hour before he felt able to shift himself.

With a loud sigh, he eventually rolled over and prised himself from the sheets, swinging his legs down onto the floor. He moved the rings around on his fingers, changing their positions. It took him ten minutes to get himself upright and a further five to walk the short distance down the hall to put on the kettle and get into the shower. The hot needles of water helped revive him, and slowly he began to line up tasks for the day ahead, not least seeing Jason Hemp over at Ardinweald. *What should I do about him? Should I keep him on the ward a bit longer? Did he present a real risk to the public?* Dr Bent massaged his temples as he considered this and other decisions he had to make that day.

It was only after the hot water began to fail that he rather reluctantly stepped out of the shower and lumbered through into the kitchen to fix his usual, strong coffee. It did the trick, and with slightly faster cognition he dressed in black leathers, checked he had everything he needed in his canvas bag and slipped out of his flat and downstairs into the small yard adjoining the doctors' accommodation block. Not far off stood the awful but necessary security fence. At that time of day, all was quiet behind it. Nothing moved. Sometimes, when the wind blew, the fences made eerie whining noises. Yet, today, the air was still. It was dry. Perfect, in fact, for Dr Bent to ride his black-and-chrome Harley.

The bike fired up beautifully, ticking over with mechanical confidence, and Dr Bent immediately felt his mood lift a notch higher, closer to ordinary unhappiness. He zipped up his leather jacket, put on the pair of goggles that pinched his eyes together and donned his round, open-faced helmet. Then he tapped the titanium "hero blob" his mechanic had custom-made and welded onto the footrest to protect the bike when cornering, slung his long canvas kitbag around his shoulders and cocked his leg back over the seat. He played with the throttle.

'Lovely,' he chirped to himself. 'Let's see what you can do.'

With the familiar *potato-potato-potato* sound coming from the engine, he pulled away and headed off down the drive and out into the unexceptional village of Foston with its small parish church, pub and post office, to the long, quiet country road that led into the outskirts of Nottingham.

Once on that near-deserted road, Dr Bent opened the bike up with a determined twist of the throttle, his head and body shifting backwards, and part of his false hair escaping the helmet and streaming behind him like the rather heavy tail of a kite. He released more and more horsepower until the wind bashed and rippled his exposed jowls. Sixty. Seventy. Eighty. Ninety. He was trying to blow his depression away. By the look of his gritty, distorted smile, as he reached a ton, it was working. He had to focus on the view ahead. He could not think of gloomy things. He did not have the leisure to despair. His mind was unable to turn in on itself at this speed. It was as he slowed down and hit a left bend in the road, with the surface coated in dew and blurred by motion that his mood lifted further. Harleys were not made for corners, and it would be an exquisite challenge to get round at speed. Dr Bent tipped the machine over and applied more power, testing the limits of friction. With the hero blob beginning to spark against the ground and the back wheel starting to slip and slide from under him, he gambled with his life. There was no hedgerow at the side of the road to catch his body should he lose control. Instead, there was a barbed-wire fence. Dr Bent felt a spike of fear as he rounded the corner, balancing the bike's ungainly power, the hot rubber and centrifugal force. He fought hard to find a final margin of grip, the hero blob going like a firework. When he held on, the feeling of relief and the high of staying on the road at an acute angle was better than any medication.

†

Dr Bent went through the familiar security procedures at Foston Hall's X-ray machine. He had already taken off the rings from his fingers and the silver ear tunnels, leaving unsightly holes. Then he removed the tail of hair that ran down his back like an external spine and placed it, along with his canvas bag, ornate belt, black boots and jewellery, in his personal locker nearby. Slipping into his pair of standard-issue black shoes, he approached the security personnel. They were polite but efficient as they patted him down for concealed items. With a tap on his shoulder, he got the all-clear and used his security card to progress through the two security chambers into the main enclosed campus of the hospital, largely deserted at that time of day, when staff rarely transferred patients along the red tarmac paths between the blocks and facilities. Much of that movement occurred in the morning or around four o'clock in the afternoon. Then the patients at Foston Hall became more visible to each other, heading to or returning from the gym, swimming pool, library, café, occupational therapy building or multi-faith chapel.

As usual, Dr Bent headed left towards the newly built block that held the bright, modern café for the Foston Hall community. The café was as attractive as the best establishments open to the public and adjoined an upgraded self-service canteen. It was one of the *wonders* developed by the psychiatrist and sent out the message that forensic hospitals should never be prisons. Instead, he saw Foston Hall as a sanctuary, a place of safety, where those unable to be among the public due to their disordered minds could find purpose and respite. The café also helped to elevate his own mood and concentration.

With a passion for the civilising power of coffee houses, Dr Bent had also insisted on the appointment of a properly trained barista to prepare quality drinks.

Dr Bent knew that he required a jolt of caffeine to start the afternoon. His late rising had left him sluggish, without the vigour and animation for work. As he ambled through the pleasantly laid out garden, produced by the patients as part of Foston Hall's green therapy initiative, the psychiatrist's head was lower than normal. He did not notice or smell the flowers.

As he entered the café, James, the young barista, greeted him and immediately set to work tamping down freshly ground beans in the portafilter.

'Good morning, Dr Bent,' he said with a cheery smile. 'Large black Americano?'

The place was quiet, with a few staff who supervised patients sitting on the leather and chrome chairs. Other staff were picking up an early lunch in the adjoining canteen.

'Yes, please, James. Let's have a double shot.'

'Yeah, sure. Take a seat, I'll bring it over.'

Dr Bent thanked him and sat alone in his favourite corner, his back to the reproduction wood panelling, next to the table with its spread of daily newspapers. He read the headlines.

Soon enough, James appeared sporting a dark brown apron, placing the drink carefully on the table.

'There you go,' he said. 'Would you like me to bring over some lunch? There's pie and chips today. I know you like that.'

'No thanks, James. I'm not very hungry,' he answered, speaking slowly, as if having to think about each word before stringing them together.

'OK, just give me a shout if you need anything else.'

Dr Bent raised a brief smile and began drinking his coffee, closing his eyes, savouring the taste and awaiting its effect. As he drank, lethargically at first, he began to consider what lay in store for him that afternoon. In particular, he was ruminating on the case of Jason Hemp, whom he found rather inscrutable and difficult to interpret. He wondered if he had made the right call in discharging him; whether he might continue to act out his grief in similarly dangerous ways. Yet there was no clinical reason to hold onto him. He was mulling all that over when Dr Sargent appeared at his table.

'Mind if I join you?' he asked brightly, not waiting for consent and plonking himself down in the free chair, calling over to James for his usual coffee.

An eminent scholar in the field of personality disorders, Dr Sargent had been a colleague for the last twenty years and someone who had worked tirelessly to help Dr Bent set up the court-diversion scheme with Ardinweald Mental Health NHS Foundation Trust. He was also someone Dr Bent trusted implicitly. Sartorially the opposite of his superior, wearing a jacket and open-neck shirt, Dr Sargent wasted little time examining the medical director's general demeanour.

As he did so, James brought over an exquisitely decorated flat white.

'Wow,' Dr Sargent enthused. 'That is a work of art, James! Ooh, a peacock! Fantastic, thank you!'

As James turned away, flattered and with his chin a little higher for the comment, Dr Sargent addressed his colleague.

'How are you? *Really?*'

'I've been better,' Dr Bent told him, looking up briefly into his colleague's kind face, avoiding direct eye contact.

'OK, so a bad day or bad week?' asked Dr Sargent, his nose nearly erasing the peacock image as he took a sip of the flat white.

Dr Bent pursed his lips and sighed deeply, slowly setting down the large ceramic bowl of coffee. 'I hate depression,' he admitted. His voice continued, slow and monotone, 'And even more than I hate it in others, I hate it in myself.'

He looked out of the window at the high, black fencing that surrounded the sprawling buildings of Foston Hall. He had suffered with depression most of his adult life, and now in middle age, it was at its worst. Depression was what had brought him to work in psychiatry in the first place. He had tried all the medications and psychosocial interventions for the condition, even volunteering for countless trials of new drugs or taking up regular exercise and dietary changes. He had self-prescribed, of course, taking quite literally the dictum "physician, heal thyself", but nothing fully alleviated his mood disorder. He only ever achieved a temporary benefit, allowing him to function in public and get on with his valuable work for a while. At his bleakest moments, he had even considered taking a course of electroconvulsive therapy. He knew exactly where his breed of "black dog" came from. Dr Gluck's psychoanalysis had delivered the origins of the assault and revealed the ultimate death of trust, yet could not resolve the broken architecture of his mind. In the end, it was through sheer psychological effort and determination, self-dialogue, strong coffee and riding his motorbike at high speeds that Dr Bent managed to haul himself out of the pit he slipped into on a regular basis.

'Anything I can do to help?' asked Dr Sargent sensitively, always supportive, practised in talking about depression as if it were no more than a flare-up of psoriasis, IBS or arthritic joints.

'No, Tim, thank you. It is just the usual, you know.'

Dr Sargent nodded and then automatically reached up and fingered the rondel of scalp showing through the back of his brown, escaping hair. 'Well, you should be proud of what you have done here,' he told him, opening his arms to indicate the café as one of Dr Bent's developments at Foston Hall.

'Thanks, Tim, that's very kind,' Dr Bent said, finishing his drink, starting to feel the expected chemical buzz.

He was gradually coming out of the fog and lassitude. In part to avoid further introspection, Dr Bent turned his attention to what had been happening on Dr Sargent's patch: the refurbished Cedar Block at the northern end of the hospital, housing patients with Dangerous and Severe Personality Disorder. It was all part of Dr Bent's enhancements to Foston Hall, but had several teething problems, not least, mistakes in the design.

'So, how are things now over at Cedar?' he asked.

Dr Sargent's head dipped a little. 'Ah,' he answered. 'No further injuries, thankfully. The builders have been back in and replaced the screws.'

'They shouldn't have installed outward-facing screws in the first place, right?'

'Well, exactly. Not great, I know.'

'Did any other patients manage to remove them?'

'No, just the one, mercifully superficial self-harming. Estates have checked through and confirmed this as an isolated incident. There have been no additional removals.'

'Good, good,' said Dr Bent, rolling a finger through the large hole in his left ear, feeling more alert. 'That kind of thing makes the Home Office jumpy.'

'It could have been worse,' admitted Dr Sargent. 'A screw can be used as a weapon. I have asked Dr Wang to follow up on the self-harm side of things.'

'Excellent.' Dr Bent eased himself up out of his chair, moving more quickly than when he entered the café. He felt less washed out. 'I must get on. Good to see you, Tim. Let's catch up later.'

With that, Dr Bent headed off to do his rounds.

23

Jason sat with the inimitable Dr Bent in an interview room larger than the one they met in previously. There were several other members of the multidisciplinary team present, not least the charge nurse, Mr Singh, but the discussion had been brief and functional. The emergency section had lapsed, and the team decided that Jason did not require further medication. Dr Bent exuded calm during the meeting, speaking in a dignified and thoughtful way about the difficulties that Jason had faced with the death of his twin brother. All the laboratory tests had come back in the normal range and Dr Bent considered the emotional crisis and acting out on campus to be part of the grieving process.

Jason waited in silence, anxious to learn if the psychiatrist would discharge him. He really could not face spending any more time in the hospital. As he wrung his hands and waited for Dr Bent to finish writing in his notes, Jason hoped and prayed that the Mental Health Act would not rear its ugly head. He reached over, pulled a tissue from its box and blew his nose. Then he watched as Dr Bent looked up briefly and scrawled in the case notes. Jason felt his sectioning unjust and considered taking Dr Bent up on his invitation to add a rejoinder in the document, but he kept silent and waited. With the occasional sniff, Dr Bent wrote a few more lines before adding a couple of bullet points. Then he laid down his pen in the crease of the notes.

'Right, Jason,' he said. 'I have decided to discharge you on the condition that you get more help with your grief reaction and managing your emotions. I would like you to see one of our psychologists as soon as possible, but there is quite a waiting list. So, in the meantime, I will review you at our outpatient clinic, once a week initially, for a month or so, and take things from there.'

'Are you prescribing medication?'

Dr Bent shook his head. 'No, no, the treatment for grief is time.'

'Good,' said Jason feeling a weight lifting from his shoulders.

'So, how does that sound to you?' asked Dr Bent softly.

'That's great. Thank you, Doctor.'

Jason smiled at Dr Bent and the rest of the team.

'I hope your stay has not been too distressing,' pursued the psychiatrist. 'It's not always the best place to be.'

Dr Bent's candid words surprised Jason. 'It's been OK,' he told him, looking and nodding reassuringly at Mr Singh, too relieved to be critical.

'Well, that's good. We will see you in a week's time at the outpatient clinic. Yes?'

'Yes, thank you.'

Jason could not quite believe he was free to go. He left the room on a high, accompanied by Mr Singh, leaving Dr Bent to take up the case notes of another patient.

Now discharged, Jason gathered his personal belongings in a black bin liner and waited for a taxi.

When it arrived, Mr Singh shook Jason's hand and wished him well.

'Now keep out of trouble,' he said, a newspaper tucked under his arm. 'Otherwise, we might see more of each other.'

'Don't worry,' said Jason. 'You won't see me again.' Then with a quick glance at his mildly radioactive watch that was back on his wrist, Jason headed off.

'Where to?' asked the taxi driver.

'Out of this place,' he said, settling the bin bag on his knees.

'Then where?' asked the driver.

Jason thought for a few moments and answered him, 'Ardinweald Cemetery.'

The driver raised his eyebrows, did a quick check in his mirror and shook his head. He responded to a radio call requesting his status and drove off with a wary eye on his passenger. As the taxi sped down the service road and through the arched gateway onto the main road, Jason looked back at the receding building with its pyramid-topped towers and vowed never to return.

†

Jason sat on Umbie's tombstone, thinking about his own state of mind. *I am not mad*, he reminded himself. Even Dr Bent had admitted as much: "You are grieving. But it is the kind of grief that comes without holidays". The bin liner lay at his feet and the beech trees whispered in the breeze, their spear-like buds awaiting a stronger sun. Jason stroked the headstone with the palm of his hand, glad to be out of hospital and deemed sane. As he stood there, rhythmically stroking the white stone, he revisited the sights and sounds of the mental hospital: medication rounds, burbling television and overcooked food. He saw Mr Singh's toothy smile again and marvelled at Dr Bent's skin-tight black trousers. He sighed with relief at being back outside in the fresh air. Even a cemetery offered a less bleak setting than a ward of broken people.

Jason looked up. Danny the gravedigger was passing by with a wheelbarrow full of soil. Jason acknowledged him, briefly lifting his hand. The gravedigger nodded and pulled up alongside the tombstone.

'How's it going?' he asked in a quiet voice, letting his barrow rest. A sprinkling of sandy soil tipped over the edge.

'Not so bad.'

'I've not seen you around for a few days.'

Jason hesitated. He did not want anyone to know where he had been. 'I've been away. A short break,' he explained sheepishly.

'Ah well,' said Danny scratching his red, raw neck, 'as you can see, I've kept the grave for you.'

Jason noted the sharply cut grass and weeded clods of earth. 'Thanks for that. You have done a great job. I'm really grateful.'

'It's not much, but it's something. It is not easy when you've lost someone.'

Jason appreciated the comment, patting the headstone and looking around. 'This place must keep you busy.'

'Oh yes, indeed it does,' said Danny, surveying the thousand graves. 'There's plenty to keep me going.'

Jason opened his nostrils wide and caught the smell of whisky in the air. He looked at the spider veins on Danny's cheeks and nose that declared years of heavy drinking. The whites of his eyes were yellow and bloodshot and his brow gathered a veil of sweat. In a natural lull in the conversation, Jason thought again about the shotgun. He considered asking the gravedigger how he could get hold of one. Yet he could not quite broach the topic, not here, not now. Besides, Danny had already lifted the rusted arms of his barrow and begun to move away.

'Bye for now,' he said, the deflated wheel of the barrow squeaking for lack of oil.

'I just—' began Jason, but his voice trailed into silence as Danny headed off at a determined pace.

Alone again, Jason decided it might be better simply to steal the gun rather than ask the gravedigger about it. Besides, he had to find the killer first. The weapon could wait. He needed to take a step at a time and be business-like. There was no point possessing a gun for longer than necessary. As he thought about his next move, with bile in his throat and the desire for revenge gnawing away, he heard shouting coming from the observatory ruins.

Two youths were jumping from the tangled grass onto concrete blocks. They carried white plastic bags. Jason stood up to see what they were doing. With their backs to the broken walls, they attached the bags to their mouths and blew into them. In and out they breathed, their heads tilted down, feet stretching out over the concrete. All that time, Jason looked on, fascinated by the sniffers. A few minutes later, the boys struggled to their feet and tumbled onto the grass. They laughed and rolled around drunkenly before settling on their backs in a manufactured paradise of fumes.

Jason shook his head. It seemed wrong that his brother was six feet under while these kids were alive, happily destroying their brain cells. He recalled the simple ways he and Umbie got their kicks. There was not such desperation for fun when they were children. There was the old locust tree with its rope, making water bombs or setting off bangers. Those were different times. Back then, life's trials seemed far away. The brothers could never have imagined murder in their shared future. Yet there it was, and Umbie's death had changed everything.

Jason gazed at the black bin liner that held his dirty clothes, noting the elastic band wrapped tightly around its neck and the sticky label with his name on it. The trash bag was a hobo's suitcase. Although he was far from homeless, he suddenly felt undignified and downcast. His social decline and short spell in the mental hospital irritated him. The hand of the killer was extending beyond the murder of Umbie. It had a hold on his life. It was taking him down, too. This notion drove Jason to kick out, sending the bag skidding across the gravel into a ridge of last year's beech mast. He felt better for this sudden outburst and let out a long sigh, resting an elbow briefly on the headless angel's wing nearby. Then he took up the bag and swung it over his shoulder, deciding to get home to Poppy. She would be wondering where he was, and he feared she might call the police to search for him. The thought of seeing Inspector Mosby's piebald face again made him walk more quickly than his drained body wanted to. As he left the cemetery, he saw the white tails of bramblings taking to the sky, heading back to Siberia. He envied their freedom.

†

'Thank God, you're out!' cried Poppy, relieved when Jason walked in through the door.

She put Juju down and threw her arms around her husband, kissing him so hard that the bridge in his bottom teeth threatened to slip between her fervent lips.

'Of course I'm out!' he said emphatically. 'I'm not mad. I'm as sane as you.'

Jason was much taller than Poppy, and she stretched her whole body to greet him. He looked over her shoulder at the hallway and the lounge. The place looked like a tip. Yet he did not say anything. Poppy had obviously been struggling to cope.

'And no tablets?' she asked.

'No.'

With that, Jason crossed the threshold, the bin liner hanging from his fist. Poppy stepped over Juju onto the hall carpet and followed Jason through into the sitting room, dabbing at her dry, weary hair.

'Tea?' she asked.

'Please. I haven't had a proper cup since I went into hospital.'

Poppy moved through into the kitchen and put the kettle on. 'Did the doctor have anything more to say?' she shouted through to Jason.

There were a few moments of silence when Jason set his thesis back against the door, pushed stuff out of his path with his feet and sat down in his armchair.

'Not really.'

'Do you have to see him again?'

'Yes, in the outpatient clinic.'

'He seemed nice,' Poppy said chirpily through the bubbling of the kettle. 'I mean, he seemed to care.'

'Yes, Dr Bent was OK,' admitted Jason, 'although a bit on the strange side.'

After a few minutes, Poppy reappeared.

'There you go,' she said, carrying in a tray of tea and biscuits.

With the hot, sweet tea in his cupped hands, Jason grew more animated. He enjoyed the steam from it, slurping happily, his eyes closed and a glow rising in his cheeks. He felt more like his old self.

'I'm so glad to have you home,' Poppy admitted, leaning over and putting a hand behind his thick neck. 'I was so worried about you. I thought they might give you that dreadful electric shock treatment.'

'Really?' asked Jason, returning her affection, clasping her free hand and squeezing it.

She hugged him again in a desperate, intense way.

'Steady on,' he complained. 'You'll spill the tea.'

'I didn't know what was going to happen to you,' she said, starting to cry. 'It's been so frightening.'

Jason put his tea down and pulled her into his arms. He kissed her cool forehead and stroked her quivering spine. He traced a finger around her creased eyelids, wiping her tears into the wrinkles at either side. Her whole body jerked, and Jason embraced her, trying to contain the fit of emotion that rippled in spasms through her body. He noted the bottle of Valium on the mantelpiece.

'All right, Pops, I'm here now,' he soothed, feeling guilty, but her sobbing deepened with his show of compassion.

She was gulping for air. He squeezed her closer, her mouth gaping. It was several minutes before her body stilled. Jason continued to hug her.

'Promise me,' she whispered finally with hot breath in his ear.

'What?'

'You won't do anything silly again.'

Jason said nothing. He knew there were things he had to do to avenge his brother's death. *Silly but justified things*, he told himself. He held Poppy's face between his hands, gazing into her eyes, searching for a deeper connection. He stared intently into the wide pupils that seemed to exclude him from her world.

'Of course not,' he promised.

She did one of her brave smiles and returned comforting touches, stroking his hands and rolling the skin over his knuckles.

'How's Mum?' he asked finally, enjoying being in his own house again. Anything was better than the smell of the ward.

'How do you think she's been?' she said. 'I think you should call her.'

'I'll ring later.'

'No, call her now,' Poppy told him, straightening herself.

'OK,' Jason sighed. 'But let me have a rest first.'

'Well, you're back. That is the main thing. I suppose you'll want a second cup?'

Jason smiled broadly with eyes shut and his body already moulding into the shape of the comfortable armchair. 'That would be lovely.'

As Poppy slipped away into the kitchen again, Juju came into the sitting room and curled around Jason's leg, his tail erect and caressing. Jason reached down and ruffled his fur.

'Oh, I forgot to say, Professor Porter rang while you were in hospital,' Poppy called out from the kitchen.

Jason grunted, twisting in his chair, holding his head as if a migraine had just started.

'Jason?'

'Yes, I heard you,' he said. Truth was, he had pushed the university to the back of his mind. He did not want to think about it. He knew only bad news would be waiting for him there.

'He was very nice,' she reassured him. 'He even sent a card. It's on the mantelpiece.'

Jason had failed to notice the small card standing next to the clock. He looked across at it now, squinting slightly at the embossed "Get Well Soon".

'That was nice,' he said loud enough to carry through to Poppy. 'I thought they'd give me the cold shoulder.'

'Why should they?' said Poppy. 'We all have our problems. You're a good teacher, Jason.'

'I suppose so,' he agreed, finding it hard to imagine returning to work.

'Anyway, he wants to see you. He was very sympathetic. You know, it didn't sound like he was going to—'

'Sack me?'

'Yes.'

'Well, I wouldn't bet on that not happening. The guy's a robot!'

'I think that's a bit harsh,' chided Poppy. 'Now look, promise me—'

'Yes?'

'Promise me that you'll give up all this revenge nonsense.'

Poppy brought in his second cup of tea and a few more biscuits. Jason could see she was anxious and he did not want to do anything to make things worse for her. He put on a little show for his wife.

'I promise,' he told her, avoiding eye contact and covering his mouth for fear real thoughts might slip out. 'I'll leave everything to the police.'

'Oh, Jason, you don't realise how good that sounds!' she cried, her body trembling and juddering in a release of emotion.

She kissed his balding head. Jason felt her red, raw lips on his bristled chin. Despite his tiredness, he returned Poppy's kisses, and it was not long before he found himself fumbling like a boy for the hem of her skirt and showing utter contempt for buttons and other fastenings. As the tea began to cool, Poppy's heels finally lifted and her legs shuffled off the last of her clothing, revealing the mole he so loved.

24

Jason stood opposite the barbershop, drawing in his collar, trying to fend off the sharp wind blowing between the buildings. He watched the glamorous troop of hairdressers parading back and forth, manipulating the heads of customers, making small talk, laughing at their jokes, no doubt spotting dandruff and recommending expensive, face-saving remedies. As Jason stared, the shop front glass behind him wobbled and shook ominously in the wind. He had nothing to lose, he decided. He needed to see loan shark-cum-proprietor Ryan. Despite mounting anxiety for his safety, he had to know what kind of relationship he had with his brother. After a few moments, steeling himself, Jason crossed the road and entered the building.

A cracked bell over the door sounded and announced his entrance. A few of the customers waiting on the long bench sized him up, but soon lost interest and returned to their reading or staring out the dead time. A young woman with bulging, rouged cheekbones standing behind a small counter smiled and asked him to take a seat. The room smelled of wet men. Combs, brushes, razors, gowns, sprays, waxes and dryers adorned the walls and shelving.

Jason had never liked going to the barbers. It was like having a bloodless operation. He had far too many memories of his failing hair tossed dismissively from side to side. The shame of depletion affected him so much he had even considered going the whole hog, shaving his skull.

'What would you like done?' asked the young woman behind the bar, seeing that Jason did not automatically join the bench and wait his turn.

'Sorry?'

'Just a trim?' she pressed, choosing the common denominator, her eyes perusing his head.

As Jason opened his mouth to speak, he was surprised to find her suddenly at his side, moving her hand through his defiant flags of hair, gently inspecting what little there was.

'How about bringing back some of the natural colour?'

'What?' he gasped. He moved away from her. 'I'm not here for a haircut.'

Yet she was not listening.

'It will make you look younger,' she said quietly, smiling with bright red lips.

'No, no,' said Jason, coughing and feeling awkward. 'I haven't come for any of that! I've come to—'

In the brief hesitation, the girl appeared to twig what he wanted. 'I understand,' she said, linking his arm and leading him towards the back of the shop. Her voice had lowered substantially. 'I should have guessed. I wondered why you were so jittery. Now, we have a wide selection of hairpieces. They look very real. You can't see the join.'

'Good grief, no! You misunderstand me entirely,' Jason flapped, his cheeks flushing rapidly, a lock of discarded grey hair stuck to the toe of his shoe. 'I'm here on business.'

The waiting men looked up again before dropping their eyes and continuing to flick through magazines.

'Business?' asked the girl, staring hard at him, training her beady eye on his ill-fitting coat and shadowy chin.

'Yes, I'm here to see Mr Ryan,' said Jason trying to shake off the spray of hair still firmly stuck to his shoe. 'I need to speak with him.'

'Who are you?' she enquired, looking at him with suspicion and cold detachment, as she headed back to the counter and perched on a high swivel chair.

'Dr Hemp,' he said, lightly rubbing his nose, hoping that his title would work some magic.

It had worked before. It had bought him more time with his GP and sometimes an upgrade to business class on flights. Poppy always protested at this. "You're not a medical doctor, Jason. What are you going to do if someone falls ill," she would say, "read them some poetry or set them an essay assignment?".

The young woman in front of him seemed equally unimpressed, casting her blue eyes at the flakes of broken skin on his cheeks and tapping buttons on an intercom system.

'Dr Jason Hemp,' repeated Jason drily. He was anxious now.

'I heard you the first time,' she said, pulling a face, waiting for the continuous buzz of the intercom to end like a swatted fly. 'Jim,' said the girl in a fruity, full voice, 'there's a man down here asking for you. Sorry, who did you say you are?'

'Dr Hemp.'

'Somebody called *Mr* Hemp wants to see you.'

There was a lengthy silence. Intermittent buzzing resumed. Jason narrowed his eyes at the way she demoted him.

'Yes, OK,' her voice withered as she put down the handset and slid off the swivel chair, sucking her tongue as if it were a *bonbon*. 'This way, *Mr* Hemp.' She led him over the shiny, black tiles to a doorway at the back of the shop. 'Top of the stairs and left,' she said and returned to her desk, her hips rocking.

Jason looked up the steep, narrow staircase and felt his heart thumping away. He closed his eyes and tried to prepare himself to meet the mysterious Ryan. *Would he have a patch of hair missing? Would it be the right colour? Was he Umbie's murderer?* Jason's mind whirred as he grabbed the banister, taking a few moments to gather himself before climbing. He half expected a gang to descend upon him and beat him up. Yet, as he crept towards the top of the stairs, nobody appeared except a rather small man dressed fashionably in a white T-shirt. He looked sleep-deprived with dark eyes sheltering beneath swollen, bluish lids. Above sleek, black eyebrows, he was as bald as a coot.

'Jim Ryan,' he announced, holding out his hand in greeting.

Jason shook it, holding on a bit longer than was comfortable. The grip was a kind of question.

Ryan led Jason through to a large office overlooking High Street. Jason found it ironic that the barber did not have a hair on his head. He wondered if he shaved his head or was naturally bald. Either way, his eyebrows were a different hair colour to that which Jason had torn from the killer's scalp.

'We were all sorry about what happened to your brother,' he said with warm deference. 'It was a great tragedy.'

Jason was speechless. The man was talking about Umbie like an old, familiar friend of the family. Yet Jason had never met the man before.

'Come in, take a seat.' Ryan was relaxed and softly spoken, palming him to sit on one of the available chairs. 'Please, make yourself comfortable.' The barber's voice was deep and gentle.

'Thank you,' Jason managed, quite perplexed by the genuine regard that Ryan demonstrated.

Jason remained cautious, however, checking over his shoulder like the paranoid patient he encountered at the mental hospital. He half-expected the footfall of Ryan's men as he inspected every corner of the spacious, well-furnished room. He examined the dark blue floral wallpaper and Ryan's enormous, executive desk. On it, within easy reach, was a vintage phone and redundant bronze inkwell shaped like an old bathtub. Jason looked at its four snake handles and lion's feet.

'Can I get you a drink or anything?' Ryan asked.

'No, no. I'm fine, thanks.'

'Are you sure?'

'Yes, thank you.'

'OK. Well, it is good to see you. I wanted to talk to you at the funeral, but I did not get the chance. I wanted to say how sorry I was.'

'You were at the funeral?' asked Jason, scratching his head, trying to recall the figure of Ryan, yet he could not get past Poppy, his mother and the coffin. There were a few parishioners, but no one else swirled into view. All were a blur, indistinct.

Ryan nodded several times. 'Yes, of course. I slipped in at the back, so you probably did not see me. Besides, at these events, everyone around you becomes—'

'Invisible?' offered Jason.

'Yes, exactly. Now, are you sure about the drink?'

'No, honestly, I'm fine, really.'

Jason remained on the edge of his seat, perched, alert, staring out of the window.

'It was a terrible thing to happen,' sighed Ryan. 'I think of him all the time. How could someone do this? Who would want to kill your brother?'

Jason shook his head and felt confused. He had no conception of Umbie having friends. Companions maybe, people he worked with, but not friends outside their established circle as such. Just when he thought he knew his brother, Umbie slipped right through the net of his mind.

'I didn't know you were a friend,' he said quietly, deliberately.

'No?' questioned Ryan. 'Of course, we were friends. We have been friends for years. He didn't mention me?'

'No.'

'He never talked about me?'

'No, I'm afraid not.'

Ryan raised his hands in exasperation and shook his head. 'So, you don't know anything about me?' he said.

'Only what I hear from people *generally*.'

Ryan frowned heavily now. 'And what's that?'

'They say you are a loan shark,' Jason told him directly.

Ryan's eyebrows flashed in surprise. 'A shark without teeth perhaps,' he said, quickly pulling out his false upper set and briefly waving them humorously to reinforce his point. He eased them back under his collapsed lip before continuing. 'This business makes good money, and sometimes people ask for loans,' he admitted with a heavy sigh. 'You know, they come in for a haircut and talk about their problems. This has happened. That has happened. The banks will not help. I feel sorry for them and—'

'You loan money,' Jason cut in.

Ryan shrugged. 'Yes, but I'm no shark. I only charge slightly more than the banks, right?'

Jason could see that he wanted to change the topic. 'So, is that how you got to know my brother?'

'No, not at all. We were good drinking friends, you know, at The Sow's Ear. Your brother was good at dominoes.'

'Ah, that makes sense.'

Jason fell silent for a while, revisiting the last time he had joined Umbie on dominoes night.

'But how do you know about me if your brother kept me quiet all this time?'

Jason looked into Ryan's eyes for a few seconds, noting his solicitous expression. 'Mrs Honeybourne mentioned you.'

Ryan seemed a little puzzled, before his eyes widened in recognition. 'Ah, the matron at Saint Martha's. Yes, I sometimes walked over to meet him there. Are you sure your brother did not mention me, even in passing?' He stood up, jamming his hands in his pockets and shuffling back and forth with beetling brow. 'It seems strange that he kept silent about his friends, especially given that you were twins.'

'*Are* twins,' Jason corrected him.

'Sorry, yes, of course,' Ryan apologised. 'I'm shocked to hear this. He didn't mention me, even once?'

'He never spoke about you.'

Ryan let out a low whistle and shook his head. 'That is strange,' he said. He sat down again, pursing his lips, kissing the air and still shaking his head rather dejectedly. Then his expression lightened and he fidgeted with the gold chain around his neck. 'The matron's a delightful woman, isn't she?' he said with a smile.

'Yes,' answered Jason staring at the letter R inscribed on a ring on the proprietor's middle finger.

For a moment, Jason lost all sense of where he was and why he was there. The meeting had not been what he expected. He had anticipated a conflict. He thought he might learn something. Yet, as things stood, he had only gleaned that Ryan was not the killer, unless he had dyed his eyebrows, and his brother was not who he thought he was. *Why did Umbie keep secret friends? What was all that about?* He was dwelling on this when Ryan's voice gradually registered.

'Now, please tell me what I can do for you.'

'I don't need any help,' Jason found himself saying.

'Are you quite sure?'

'Honestly, but thank you,' Jason told him. 'I just wanted to meet you.'

The two men sat in silence for a minute or so before Ryan spoke again.

'How are the police getting on with their investigation?' he asked.

'It's hard to tell,' admitted Jason. 'They say they have a lead, however, I'm not so sure.'

Ryan leaned forward over the desk now, interested. 'What kind of lead?'

'They won't give specific information.'

'Sounds like they are onto something,' Ryan concluded.

'Perhaps, but to be honest, I think they are putting a finger on someone, anyone, to make it look as if they are making progress with the case.'

Ryan smiled sympathetically and ran his finger around the neck of his white T-shirt. Jason took a long look at him and found nothing particularly disturbing about him. The meeting with Ryan had left so much unanswered. Jason clearly did not know a great deal about his brother—what he did, where he went—the most banal things. He had always assumed he knew everything about Umbie. He had always professed that he knew his brother more than he knew anyone else. Yet this was embarrassingly not the case.

'Umbie used to come here to get his hair done,' Ryan added. 'He didn't like the girls cutting it, so I did it.'

'That's news to me too,' Jason admitted, floored once more by the gaps in his knowledge about his brother's life.

'He was always very self-conscious about his hair,' Ryan told him, 'trying to comb it back, but it had a mind of its own. You know, the way it stuck out over his ears like—'

'An umbrella,' Jason finished for him.

'Yeah, exactly, that's right,' Ryan chuckled quietly.

Jason wondered if Ryan was hiding anything about his relationship with his brother. He could see his brother now holding the dominoes in a line in his palm, figuring out the odds. He had no recollection of seeing Ryan at The Sow's Ear or The Half Moon for that matter. Yet he claimed to be a good friend, albeit an unknown one, and Umbie's barber to boot. Jason felt he was getting nowhere. He was no closer to finding his brother's killer. All he had upturned were soft, useless facts. So much about his brother seemed out of view, *postmortem*. Ryan's commonplace revelations seemed to say the world was not nearly as terrible as he thought.

Jason sunk back in his chair, stared at the snakes curling into the sides of the inkwell and began to talk to Umbie in his head. *Why did you keep your friends secret? Why didn't you tell me about them? I trusted you!* It hurt Jason deeply to think his twin brother had lied to him all these years. They were supposed to be close. Under the dome of his skull, in a part of his brain above the right ear, Jason was trying to create Umbie's voice, but nothing came back. No answers, nothing. Just the chilling certainty that he had gone for good, and they would never meet again.

It suddenly struck Jason that most of the memories of his brother came from childhood. These stood foremost in his mind. His memories of Umbie as an adult were much less prominent. Beyond watching a football match or drinking together, there was little to remember. They had different jobs, went on separate holidays, did not share a hobby and rarely gathered for family occasions except the odd christening, wedding or funeral.

Jason began to question how well he knew his twin brother. After all, both Mrs Honeybourne and Ryan had highlighted gaps in his knowledge of Umbie. It looked like he was the last to know his habits and preferences, even where he got his hair done. Yet Jason tried to put things in perspective. *It is impossible to know everything about another person. Why should I know every drinking friend of my brother or his choice of barber? There are gaps. So what! Nobody can have total knowledge of another person, even someone close. Something always escapes notice.*

As Jim Ryan looked back across the desk and began checking his watch in an obvious way, Jason's eyes grew wide with a sudden realisation. He wondered why it had not entered his mind before. It was staring him in the face. He smiled suddenly in a detached, dreamy way. Perhaps his visit was not such a complete waste of time after all. He lifted his hand and slapped his forehead lightly, allowing himself a burst of happy, contented laughter.

Then Jason just stared at the gnomic ring on the barber's finger.

'For Ryan,' said Ryan, noting his interest. 'Something wrong?'

he questioned, rotating the ring of his finger.

'Not at all,' claimed Jason joyfully, almost gratefully. 'You are the very man I need.'

†

That evening, Jason sat in his armchair by the fire, stroking Juju, waiting for his mother to visit. All afternoon he had pottered about in the garden, tidying the pool, dredging it of last year's leaves, sweeping the path and making pots of tea. Now he rested up while Poppy busied herself in the kitchen, preparing a cottage pie for supper. As she chopped the onion and carrots, she talked about the future. She had begun applying for jobs at local laundries and hoped something would come along soon. Jason looked at his wife, framed in the doorway, her back to him. He heard the tail end of her complaint about job opportunities before fading into himself again. He was thinking about what he asked Ryan to do. Satisfied that his luck might change with the barber, one of Umbie's friends, Jason sensed he was closer than ever to catching his brother's killer. There was no doubt in his mind that Ryan was going to prove very helpful. At that moment, on a cool evening, with Juju in his arms, he felt enlivened and confident.

As the cottage pie warmed and started to brown, filling the air with a homely smell, Jason breathed deeply, regularly. His muscles relaxed for the first time in ages and his heart squeezed quietly. He felt a million miles from the mental hospital and could hardly believe that he had ended up there in the first place. Only a day had passed since he had been in that most alien of environments. Now, here he was, in familiar surroundings, enjoying the purr and rumble of his cat, the hissing fire and the tick-and-tock movement of the clock. He even savoured the *bing-bong* of the doorbell, although he knew the arrival of his mother would disrupt his newfound composure.

'I'll get it,' he said, stirring and dropping Juju onto the cold tiles.

When he opened the front door, he felt completely taken aback by his mother's reaction to seeing him. She jumped forward and hugged his chest, pressing the side of her head tightly into his ribs. It was the first open show of affection from her in years, and Jason did not quite know how to respond. He stood with his arms out at the side, reddening slightly, bowing down until his chin rested on the crown of her head.

'Thank God, they discharged you!' she said, standing back now, but with both her hands on his chest. Tears filled her eyes, and pink lipstick smudged her downy lips.

'You'd better come in off the step,' Jason advised, raising a hand to Mr Norris, who was out cutting his hedge, his eyebrows high from witnessing such a profound display of affection and on hearing the word "discharged". Jason could see that his brain was whirring as much as the electric trimmer he switched back on. No doubt, he was putting together all kinds of drama behind the word.

'I've worn these knees out praying for you,' announced Mrs Hemp safely inside the vestibule, wiping a stubborn tear from her cheek.

As she did so, Jason spied her bitten nails, chewed to the quick. The buckled moon shapes looked raw.

'I've had so many masses offered up!'

'Hmm,' said Jason, unmoved and disinterested in her relentless attempts to promote the old religion. He showed his mother through into the sitting room, taking her coat with its artificial fur trim and placing it on the hook behind the door.

'Where's Poppy?' she asked, dabbing her eyes with the corner of a handkerchief.

'She's through in the kitchen doing the dinner.'

'Poppy!' Mrs Hemp shouted through, crossing the room, her shiny blue slacks crinkling at the knees.

'In here, Mum.'

Mrs Hemp entered the kitchen as Poppy struggled to spoon peas onto each plate of cottage pie. Her muscles had grown twitchy since losing her job and suffering Jason's public shaming. She managed to spill them.

'Here, I'll do that,' offered Mrs Hemp, moving forward.

Poppy let her mother-in-law take over.

Jason followed his mother into the kitchen and began setting out the cutlery before taking his seat. Juju curled around his leg, expectant of titbits. Jason reached down and stroked him, all the time watching the two most important women in his life finishing the preparations.

'Well,' said Mrs Hemp, putting the dinner in front of her son and drowning it with gravy, 'going into hospital doesn't seem to have done you any harm.'

Jason was not so sure, but he nodded and looked on as Mrs Hemp set down the gravy boat and went back for her own plate.

'He's a bit sorry for himself, yet I think he's a lot more settled now,' said Poppy.

'Perhaps those places have changed for the better,' argued Mrs Hemp, sitting opposite Jason, polishing her knife and fork with a tea towel.

'Well, I don't know what they did to Jason, but he seems better,' Poppy said. 'He is not so preoccupied with revenge. At least, that is what he tells me. He's promised to leave Umbie's murder to the police.'

'That's good,' said Mrs Hemp, reaching over and patting the back of her son's hand.

'Things couldn't get worse, could they?'

Mrs Hemp turned to face her daughter-in-law. 'Let's hope not,' she croaked ominously while Jason dipped his head, ashamed. 'Our family has been getting a bad spin of the wheel lately.'

25

Jason sat at one end of the common room, away from the other lecturers who were clearly wary of him. Isolated, with empty chairs around him, he waited for his appointment with Professor Porter. Jason imagined tongues fluttering about what had taken place in the lecture hall. Now and then, he caught the eyes of colleagues who looked quickly away. It was as if they might develop madness by simply being in his presence. Dr Millicent Walker was there, her shoulder curled inwards, whispering in an urgent way to the gathered academics. Her lips pecked the air and she kept placing a hand over her mouth like a lid. There was the relentlessly dull Dr Amy Reilly in her darkest beige skirt who joined the garrulous Mick O'Rourke, blanking Jason completely. In turn, they bantered with a resplendent Valerie behind the refreshments counter, her hair newly dyed a rust colour. Jonathan Darling was there ordering a coffee, tamping his bushy eyebrows. Eventually, he joined the others, sitting on the edge of his seat, as if he did not belong in such company, his legs under him like a grasshopper. Only Barney Hill, the famous forensic linguist, gave Jason a brief nod when he entered the room, acknowledging his existence. Then he sat with the others, his back turned.

'Well, fuck you too, Barney,' Jason whispered under his breath, twisting in his seat and looking out of the tall windows at the blotched, windless sky, his fingers intertwining and separating.

He began picking at his nails, knowing that his colleagues were talking about him. He wondered whether Professor Porter would treat him any better. He guessed not and prepared himself for bad news, his palms sweaty and the inside of his mouth as dry as rice paper. He slopped his tongue around to moisten it, yet decided he needed another drink. The refreshments counter was clear now, so Jason went up with his dirty cup.

'What are you having?' asked Valerie, smiling warmly. 'Another tea?'

Jason smiled back, but in a restrained way as if in pain. As ever, the secretary-cum-cafeteria assistant did not seem any different in manner towards him. She did not freeze or appear preoccupied with her personal safety given his recent behaviour and visit to the mental hospital.

'Yes, please,' Jason answered, watching Valerie adjust her skirt before stretching over for the little metal teapot.

As he handed over his money, admiring her ruddy hair, her fingers touched his for a fraction longer than mechanically required to capture the falling coins. His mouth sprung open slightly with the contact, and when he took his tea back to his seat, her gesture was all he could think of. Valerie had touched him intimately, knowingly. She had lingered.

At that point, Dr Patrick Kilkenny made his usual dramatic entrance.

'Afternoon everyone!' he shouted, clapping his hands once and rubbing them, sending shock waves down his baggy corduroys. 'Ah, you're back, Jason. How's it going?' he asked, rolling up his sleeves, exposing his wiry, ginger-haired arms. Yet he did not wait for an answer, turning his attention to Valerie. 'Coffee please, Val! No milk,' he reminded her.

Soon enough, with coffee in hand, Patrick headed over to join Jason, breaking the quarantine of empty chairs.

'Good to see you!' he said genuinely. 'I hope things are getting a bit easier.'

'We're managing,' Jason told him. 'Just.'

'Glad to hear it.' He paused for a few moments before opening up again. 'Has that, er, you know, business with the student been sorted?'

Jason scrunched up his face and squinted.

'Oh, right, I see,' said Patrick. 'Sorry.'

'I'm here to see Prof. Porter,' Jason told him. 'I assume he wants to talk about—' He then fell silent.

'Right. Tricky, huh?'

'Tricky is not the word!'

Patrick tutted and sighed. 'Well, maybe it won't be as bad as you anticipate,' he advised before slurping some of his drink.

'Oh, it will. I am sure of that. I think I'll be getting my cards,' Jason told him, gazing at the reflection of light in the teaspoon that rested in the saucer.

The finality of his words made his colleague rub his lips together and stare intensely at the floor. 'It couldn't be worse, then?' he said inanely.

'No.'

Patrick rummaged in his pocket for his vape pen and, finding it, put it away again. 'I wish you luck anyway,' he said, blinking his large eyes.

'Yeah, thanks. Look, I think I'll go and knock on the big man's door,' Jason told him gloomily, his stomach tight with nervous gas. 'He should be in now. I cannot bear waiting. I feel like a condemned man out here.'

Patrick smiled weakly, trying to dole out a comfort he was unable to give as Jason stood up, tucked in his shirt and left the room, scratching the back of his prickled neck, feeling agitated, paranoid and alienated with every footfall. Professor Porter's office was at the darker end of the corridor. A fan of light moved out from under his door. It was a door covered in outdated tutorial sheets.

'Shit, he's in,' Jason whispered under his breath and cocked his ear to see if he was alone. There were no sounds of conversation, so he knocked lightly and waited. When there was no answer, he gave the door a heavier tap.

'Come in!' summoned Professor Porter, his voice detached, serious.

Jason did so, closing the door behind him and touching the head of school's doctoral robes hung on the back. Porter glanced up, put down his gold-nibbed fountain pen and palmed at the empty chair. Jason sat down, the sweat gathering in the creases of his skin.

There was a heaviness and solemnity behind the head of school's expression. The frown on his face cut deeper than usual. There was the bitten lip, fidgety nose and general reticence. The expectation of bad, irrevocable news overcame Jason and he began to panic inside. He sat down, his fingernails catching the armrests and his mind trying to prepare itself for bad news.

'I'll get straight to the point,' said Professor Porter, using his favourite phrase. It was predictable and business-like, and he was unable to look Jason in the face, never mind the eyes. 'We've got a sticky situation on our hands.'

'Yes,' muttered Jason numbly, half listening.

There was a long pause before the professor spoke again.

Jason winced, one eye completely closed, ready for the shot, for the kill. Then it came.

'After what happened, we are going to have to let you go.'

The dismissal tore through Jason. He was thinking about all the years he had been at the university. He could not begin to count the hours he had pinched from Poppy to write into the night. He thought of his seasonal indigestion when new intakes of students took away his lunch and the endless slog of marking. Now the university he had given much of his working life to was casting him out. He was losing his tenure. *What kind of job will I get now? Who will want me? My CV is shit.* With these thoughts, he lowered his head into the only place Jason had left, the bowl of his hands.

'When?' he asked finally, uncurling his back. It was all he could say, staring at Porter's striped, pink tie.

'Ah, well, that's just it,' Porter said reluctantly. 'The vice chancellor wants you to leave with immediate effect.'

'I'm sacked? Just like that?'

'Yes, I am afraid so, Jason.'

'After what has happened to me?'

'Well, I am sure the VC took on board those mitigating circumstances. Still, with the student suing the university—'

Jason coughed, held his brow and tried to think. He fought to understand, reflect and build a defence. It was like receiving the gloomiest diagnosis. He froze and felt overwhelmed. For a moment, Jason considered getting the union involved, but then realised he had let his contributions lapse to preserve his salary. He looked up at the framed logo for the university on the wall—*Sapientia et Virtus*—wisdom and virtue. There was no wisdom or virtue on offer. Jason looked back into the steely eyes of Professor Porter. The head of school's unmoved expression underlined the fact that his career at the university was over.

As he sat, stunned by the news, even though he had anticipated it, Jason gradually sensed there was no point contesting the matter. He had made the unforgivable mistake of assaulting a student. There was no way back. Any struggle would only make things worse. The VC had fired the shot and Professor Porter had merely stood aside and watched it tear into Jason's mediocre career. As Jason thought about all that, he could hear the muffled words of the head of school pretending to be helpful and constructive. Jason did not wish to stay a moment longer in his office. He stood up, apologised for the mess he had created and excused himself. Yet, at the door, he hesitated and turned his head to speak.

'Please tell the vice-chancellor to go fu—'

At that very moment, the fire alarm test sounded and robbed him of even that bleak satisfaction.

†

When Poppy found out Jason had lost his job, she berated him for not putting up a fight about the decision. She urged him to restart his subscription to the union and ask for advice. She even suggested that he swallow his pride and apologise in person to the vice-chancellor. After all, there were such compelling mitigating circumstances. Jason had been under great stress following the death of his brother. It was not as if he made a habit of beating up students.

Poppy's anxiety was such that she hardly slept all night despite taking a dose of Valium, waking Jason frequently, asking him how they would manage the mortgage payments on the house. These were modest, but still bled them, slowly. Then there was the high local tax for the property and all the other bills to pay. Their credit card debts had also mounted significantly after Poppy lost her position at the laundry. Poppy told him she did not want to dip into her inheritance to survive. She had set that aside as a cash pension for later.

Tired from his wife's sleeplessness and pecuniary worries, Jason felt as low in mood as he had after his brother's death. It was a sensation of total and absolute defeat. His tongue did not taste the soggy cornflakes in front of him. His chin rested on his ribcage. He did not know what day it was except that it followed the one before. He had lost the *when* of his existence. As a sort of hooligan teacher and part-time mental patient to boot, he felt he had kissed goodbye to getting another meaningful position elsewhere. His sacking was inevitable, of course. He knew that the university could dispose of anyone for more trivial misdemeanours than assault.

Jason sat knit in silence, frozen by the thought of aimless, unemployed days spent with his wife, getting on each other's nerves.

He anticipated continual bickering and arguments about money. He feared that domestic boredom would inevitably encroach and settle into every fibre of his being. There would be a tyranny of chores—new and largely futile tasks such as dusting or cleaning out cupboards. He dreaded the prospect of applying for other lesser teaching or research posts. Yet he would have to do this to avoid an oppressive, indoor life, a social lockdown.

Jason sat motionless, his hands inert on the table, his spoon sticking into the air. It was some time before he played with the cornflakes apathetically, looking up occasionally at Poppy's raw, reddened face. He suddenly feared the loss of routine available in his lecturing work, burrowing into archives, resurrecting dead authors and writing articles, chapters and the occasional book. Now subject to domestic lassitude, without structure to his day, he found himself listening to the jingling progression of the only surviving milk float in Ardinweald, moving steadily along the quiet road. He tracked its sound, a shaft of hot, early sunlight falling across his tense, stretched neck.

'Late again,' he said, barely surfacing.

Poppy slapped her spoon down onto the table and stood up. 'Do I look as if I care whether the milkman is late?' she told him, unable to contain her tiredness and anger.

Jason felt acutely ashamed of his emotional incontinence, putting everything at risk: their home, their marriage and their health. He watched as his wife twisted the cold tap fully open and blasted water into the kettle before switching it on with venom.

'You've lost your job. We are both out of work and you are complaining about the milkman! Who cares about him? Most people don't use them anymore!' As she fumed, Poppy picked up a scouring pad and set about the dirty dishes with manic intensity.

Juju circled the thick kitchen table leg, brushing against Jason, who kept quiet following his wife's outburst and continued to play with rather than eat his breakfast. He wondered how to prevent himself from turning into a cleaning machine. He watched his wife cut through the grease even though they had a dishwasher. She *wanted* to do the washing up. She was *choosing* to do it like therapy. She did not have to. As he studied the white bubbles covering her forearms to the elbow, he felt ineluctably drawn to join in or take the vacuum cleaner from under the stairs and do the whole house from top to toe—something he had avoided for a very long time.

Yet Jason shook thoughts of cleaning carpets, wiping surfaces, disinfecting toilets or emptying the overfilled pedal bin from his mind. Instead, he thought about his personal mission to track down Umbie's killer—an enterprise that would surely benefit from his unemployment. Now he could really focus on hunting him down, without distraction. He would be able to devote as much time as he pleased to this, at least in the short term.

'I don't want you moping around the house,' Poppy told him, rinsing a plate mercilessly. 'I want you out there looking for jobs. Talk to the union. Go down the job centre. I want you off that arse of yours and out from under my feet.'

'Tell it how it is!' snapped Jason, pushing his bowl away, milk slopping over onto the table.

It was not the thing to say. Poppy took a cup from the sink and threw it down on the floor. It exploded, sending a fallout of porcelain and soapsuds across the kitchen. She stormed out with Jason in tow, picking his way through the broken crockery, trying to placate her. At the sitting room door, she picked up his doorstop thesis and hurled it across the room. He watched it open in the air like a plump grouse with stunted wings before falling to the floor.

'Just get out!' she cried. 'Go on! Get out of my sight!'

Jason did just that, hurt by the sudden harshness from his wife's lips and wisely not attempting to recover the fallen tome. It was unusual for her to speak or act in this way, and his heart raced at the thought that their marriage might be in serious jeopardy. He quickly grabbed his coat, leaving the house without exchanging another word.

Outside, Jason walked around his dusty Volvo, relieved to be beyond his wife's anger. It was clear that life at home was not going to be easy or straightforward after all that had happened. He looked up at the clouds hanging low over Ardinweald, keeping the intermittent yet burgeoning sun in check, and he sensed that his post-university existence would be a challenge. Yet, for now, he coached himself to stay focused on the prize. He headed off along the bone-dry, glistening pavement, dark patches forming under the arms of his shirt. He had rushed out of the house without his usual spray of antiperspirant and without questioning the need for a coat. He left it open, ventilated.

Despite Poppy's instructions to claw back his job, Jason quickly dismissed the idea. He knew that the teaching union would not defend his behaviour towards the student, and he had no appetite for brown-nosing the vice-chancellor. Poppy would have to face it; he was out of a job too, at least for now.

Instead of heading towards the university, Jason took an entirely different route. He needed cheering up, even in a dark way. He decided that there could be nothing better than paying a visit to Headquarters. He needed good news and Ryan was just the man to deliver it. In anticipation, he sped up, sudden bursts of sunshine making him shield his eyes and wish he had decided to leave his coat behind.

With long, eager steps, Jason strode along Ardinweald High Street. It was only a few minutes' walk to the corner of High Street and York Road, but there was a large crowd of shoppers and his irritability grew as he weaved along the pavement. He was sweating profusely by now, taking his trusty handkerchief from his trouser pocket to dab his face before negotiating yet another slow-moving

Ardinweald resident.

By the time Jason reached the barbershop, his skin prickled. Only the faintest of breezes refreshed his hot face before he slipped beneath the red-and-white pole and into the barbershop, praying Ryan had news for him. The more logical part of his brain told him that it was far too early, a waste of time, but he did not turn around. The little bell over the door rang out, making him jump a little. He tried to remain optimistic. *This might be my lucky day. It could be a day that sets everything in motion. What is an arrow without a target, or a bullet without a body?* He badly needed Ryan to set him on his path.

No sooner was Jason inside than the sulphurous odour hit his nostrils, making him grimace. He wondered which of the oily-haired men were having special chemical treatments. He removed his coat and placed it over his left arm.

The glamorous receptionist recognised Jason and pulled a face, but then quickly flashed a neutral smile and waited for his request. This time she used his proper title.

'Morning, *Dr* Hemp. Are you here to see the boss?'

Although unintentional, her reversion to his special title made Jason uncomfortable. He was now a sacked, redundant doctor, after all.

She picked up the handset and checked with Ryan that Jason's visit was convenient. 'You know the way,' she said languidly after a few moments, her lips more fleshy than plastic today. She stared at the dark patches around Jason's armpits and drew in her nose.

Jason took a long, deep breath before heading upstairs, butterflies in his stomach, hoping for positive news from Ryan.

Ryan did not greet him on the landing this time, instead calling Jason through into his spacious office, where he shook his hand firmly and offered him the same seat as the last time they met. The barber still wore a white, albeit fresh, T-shirt. He smiled warmly at Jason.

'How are you?' he asked.

'Not too bad. And you?'

'Up to here,' Ryan announced, chopping his neck. 'I've got lots to do.' He twiddled his ring, smiling cordially, rubbing his lips together.

'Well,' said Jason. 'If you want a job doing, ask a busy man.'

'Yes, that's very true. Please, sit down.'

'No, it's OK. I just— I was wondering if you had come up with anything?'

'Ah, that,' said Ryan apologetically with a sharp intake of breath. 'Nothing yet, I am afraid.'

Jason's face sagged, his eyes retreated and his lips kicked out like a pouting child. 'Oh,' he muttered, gazing at the edge of the desk.

'I know it's disappointing. I'm sorry,' Ryan told him, his hands unfurling. 'But, as I said, these things take time. Look, I will do all I can, I promise. We get a good look at people's heads here. As soon as we spot something, I will call you. I have your number here.' Ryan held up the little card with Jason's mobile number scrawled on it. 'I have also asked the girls to keep their eyes peeled.'

Jason pulled his lips to one side and stared fully at Ryan's sincere face. He was thankful that someone else was on his side. Revenge was a lonely business and Jason was grateful for the barber's support. He had heard nothing more from Inspector Mosby and Jason was sure that the case was stalling. There had been no further mention in the newspapers of progress in the investigation.

'You have my word,' said Ryan, 'we'll find him.'

'I hope so,' said Jason, staring at the barber's shiny head, overwhelmed. He felt raw and fragile, hardly an avenger.

'If we see anyone with brown hair and a patch missing from his scalp, you'll be the first to know. I want to find him just as much as you do. Umbie was my friend. Look, I will call or text you if anything turns up. OK?'

'It means a lot, thank you,' Jason told him, drawing his lips together to preserve a masculine dryness.

'It's nothing,' Ryan told him. 'It's the least I can do. We will find him, don't worry!'

26

On returning from Headquarters, Jason found that he had the house to himself and decided to take a much-needed bath. In his obsessive quest, he had failed to maintain his usual standard of personal hygiene. Now he sat in the tub, flexing his legs until his big toe caught the plug chain and his bottom settled into position. He felt the urge to urinate, but resisted, wallowing in the steaming water, rubbing the white soap over his hair-sprinkled chest and staring through the mist at the cold tap.

He began steeling himself for visiting the university one last time. He really did not want to go in, yet he needed to collect all his personal possessions and had already placed several flattened cardboard boxes and duct tape in the back of his Volvo to do just that. Apart from emptying the shelves of literary works, Jason wanted to gather all the research about the murder that he had stuck to the wall of his little office. There were literally hundreds of fragments of information from his enquiries. He had drawn maps of the likely routes the murderer would have taken after the attack. He had spoken to taxi and bus drivers—their comments scrawled on odd bits of paper, even the back of receipts. There were numerous photographs of the murder scene taken long after the authorities had removed Umbie's remains for autopsy. Jason was keen to have all of this information to hand, yet at the same time, he felt nauseous at the prospect of bumping into ex-colleagues. As he stared at his toes, he fell asleep. It was not long before an image swelled in his dozing mind.

It was Poppy, moving through the grim, northern waves of

Scarborough, her cheeks scoured by salt. She was wearing the frumpy clothes her mother bought for her. The garments were sodden and she was carrying a beach ball. She looked deeply afraid.

'What is the matter?' Jason asked as the bathwater and sea joined in his mind.

She was pointing behind her at the vast, grey expanse. He looked into it, but saw nothing. Now Poppy was trembling, the skin of her face turning bluish, juddering from the cold air that came with each roll of water. A deceitful sun carved her into a brown rock. Jason closed in, putting his arms around her. She pushed him away with force and drifted backwards with a smooth, unnatural acceleration.

Suddenly the surface broke and he saw his twin brother, sideways on, his left hand reaching over and pulling open Poppy's dark blouse. One of her breasts tumbled over the fabric like a large, pale anemone.

'Hey, Umbie, leave her alone!' Jason was shouting. 'She's mine now!'

As Umbie turned in the foaming water, blood was spewing from his eye. The flow trailed from his head like an exotic form of seaweed, moving across the surface of the waves towards Jason.

Jason started, gripping the bath's edge and shaking his head into stiff wakefulness. He reviewed the image of Umbie, with his bloody eye, the eye he had seen in the subway, split in two, catching the glow of a sodium lamp. Despite the warm water, Jason shuddered involuntarily. He lay back, slipping deeper into the tub, his knees bending and chin touching the water. He stayed like that for some time, rarely blinking, thinking again of that terrible night after drinks at The Half Moon.

It was not until the front door slammed that Jason fully stirred. Poppy was back. He lifted himself from the cooled water, his fingers puffed up and waterlogged. He shook each foot before placing it on the linoleum and pulling the plug. He dried himself with the damp towel Poppy had used before him that morning and got dressed. The sun still shone, splintering through the frosted glass and falling across the wet-skinned, gurgling bath. Jason quickly finished putting his clothes on and joined his wife. Poppy was opening a can of tuna and Juju was meowing expectantly. Jason plastered his wet hair behind his ears and entered the kitchen.

'Where have you been?' Poppy asked, bending the lid of the tin, careful not to slice her fingers.

'I've been in the bath.'

Poppy's eyebrows raised a notch, handing down the saucer of food to Juju's already protruding tongue. 'I meant before the bath.'

'Oh, nowhere really,' he lied and then deflected the conversation by telling her that he was going over to the university to get his stuff. After that, he would visit the local job centre and see what vacancies they had for tutoring. 'What have you been up to?' he asked. He could see that she was in a much better mood.

'Well,' she said rather pleased with herself. 'I've got a job.'

'Seriously?'

'Yep,' she said, brushing bits of fish from her fingers and rummaging through the contents of her handbag. 'The letter came this morning. I start tomorrow.' She handed him an envelope.

He turned it over before pulling out the headed notepaper with "Glo-Bright Laundry" across the top. It was reassuring that the day after Jason had lost his job at the university, Poppy found work.

'We won't starve then,' he said, noting the half-decent salary before handing the letter back to his wife. 'That's good news.'

'It's not as high up, but it's a foot back on the ladder.'

'Absolutely!' he enthused. 'At least we'll be able to keep up our mortgage payments on the house. I got a letter from the university this morning with my final pay statement. I've also got to go in and get my stuff.'

'Your books and everything?'

'Yeah.'

Poppy caught his deflation. 'Something positive had to happen to us,' she insisted. 'And now it has!'

Jason was not so sure. 'Your job's good news,' he mumbled, switching on the kettle.

Juju circled Poppy's leg, tail in the air, as she bent down with a second helping of fish.

†

The next day, Jason drove through the campus for one last time, skirting the lake, passing the Wright Gallery to the Dyson Building, lifted high and white above the water. He exceeded the speed limit as usual. A few people were out with their dogs on the parkland, but mostly the campus was busy with students. Jason wished to remain unseen, but the smoky exhaust from his old Volvo attracted attention. He was sure that one or two spotted him so pretended to adjust the mirror to shelter his face.

Normally, he would have enjoyed this idyllic scene above the lake, capped with a flawless blue sky, yet his spirits were low. Already he dreaded meeting former colleagues and having to run the gauntlet of their office doors. As he drove past the students' union at the Alan Sillitoe Building on his right, his heart squeezed and he felt breathless when he thought he saw Bradley in an arm sling. Yet it was just his guilty mind and an entirely different, damaged student. He blew out a couple of times and gritted his teeth. For a moment, he considered turning round and going back home. However, he needed to get his stuff, not least his collection of literary works and notes from his murder investigation.

With some relief at not meeting any students he knew while parking up, Jason entered the Dyson Building, punching the disabled button to open its heavy doors. Quickly, with his chin pressed down into a bundle of collapsed cardboard boxes and with a bangle of parcel tape on his wrist, he sped along the main corridor and into his office. As soon as he opened the door and kicked it shut behind him, he looked around. The cleaners had not touched the place. Nor had the porters moved any of his stuff. Everything was as he had left it. He put the flattened cardboard boxes down and began to rebuild them. He felt like an intruder now, half expecting a visit from one of the security guards. As soon as he finished, he began gathering up his murder notes and pictures. Most of his detective work had led nowhere. It had been a process of going up alleys to find they were blind. As he put each fragment of information into one of the boxes, he wondered when he would hear news from Ryan. He checked his phone for messages from him, but there was just one from Poppy instead, wishing him well on campus. Jason continued with the packing, carefully removing various items from the walls and placing them in the boxes. As he moved around the room, the space began to look even more alien and forlorn. He stopped, threw off his coat and continued breathlessly.

When he finally completed stripping the room and filling the boxes, huge sweat patches gathered under his arms. He sat on his creaking office chair and waited for his heart and breathing to fall back to normal. As he did so, he gazed at the blank yellow walls, shadowy rectangles left where posters had once hung. *Soon enough, someone else will inhabit this room*, he thought, *running seminars and tutorials, mopping up the anxiety of first-year students.* Another lecturer or professor would be sitting in his chair. Jason pitied him or her. *How many years will they serve? Will they explode at the desk from too much stress, poor diet and lack of exercise?* He imagined Professor Porter's response: "We'll have to get another member of staff. We've broken this one". For an instant, Jason enjoyed the sense of escape. He was out of all this now. *No more lectures to plan. No more marking. No more departmental meetings.* Yet these thoughts quickly soured. He was leaving short on years for a meaningful pension.

One by one, Jason hauled the boxes of papers, books and pictures out of the office, down the corridor and through the fire door to the parking lot to avoid his colleagues. Picking up the last box, he glanced briefly around the office he had once been so proud to inhabit, dwelling on the now empty bookcases. He had completed his forced evacuation. There was nothing left for him at NEU. His colleagues had already become ghosts. He knew that soon enough they would forget he had been among them. As he filled the boot and stacked the boxes on the back seat of his Volvo, he realised he had forgotten a personal item and went back inside. Walking quickly along the corridor, hoping to avoid meeting anyone, he quickly opened the department's unlocked display cabinet and removed the copy of his one and only serious book, *Reading Emotion in the Renaissance*. Then Jason headed home, where he placed everything, including his singular creative work, in the garage. Poppy rarely visited the place. It was where he could freely examine the evidence he had collated about his brother's murder.

27

Poppy left the house early with a spring in her step for her first day at Glo-Bright Laundry, while Jason stretched out on crumpled, sweat-absorbed sheets, listening to the awful, domestic silence that depressed him and reminded him of his unemployed, housebound condition. He turned back and forth under the duvet. Closing his eyes, picking over a flimsy, unfinished dream, Jason wondered how he might spend the rest of the day. He envisaged a life of shopping, vacuuming and succumbing to daytime television. He thought of revisiting the box of evidence in the garage, migrating the books into the study or checking on his brother's grave. Perhaps Ryan would soon provide the breakthrough he so desperately needed. After dozing with his thoughts until late morning, he checked his phone for any news from Headquarters. There was nothing. Cocooned in the duvet, his toes stretching out the bottom, his lips sticky in the corners, he thought about what the barber might tell him. Headquarters was without doubt the busiest barbershop in Ardinweald. In fact, it was *the* barbershop and there was every chance that the murderer was a customer.

After several attempts to stir, Jason finally threw his body to one side and sat up, his mouth wide, stale breath trickling from his lungs. He punched the air with his fists, swung his legs over the edge of the bed and rubbed his eyes, tiny silver dots filling his vision. Yawning, shaking his head, breathing deeply, poking his ears with his little finger, Jason stumbled towards the bay window and drew back the curtains. The weather was resolutely dull. Clouds like sandbags hardly budged. Along the road, Jason spotted the postie with his overlong fuzzy grey hair. He walked right past the house with not even a bill to stick through the letterbox and break the sound of isolation.

Jason turned from the window and went out into the bathroom, coughing phlegm from his lungs and inspecting his furry tongue in the mirror. He welcomed the hiss of the tap running and the routine of brushing his teeth and coached himself to get going with his day. He jumped in and out of the shower, dressed in a green polo neck and loose-fitting jeans and went downstairs, carefully stepping over Juju on the bottom step. He stared briefly at the empty mat by the front door and went through into the kitchen, flicking the kettle on to make a brew.

He could see Mr Norris already out pottering in his garden. Jason watched him cross his perfect lawn, armed with a big pair of secateurs. He headed for the boundary fence where wild roses and blackberries had sprawled over from Jason's side. With a look of disgust at his neighbour's inattention, Mr Norris clipped back the untidy growth. Such was the poor state of Jason's land that the gooseberry bush was now lost midst rampant weeds. Towards the rear, the pool lay still, surrounded by gnomes.

The last thing on Jason's mind was the upkeep of the garden. He had far more important things to consider. When the kettle boiled, he made himself a builder's tea and sat down at the table, drawing the mixture of hot liquid and air through his pursed lips. He thought about the cake he had eaten and its sacramental force. A phantom of its burnt, bitter taste returned. *What a strange but powerful little ritual*, he decided now, recollecting Heywood's proverb: "*A hair of the dog that bit us*". His thoughts shifted back to Ryan. Jason pictured him among his staff of pretty hairdressers, studying the heads of customers, drawing back their locks, peering and scanning for a camouflaged bald patch.

Jason smiled broadly. *Vengeance will not escape me.*

When he finished his tea, Jason ate the last of the crumpets. He barely tasted them, munching away in a mechanical rhythm. When he finished adding fuel to his body—for that was all it was to him for now—Jason put on his shoes, threw on his coat and left the house. He decided he would do something he had not done for a long time, sit and read for a few hours in the local library. It felt like the best place to inhabit after leaving the university—a kind of academic detoxification unit. Gradually, such visits might weaken the scholarly addiction to sources and footnotes and help him simply read for fun the kind of books that never got onto course reading lists. Although he was an expert on how reading can lift people's moods, his mind was set ironically on reading everything the library had on real-life crime and detection.

On his way out, stepping around the old Volvo, he noticed a battered white van parked across the street. He had seen it on the road a few times now. It seemed odd, conspicuous. Jason studied it a little more closely. On its side, he read the letters "AR" and "CHER". *What is it doing here?* Although he suspected it was just a plumber, window cleaner or gardener on his rounds, the vehicle made Jason feel uneasy, on edge, threatened even. There was something about it that made his hair stand on end—the intimation perhaps, that whoever sat inside was up to no good or keeping a watch on him. Certainly, something told him the van did not belong to a tradesman.

Just as Jason steeled himself to go over and take a closer look, the wheels of the van spun wildly, burning rubber, sending up a cloud of smoke that trailed back in the breeze. Standing in the middle of the road, Jason watched it disappear around the corner. It was then that he suspected Inspector Mosby had ordered some of his men to keep a close eye on him.

†

Ardinweald Library stood proudly at the far end of High Street. Built in 1906 following a donation from the philanthropist Andrew Carnegie, it was one of the most striking of the local red brick buildings. Dressed in ashlar, with Ionic pillars and an Edwardian interior, it stood beside the equally impressive Public Baths. Jason appreciated the resource. There were fewer and fewer libraries open across the city. This Grade II listed one had managed to retain its funding. Stepping inside through its heavy wooden doors, Jason felt suddenly and unexpectedly overwhelmed and tearful. Stack after stack of books on the original shelving were like old friends, even more so following his fall from grace at the university. For a moment, he wondered about taking up a new career as a librarian or even joining as a volunteer. However, this thought was soon lost as he began to locate the shelves of most interest, where he might find guidewires to his detective work. Mercifully, these were far away from the children's section where a teacher was opening a very large picture book and crouching forward with wide eyes and an animated voice to keep the attention of her class.

As Jason sat in the library, scanning the book spines with his head cocked to one side, he felt himself relax a little despite the subject of his enquiry. The library had a decent collection of reference books on crime and detection. He took a pile of several titles away to one of the long reading tables. A few Ardonians sat here and there, one or two dozing in the quiet and stillness. Jason pored over the books, methodically comparing and contrasting his own amateur sleuthing with that of others.

After a couple of hours and with the blood supply to his legs failing on the hard reading chair, Jason got up and went back to the stacks. He had digested the selection of books and searched for more. After several minutes and with pins and needles relieved, he returned with an even bigger set of books and began consuming these, relying on his hard-won skimming technique. After a life in academia, Jason knew how to flick his eyes back and forth to capture the substance of any book. He always began by reading the index of a book, if it had one. This gave him a general skeleton for what lay inside. Then he flicked through the contents page, which gave the broad shape or logical progression of the work. Then he gutted the book like a fish, proceeding with lightning speed, paying attention only to the start of each paragraph. He imagined that anyone observing his eye movements at such times would suspect that he had succumbed to a gross neurological disorder.

As he sliced through a biography of Jack Slipper, the detective who investigated the Great Train Robbery, Jason's phone pinged. He dug it out from his trouser pocket and stared for a long time at the text message. It was from Ryan. Jason saw an emoticon of a smiley face: "Good news. Drop by". It could only mean one thing—Ryan had information on the killer. Jason felt suddenly enlivened by the possibility of an end to his quest. He quickly thumbed his reply: "On my way!" Jason left the books he was studying scattered on the reading table.

Within minutes, Jason was running along High Street towards the barbershop, dodging through the crowd. Now, more than ever, Jason believed in the efficacy of the sacrament, his coat trailing behind him, sweeping by the police station yard. On he sped, past the carpet shop, charity shops and the string of boutiques before arriving in the shadow of Ardinweald Parish Church, its famous bells ringing and calling to no one. *This is it*, Jason thought, racing forward and turning towards York Road. *Now I will know who killed my brother. The hammer will fall*. He wondered if the murderer sported a hat or hood to cover his sins or whether he was so hardened that he had left the ripped out bald patch on show like a badge of honour. Yet, as he approached Headquarters, one of Poppy's comments seeped back into his mind: "You don't know what you might get yourself mixed up in. Everything's clouded and difficult and frightening". Jason shook off the warning. He was not going to give up on his quest, not now, not ever.

The bell over the door of the barbershop sounded as always, yet did not make Jason jump this time. He arrived with a mission, an unwavering focus. Already, the bench was full and the red leather chairs occupied. The familiar background stink was in the air and the hairdressers were busy chatting with the mirror images of Ardonian men, clipping away. One of the gowned customers grunted in satisfaction as one of the young women began with the popular head massage routine.

Jason approached the counter and the receptionist, whose rouged cheeks and eyelashes stood out more than ever.

'Go straight up,' she told him with a flick of her hand, nothing more. She did not bother to call through to her boss.

Jason did not waste any time, stepping through to the back and climbing the stairs.

Ryan was on his feet and waiting for him in the office, breaking into a wide, enthusiastic smile. Jason responded in kind, shaking the barber's hand and patting his arm, saying how glad he was to see him. No sooner was the greeting over than Ryan took his seat at the huge desk, signalling for Jason to sit opposite him. He did so, perching on the edge of the chair, expectant, focusing on the ornate inkwell and then on Ryan's tired eyes. In the background, music burbled on a radio.

'Well, Jason,' said the barber leaning back in a self-satisfied way. 'What would you say if I told you one of my girls spotted him?'

Jason's belly cramped. 'No?' he gasped excitedly, rubbing below his ribs and burping successively. Already, he had jumped to his feet, wondering if Umbie's murderer was still in the building. Perhaps he was the one moaning with the head massage.

'Please, sit, sit,' Ryan told him. 'He's not downstairs, OK? He came in yesterday and I wanted to do a few checks before I got in touch.'

Jason did not know what to say, his teeth parted, his spine tingled and his heart was pounding under his ribs. 'You think it's him?'

Ryan nodded rather than spoke.

'Was he wearing a hat or hood?' Jason asked, trying to contain the rush of emotion.

'Neither.'

'Was he trying to hide the mark?'

'No,' Ryan informed him.

Jason was shaking his head. 'And he had a—'

'Patch? Yes, he did.'

'Where?'

'Right on top,' said Ryan fingering his own head. 'I went downstairs and looked for myself.'

'Did you ask him how he got it?'

'No, but he seemed anxious about it.'

'How do you mean?'

'Well, he kept touching it and asking if it would grow back fully. You know, with root damage and everything.'

Jason went stony quiet. Now he knew that he had his man. 'How big was the patch?' he asked, his heart in his throat as he waited for Ryan's answer.

'It was fairly substantial, the kind of thing you get after someone has really had a good hold and—'

'Ripped it.'

'Exactly.'

'And the hair was brown?'

Now the barber paused. He appeared unsure, yet finally gave a confident nod of his head.

'Yes!' cried Jason, punching the air as if he had just unfolded a winning lottery ticket.

'Now you will be able to settle things,' Ryan added. 'And I feel that I have done my best as a friend of your brother.'

For a time, Jason remained speechless. He stared at the lion feet of Ryan's inkwell, its claws and the sinuous snakes at either end. His mind filled with all kinds of thoughts and his eyes felt like they would pop out of his skull with cranked-up blood pressure. He wished he had been there when the man came in. He began fantasising about what he would have done. In his mind, he was taking over from the girl who spotted him. He was tilting back the man's head into a white basin and then flicking open a cutthroat razor, smiling at the reflection of his special customer.

'What's he like?'

Ryan pulled at his chin and looked up to the left. 'I'd say he is a similar age to you, not very tall, with big hands. Well, they seemed big compared to the rest of him.'

'It's not much to go on!'

'The thing is, there's nothing unusual about him. Well, apart from his nose, which is slightly to one side. But there's no mistaking the bald patch.'

Jason felt deeply grateful to Ryan. Finally, luck had come his way. It seemed that the cake had worked its magic. The unfathomable force of the sacrament had moved things in the right direction. He clenched his fist and bit his teeth until they hurt. Then his mouth opened into a broad smirk. It divided his rigid, staring face.

'How will I find him?' Jason asked.

Ryan stroked his chin, looking at Jason with determined, narrowed eyes. 'Well, that's the easy part,' he told him.

'Why?'

The barber paused dramatically. 'He drinks at The Sow's Ear.'

'Oh my God!' cried Jason, his eyes wide. 'He's a local man! That's what I told the police, yet they didn't believe me!'

More than that, the pub was just spitting distance from the

cemetery.

'Murderers are often local,' confirmed Ryan with several long nods of his head. 'And now we know *who* it is.'

'Yes, thanks to you,' Jason managed. 'Thank you so much!'

He reached over and squeezed the barber's shoulder, gritting his teeth and making agitated, butting movements with his restless head before sitting back down again. Pinching his nose and breathing heavily, his mind raced. He was back fantasising about the cutthroat razor. Now in his mind's eye, he drew the thing across the customer's neck.

'Do you know his name?' he asked.

Ryan shook his head. 'No, but you will find him there on dominoes nights.'

'He plays?'

'Yes. He is a new player. He only started recently by all accounts. Perhaps your brother had an argument with him. There are some nasty people out there.'

Jason bit his lip, trying to visualise the man Ryan described, wondering why the domino player would want to kill Umbie. *What is his beef? What grudge does he hold against my brother? What did Umbie do to hurt or upset him? Perhaps Umbie lost a big game and failed to come up with the money or messed around with his wife or girlfriend.*

'I'll get him!' he vowed in a deep, guttural voice, enraged that the man with the bent nose could still play dominoes while his brother lay mouldering in the ground. He imagined the raw patch of skin on the crown of his head and heard the sound of dominoes slammed onto the tables as each man took his turn. 'So the guy is not a regular,' mused Jason, wishing that he had taken to drinking in The Sow's Ear instead of The Half Moon.

'I don't think so,' Ryan admitted. 'As I said, he is a new punter.'

Jason held his chin. 'They play dominoes on Friday nights, don't they?'

'Yes, that's right,' the barber answered.

Jason was nodding rhythmically, biting his lower lip, occasionally flashing his eyebrows as Ryan added other details. He imagined the killer with beer slopping into his mouth, teeth riveted with silver fillings, laughing, wiping the back of a veiny hand across his imperfect nose, matching domino dots and thumping each block on the table with the customary, triumphant cry. That was how they liked to play the game at The Sow's Ear.

Jason felt well and truly fired up.

'Now I know where he is going to be, I'll kill the bastard!' he declared.

†

Poppy returned late from work to find Jason in an agitated, excitable state, pacing the sitting-room carpet and wringing his hands, with sweat pouring from his skin. He looked at her with frenzied, weird eyes and held the back of his neck as if accused of some mischief. She wondered why he was so ruffled. Frowning, Poppy chewed her dry lower lip. Then she started on him.

'What have you been up to?'

'Nothing.'

'I know your nothings,' she charged. 'Come on, out with it! I know you've been up to something.'

'I haven't done anything,' he argued.

'It's written all over your face!' she continued mercilessly. 'What are you up to?'

'Absolutely nothing,' insisted Jason, unclasping his neck and slumping into his armchair.

Now Poppy turned to house matters. 'Look at the place! It is a complete mess! I don't suppose you vacuumed?'

'No.' Jason's eyelids began to droop. He hated it when Poppy went on and on about the house. It was not as if she was the tidiest person in the world.

'God, I'm getting fed up tidying up after you!' At this point, she crossed the room and looked into the kitchen with its pile of dirty crockery stacked up. She gave out a cry of despair.

Jason poked his fingers into his ears to muffle Poppy's shrill complaints.

'Why do I have to come home to this mess? What have you been doing all day?' she railed. 'I've been working myself to the bone while you've not lifted a finger. You didn't even bother to ask me how I got on at Glo-Bright! It was my *first* day!'

Jason unplugged his ears. 'I'm sorry,' he offered. 'I've just been distracted, that's all.'

'Distracted? What are you scheming about this time? And don't tell me it's anything to do with—' Jason could see she just did not want to say it. 'Well, you better shape up and get yourself together and find a job because Umbie can't help us with the bills. My new job will help, but it is not enough.'

'I went to the library to see if they had any vacancies,' he lied, hoping to assuage her and limit discussion.

'The library?'

'Yes.'

'You are thinking of being a librarian? Do you know how little they get paid?'

Jason decided not to defend the point. When Poppy was in this mood, he had learned that it was best to keep quiet. He knew she wanted a more amenable husband, yet he had things he had to do. After a long silence, he saw Poppy's tense shoulders drop. She was relenting, softening, as she always did. It just took time.

'I'm going to make some dinner,' she finally offered. 'What do you fancy?'

'I don't want anything,' Jason told her. 'I've lost my appetite, to be honest.'

'Right, suit yourself then,' she said entering the kitchen and closing the door behind her.

†

'I can make the delivery now,' said Dazzler parked up outside a house on the opposite side of the city to Ardinweald, adjusting his balaclava in the mirror. 'I'm right outside.'

As he spoke, he patted the trusty Walther PKK pistol lying on the passenger seat. There was a delay of a few seconds then the voice came back through the air to the burner phone.

'No. There has been a change to the order.'

Dazzler had not expected this answer. He tried to hide his disappointment. 'OK, no problem,' he said.

The voice picked up again. 'Here's what I want you to do.'

'Yes.' Dazzler listened intently to the information, his eyebrows notching higher and higher. 'Say that again,' he asked, surprised by the weird suggestion. 'Wouldn't it be easier to make a direct delivery? Are you sure?'

'Yes, that's the order, OK? This way, we will get him to do our work for us. Two birds and all that—' the voice came back carefully staying in code.

'I see where you are going with this but—'

He got his answer quickly and dispassionately. 'Please complete the order as requested.'

'OK, I think I can do that,' he said and signed off.

He placed the gun under his seat and reached back to root through a toolbox. He found what he needed, turned off the engine and waited.

†

Jason woke from his nap. All his reading at the library and the emotional hit of Ryan's news had exhausted him. For a moment, everything seemed right with the world. The clock ticked in a reassuring and homely way. He could hear his wife busy in the kitchen. Jason stretched and rubbed his dry eyes. His mouth felt dry and he massaged his tongue to free saliva, rehearsing his visit to The Sow's Ear on dominoes night, spotting the man with the bent nose and killing him. He thought about getting hold of the kind of shotgun that Danny the gravedigger had in his possession. He visualised the murderer's head exploding graphically like that of JFK.

Despite these workings through, Jason had an overriding sense of his impotence. *Can I kill? How will I do it? Can I get hold of the gravedigger's gun? Can I walk through the bar door and shoot my brother's killer?* Slowly, he tried to talk himself into being a man of action. Yet, sitting there, a pudgy ex-academic, he doubted he had it in him. Despite his threats to avenge his brother's murder, he did not know if he could *actually* kill another human being.

As he thought it all through, Jason wondered whether it would be best to identify the man on dominoes night and then pass the information on to Inspector Mosby. That would be the normal course of action. Yet he convinced himself that Umbie's murderer might slip the net of justice. He knew people guilty of crimes often smiled at news cameras on their way out of courts and back onto the streets. In the end, he felt that he had to put himself in a strong position first to apprehend the killer and leave the consequence until its time.

28

The gravedigger's lodge stood at the far side of the cemetery, beyond the observatory ruins. The black gothic building with tiny, barred windows rationed its poor interior light. Jason suspected Danny kept his gun there. It is where he lived, and he would hardly leave the weapon unsecured anywhere else in the grounds. More spectacular than a knife, Jason entertained the gun destroying the murderer's head as easily as bursting a child's balloon. More than anything, it would offer him the means to kill at a distance, remotely, anonymously even, compared to the intimacy of a blade, something he found undeliverable in his dreams of impotent assaults.

Jason approached the building cautiously, picking his way through the clumped grass and alert to the darkness that closed in around him. It was a palpable, more than visual darkness. It came with a quality of silence that set the nerves on edge. What Jason did not want was any sudden, unexpected noise. Yet that is what he got as his phone went off. At first, the ringtone was light, barely noticeable, but then it swelled in volume.

'Shit!' he cried, almost jumping out of his skin and panicking to silence the thing, shoving his hand into each coat pocket before locating it and thumbing the mute button.

In the darkness, his face lit up like a small, Halloween pumpkin. It was Poppy. There was no way he was going to answer her call. With gritty determination, he switched the phone off, stuffed it back in his pocket and carried on towards the lodge, keeping close to the thicket, trying to determine if the place was empty. There was only a single light in the archway that brightened the worn cobbles. The rest of the building was dark.

Crouching down on his heels at the small bay window of the lodge, Jason guessed Danny would be drinking with the other gravediggers at The Sow's Ear. He gave the window a sharp tap to confirm the property was empty before hiding behind one of the nearby bushes. Jason looked for any changes of light in the building, discerning for movement. There was no response. The dark, winding drive leading to the lodge was also completely deserted and silent, as unoccupied by life as the cemetery at Jason's back.

Growing confident that he was on his own and that Danny was not there Jason inched forward, peering at the small, pointed door beneath the archway and the ground-floor windows. First, he tried the windows, repeatedly knocking the frames to release the old, loose metal stays. They were too tight. Breathing heavily and with blood thumping in his ears, he tried again, unsuccessfully. Next, he wiggled the iron ring handle on the door. There was no joy there either.

Jason cursed and went back to the nearest window, peering inside. He made out the gun leaning against the wall to one side of the empty grate in the small, austere and poorly furnished room. It looked as harmless as a slightly crooked stick. Jason studied it carefully, his teeth massaging his bottom lip. In the low light, the metal appeared soft, almost silken. It was only then that Jason noticed something much closer by on the ledge just the other side of the glass. At first, he thought it was a jar of sweets or beads. Yet he soon realised that the little coloured objects were the gravedigger's collection of racing pigeon rings. He shook his head in disbelief and drew back.

Jason contemplated whether he could force the door of the lodge. He had not come tooled up and had little choice, if he wanted to get hold of the gun, but to use his body as a ram. Stepping back, he quickly attacked the door with his shoulder. The heavy collision shunted air out of his lungs and provoked a cracking sound that left

Jason wondering if it was the wood or his bones that had given way. He rubbed his painful shoulder and arm before trying a different part of his anatomy to open the door. With a short run-up, he lifted his best foot and kicked to the side of the handle. He used all the force he could muster. Once again, the door stood firm and the impact left Jason with a jolted knee. Hobbling away into the woodland, he accepted that unless he went back home to get the right tools, he would have to give up on the shotgun and rely instead on another kind of weapon. He stumbled through the trees and back out to the perimeter of the locked cemetery and the gap in the railings used by grave vandals, glue sniffers and lovers.

†

It was Friday and Jason prepared to commit the ultimate sin. He had come to terms with what the act might mean. He had replayed the tragic night when he lost his twin brother, whose eye took the attacker's blade. He felt the killer's hair caught in his fist. Over the days since Umbie's death, Jason had lived and slept revenge. With his emotions out of control, spending time in the local mental hospital and losing the job he had worked so hard for over many years, it did not seem to matter anymore that he could end up in prison. He was already at rock bottom. He softened the idea of prison with thoughts of an enforced sabbatical, reading library books all day. In core ways, it would not be so different from an academic life. After all, universities can be imprisoning, limiting and confining of those who think unusually deeply about topics. In prison, he would not have to ration his reading time to serve a heavy teaching load. He suspected Poppy would cope alone. Yet they had already started to drift apart, relying less on each other anyway. All that mattered now to Jason was completing the job, relieving the burden of survivor guilt by serving justice.

Without allowing new shadows to fall across his plan, Jason threw himself out of his chair and set about putting on his shoes. He wanted nothing to detract from his mission. He gritted his teeth, willing his skin, muscles and bones to grow as hard as iron. It was time to end his grief. He would take out the man who killed his brother. Even if he had to do it with his bare hands, he would succeed. He had no doubt about his strength and determination. It was total at this point. His whole body felt like a primed weapon.

While Poppy sat alone watching television with JuJu on her lap, Jason slipped into his black coat. He felt restored by the little sleep he took earlier and his lips formed a strange, manic grin. He swallowed repeatedly, shunting wind into his hungry, neglected intestines. With an aching belly but focused mind, Jason continued to mentally prepare for what he was about to do.

'Jason?' Poppy called out suddenly, twisting her head round.

'Yes?' he managed, slipping on his coat.

'Can you put the kettle on?'

'Sure,' he shouted back over the canned laughter of one of Poppy's favourite shows that bled through the half-open doors separating them. He was already in the kitchen.

He filled the kettle with water and clicked it on. Then he reached into the cutlery drawer, took out the only sharp meat knife and put it inside his coat along with the roll of tape to bind it to his wrist. *If the tactic is good enough for terrorists, it is good enough for me,* he decided. Yet a different interior voice questioned him. *What are you doing? Leave it to the police! Do you really want to do this?* Jason fought to block this more reasonable intracranial voice. He hesitated as the kettle started to boil and the canned laughter lifted again in the background. He thought about the consequences. He pictured Poppy sitting across the other side of a prison table, crying and telling him how she was taking Valium for breakfast. In his mind's eye, he looked at her distraught face. He felt a strong urge to put the knife back, go into the lounge, throw his arms around her and melt. Yet his grief-driven obsession with revenge generated a different response.

I have to do this, he told himself.

He left the kettle in a sonic tussle with the laughter from the television and walked out of the house through the side door.

†

At the rear of The Sow's Ear, Jason waited, crouched down out of view on the unlit side of the old toilet block, summoning the courage to enter the building. He could already hear the slamming of dominoes through the open windows and see Frank, the owner, and his sons behind the bar. The place was full. A few regulars stood outside the back door smoking. Dominoes night was still as popular as ever. The thought that Umbie's killer sat at one of the tables with a palm of dotted bricks in his hand set Jason's heart racing. He remembered the few times he drank there with his brother instead of at their usual pub, The Half Moon. It hurt that his twin was now a stone's throw away lying in the cold ground. With fire in his belly, Jason narrowed his eyes and scanned those he could see through the windows, trying to catch sight of the displaced nose of Umbie's killer. Apart from the owner, his sons, Danny and the other gravediggers propping up the bar, he struggled to identify anyone else he had seen before. He was also too far away to survey the noses of strangers. There was little choice but to go inside and do some reconnaissance.

Jason straightened up to his full height, the handle of the knife in the inside pocket of his coat like an extra bone against his chest. He patted it. He was trying to remain as calm as possible, yet it was hard to resist the temptation to tape up the knife right then, search out the man and do the same to him that he did to his brother. Yet the thought of long years in prison brought him to his senses. If he could avenge his brother and remain free, then he would do just that. First, he would make sure the killer was there, then wait for closing time and see what opportunities arose to rivet the knife into his skull. This seemed the best way to complete his dark task.

Jason straightened his coat and combed at the hair over his ears. He knew he would have to act like any other visitor to the pub and not attract attention. Thinking about killing someone was the easy part. Planning to do it was something else. His whole body felt heavy now, burdened with the mission ahead. He was sweating hard as he ambled around the toilet block and down to the building, trying to keep calm and getting a grip of his emotions. *Come on*, he coached himself. *You can do this.*

†

In The Sow's Ear, the din intensified as the domino players moved half matchsticks on cribbage boards and secretly wagered money. They slammed down the little white blocks on the tables, sending ripples through the glasses of ale. The whole place was heaving now and developing a familiar piss smell. The owner Frank's youngest son, Tom, was moving around collecting the empties and checking that alcohol-fuelled arguments were not about to start. There was real money won and lost at the tables. At times, the stakes could be very high and any cheating, such as hiding a domino, usually ended in a fight. Frank had five other strapping sons, much bigger and intimidating than Tom, and could call on them should anything kick-off. For now, things were serious at the tables, yet jovial.

'He fucking well does!' insisted a player in the far corner of the room, laughing, his beer belly challenging the buttons of his shirt.

'I can't see anything,' said another, studying the person in front of him.

'I'm telling you he does. Look!'

All the players at one of the tables flicked their eyes at the new player with the displaced nose.

'He's right mate, you do have a bald spot!' agreed one of the young gravediggers.

The slightly built man just shrugged it off and coolly checked the dots in his hand. He was a decent player, counting the dots, eyeing the remaining pieces in his cupped hand and adding a slab to the snake of dominoes on the table. Now and again, he reached up self-consciously to fiddle with his hair, trying to cover the gap in his locks. He was still mystified why anyone would knock him down outside his house, leave his wallet untouched and remove a chunk of his hair. When he came round, he had not been aware of the loss. It was only when he went back into the house and looked in the bathroom mirror to inspect his bruised jaw that he caught sight of the missing hair on his pate. His first thought was that he had randomly fallen victim to a deranged individual. Yet, given his work on the Hemp case, it was also possible that someone wanted to warn him off the investigation.

Inspector Mosby had sent him undercover at The Sow's Ear to see what he could find out about the murder victim's circle of friends. After all, the police knew that the place was popular with the criminal fraternity. Now he was back at the dominoes table, wondering if someone at the table knew he was a cop and not the ex-con and gambler he pretended to be. He felt more anxious than usual as he studied the players around him, but if they did know, it was not obvious. The mood had not changed. Even so, he sensed he had to be very careful just in case. He had to make sure he was downing pints like everyone else. He had to stay within the fold and build on the information he had gleaned so far. What was going on in Ardinweald was much bigger and darker than gambling. What he knew already would make the hairs on any neck stand up. He needed to stay in a game bigger than dominoes.

'OK, let's go again,' announced Dazzler, turning the slabs over and jumbling them on the table with his big hands.

†

Dipping his head through the low doorway, Jason entered the pub and moved quickly through the crowd. The place was heaving and the sound of the dominoes slammed onto tables filled the air. He squeezed between the locals, apologising as he shifted this way and that, careful not to nudge beer arms, keeping one hand pressed onto the hidden shaft of the knife and roll of duct tape. He eased into a space at the bar, resting an elbow on a sodden beer towel, waiting to catch Frank's eye by holding a twenty-pound note in his fist. As he tried to fit in and look relaxed, setting a foot on the brass rail, he checked out the noses and scalps of those around him, casually turning this way and that, as if taking a general interest in his surroundings. Eventually, Frank asked for his order.

'What are you having, pal?'

Jason hesitated and looked down the line of hand pumps. 'A pint of your best,' he asked.

'That'll be the Monk's Head then,' Frank told him, and started to pull the beer.

Jason quickly paid for the honey-coloured ale and lifted it blindly to his lips while looking around, continuing his surveillance.

He saw Danny the gravedigger heading off early looking worse for wear as always, but his younger team were still in the far corner. Jason did not recognise any of the remaining punters and although he felt conspicuous, there were several men seemingly drinking alone in the pub. Most of them looked beyond the shame of having no mates. They appeared worn down or hard as nails, unperturbed by sitting or standing in isolation. The majority of the clientele seemed tough, on the margin of what Jason considered acceptable company. The customer base had certainly deteriorated since the last time he visited with his brother. He could guess the breed of dogs some of the regulars kept at home and imagined wives or girlfriends under the cosh. Clearly, Umbie had been mixing with the wrong company of late. As he kept an eye out, Jason found he had quickly drained his pint of ale and turned back to the bar for another.

'Same again?' Frank asked.

'Please,' said Jason, wondering about the best tactic for methodically observing the crowd, not least those banging their dominoes.

Jason feared that the man Ryan identified had not turned up. Perhaps the barber had made an error or lied to him. Yet this was the only lead he had now, and besides, Ryan was undoubtedly on his side, a friend of his brother. He had to trust him and do a proper search. He drank the fresh pint of ale that Frank set down in front of him—the taste reminding him of happier times at The Half Moon—and began to chart his passage from table to table. Others in the room were moving around, spectating, so he would do the same.

With glass in hand, Jason set off, slowly emerging at the outer perimeter of each table audience, showing a keen interest in the state of play and chatting away to the other lurkers. As he went around, the ale made his head feel lighter and he sighed contentedly, wiping his mouth with the back of his hand. For a while, he lost track of his mission and the heft of the knife under his coat. So far, he only spotted the odd gambler with a broken or asymmetric nose, but none sporting a bald patch on their heads. Slowly he inched his way around, less considerate and polite in getting into the best position at the tables to scrutinise the players properly. Eventually, he arrived at the far corner where the young gravediggers sat. The play was lively and noisy, and by the look of the cribbage board, very much in favour of a man with both a bruised jaw and skewed nose. Yet even this man did not show a bald patch in his thick brown pate. That is, not until he dipped his head to study the dots in his hand.

Jason suddenly gripped the handle of the knife with his free hand as he realised who now sat within striking distance. His whole body sharpened and sobered up. There was Umbie's killer, thumbing his nose even more to the left as he apologised to the players around the dominoes table for winning yet again. Jason hesitated, his eyes glued to the man on the stool with his back to the wall. He would not stand a chance if Jason lunged at him. There would be little to stop him from executing the attack. Jason sensed he would not need to bind the knife to his wrist. He was not going on a killing spree after all, and by the time anyone realised what was happening, it would all be over and done. He shook his head in disbelief, grateful now that he had visited Ryan and that his brother had decent friends he did not know about. He watched as the man with the misaligned nose picked at the hair around the bald spot, trying to cover it and make it less visible. Jason clocked this and immediately interpreted a guilty conscience. A chunk was missing of similar colour to the hair he had added to the cake, a sacrament of revenge that had worked its magic. Yet, as much as he wanted to jump forward and stick the knife into the man's sorry skull, Jason felt the call to self-preservation, to strike anonymously on his own terms. He would save it for later when the pub closed. He would be out there, in the darkness, waiting for him. As Jason turned to head back into the main crowd away from the table and out of the pub, he thought he recognised one of the other players. He studied him closely too and recalled that he had once cleaned his office at the university. Jason shrugged. He guessed even cleaners had to boost their income by gambling.

Back outside, Jason reeled from the shock of seeing Umbie's killer. His heart was pounding still and he could feel the blood shunting up his neck. His muscles had balled up, ready to spring for the murderer. At one point, his urge for self-preservation weakened and he turned back towards the pub, gripping the knife, but then relented and dropped away. People coming and going from the pub, frowned at his awkward stance and manic expression. Still rather light-headed and stumbling into the gutter, Jason knew he needed to find somewhere to bide his time until the pub closed. He looked through the tangerine of sodium lights into the darkness of the cemetery. The place was becoming a second home, he decided, and offered the best cover. No one would see him there and he could keep his eye on the front of The Sow's Ear.

With the knife against his breast, he found the gap in the railings and slipped once again into the dark interior, his hands out in front of him like a zombie. This time he headed towards the field of headstones and away from the lodge. As he went, something stirred in the bushes and caused his skin to pull tight over his large frame. Yet it was just a fox. It stopped briefly to stare at the intruder before loping off with a rabbit in its mouth. Now Jason was alone, finding the path and his feet crunching the gravel. Gradually his heart and lungs slowed down and he circled the inky, rotten crucifix on his way to Umbie's grave. There, he greeted his brother, held onto a wing of the headless angel and emptied his bladder. He could see the railway track down below and the stars in the wide sky over the valley, like buck shot from the gravedigger's gun.

29

Jason stood beside Umbie's grave, looking out at the unlit Parish Church and finally back at The Sow's Ear. He took the knife from his pocket and held it before his eyes, running his thumb against its point, just short of cutting the skin. He could hardly believe the day for vengeance had come.

'Not long now,' he whispered as much to Umbie as himself, looking at the luminous dial of his watch. The sacrament had worked mysteriously. It had led him to the killer. Now he knew its power.

Something lay on the neck of the headless angel. In the vestigial light, Jason stared at it, trying to fathom what it was. He moved forward across the path and pushed his face closer, inspecting it with frowning eyes. He drew back his head, disgusted, and used his knife to flick a condom into the grass. Turning back to Umbie's grave, he sat down, the cold of the stone rising through the seat of his pants. He sat like that with his knees drawn up and his hands joined across his shins for an hour or more, wondering how best to kill Umbie's murderer. He continued to fear that paralysis would overtake him. *Perhaps someone might intervene and save the man.* Such thoughts ruffled Jason, making his heart judder once more. *Can I do it?* The question haunted him. *Can I really kill a man?*

Such was his jumpy state that when an owl hooted in the trees above, Jason started, brandishing his knife and looking nervously around. The bird hooted once more, flapped its invisible, inaudible wings and swept like a shadow to the far end of the cemetery. Jason tried to relax a little and laid the knife on Umbie's tomb. Stroking the hair over his ears, he looked out again along the valley. He followed the silver threads of railway track extending beyond the lights of Ardinweald into the dark, fathomless countryside. With a shrinking feeling, he recalled all the days, weeks, months and years he had spent growing up with his twin brother. There had been so many good times and so much fun. Now, the fun days had gone for good.

†

It was only when he heard distant laughter blooming in the night air that Jason realised it was closing time at The Sow's Ear. He had been in a reverie of memories about the past and now they congealed like a wound. He shook himself into action, grabbing the knife, fearing he might have missed his chance. From his vantage point, he looked across Barnabus Lane and saw shadowy figures pass under the trees, beneath the sodium lamps, slapping backs, saying goodnight and laughing from their bellies.

Jason quickly skipped around Umbie's grave and raced along the path, his hands protecting his eyes from unseen twigs, the knife dancing in his pocket. Through the gap in the railings, he dived, twisting, nearly tripping over his own feet and stumbling into potholes along the driveway. Out into Barnabus Lane he ran, barely keeping upright, his lungs wheezing and his face flushed from such unexpected exercise.

Down the lane, he sped with long, careless strides, his coat a restrained cape. Faster he went, his muscles fighting to keep him upright, his heels thumping the pavement, his jaw bouncing and knees jolting. When he arrived opposite The Sow's Ear, out of the direct streetlight, he came to a stop and caught his breath, doubled over with his hands on his knees. From beneath the shelf of his forehead, his eyes scanned the people leaving the bar. Regulars left in clumps and dawdled on the forecourt. Some struggled into their cars and drove away at disinhibited and unnecessary speeds, sounding their horns. The majority left for their homes on foot. As each one departed, Jason looked out for his target, but he did not show.

Jason feared Umbie's killer had already left. After a while, Frank locked up the main door, sliding the bolts. Nobody else emerged and soon enough the lights went down. Jason cursed under his breath, knowing he would have to wait for another opportunity. He ran his hand over his head and around the back of his neck, frustrated, regretting that he had not attacked the man when he had the chance.

Jason turned away dejectedly and began walking down the lane, the knife redundant in his coat pocket, chewing over his miss. As he descended the lane, it dawned on him that Poppy would be at home fretting. Worse still, she may have notified the police. After all, he had said nothing of where he was going or what he was doing. She may have also spotted the absent knife and suspected he might be about to harm himself, never mind others given his recent, unpredictable state. A terrible nausea gripped Jason. Once again, he had put himself in the firing line. He imagined that Mosby and the rest of the police in Ardinweald were scouring the streets for him already. If they found him with the knife, he might spend time in prison or even a secure institution. He knew that folk deemed dangerous and mentally ill could find themselves banged up indefinitely.

Soon enough, he reached the tunnel under the railway track. The hood of brick above his head echoed the sound of his falling feet. Shaking his head now, Jason imagined blue flashing lights outside his house or the tall, imposing figure of Dr Bent awaiting his cue with that slightly tilted head and curious expression. He could almost smell the psychiatrist—his characteristic odour accompanying the glistening, skin-tight, gothic clothing. Worse still, Jason had a vision of Mr Singh or one of his staff, wielding a syringe. It would be like the first time when the needle ripped his buttock and dented itself on bone.

As Jason moved through and beneath the railway embankment, he started to consider how best to rid himself of the knife rather than return home with it on his person. He had begun to look out for a drain to dispose of it when he heard another set of feet behind him. Jason looked back and saw a man struggling to walk in a straight line, banging against the wall like a fly, his collar turned up to his jowl. The stark, caged lights played across the man's face and revealed a familiar misaligned nose. When he saw it, Jason faltered in his steps. His flesh crawled, the hairs on his neck stood up and his entire body flooded with adrenaline, sending him into an overload that caused an unexpected response. Rather than racing towards the man with his knife held outwards like a bayonet, he found himself heading in the opposite direction at speed. Was this the impotence marked in his dreams? Was he only capable of talking about revenge but not walking it? *I am a coward*, he decided. Feeling perplexed by his reaction, Jason reached the far end of the tunnel and fell back into the darkness where an old, rusting wire fence sagged at the bottom of the embankment.

In this dark corner, Jason struggled to breathe and pull himself together, and considered his options. The knife was still in his coat pocket. He began to fear using it now. He worried that he might fail. Perhaps the man would fight and manage to use it on him instead. Quickly, Jason pulled it from his pocket and began to bind the tang, scale and bolster of the knife to his hand and wrist. Then he clasped it tight, preparing himself to strike. The only time he had used such a knife was to cut beef, pork or chicken. In the seconds that elapsed before the man appeared, Jason contemplated how it would feel to stick the blade in human flesh, the eye.

The murderer was coming. Jason heard his staggered footfall and could hardly believe it. Now he was only yards away. With the proximity, Jason grew severely apprehensive. He stood out of sight at the corner where the tunnel ended, his knife ready, an orange sodium lamp jigging in its polished, mirror surface. The man was almost upon him. His brother's killer, unsteady and slow, weaving, came into striking distance. Suddenly breathless with the enormity of what he was about to do, Jason felt himself freeze and wilt. He shivered and bit his tongue. Umbie's killer was now merely one steaming breath away, clearing his throat, mumbling. In a whirl, Jason jumped forward, the knife up and ready. The bent-nosed man recoiled in slow motion. Everything happened as in a dream with the knife flashing back and forth, yet not connecting.

Jason carved only the air, failing to strike. Jason's dream of paralysis had come true. He wanted to stab the man, but he could not do it. He could not command his arm to do what he so desperately wanted. The knife sliced or jabbed nothing as he danced around. The man began to defend himself, kicking out and shoving Jason away. He was quite strong for his size, clasping Jason's wrist attached to the knife and twisting it painfully. Yet Jason was the bigger man, and managed to drive his drunken victim against the tunnel wall, winding him. Even with a clear chance to finish him off, Jason could not stab him, however, he suddenly thought of a way through his own impotence. In a fit of anger at himself and the man before him, he dragged him around the shadowy corner and through a dip in the fence, holding the knife under his ear.

With the knife at his neck, the man's early courage and robustness evaporated. He began to apologise profusely, drunkenly. He did not know what he had done to upset Jason and spoke incoherently, whimpering as they climbed along the worn path in the embankment. He was shaking and breathing heavily, blood felt but unseen running down his neck.

'Do you want money?' he cried, holding up his wallet in the air. 'Take it! Take it!' He fumbled and dropped the folded leather as Jason pushed him onward.

'Just climb!' Jason ordered, holding the man's collar tight and finding the resolve to keep the knife pinned to the flesh of his neck.

The man clambered up the bank of dirt, afraid of further upsetting his attacker. The stars above hung indifferently in the huge bowl of sky. No one interrupted the two climbing figures. Over the top of the bank they went, Jason more resolved now to the role of perpetrator.

Onto the railway track, they stumbled, away from the lit street. Jason forced the man to lie face down on the stones at the side of it. As he lay there, Jason's knee was in his back, with the knife one jerk away from the man's artery, pulling his head back to spy the bald patch.

'You bastard!' cried Jason, punching the man in the kidneys before jamming his face down into the stones with the heel of his free hand and shouting more obscenities into his ear, leaving a trail of spittle hanging there like a spider's dew-coated silk. 'You killed my brother!' he screamed, hitting him in the head with the knife's pommel.

'What are you on about?' the man shouted, incredulous. 'Who are you? Please, I have kids.'

'Shut up about your kids!' Jason warned him, pounding him once more. 'You remember Will Hemp, don't you? His friends called him Umbie?'

Jason decided the stunned hesitation that followed was far too long for the man to be innocent. He pressed down hard on his neck, feeling him swallow.

'Yes, yes, you remember *now*?' growled Jason.

'I know about your brother,' the man admitted, spitting out the words. 'But I didn't kill him. I swear to you. Look, this is a mistake. You just don't understand.'

'Oh, I understand all right, pal. You can't get out of this.'

'What? What are you on about?'

Jason leant more heavily into the man's slight back, jabbing him with the knife to ensure compliance.

'OK, OK, don't do this,' the man pleaded. 'You really don't understand.' He was struggling to speak now out of fear. 'What are you going to do?'

'Nothing,' spat Jason. 'I'm not going to *do* anything.'

The man relaxed a little. He laughed nervously. 'OK, just let me go,' he coaxed. 'It's a misunderstanding, right? Look, I can make a call that will clear up everything. Just let me make the call. Listen, I'm a—'

'Shut it!' bellowed Jason, sticking the knife below his ear again.

'I'm an undercover police officer,' the man persevered despite the knife, panicking, his lips pressed down against the sharp stones.

'Yeah, right, sure you are. You expect me to believe that?'

In the seconds that followed, with the darkness unchanging and the silence deepening, nothing more came from the man's mouth. For a moment, Jason wondered if the knife had slipped deeper and cut the vital flow of oxygen to his brain. The scent of beer-pee took the air as one second yawned into the next and Jason looked expectantly along the railway line. The long nuclear waste train would soon thunder its way through Ardinweald. He checked his luminous watch. It was five minutes past midnight. *Not long now*, Jason thought. The man was whining, incoherent, sensing that his attacker, now known to be Will Hemp's brother, would reject anything he said. His steamy, panicking breath trickled past his bared gums, across his frozen cheek and disappeared. Just then, the ground around them and the silver track began to vibrate, gently at first, then with more vim. The train was on its way. It was coming. Jason stared down the line into pitch-black darkness and willed it on.

'I've got two kids, for Christ's sake! Please!' Now the man began squirming for all he was worth and crying out about his children at home as he heard the rail singing. 'No!' he screamed primitively, wriggling under Jason's weight, finding little grip despite his fear and being conscious of the knife at his neck.

He did not have time to play with. This was all down to the tiniest of intervals as the train's white light glided at speed down the track. It was upon them faster than a brain can make a sentence perform on a tongue. Jason held firm in those seconds when the man begged for escape, the track bouncing noticeably, and the train approached the two dark figures relentlessly and blindly. Jason smiled weirdly as he jerked the man's head over the track.

'Now I have you!' cried Jason above the tumultuous din. He tasted again the phantom cake in his mouth.

In a final struggle, the man tried to free himself, but the weight of Jason was too much. His condemned head shook horribly.

'Umbie!' hollered Jason. 'We have him! We have our dog!'

The man managed to turn his head enough for Jason to see one eye struggling upward as if to escape his skull, the gravity of death. The train tumbled down, the wheels churning, the air rushing, roaring, biting. In a timeless space, Jason imagined the killer's head dismantling under the tonnage of the train and its radioactive cargo. The train, a proxy avenger. He anticipated the sound of his victim's skull bursting like a balsam pod squeezed between the fingers. Yet, powerfully and urgently, a different image filled Jason's mind. It was of two young children grieving the loss of their daddy, with fists in their eyes and the corners of their mouths turned downward. As the train's horn blew, a remnant of Jason's rational mind held sway with doubt about the man's identity unravelling his determination. He rolled back from the track, bringing the man's head and shoulders clear of danger.

30

Dazzler parked his white van near the tunnel under the railway as the night train passed over, sounding its horn. His small head tilted as he listened carefully to the voice on his burner phone, the windscreen misting up, his Walther PKK tucked away under the passenger seat. He rubbed the windscreen with his fist and looked outside. There was no sign of Jason or the undercover police officer. Both had disappeared without a trace. He had followed the worse-for-wear officer after closing time to see when and if Jason might strike. After all, Jason had visited the pub and watched the dominoes match, with Dazzler clocking his murderous look when he identified the person he thought killed his brother. He also saw his glance of recognition. Now Dazzler reached down and brought out the gun, maintaining his observations through the porthole of cleared mist. He saw no movement. Everything was quiet.

'I've lost sight of them,' he said, frustrated and forgetting his usual coding. 'The Hemp brother found the target, but they've both disappeared. I think they might be up on the railway embankment. What do you want me to do?'

He was tapping his gun on the gear stick impatiently.

No answer.

'Do you want me to make a double delivery?'

'No,' the voice resumed.

'Why not?'

'I don't want more drama. It will leave an even bigger trail.'

'OK.'

There was silence again and then it broke.

'I'll be in touch if I need you to mop up.'

Dazzler put the burner phone in his pocket and shoved the pistol back under the passenger seat. Then he turned on the scanner to pick up police transmissions. He liked to keep track of them at moments like this. It was possible that the undercover officer had called in or asked for help. Dazzler knew that this would be far from ideal. As he listened, he hoped that Jason had succeeded in his mission to avenge his brother's death by hitting the wrong man. That way, everything would remain tidy. Jason's amateur sleuthing would end with the disruption of the undercover investigation on the gang's operations. As Dazzler listened, police communications were light. It appeared that nothing much was going on this side of the city. There was a domestic incident, a stolen car and a burglary in progress. Dazzler twisted the ignition key and kicked the accelerator pedal. He hated it when the promise of a delivery, and a double one at that, vanished. It made him feel worthless.

†

Jim Ryan put down the phone and sat at his desk at Headquarters, building a very precise line of dominoes. Now that he had tricked Jason Hemp to remove the undercover police officer, he felt more optimistic. If, as he hoped, the ruse proved successful, he would have killed two birds with one stone. He could return to his favourite game at The Sow's Ear and his latest scheme would remain undiscovered. Now, carefully nudging the little bricks into order, he could do nothing but wait. Even though Will Hemp was long dead, he was still angry with him. *If he had not been so greedy, none of this would have happened. Why had he gone and rocked the boat? Everyone was happy. The money was coming in. Why had he taken more than his share?* Frustrated, Ryan pushed his thick fingers over his bald, bony skull.

Then he flicked the first of the line of dominoes, watching them fall. The gentle whirr of the line collapsing relaxed him. He set them up again. He wished things had turned out differently. He hated mess.

He was just beginning to breathe more evenly when the phone rang again. He immediately suspected bad news.

'Yes? What's happening?' he said, beginning a fresh line of dominoes, expecting to hear Dazzler at the other end, but it was someone higher up, with cleaner hands, reminding Ryan that he was still at the low, dirty end of the business.

'It's Gerry.' There was a new, savage tone to his posh voice. 'Do you have everything under control?' he asked.

Ryan swallowed heavily, unable to place the next domino, working hard to have the right tone to his answer. 'Yes,' he told him. 'We are neutralising any threat.'

'That is good to know,' said Gerry. 'Let's keep it that way, OK, for your sake?'

†

With the final blow of air from the last carriage of the train, Jason stood up in a daze, knife still bound to his hand, the man he had nearly killed curled up at the side of the track, whimpering quietly, his head next to a clump of grass as if the precious hair of his son or daughter. Jason tried to figure out how the man he thought was Umbie's killer could possibly be an undercover police officer. His visceral call for mercy over his children seemed real. As Jason hovered over him, retching from the anticipated trauma yet still wanting to avenge his brother, he now doubted the ease with which Ryan had presented his quarry. Things did not stack up. He also began to wonder if the police had been directly involved in Umbie's death. The words of Poppy held in his mind: "You don't know what you might get yourself mixed up in". Despite his desire for vengeance, he felt a spike of panic about what he had so nearly achieved and the consequences of his actions, especially if his intended victim turned out to be an undercover officer after all. Unable to make sense of the situation, Jason found himself compelled to do one simple thing: run away. He hesitated for a few, numb seconds, stepping forward then backwards, before unwinding the tape and throwing the knife into the darkness, scampering along the trackside and stumbling as he went. He felt guilty that he failed the pact of twins to stick together, to look after each other, never to part. He had been unable to do anything to avenge Umbie's murder and the memory of him lying soft and cooling in the subway.

Jason looked back over his shoulder at the man he had so nearly decapitated starting to get to his feet, dazed, moving away from the track where his life had so nearly ended. As the man reached inside his coat and pulled out a phone, Jason quickly headed off back down the embankment, keen to put some distance between himself and his intended victim. Stepping over the depressed wire fence, he turned in the only direction that meant anything now: home. He ran through the deserted streets, the stillness of the night in Ardinweald broken only by the occasional taxi, which brought Jason to a walking pace as he tried to be less conspicuous. Jason knew that if his designated prey was an undercover cop, each step might prove his last as a free man. Breathing hard, he kept away from main routes and the array of CCTV cameras on their stalks.

As he went, he caught sight of his reflection in the window of a newsagent close to home and imagined how he might have looked plastered in the liquid rust and knots of brain that had once carried the suspected killer's memories. Yet there was nothing to see, no veil of trauma, just his own manic, stretched face staring back at him—a face he struggled to associate with himself. He peered long and hard as if he had become a different kind of being. He felt light-headed, floating in an adrenaline bubble. There was a sense of elation and a roiling despair. The hair-filled cake seemed to have worked its magic, but he had failed to do the deed. He had desperately wanted to keep his promise to his dead brother. He had wanted to be more than a man of words. Yet, when it came down to it, he just could not be that person.

†

No sooner had Jason begun slowly walking down the road to his house when everything suddenly lit up on all sides with flashing blue lights, squad cars fanning out in front and behind him and officers shouting repeated commands for him to lie face down on the ground. He did as he was told, quickly kneeling and then prostrating himself for fear of receiving a Taser or worse. In a trice, he felt his body pinned by flesh and gravity, his pockets searched and his arms pulled back into cuffs. Several neighbours were already peering out from the double-glazed security of their windows, not least Mr Norris. Poppy ran outside in her dressing gown just as Inspector Mosby stepped out from one of the vehicles to take charge.

'Jason!' cried Poppy. She ran towards him, but one of the female officers held her back.

'Please stand back, madam,' she ordered. 'Let us do our job.'

'He is my husband,' Poppy complained. 'He hasn't been right since his brother got killed. What has he done this time?'

'Sorry, we cannot give you any information. Please step back.'

Poppy did as the officer told her while holding up her phone camera to capture everything. She called out to Jason. 'What happened to you?' she cried. 'Are you hurt?'

'Pops!' Jason shouted back. 'I couldn't, I didn't—' But his words were cut off as the circle of officers lifted him onto his feet and walked him to the custody van which had reversed into position.

As he went, Inspector Mosby came up beside him. 'Let me

tell you something,' he began, holding his barely divided thumb and forefinger right in front of Jason's face. 'We were this far from finding out who killed your brother. This far, right, and what do you go and do? Nearly take out our undercover officer, you stupid fu—' Yet Mosby tidied his mouth, aware of the crowd gathering on the pavement and phone cameras raised in the air.

Jason looked at the detective's face and the way he held his mouth tight in disgust, as if about to punch his lights out.

Then Mosby drew close and spoke in a quieter, altogether more restrained voice. 'You think you knew your brother, but I will show you that he was a complete stranger.' Then, he turned to the officers. 'Just get him in the van,' he told them, shoving Jason forward and turning away in despair.

Confused and overwhelmed as the officers forced him into the small mobile jail, Jason wondered whether the police had been involved in Umbie's death. *Can I trust Mosby? Can I trust Ryan? Could I trust anyone now?* The man he nearly decapitated with the train wheels was gambling in the same pub his brother frequented before his death and had a patch missing from his hair. He doubted Mosby would find it easy to explain that away.

'This is madness!' Jason shouted, protesting and pushing back against the officers who subdued him, slamming the van door shut.

Inside, Jason was shouting for all he was worth, his face pressed to the grid of bars, accusing Inspector Mosby and the police of corruption. He suddenly felt suckered by his intended victim's pleading about his children.

'I should have killed him when I had the chance!' he shouted and started kicking out at nothing in the metal box.

31

At Ardinweald Police Station, Jason sat in a small, sparsely furnished, windowless interview room, struggling for answers to the slew of questions from Inspector Mosby. He felt utterly confused about the chain of events surrounding his brother's killing and his own attempts to put things right. Now facing a serious charge of attempted murder of an undercover police officer, he became almost speechless, the opposite of his life as a university lecturer when he would set forth on almost any topic of interest. The chemical yet indeterminate odour further inhibited him. He now sat in alien territory, completely cut off from the comforts and familiarity of his own home. It was as if he were taking his doctoral *viva voce* all over again, but without command of the topic. His brow poured with sweat and the interior of the cuffed fists in his lap grew wet with anxiety.

After a long silence, Inspector Mosby turned on the black, unlit TV screen fixed to the wall. An image of dry grass appeared. Mosby paused the film and set the remote control on the table. Jason looked up at the stilled image.

'So, you think you knew your brother?' began the detective inspector.

Jason swallowed heavily, wondering what he was about to be shown. He did not know how to answer. He suspected that some kind of cover-up was going on. He had begun to learn that he did not know his twin brother as much as he first thought, yet could not bring himself to state this. He gave Umbie the benefit of his increasing doubt, choosing to remain silent.

'Well, I can tell you, Jason, Umbie was far from innocent.'

Jason immediately objected, standing up. 'Don't you ever use that name!' he warned the inspector. 'It is my name for him. I made it up. Only his friends called him that.'

The officer guarding the door moved forward, but Inspector Mosby held up his hand.

'Please, sit back down, Jason. Look,' Mosby continued, 'your brother, Will, was up to no good. He was a criminal. OK? That's the truth and I'll prove it to you.'

'You're lying!' Jason cried.

'I wish I were.' Mosby picked up the remote control.

'You're a fool!' challenged Jason. 'I told you before that he was a blank. He wouldn't hurt anyone.'

Mosby shook his head. 'Well, *technically* you are right about that.'

Jason sat down with the encouragement of the other officer's hands on his shoulders. 'What do you mean?' he asked, puzzled by the detective's remark, but the inspector was in no mood for further talk.

'Right,' he announced with a determined, confident voice and turned to face Jason. 'Watch this.'

Jason shrugged, his left cheek forming a cynical dimple. Inspector Mosby nodded to the officer who moved back in front of the door. Then pointing with the remote control, he defrosted the frozen image.

Suddenly, the camera angle fell away and indistinct images of yellowing grass appeared. Yet, as the camera lifted back into position, the lens caught the serious face of the man almost killed on the railway track.

Jason's jaw dropped.

'Yeah, that's right,' said Inspector Mosby, nodding, glaring at him.

Jason swallowed heavily and placed a hand over his mouth.

'Keep watching!' Mosby insisted.

There was the sound of an engine screaming with effort. Soon enough, a Land Rover became visible, struggling over a knoll, at a slant, kicking up softened grass and proceeding in low gear towards the cadavers. For a few moments, it lost its wheels to the low-lying mist before rising up again onto the higher ground. It did not drive right up to the apparatus, but held back a hundred yards or so, spewing exhaust fumes. It was an old vehicle such that when the engine died, it juddered and faltered before falling silent.

Three men got out. All wore combat gear and balaclavas. All were tall and brawny. They clotted together talking, a ball of steam rising from their combined mouths. They were laughing and slapping each other's broad shoulders before dispersing. Jason was puzzled as to why they were laughing so much in the company of the hanging dead. One of them was removing his tan leather gloves.

'Right,' he said. 'Let's get this show on the road.'

The camera zoomed in again, moving slowly but jerkily between the dead bodies. The shaky footage stopped first on the gnarled face of a man with fists clenched at his chin. Then the camera shifted to the old woman. Her bare chest remained in frame for a second or two before the camera rose for a close-up shot of the bolt attached to her skull. The thread of the bolt itself was clearly visible.

Jason watched the compelling images, his head wobbling slightly as if he were finding a place in his brain for the images to settle. Inspector Mosby was watching him instead of the screen. He had seen the film many times.

'What the hell's going on?' Jason asked.

'Just keep watching,' he told him.

The man who had been wearing gloves returned to the vehicle and took out two small spades, handing them to the others before lifting out a black metal box. Then they all crossed the damp, stooping grass to the hanging bodies. The camera tracked them, sometimes zooming in and out inconsistently. For a moment, Jason sensed the people on film were going to dig shallow graves for the people they had murdered. Yet he was surprised when they removed small, round objects from the box. The camera adjusted its focus and trained on one of the men, bending down and digging beneath the leftmost corpse. The other man did the same, though more slowly and a little deeper into the soil. Then the first man went round and dug a final hole beneath the female cadaver. The man without gloves then genuflected beneath the first corpse and planted something in the ground. He moved to the next and did the same. Finally, he pushed the woman's feet to one side and buried another object in the soil.

†

The video continued, and Jason kept watching, bewildered, as the three men sauntered back to the Land Rover, laughing and joking. He watched as the man without gloves threw the empty box into the back of the vehicle and retrieved what looked like some kind of transmitter. Now Jason was squinting, leaning forward with his elbows on his knees, his cuffed wrists under his chin. All this time, he felt the stare of Inspector Mosby and wondered what more the film would reveal. He questioned his own grasp of reality, its complexity, and his own vaunted powers of amateur detection.

Jason watched, transfixed, as the man with the transmitter waved everyone away behind the vehicle and some distance from the strange contraption and hanging bodies. Then, after a long delay in which nothing happened, a bright flash and almighty explosion ripped through the air. When the covert camera regained its focus, the first of the corpses reappeared, swaying and twisting in spectacular fashion, with mere ribbons of flesh below both knees. The boots it had been wearing had gone. Then there was a second flash and booming explosion, making the corpse in the middle of the contraption spring to life like a manic puppet before the veil of earth and smoke dissipated to reveal only one leg intact. The camera zoomed in on the limp body and the blue anchor tattoo on one of its knuckles. A final flash and blast sent the female corpse in a mad jig, her one leg bending back at a perverse angle. Yet, this time, the legs and boots remained attached. Then the film suddenly went dark.

Jason sat looking at the black screen for several seconds of mute wonder and shock. He seemed to be having a little conversation with himself before growing aware of his surroundings. Frowning heavily, he looked across at Inspector Mosby for an explanation.

'Illegal military testing,' Mosby informed him pithily, bringing his lips up to a point under his nose and scratching his head.

He grimaced with anticipated conflict and, drawing his hand down over his mouth, stroked his chin and then his neck. Here his fingers pinched a fold of skin and he sighed heavily. He raised his eyebrows and closed his mouth firmly before opening it again. There were several false starts before he could speak.

When he did so, he was blunt and to the point. 'We think Umbie was part of a scam selling corpses to the military for secret testing of anti-mine footwear.'

Jason's eyes opened wide and then his mouth. 'What the hell are you on about?' he cried, jumping up, profoundly disturbed, the chair falling back onto the floor. 'Are you kidding me?'

The other officer moved closer in case things turned nasty, lifting the chair and getting Jason to sit down again.

'Your brother was involved in procuring bodies.'

'What?'

'He was what we call a body broker, or snatcher, if you prefer.'

Jason's eyebrows were as high as they could go, his eyes staring and his tongue running back and forth along his lower lip before his teeth drew together in resolve. He was deeply perplexed.

'What the fuck! You cannot be serious! Where did you get this film? Umbie would not get involved in this kind of stuff.'

'Calm down,' advised the inspector.

It took Jason a long while to adjust to what he had seen in the footage and stop mumbling obscenities.

'Look, I know all this is hard for you to digest,' said Mosby, 'yet the fact is there was another, much darker side to your brother. It was a part of him that he kept hidden from view.'

'Umbie was not a criminal. He was a good man. As I told you before, he worked in—' A look of horror suddenly crossed Jason's face. The pumping of his blood past the stricture of the cuffs increased. He was experiencing flashbacks of the animated corpses.

'An old people's nursing home,' completed the inspector.

'Yes.' Jason's voice was suddenly light and expiring.

'We suspect that when residents at the nursing home died, Umbie was involved in identifying those without any family. The kind of person that nobody would miss or care for. The bodies were then diverted from the usual council process.'

'My brother was a body—?'

'Broker,' the detective finished, sighing heavily again, placing the remote back on the table. 'At least, that is where the facts point. We think others were involved and we are following leads on this.'

'If this is true, who killed him? And why?'

'That's all guesswork, I'm afraid,' admitted the inspector. 'Perhaps he got greedy? Who knows? He had a good stash of money in different bank accounts. This suggests he was a key player in all of this.'

This was news to Jason. He had always assumed his brother had little in the way of money. After all, he had lost count of the number of drinks he had stood him at The Half Moon.

'What about the military? I mean, how can that kind of thing go on?'

'The investigation is continuing,' Mosby insisted. 'The Ministry of Defence is making no comment. We are facing deniability.'

'Fucking hell.'

If all that Mosby told him was true and not some carefully concocted lie, he never knew his twin brother. His brother of all those years was not who he appeared to be. If it was true, he had nearly beheaded an innocent man. As he mulled over all the implications, not least how anybody could be trusted, his own fate came into question. *How long will I go to jail for?* The thought unnerved him. He dreaded what Poppy and his mother would do. *Will they disown me?*

With these thoughts, Jason's psyche rallied to defend itself. He tried to convince himself that Mosby had everything jumbled. He nodded to instil confidence in his own deduction that the police were spinning some elaborate lie about his brother. *There is some kind of conspiracy. After all, the man I almost killed had a clump of hair missing. He was the killer all right!* Jason recalled how the man had frozen when he mentioned Umbie's name. Yet he was the man behind the camera in the film. Was he really an undercover cop? It all seemed so cleverly orchestrated and unreal.

'Selling dead bodies to the military?' Jason scoffed, shaking his head, incredulous. 'Umbie wouldn't have done such a thing. He cared for the people at the home. Everyone says so.'

'Then you delude yourself,' insisted the inspector.

Jason felt his mind shrink to a pinprick and expand again, seeing the so-called undercover police officer's head on the track, the heavy metal wheels approaching in a blur. As his mind filled with the phantom image of a disarticulated brain spewing forth, Jason imagined the response of his intended victim's children: "Where's my daddy?" and "I want my daddy!".

Suddenly, Jason was up on his feet again, wordless. He was looking around the interview room, his eyes flitting, jerking and darting this way and that. He saw the serious, sour expression on the inspector's face, but he could not take it in. Inspector Mosby was talking to Jason, but he was *absent*. It was late morning, and his mind had begun to close itself down, his thoughts turning in ever-decreasing, isolating orbits. Spasms and flashes of acute realisation of what his brother may have done afflicted him. He thought again about the corpses performing the maddest, undignified dances. *Were Harry or those other lonely residents that Umbie had comforted among them? How could my brother be involved in such a macabre scheme?* Now Jason began to grunt and retch, but his stomach was empty. He began to shout out. His speaking machine groaned and then, with an astonishing shift in pitch, suddenly unleashed an inhuman, howling of grief and shock from his cavernous mouth.

'Interview terminated 09:00 hours,' said Mosby into the recorder. 'Right, let's have him back in his cell.'

†

On the other side of Ardinweald, Darren McCartie slipped through the rear entrance to the family business and began to prepare for the day's trade by hanging the fake pigs in the window. His wife was scolding him already as she put on her apron and started to mince the beef. She resented the amount of time he spent at The Sow's Ear and being out all hours. She had grown lonely with his inattention and tired of the daily grind of their business. Darren appeared not the least bit interested in addressing the dwindling numbers that came through the door. Most of their loyal Ardonian customers were elderly, desperate for chitchat with their purchases.

'Everyone's going to the supermarkets or online these days,' she shouted, as she shoved another chunk of meat through the mincer. 'We need to change.'

Yet Darren was not listening. He was pushing his way between the carcasses in the walk-in cold room. At the rear of the icy compartment, with one eye over his broad shoulder, he took out from the ribcage of a lamb the Walther PKK pistol he had wrapped in a sealed freezer bag. He checked it was in good order and rubbed a finger over his nickname before returning it to its hiding place. Then he removed a bag stuffed with banknotes, making sure his stash had remained unchanged.

'You're taking your time in there,' his wife complained. 'We need to open up.'

Darren quickly counted through the money and stuck it back next to the gun in the suspended carcass, satisfied that none was missing. He trusted no one, not even his wife. At any time, one of the domino gang might double-cross him, just as Umbie Hemp had done. Then he closed the cold room with the heel of his foot and gathered up the various trays of meat for display. He took the produce through into the shop, ignoring Mrs McCartie's wittering, and began to complete the preparations for opening. Tying a red-striped apron around his formidable body and setting a fresh white hat on his small head, he placed five fresh rabbits that Danny the gravedigger had bagged with his shotgun on hooks by the door and sprinkled sawdust at the entrance.

'Don't forget the pheasants,' his wife reminded him.

'I'm on it,' he said, going out to the yard to open up the van with its broken logo: "AR—CHER".

He studied the blistered paint and rust. As soon as he had enough money, he promised himself a new van. Then he would get a sign writer to paint in gold and black: "McCARTIE'S, FAMILY BUTCHER—Quality meat, poultry and game—Est. 1954".

When Darren went back inside, thinking of his father who had started the business all those years ago, his wife was opening the shop door and greeting the usual, small number of early birds. He moved past them, engaging in a bit of banter, and tied up the pheasants. The pheasants and rabbits were a curiosity as much as anything, enticing custom for everything else in the shop, not least their award-winning pork pies. From the street, Darren checked all the displays, catching his reflection in the glass. He held up his chin, pulled the tip of his nose downward on his small skull in the vain hope of lengthening it, and headed back inside and behind the counter.

'Morning!' he shouted in a loud, barrow-boy voice. 'What can I get you? We have some lovely steak just in. What was that? A pound of best mince? Right, you are!'

†

Ryan followed Gerry away from the vehicles, through a stile and out into the dark fields leading up to the Ministry of Defence's land. No one else was around. The grass was long and brushed their knuckles as they went. Once or twice, Ryan looked over his shoulder, but no one was following them. He felt unnerved. What did Gerry want? Why did he want to talk out here? Ryan feared he might be about to get a beating, expecting a welcoming party of military personnel to appear suddenly from the blackness. Yet Ryan could do nothing other than match Gerry's heels and torchlight. If Gerry wanted to talk to him in the middle of the lake, never mind in this quiet Nottinghamshire countryside at night, far from prying eyes, then Ryan had little choice but to go along with it. In the rural silence, he heard each rubbery squeak of his throat as he swallowed back his fear, and with his hands lifted in front of him to fend off any attacker, he fell back a little to give himself the space to turn and run away, knowing deep down that even that would be useless.

After fifteen minutes of walking, Gerry turned off the bobbing beam of light and the darkness fell in around them. Ryan strained his eyes to descry the outline of the man he rightly feared. There was no moonlight for comfort. The blackness accentuated the soundscape.

Ryan listened to his own breathing settling down as his pupils widened to bring the figure of Gerry into his brain. After a while, in the silence, he saw that the soldier was facing him, hands in pockets.

'We have a problem,' Gerry said finally.

Ryan moistened his dry throat. 'What kind of problem?'

'We think the police are onto us.'

There was a stunned pause before a panicked Ryan responded. 'Shit! You're joking, right?'

'Do I sound as if I'm joking?'

His vowels were as tight as Ryan had ever known them, like little grenades primed to go off in the darkness surrounding them.

'No, of course not. Sorry.'

'That attempt to sort the undercover guy has increased police interest.' Gerry remained silent for a long time before speaking again. 'I don't know how much they know, but they are onto us. We need a solution. Before things get out of hand.'

'What do you suggest?'

'The mop and bucket,' said Gerry.

32

Dr Bent sat at his desk in his apartment at Foston Hall, staring out of the window. He had been working on yet another editorial for the *British Journal of Psychiatry* about the development of compassionate environments in forensic hospital settings. He had lost count of the papers he had written in this area, but the current article felt particularly important. It revisited the thesis of his book *The New Asylum*. It described what his staff referred to as his *wonders*—the humane facilities he created for those people with serious mental health disorders who posed a danger to others or themselves and required long-term incarceration. At the heart of this work, he described the importance of accessing nature when held in secure and otherwise forbidding settings such as Foston Hall. Yet, as he lifted his fingers over the keyboard to progress with concluding remarks, he had a sudden failure of energy and imagination, caused by the unbidden and frequent recollection of the man who used to be his father.

At such times, Dr Bent felt jolted, as if from electro-convulsive therapy that did not wipe out bad memories but installed them instead. He revisited the consequences of bringing the historical case of family abuse to the courtroom. He remembered how his mother reacted to the news, succumbing in her grief and shame and admitting before she died that she had looked the other way. "I always told him that he was getting too close to the children," she confessed when Dr Bent visited her for the last time in the retirement home after the police arrested his father. Her frail body had slowly curled up in the chair until her head rested on her knees. Her comment before dying a week later still haunted him, threatening the fragile state of his identity. Despite his expertise in the human brain and its functioning, he struggled to get beyond the devastation of trust it provoked. After all, if one cannot trust a father *and* a mother, or a past with them in it, the notions of *home* and *roots* disappear. The mind becomes a battleground like no other.

After his mother had died and before the court case, Dr Bent faced even more losses of trust. He endured the desertion of his siblings for bringing the gross events to light so late in the day, for destroying the fantasy of a close family and even blaming him for the death of their mother. They left him to attend court alone and without support. Afterwards, and astonishingly, they chose to visit and comfort their father in jail rather than their victim brother. They overlooked their own victimhood—with each of them having had raspberries blown on their little bodies—deeming the head of the family mentally unwell and deserving of support. Worse still, they marked the grave of his parents "So Dearly Beloved". Dr Bent's arguments about mental capacity were lost to the wind. This last great abandonment was perhaps the engine house of profound bouts of his depression even more than the knowledge that the man and woman who made him were now complete strangers.

As he looked out over Foston Hall, with its high black fence, he tried to get his thoughts back on task, yet failed. Pushing the laptop away, he sunk into his chair, shaking his head and blowing out with all the sadness of a deflating balloon. Slowly, lethargically, he transferred to the black leather couch, clearing a space, removing a stack of complimentary copies of his book, and lay down on his side, wishing for oblivion. He stared at the glass cabinet against the far wall, full of old medical instruments he had collected over the years: endoscopes like dry, uncoiled snakes, early stethoscopes, forceps and scarifiers. As he lay there, he felt the chill of his patently single life.

Without a companion and a family to call his own, he felt vulnerable to the weather system of his thoughts. He did not relish yet another long evening of lassitude and dullness. Yet he lay still on the couch for a very long time, unsleeping in the fading light and only moving once to unclip his detachable hairpiece. It was quite late when he finally surfaced from the vortex of his past and sat up again. The usual torpor was setting in and he knew he had to act, do something, anything, to avoid spiralling downwards. He reached out and took the keys to his bike from the little bowl on the coffee table.

There was no chicken strip around Dr Bent's tyres to show brave cornering. The Harley stood up too much for that kind of manoeuvre and the hero blob that sparked on the ground was too prominent anyway. Yet, with his headlight burning a hole into the dark and with suddenly luminous rabbits frozen at the roadside, Dr Bent tested his nerve to the limit. Doing a ton up on a straight country lane at night was like making an incision. It had to be perfect. With the speed, his cheeks hurt and even his gloved hands started to grow numb. Despite this, behind the goggles, his eyes were alive, fixed and wide. With each bump and dip in the road's surface, his stomach and heart floated free for a delightful yet questioning moment. *Should I stay on or fall off?*

Dr Bent's existential indecision on life or death continued for more than an hour as he tore across the Nottinghamshire countryside, going further than usual, circling and revisiting its emptiness. All the time, he was thinking of the abandonment by his brothers and sisters. In the internal theatre of his psychology, he reviewed all that had occurred. He imagined them visiting the special wing of Stafford Jail at the weekend, giving their love and attention to the man they still held up as their father. He pictured the old man's duplicitous, easy banter on seeing them and knew they would never be able to uproot their loyalty. He had loved them so hard and for so long they could not sever the ties despite his behaviour. Dr Bent's sisters, Margo and Lisa, had received the greatest attention and fuss.

They normalised the blown raspberries and rationalised their father's passions as the peccadilloes of a compromised mind. Colin and Neil struggled to accept the theft of trust, but did not wish to lose contact with their sisters. There, the family split and into the crack fell the eldest of the brood, left to wonder if he would ever see his siblings again, a thought that made his heart twist.

Once again, Dr Bent opened the throttle, speeding through another tunnel of dark hedges and trees towards an unknown horizon. He slowed down when a burst of headlights dipped and came into view, tears gathering in the bottom of his goggles and threatening to blur his vision. He stopped and wiped them before continuing his solitary fairground ride.

Eventually, he came to familiar roads in and around Foston Hall and settled down on the throttle, disappointed that his high-speed and unpredictable journey had not had its usual mood-busting effect. Yet, all the same, he raced along a final stretch, with the hospital and its lights in view across the fields, tearing towards the next turn in the road.

Should I stay on or fall off?

Stay on, came the reply deep in his helmet-doubled skull.

He took the bend at speed, his icy cold cheeks bulging downwards, before easing up as he approached the entrance to Foston Hall. No sooner had he entered the grounds than his phone rang and he pulled over to answer it. He removed his gloves, took the phone from his jacket pocket and looked at the screen held in one hand while revving the engine with the other out of habit.

†

On the far side of Ardinweald, Inspector Mosby watched Dr Bent enter the police station yard on his black-and-chrome Harley, the bike's engine rumbling *potato-potato-potato*. Mosby rolled his eyes for the benefit of the duty sergeant and they both tracked the psychiatrist's slow progress towards the main entrance. Dr Bent appeared tired with his head lower than usual, listlessly carrying his canvas bag. Mosby wanted to rub Dr Bent's nose in the mess of Jason Hemp. After all, if he had not been so liberal, the undercover police officer would not have suffered his ordeal at the railway track, Jason would still be in hospital and the murderer more than likely banged up. Mosby began formulating what he wanted to say to the doctor. He wanted him to see the fruit of his soft, humane approach. In cuffs, with saliva on his chin, Jason sat in the holding room off the main foyer, looking completely spent and damaged beyond repair. A shadow of his former self, almost catatonic with the shock of his own behaviour and the assault of new, disturbing information about his brother, he kept up a constant moaning, rocking back and forth on the bench.

'He's not your usual quack,' said the duty sergeant as the psychiatrist approached the door.

'You can say that again.'

'That's some machine. They must be paying him well at Foston Hall.'

'Too well,' said Mosby bitterly.

Inspector Mosby turned to look into the holding room and considered the possibility that Jason was faking a mental breakdown. The inspector's experience over the years had kept him alert to the possibility of defendants feigning psychic collapse to avoid blame for their crimes and slip jail. Whilst Jason appeared to be in mental free fall, it was not necessarily the case. However, the inspector also knew that his misguided acts of revenge were far from normal. Jason's obsession with the attacker's hair, the episode in the shopping mall, the attack on the university student and the near decapitation of one of his undercover officers revealed an unpredictable and dangerous mind. It was ultimately for the courts to determine what to do with the spent lecturer, yet Inspector Mosby knew that one way or another the amateur sleuth would be out of circulation for a long time.

Soon enough, Inspector Mosby and the duty sergeant heard the distinctive clomping of Dr Bent's gothic boots as he entered the building. His pace was less forthright than usual, as if reluctant to conduct an assessment. The detective inspector felt a little smug that the psychiatrist had failed to listen to his warning that Jason was a danger to himself and others. As Dr Bent approached the desk, Inspector Mosby ran his fingers through his short, parted hair and stroked the half-butterfly of his birthmark.

'Thanks for coming over so quickly, Dr Bent,' he said breezily. 'As you know, Jason Hemp is beyond court diversion, yet his mental state is a concern. He may be a malingerer, of course, but you are the expert. He's over there in the holding room.'

†

Dr Bent entered the holding room with his kitbag slung over his shoulder. He felt particularly crestfallen to learn what had *so nearly* happened. Jason had put his freedom in great jeopardy and his mind under extreme duress. Placing his canvas bag on the free part of the bench, Dr Bent sat across from him, near the door. He observed him closely. Jason looked like a tormented figure, with his head down, rocking back and forth with his hands between his knees. Now and then, a paroxysm took hold of his whole body, the low moaning from his throat rising in pitch before falling again. His metronomic movement continued. Dr Bent noted the reddened flesh around the cuffs on his wrists and the matted hair over his ears, empathising with the former lecturer who had lost so much. Jason did not even clock that Dr Bent was in the room, clearly isolated in his own awful bubble.

Inspector Mosby put his head around the door. 'Are you going to give him something?' he asked.

'Please, can I take a look at him first?' Dr Bent said, irritated, raising both palms.

The detective inspector left him to it, closing the door noisily behind him.

Then Dr Bent turned back to his likely future patient and spoke gently, courteously. 'Jason? Jason? Can you hear me? It's Dr Bent.' The psychiatrist's tail of hair swung forward.

After a long delay, Jason's eyes rolled upward, blinking, mouth loosely open, his eyes revealing him lost. Yet the flicker of recognition was there, and he slowly mouthed something. Dr Bent could not hear and leaned forward, his elbows on his leather-covered knees, turning his better ear towards Jason who was licking his dry lips, working up the architecture of his voice. The wrinkles on Dr Bent's knit brow deformed the scar tissue of his cheek as he waited for Jason's response. It dawned on him what a shambles he had made of things. He should have kept Jason longer at the hospital and not discharged him so early. Now, with the incident on the rail track, it was likely that the former lecturer would end up detained for an indefinite length of time, probably at Foston Hall.

Jason's mouth opened, closed and opened again, listlessly.

'I don't want an injection,' he finally mumbled.

Dr Bent tried to reassure him. 'That is not necessary just now,' he said, careful not to promise too much.

Jason's head dipped again, and he continued rocking his body back and forth before slipping down off the hard metal bench and lying down on the floor, curled up in a ball, still in cuffs.

It was obvious that Jason was suffering stress from his current situation, and his maladaptive grieving and impulsiveness about killing the perpetrator had brought him into the category of "dangerous personality". Dr Bent was unconvinced by Inspector Mosby's charge that Jason was doing "Hamlet's trick" by feigning madness. The psychiatrist thought about the irony of this association, given Jason's profession, and recalled the famous line from Polonius concluding that the young prince was pretending to be unhinged: "*Though this be madness, yet there is method in't*".

He knew it was possible that the reality of nearly decapitating a police officer could be driving Jason to escape the penalty of the law by malingering. Psychiatry had always faced the difficulty of discriminating between people who were genuinely ill and the few who feigned it. Dr Bent had even suspected a few patients at Foston Hall of doing just that. Yet here was someone who had fallen a very long way indeed, and there was every reason to suspect his mind had been assaulted by the trauma of his brother's murder. More tellingly, he had endured deeper losses. He had not only lost his brother in the physical sense, but also the knowledge and memory of who that brother was. Worse still, his brother was his twin, an integral part of Jason's own identity.

Inspector Mosby popped his head around the door for a second time.

'I'm afraid we haven't got all day,' he complained, looking at his watch. 'If you can just give him something to calm him down, that would be great.'

Dr Bent gave Inspector Mosby a blunt, dismissive look that sent him back out through the door and to the duty sergeant's desk. Then he returned to his assessment.

What he saw before him was a man in unbounded defeat. The reality of Jason's losses had been too much and this was the result. Where once had stood a proud, capable university lecturer and dependable husband, there was now a rag of a man with spittle hanging from the side of his mouth, somatising in spasms and contortions, successively turning his spine into an exclamation point or a question mark. Dr Bent began to mull over what he had learned about the psychology of twins. He recalled an early paper on what happens to the survivor when one of them dies. As he made links and connections, he suspected that a particular kind of intervention might work just as well as any sedative, at least in the short term. That said, he knew the detective inspector would find his approach more shocking than any grisly crime scene.

As Inspector Mosby looked on through the safety glass of the holding room, the psychiatrist took off his heavy boots and got down on the floor with Jason. No sooner had he lain next to him than a freakish wrestling match began. With his hair swishing around like a snake behind him, Dr Bent struggled to keep hold of Jason as he twisted one way then the other, sweating profusely and breathing hard. Jason was wailing now in the knot of legs and arms. Yet the bonding quickly worked, and Jason's writhing body began to slow down and a womblike stillness occurred, so suddenly that when Inspector Mosby and the desk sergeant entered, there was nothing to do. There, lying in the middle of the holding room, were the eminent psychiatrist and the broken lecturer with their arms around each other.

Dr Bent indicated to Inspector Mosby that there was no need to intervene.

'You're not alone,' Dr Bent told Jason.

As he said this, he reached up and touched his patient's cheek in a tender, gentle way with the side of his silver-ringed thumb. It was not a random act. It was as clinical as any well-placed needle. The psychiatrist knew that touch was the most powerful of the senses and that it began in the womb. He understood that the first part of an embryo's flesh to develop sensitivity was its cheeks. Yet, more than this, Dr Bent recognised that the sense of touch was all the more significant for twins. As soon as their eyes open in the womb, they have no trouble finding each other's faces or even holding hands. It is here that a special bond forms and two become one. Dr Bent also knew that when all this stops, when a lifelong companionship evaporates, a lone twin always struggles.

Now, in the arms of the psychiatrist, Jason's eyes opened as if for the first time. His eyelids moved apart and the holding room light caught in his dark, rosary-bead eyes. Gradually they focused on the scar on Dr Bent's left cheek. Then they shifted upwards in little notches of movement to the psychiatrist's deep blue eyes. This time, the alienist did not look away. His gaze was steady, humane and compassionate. What Jason did not see was what Dr Bent knew: that their lives were about to intertwine much more closely, most likely for a very long time.

33

The headless angel, its arms outstretched and its garment sculpted to suggest a blow of heavenly wind, overlooked Danny the gravedigger. All was quiet. Not one brambling sang. Only the hum of cars lifted vaguely into the cemetery air as he set his feet carefully on a plank of wood garnished with plastic grass. He looked down at the polished coffin and began scooping earth into the hole. As each clod fell, it drummed mercilessly against the wood. It was heavy work due to the recent downpour and his brow filmed with sweat. Several times, he wiped it away with his gnawed, yellowed fingers, leaving stripes of mud over his rheumy eyes. He had three more burials to do after this one and he began to curse the absence of the two younger gravediggers. They had both resigned that morning, complaining of the meagre pay without the free accommodation that Danny enjoyed at the lodge. Yet Danny suspected these were not the true reasons for their departure.

Danny wanted to be in The Sow's Ear with a glass of ale in his hand instead of the worn handle of the spade. He wanted to be anywhere except over this grave in his broken-laced boots with a cheap cigarette hanging from his lip. He scowled at the sugary wreaths marked "Daddy", "Dear Son" and "Loving Husband". Looking around to make sure no one was about, he hoofed the flowers into the half-filled hole, quickly covering them over with earth. As he did so, a sudden wind struck up and knocked him sideways, making him dance along the edge of the grave, his arms outstretched for balance, the artificial grass giving way. He just about managed to keep upright. He had never fallen into one of his own holes and he was not about to start now. He kept his back straight and held his footing, but his head felt suddenly cool and light as his hat tumbled away into the grave.

He quickly filled half of the rest of the grave so he could step down more easily to pick it up, sinking into the cloying soil as he went. There was no one to see the patch of damaged hair exposed at the top of his head. Danny was glad that it had started to grow back and was less noticeable with each passing week. Briefly dabbing at it with his cracked fingers, he picked up the hat and squeezed the felt over his head. Then, with a contemptuous spit of phlegm into the mud, he clambered out of the damp, oblong emptiness and quickly filled it.

When he finished, Danny stood motionless for some time, looking out over the prickle of white headstones and down into Ardinweald Park. He was tired of his work. He did not want to spend one more day lifting his eyes to mourners with their endless requests for tin vases, directions to the water pipe or access to the old grave map at the lodge. He also began cursing the day he took up playing dominoes, falling in with Will Hemp and Jim Ryan and their scheme of selling "nobodies" to the army. It all seemed so simple, so easy. It did no harm, they argued. It was military service for the dead. Danny had access to temporary storage in the cemetery after all and no one had suspected anything. Besides, he needed the money to pay off his gambling debts. Then Will Hemp got greedy, cheating his way to a bigger cut of the money. Danny shook his head, lit up another cigarette and blew the smoke defiantly up at the curdled sky.

He took a moment to inspect the inky dirt around the tips of his fingers, reminding him of his status in the world: gravedigger. It did not matter how often he scrubbed his hands, the grime did not go away. The grubbiness irritated him as he had always hoped for better, cleaner work. He drew his knife from his jacket to clean them, running the tip under each one, knowing that it would not make a difference. When he finished, he slipped the knife back into his pocket and picked up his spade and shotgun that lay draped in an oily cloth, ready to bag the odd rabbit or racing pigeon. Standing with one foot on the most recently dead man's mound, he could see the small gathering of people and baskets in the park below and wanted to get into position behind the observatory ruins. Ardinweald Park was a regular liberation site of the Royal Pigeon Racing Association and the birds often flew directly over the cemetery. Danny would make sure that at least one more would never get home.

†

Jason stared out of the window of the prison van on the long drive that led up to Foston Hall. The first thing that struck him was the high, doubled, black fences and the dreary redbrick buildings that hovered behind them, interspersed by newer constructions. Found guilty of attempted murder with diminished responsibility, he received an indefinite hospital order. Dr Bent had attended court, supporting Poppy and providing a moving account of the magnitude of the insult that Jason had received in the violent death of his twin brother. His expert report convinced the judge that a longer period of assessment and psychological interventions in a high-security hospital setting would likely return him to more normal, predictable behaviour. He argued that his condition deserved a clinical response, a real chance of recovery, of restoration, while at the same time, given the calamitous nature of the near decapitation, ensuring public safety. He hoped Jason's aggravated and misplaced grieving would subside and allow for a speedy transfer in time to a less secure setting.

As Jason approached the main entrance to the facility, sweat gathered in the dent of his skull and his fingers trembled. He wondered if Dr Bent would be there to greet him. He feared the *indefiniteness* of the hospital order. *How long will they hold me here? Will they throw away the key?* Yet Jason felt relieved that he was not heading into the city's jail, HMP Sherwood. He had heard such bad things about the place, overrun with drugs and casual daily violence. The knowledge that Dr Bent was the medical director at the institution also brought some comfort to Jason. After all, the psychiatrist had shown great sensitivity towards him. Even so, escorted in cuffs to the main reception area, Jason swallowed heavily, his clothes damp from fearful sweat. In the few last steps before going through a sliding door, he tried to get his bearings and sip the free air.

Inside the reception area, everything was bright and modern with a little café for visitors. There was a busy administration office behind a large, glass partition and on the far side of the extensive dark blue floor space, the same kind of security area found in airports.

'Hello,' said a young Asian woman. 'I am Dr Alice Wang, welcome to Foston Hall. I am your psychologist. Let us get you checked in.' She palmed him towards a comfortable seat in front of a swish desk while the escort officers slipped into the background.

For a moment, Jason felt like he had just walked into a hotel or bank instead of a secure hospital. The young woman was remarkably friendly, even giving Jason a genuine rather than perfunctory smile. Jason shook his head a little, puzzled by this.

'OK,' she said, 'if you do not mind, we will just take your picture. We do this for all patients.' She moved a white screen behind him. 'If you could just look at me,' she asked, holding a camera.

Jason sat up straight and looked ahead.

Dr Wang checked the image. 'Yes, that's fine. Now we already have all your transfer details from the court and as soon as you go through security and get those cuffs off, we will take you to your accommodation.'

'Accommodation?'

'Yes,' said Dr Wang.

'It just doesn't sound like a high-security hospital,' Jason admitted.

'Exactly,' said the psychologist. 'That is what we try to avoid here, sounding like one. It is all part of—' Dr Wang paused, deciding it best to leave the new patient to learn about the facility's new ethos in his own time.

'I must say, I am pleasantly surprised. I did not expect this kind of reception,' he said, relieved that he was not in the shabby, overcrowded local prison.

'Great, that is what we like to hear! It is a hospital after all.'

'Can I ask something?'

'Sure.'

'Is there a library here?'

'Yes,' Dr Wang confirmed. 'There are very good resources here at Foston Hall. The library is in the oldest part of the hospital and well stocked with over six thousand books. I gather from your notes that you are a writer.'

Jason nodded reluctantly.

'It says here, you wrote *Reading Emotion in the Renaissance*. That is impressive. And a novel too?'

'Let's not talk about that. I am more of an academic,' Jason told her, with a fragile smile. 'But even then, not really an academic now.'

'*Reading Emotion in the Renaissance* sounds like an important topic,' said Dr Wang. 'I will have to read it.'

Jason dismissed the idea. 'It sounds more psychology than it really is. Although my later work was all on how reading can—'

'Yes?'

'Well, improve mood.'

'Ah great, that sounds fascinating.'

'Well, that's all gone now, something I did in the past.'

Dr Wang sympathised with his position and let the topic lie, focusing on the remaining checklist items about his possessions, general health and family contact details. As he sat, his cuffed arms resting on his thighs and answering as best he could, his mind turned to Poppy. *How is she? Is she thinking about me? Will she visit me here?* He visualised the house with the dusty Volvo outside and tried to spirit her body into the tiny theatre of his skull. Yet she would not appear for him. However much he tried, she eluded him and turned fuzzy. He strained for her features, but they would not draw together into a face. He focused on tiny details—the mole on the inside of her leg, the pink of her nails, the philtrum of her nose—yet even these would not manifest themselves. He felt suddenly and painfully abandoned by his mind.

Once Dr Wang completed the standard online information sheet, she invited Jason to head over to the security area before entering the main hospital and transferring to his accommodation.

It was at this point that the atrium filled with a distinctive clomping sound. Jason recognised the footfall immediately and turned in his chair, catching Dr Bent's clear radio voice as he chatted to the staff in the café.

'No, thank you,' he told them, declining a coffee. 'I am already up to operating pressure!'

Now Jason relaxed a little more. He trusted the psychiatrist and sensed that he really cared about him. He had not forgotten his unorthodox and compassionate treatment at the police station. Dr Bent spotted him.

'Jason,' he said, heading over and smiling warmly, lightly touching his shoulder. His smile crinkled at the corners of his blue eyes. 'Good to see you!'

Jason caught the fruity, bike scent and followed the psychiatrist's gaze to the half-empty bin bag on the desk. He did not know quite what to say. Dr Bent's breezy greeting made him feel he was visiting a country house run by the National Trust when really he felt like a vagrant.

'I will leave you in the capable hands of Dr Wang. She will help you settle during your assessment here. How are you feeling?' Dr Bent's eye contact flitted away as he waited for Jason's response, pulling at one of the rings in his ear.

'I don't really know to be honest,' he confessed, facing another dismal chapter in his life.

Dr Bent's face tightened and nodded as he pressed his lips together. 'Well, that is to be expected,' he said. Then he turned to Dr Wang. 'Alice, are you ready to go through onto campus?'

'Campus?' asked Jason, surprised by the use of such a familiar term in a secure hospital.

'Ah, yes,' said Dr Bent. 'We prefer this to words like *grounds* or *site*. More colourful and positive. I hope you agree.'

'Absolutely,' chimed Jason. 'A different kind of university?'

'Exactly,' Dr Bent underlined, smiling warmly. 'We do not underestimate the power of language here. As a doctor of philosophy, no doubt you will appreciate this more than many.'

'Yes, I do,' said Jason his voice softening, feeling comforted.

'Excellent, now try not to worry,' the psychiatrist said. 'We will do our very best for you while you are with us. OK?' With that, Dr Bent joined Dr Wang in guiding him over to have his biometric fingerprints taken and to proceed through the security scanners.

†

The bramblings had long gone and the cemetery was hot in the first real sunshine that year. Danny the gravedigger was working alone. With his hat tilted back on his head and a fag dangling at his dry lip, he shovelled the earth back over his shoulder. He stopped to gather up the sleeves of his shirt and fathom the depth he needed to dig. It was always awkward with "family stacks" like this one. There were already three coffins in this particular plot and he tried to gauge how far he could drive the spade short of the "penthouse".

He miscalculated and drew back, wincing as the wood cracked. He hated orthopaedic sounds.

'Shite,' he growled, pulling the nub from his lip and flicking it away. He climbed out of the shallow hole and covered the split coffin until it disappeared from view again. 'That is about the closest you'll get to a fucking resurrection,' he muttered. 'And you'll have a big fat bastard right on top of you before long.' Danny caught himself. 'Jesus, I'm talking to myself again!'

Danny looked around, took off his hat, threw it to one side and combed through his sweaty hair with both hands. He lit another cigarette, taking a few quick puffs and then slowed down, focusing his eyes on the park. There was no pigeon racing today and he had gone nearly a week now without using his gun. It lay under the oily cloth next to the rolls of artificial grass and he was tempted to take a few potshots at the gravestones in the same way that he used to shoot ducks at the fairground when he was a young man back in Dublin. Yet he did not like the spit of lead onto granite, and besides, it was a waste of cartridges. Instead, he got back to work, setting the planks along the sides of the hole and unfurling the plastic grass over them. He tidied each piece with his boot then looked to head back to the lodge for a brew before the funeral cortege arrived.

Danny bent down to lift the spade and the gun from the ground. Something moved. He froze, still crouched over, with only his eyes lifting, then narrowing and studying the clumped and long grass at the back of the cemetery. All went suddenly quiet and the air shushed through his alert, flared nostrils. There it was again. Then Danny's face brightened as he caught sight of a rabbit, lean, tight, nervous, sitting up on its back legs, ears pricked. Slowly, the gravedigger put down his spade on the mound of clay and gently shook the oily cloth from his gun. He rarely missed the chance to bag a few rabbits, pheasants or pigeons for McCartie.

Danny's eyes were firmly on the rabbit. It hopped in the

lush, untrodden grass, occasionally stopping to test the air. The gravedigger went slowly for his gun, in little increments of descent. Now he was lifting it in slow motion, the butt onto his firm shoulder, the metal against his cheek, the dirt-grained finger at the trigger, his eye lining up the shot. As his finger began its deadly curl, the rabbit looked directly at him, yet there was no expression that it perceived the threat. Then Danny heard the click of a safety catch. It felt as if the noise came from within his skull. Suddenly aware that now he had become the rabbit, he turned as quickly as he could. He saw the Walther PKK, the fist gripping it, the arm and then the face.

'Dazzl—'

34

Jason found himself allocated to Redwood Block, one of four residential structures within the grounds of Foston Hall. The windows of each block faced into the hospital campus. Designed like abstracted horseshoes, these buildings divided into three wings comprising six segregated *houses*, with ten patients in each. Shortly after arriving through the card-release security doors into his allocated *house*, Dr Wang introduced him to his named nurse, Milly Palmer, and then briefly to the other patients who were sitting around in a kind of small day room. One or two acknowledged him as Dr Wang showed him through to his own small, safely furnished room and allowed him time to settle in. Throughout the rest of the day, Dr Wang and the other staff attached to Jason's *house* provided a steady induction into the rules and schedule of assessments and activities. It was all so overwhelming that when Jason finished eating a plain chicken dinner provided by the hospital kitchens, he took to the privacy of his room and stood for a long time looking out of the thick window, with its internally secure blinds, at the other blocks called Cedar, Pine and Oak across an expanse of bland grass. All the noises from his particular *house* were unfamiliar. Now and again, something kicked off and the place sounded like a monstrous bear pit.

By late in the evening, the intermittent agitation fell away and solitude became guaranteed behind locked doors. It was then that Jason's first long night at Foston Hall began, frequently broken by anxious dreams. When he woke, he waved at the embedded sensor for light and looked around the room. It felt like a prison cell despite the green pastel shade of the walls. In the fug of his own bodily odours, the chill factuality of his predicament, his peculiar kind of house arrest, crept in. It sent him back under the hospital issue blue duvet, with the passage of the night marked by the regular footfall of the staff and their accompaniment of slightly jangling keys. He felt *utterly* alone.

†

After his first few, difficult and slow days at Redwood, Jason went to the staff room to speak with his care coordinator, Dr Wang. In the quiet periods between the *beep-beep-beep* alarm of his *house* and assessment meetings, he had gutted the few books on offer in the day room. Now he craved more substantial and chosen reads, if only to buffer the loss of purpose in confinement and to counter the shock of finding himself away from Poppy, from his former, settled university life, in a high-security hospital for an undetermined stay. So far, he had kept himself to himself as much as possible. Apart from his key worker, he had shared little with the other staff or residents. When he did speak with them, it was for practical reasons or about safe topics such as the weather, air temperature or the quality of the catering. His trust in others had gone. He felt cooped up in the secure hospital grounds, then Redwood Block, then a *house*, then his room and finally in himself.

The staff room was next to the day room, its door generally propped open. He looked around and caught Dr Wang's eye.

'Any chance of visiting the library?' he asked.

Dr Wang stopped typing and looked up from the computer screen. The other staff, including his named nurse, Milly, continued with their work.

'Sure,' she said. 'How about we head over there after lunch? We can also add weekly visits to your timetable.'

'That would be great,' Jason said, relieved by the prospect of seeing a fresh, new place and the chance to inspect the library's stock of books. 'Can you also ask my wife to visit?'

'You can do that yourself from the hospital phone,' Dr Wang informed him.

At that point, Milly came over with a leaflet. She handed it to him. 'This has the key information to discuss with her before she visits. It explains the security checks at reception.'

'If she visits,' Jason corrected the nurse's optimism.

'Well, let's see,' she said. 'I am sure she will. It can take time to come to terms with everything.'

Jason examined the colourful leaflet. It listed what visitors should not bring into Foston Hall. He read it carefully.

THE FOLLOWING ITEMS ARE PROHIBITED:
- *holdalls, large bags, laundry products*
- *cameras, tape recorders, mobile phones, radio scanners, smart watches, fitness trackers, laptops, iPads or other electronic items*
- *compact disks, floppy discs, USB sticks*
- *weapons, sharp or glass products, matches, lighters, safety pins, needles, brooches, pencils, pens*
- *alcohol, drugs, drinks, food, sweets, chewing gum*
- *passports, driving licence*
- *credit cards, money*

†

The library stood in the original Foston Hall building internally renovated to the required security standards. No sooner had he arrived, accompanied by Dr Wang and a male staff escort through several security gates within the grounds, than he smiled the broadest of smiles. In a wing of the capacious interior to the once grand country house stood stack after stack of books, all perfectly arranged and catalogued. Behind a large traditional oak desk sat two hospital librarians. They were welcoming, friendly and open, yet characteristically quiet. A large family portrait hung over the vacant marble fireplace. Jason examined it and read its inscription: "The Vaughan Family". A finely dressed man stood over his wife, all in white, with two sons at his side, one holding a flute, the other a telescope.

Jason turned to Dr Wang.

'The place really is a campus,' he told her.

'It is a wonderful resource,' she said tucking a fall of her dark hair behind an ear. 'It is all part of Dr Bent's vision. He wants the hospital to be less prisonlike—a *new* kind of asylum.'

As they found themselves by the poetry section, Jason could not refuse the didactic bones in his body. 'Now asylum is one hell of a word,' he explained while fingering the spines of several volumes. 'It comes from the Greek *asylos* meaning a refuge or fenced territory.'

Dr Wang was not familiar with the etymology, but showed interest in his learning anyway. 'Really? I didn't know that,' she admitted.

'We have a pretty big fence, right?'

'Yes, we do.'

Just then, Dr Bent, the architect of the new asylum, entered the library at exactly this definitional juncture. For a moment, Jason wanted to take up a conversation with him about his mission to enhance conditions for the inmates behind the high black fence at Foston Hall. Dr Bent was clearly attempting to do something positive in an otherwise dire and unyielding environment. Jason watched the medical director as he stomped to a section marked "Staff Only" behind the library counter and took down the latest version of *The Diagnostic and Statistical Manual of Mental Disorders*. He watched him searching through the large book. The psychiatrist seemed particularly engrossed, so Jason did not attempt to disturb him.

'How many books can I take out?' Jason asked Dr Wang.

'Three maximum,' she said, 'and only from the main shelves A to Z.'

'Fair enough,' said Jason, setting off to browse the collection.

†

It was a few weeks after seeing Dr Bent in the library at Foston Hall that Jason met him again. After regular sessions of Cognitive Behaviour Therapy with Dr Wang for grief trauma, and occupational therapy assessments on the opposite side of the campus to the library, Jason was next to see the medical director at his monthly clinical review at Redwood Block. Like the other residents, Jason waited in the day room until Milly, his named nurse, called him through into a generous yet windowless interview room. As he entered, he saw immediately that Dr Bent looked worn out and tired. The psychiatrist's skin had a vague, bluish hue, and he sat with the posture of a tortoise in one of several identical, light green chairs, his feet crossed at the ankles.

'Ah, good morning,' the psychiatrist managed sleepily, uncrossing his feet slowly and sitting more upright. It seemed to Jason that his movements took some effort. The word *torpid* sprang to Jason's mind. 'Please, take a seat.'

Jason sat on one of the free chairs, the familiar bike scent commanding the air. Dr Wang, Bethany Wall, the occupational therapist, and Milly were all there with their files open. Jason assumed they held information about him.

'I understand from the team that you are settling in,' said Dr Bent.

Jason nodded.

'Not easy, I know,' he offered. His voice came flatter than usual. He fidgeted with one of the holes in his temporarily unadorned ears.

'The first weeks are, well, a shock to the system.'

'Yes, indeed,' Jason confirmed, wanting a window to look out of now, a horizon to focus on.

He remained silent and Dr Bent turned his attention to Jason's named nurse who had been nonchalantly inspecting and stroking the freckles on her arm.

'Milly, have all the care plans been updated since the admission?'

'Yes,' she said, almost dropping her file. 'No meds. Psychological interventions as planned. Occupational therapy. Social worker assessments not yet completed.'

'OK, please chase up on that. Alice, how is the CBT going?'

'Jason is making good progress on the *You Deserve to Be Happy* programme,' answered the psychologist in a business-like way. Then she handed him a sheaf of papers. 'Here's a summary of scoring so far.'

Dr Bent flicked through the results, looking satisfied with the tables and graphs. 'Excellent. Thank you.'

Jason suddenly felt like a university student at a *viva* examination.

Dr Bent turned in quick succession to Bethany Wall. 'Anything to report your side? I gather Jason has been regularly attending occupational therapy.'

'Yes,' she reported, the file open on her lap, a fleck of red acrylic paint on her cheek. 'Jason has been quite taken by the clay modelling workshops, haven't you?'

Jason was pleased with how Bethany brought him into the conversation. It made him feel less of a patient. 'It's not something I ever thought of engaging in, to be honest,' he admitted. 'But very relaxing.'

'Jason has also joined the group drumming,' Bethany added, her legs folded back tightly under the chair, back straight.

Dr Bent looked suitably impressed, nodding away. 'Excellent, excellent. Very good for—'

Jason noted his hesitation.

'Depression,' he finished, his eyes dodging contact.

For a moment, Jason wondered whether the psychiatrist might need to self-prescribe group drumming. He looked afflicted by the black dog. The sparkle was not there.

'I didn't know that,' Jason told him. 'That is interesting. My own work showed how reading was as good as anything on the market for low mood.'

This got Dr Bent's attention. He looked up, squinting a little and clearly thinking, albeit slowly. 'Is that so?' he pondered. '*All* reading?'

'Not quite,' confirmed Jason. 'But there are many books that can help. Some GPs have even started giving books on prescription.'

'Instead of pills, right?'

'Yes,' confirmed Jason.

'Very interesting,' Dr Bent concluded with a nod and making a note. 'Now, have you had any visitors?'

Dr Bent's question underlined Jason's main and current fear—abandonment by Poppy.

'My wife has still not visited,' he told him.

Dr Bent's head dropped a telling notch. 'That must be difficult for you, Jason. Give her some time. She will be going through all sorts of emotions herself just now. In the meantime, would it help if you had a visit from one of our volunteers at the befriending service?'

Jason shook his head quickly, decisively. 'No, thank you. I don't want to add to the strangers in my life.'

†

It took Jason several months to get used to the residents of his particular *house* in Redwood Block and their ways. This group were there for serious albeit comparatively lighter or borderline offences compared to those in the other blocks, notably Cedar, where seriously dangerous personalities and the most famous patients lived, unlikely to be released given their unthinkable crimes. Jason's *house* was an assessment unit for possible early transfer to less-secure settings despite indefinite hospital orders applied by the courts. The patients of the *houses* in each block lived separately. Only those from the same block might meet under supervision within the various facilities at Foston Hall such as the sports hall, swimming pool, occupational therapy unit, library or multi-faith centre. Most of the time, Jason kept himself to himself on such visits, even during group drumming or other workshop activities devised by Bethany Wall and her team at occupational therapy. He only attended a minimum of exercise classes and had no time for the competitive sport on offer, chiefly basketball and five-a-side football. Nor did he partake in swimming in the new, modest pool that Dr Bent had brought to the site. He avoided all offers of religious observance, not wishing to re-enact a misguided, sacramental past. As to be expected, he gravitated to the library, where he read avidly and enjoyed conversations about literature with Dr Bent, a frequent visitor, the kindly librarians and similarly bookish patients. It was where he found the greatest comfort.

It was comfort he needed half a year into his enforced stay at Foston Hall when two pieces of sudden and devastating news magnified his growing sense of deep abandonment. First, his mother died. As if this were not bad enough, Poppy then notified him that she wanted a divorce. The legal papers arrived soon afterwards in a thick manila envelope. He should have guessed this might happen given her reluctance to visit him at Foston Hall. It hit him hard, all the same.

Dr Bent, as the Responsible Clinician or RC, gave permission for him to attend his mother's cremation under close supervision. There, he saw yet did not speak to his estranged wife, guarded by her circle of friends who all gave looks that could kill. On his return to

Foston Hall, Jason took to his bed at Redwood Block for as many hours as the staff allowed for the best part of a month. He ate and drank sparingly, crying the nights away. He had never felt as alone as he did at these times. His trust in others and in himself had been devastated. As he began to surface again, very slowly, he started to accept the new reality of his situation, repeatedly murmuring words he knew so well:

"I am—yet what I am, none cares or knows;
My friends forsake me like a memory lost."

Yet Dr Bent, Dr Wang and Milly Palmer showed they cared through their unconditional positive regard. From time to time, Dr Bent popped into the *house* in Redwood Block to check in on Jason, to see how he was managing the recent, difficult news. He would sit with him in the day room and shoot the breeze or suggest they move to an interview room as appropriate. He even suggested that they have a walk together in the grounds when he felt up to it. Jason appreciated the offer. He had developed a pallor from the prolonged indoor life. Dr Wang was also kind and thoughtful, reducing the timetable of assessments and CBT to let Jason adjust to the intense emotions brought on by the one fell swoop of losing both his mother and, it appeared, his marriage. Milly arranged for a social worker and took care of his day-to-day needs in the house. She also met with him regularly, actively listening to his pain, showing him through body mirroring as much as her words, that anyone would find these compounding events bewildering, at least initially.

35

It was a bright, beautiful day when at the far side of Foston Hall, Dr Bent made good on his suggestion of a walk and swiped his security tag to gain access through various electronic gates before leading Jason up the now famous raised ground behind the visitors' centre. Dr Wang accompanied them, as per policy. This newly landscaped slope or elevation was the core feature of Dr Bent's *wonders*. It comprised a broad, gentle mound that rose to a plateau offering the illusion of freedom and an uninterrupted view of the surrounding countryside. The grass on the raised land was wet from the overnight rain, and Dr Bent, Jason and the psychologist kept to the path lined with several abstract fibreglass sculptures designed by a local artist in consultation with a focus group of Foston Hall's patients.

'So,' said Dr Bent. 'Tell us more about your mood-busting books. It is an entirely new area for me.'

'And for me,' Dr Wang acknowledged. 'Which books can do this?'

Dr Bent walked slowly, his head dipped, though his expression was lighter than it had been in recent times. Dr Wang, as deferential as ever, hovered slightly behind the medical director.

Still fragile after his mother's death and the beginning of divorce proceedings, Jason welcomed the conversation turning to books and began a disquisition on the power of the written word. He spoke on the neurology of reading—a topic of particular interest to Dr Wang—and how books generated *textual hallucinations* that could transform the mind. Jason cut a less impressive figure than Dr Bent did as they walked across the plateau, Dr Wang in tow. Here, a large lawn area tapered away to a viewing point with attractively moulded, colourful fibreglass seats, of the kind one might expect in the gardens of a contemporary art gallery. From there, came an endless, stunning panorama of banks of trees, a shallow lake and miles of open fields. The fence preventing access to the water below remained largely invisible. The careful landscaping created a wonderful fake freedom.

'It's quite a view, isn't it?' said Dr Bent, still marvelling that the substantial funding had come through to bring such change.

'Your *wonders*, right?' said Jason.

'Yes, I suppose so,' answered Dr Bent not feeling the thrill of this description.

'Would you call this a hill?' asked Dr Wang gently.

'Well, I am not sure it would be classed as such,' answered Dr Bent. 'A rise perhaps.'

Jason trawled through his extensive, lexicon. He thought of words like *eminence, bank, height, hump, prominence, summit, hillock* and *knoll*. His long years of studying dictionaries further yielded *altitude, peak, promontory, ridge, upthrow* and more unusual tokens such as *tump, koppie, scarp, knob and glob.*

'I would call it a *tump*,' he said finally, unsolicited.

'That sounds about right,' said Dr Bent chuckling at the odd, poetic word, not knowing its meaning, and palming Dr Wang and Jason toward the colourful seating.

As they ambled along, they could see out towards the city, barely a smudge of grey in the distance. Dr Bent caught sight of the long, straight country lane down which he liked to run his bike and the corner where he would pit himself against centrifugal force to shock happy chemicals into the gaps between his brain cells. Yet today he did not feel quite so flat. He did not *need* his bike. Now, as he looked out, a heron glided down, settling at the edge of the kidney-shaped lake. Its smooth passage through the air was a natural tranquilliser, and even Jason seemed to lose himself for a moment to study the bird's eventual, dignified pose. Such a creature would never have landed in this part of the country had it not been for Dr Bent's *wonders*. As the psychiatrist examined the reflection of clouds moving briskly across the water, the whole scene reminded him that he could transcend the torpor of depression, if only briefly.

'It's lovely here,' Jason ventured ironically, enjoying the breeze. 'You don't feel locked up.'

Dr Bent nodded deeply in agreement. 'I'm glad you like it. I wanted you to see that this place is not *against* you. You are here to recover and find your way back into society.'

A period of silence followed; not the awkward kind that blighted conversation, yet one that confirmed engagement and mutual regard.

'So,' said Dr Bent, fingering the scar on his cheek, 'bring us further up to speed on these mood-busting books. Are they something we should get for the library? We have a little money left from our project funds.'

'Yes, I think so,' Jason told him. 'If you want, I can put together a list?'

'That would be great,' said Dr Bent. 'Perhaps you could even give a talk on this topic to staff and patients?'

Jason felt a spark of joy in this recognition of his knowledge and skills. 'I would be happy to do that,' he said.

'Well, that's why I like walking outside,' said Dr Bent. 'It opens up the mind to new possibilities.'

Yet Jason was not listening at this point. His head was out over the fields and trees. 'You can see for—'

Jason froze, becoming suddenly quiet and keen to scan every detail of the horizon as it became clearer what he was seeing.

'What is it?' asked Dr Bent.

Jason did not speak. He was too busy turning his head as if his eyes were behind a pair of binoculars. He could see Round Hill, lifting above the distant fields and city suburbs, much higher than the tump he stood upon, a large white cloud billowing up behind it. In sharp relief, Jason made out the locust tree, like a little black crack in the air itself. The view provoked thoughts about his twin brother and all the estrangement and abandonment in his life. For the first time in ages, the muscles of his belly juddered with the release of deep emotions. He began to cry noisily, freely, his mouth opening. He did not stop the tears. He did not wipe them. His arms hung heavily at his sides, in catharsis, in submission to the pull of gravity. Each tiny ball of grief rolled out of his head and down his face. Dr Wang turned towards him, placing a comforting hand on his heaving shoulders.

Through the tears, Jason was mumbling something.

'Sorry, Jason, I didn't catch that,' Dr Bent apologised.

'Orphan,' Jason repeated, the heels of his hands now pressed into his eyes. 'I feel like an orphan.'

†

That night, Dr Bent woke in a blurred moment, a stunned unknowing. He looked around, trying to focus, struggling to figure out what had happened. He perched naked on the hard double bed in his accommodation at Foston Hall. In a wobble of disorientation, he touched his chest and legs, breathing hard and squinting around the dark room. His depression was bad, and he suddenly regretted agreeing to give a talk to visiting dignitaries about his *wonders* later in the week. He stared out into the living room, past the low coffee table and couch, at the red standby light of the open clam of laptop. He had not managed to finish writing his speech. He got up and headed for the toilet, but as he placed one foot in front of the other, he found that his legs had parted a little from their normal trajectory. Disconcertedly, the floor had moved. Soon afterwards came a loud knock on the door and a voice.

'Doctor Bent!' It was Alice Wang. 'There's been an earthquake!'

He quickly slipped into a clean pair of Lycra leggings, grabbed one of his silk black shirts, before jamming his slightly swollen feet into his boots and opening the door.

'Hurry!' she cried, pulling at his elbow, guiding him into the corridor and towards the emergency exit. 'It was quite big. Come on!'

At first, still dazed, Dr Bent moved slowly, reluctantly. He was fiddling with his shirt buttons. Although small, Dr Wang was strong and she urged him forwards, tightly gripping his elbow.

'We have these back home in Taiwan,' she told him. 'It is best to leave the building.'

Dr Bent moved in a lumbering manner, somewhat thrilled by the new and different exposure to apparent peril. He had not experienced an earthquake before.

'You are too slow!' she chided, hitting the push bar, her olive black hair swishing and her dark eyes imploring him to get a move on.

She guided his descent. Down, down, down. Her feet barely touched the concrete steps, with Dr Bent behind, a heavier, tall, middle-aged man with a thinning fuzz of grey hair dishevelled in the nightmare rush.

They finally reached the ground floor and burst into the open air, next to his parked bike that had toppled over. He set it back upright. There was only slight scuffing that would polish out. Dr Bent felt instant relief. He looked around, half expecting some visible damage elsewhere, but there was nothing. The buildings nearby seemed intact beneath the looming cloud. Nearly all of Foston Hall's resident staff were standing out in the car park.

'Wow,' said Dr Wang. 'I didn't know you had earthquakes *here*!'

'It woke me up,' said Dr Bent, looking around at the unfamiliar scene of the hospital staff from the accommodation blocks in their various nightwear. He pushed his fingers over the dry hairs of his head and puffed, trying to clear his mind, his heart still racing from

Dr Wang's urgency. He watched everyone milling around, chatting, concerned and jumpy.

'Will it be safe to go back in?' someone asked.

'Let's wait and see,' said Dr Wang, joining the throng with Dr Bent in her wake.

'It is probably a collapsed mine,' explained Dr Sargent, securing his blue dressing gown to preserve his dignity. 'This part of Nottinghamshire is riddled with old coal mines.'

'You think one collapsed, right?' asked Dr Wang.

'Possibly,' said Tim, now looking for breaking news on his phone. 'It was a good one, though. Normally they don't cause ground motions.'

'I can't see any structural damage,' observed Dr Bent. 'So, it's probably safe to go back inside.' The notion of expiring under a pile of rubble was not particularly at odds with his mood. Besides, he had a speech to finish, and he decided he might as well get on with it now he felt so wakeful.

'Let's wait a while longer,' advised Dr Wang, placing a tender, stilling hand on his gothic arm.

36

At Foston Hall library, Jason revelled in suggesting titles for a new section on mood-busting books. Dr Bent had allocated a decent budget for this and added Jason to the regular programme of evening lectures at the library. As a result, Jason felt some of his old confidence return after the early turbulent and lonely months at the hospital. It still hurt that Poppy refused to visit him and had filed for divorce and he ached to belong again, to enfold into family. Yet, with the help of Dr Bent, Dr Wang and the other staff, he had now at least begun to express his grief for his losses and explore his feelings without turning to violence. He had started to understand, own and regret his extreme behaviour. He even penned apologetic letters to Bradley, the student he attacked, care of the vice-chancellor of NEU, and the near-decapitated undercover police officer through Inspector Mosby. Although he did not quite believe he deserved to be happy, he aimed instead at being content despite the environment. He also wanted to increase his chances of an early release to a less secure, rehabilitation unit, by being a model patient.

Sitting at the end of his bed, with his back to the wall, a small tower of library books to hand on the little desk, Jason felt as if he could be in student digs. On his lap, he had a blank notepad on which he was scribbling ideas for his talk. He lifted the floppy pen staff had provided for safety reasons and wrote a few possible titles, crossing out each in turn before landing on *Can Books Save Your Life?* He felt that would hit the mark and make his intended audience sit up and listen.

†

Dr Wang joined Dr Bent and the other psychiatrists in the canteen. The visiting dignitaries, including both the health and justice ministers, were having a tour of the facilities, led by Yvonne Cooper, Director of Estates, John Carr, Director of Finance, and Saif Ali Khan, Director of Human Resources. Dr Bent left them to it. Although he was pleased key politicians from the newly elected right-leaning government wanted to scrutinise his *wonders*, Dr Bent did not relish the brown-nosing that inevitably accompanied such events. Although his low mood was such that the idea of giving his speech proved almost overwhelming, at least he had finished writing it thanks to the earthquake. All the talk that morning had been about the seismic event that had rattled Nottinghamshire and felt as far away as Birmingham, Leicester and Manchester. News channels had started to report on the various decommissioned collieries suspected of collapse. As Dr Bent sipped his thick, black coffee, he found himself staring distractedly at the slightly twisted front teeth of Dr Wang.

'I am looking forward to your talk,' she told him, self-consciously covering her dentition with her tiny hand.

'Sorry?' asked Dr Bent homing back in.

'Your talk,' she said. 'I am looking forward to hearing it. On Cedar, right?'

'Yes, that's right,' said Dr Bent. 'Excellent.'

Dr Bent looked at her kind round face, brown eyes and little black spot above her full top lip. He broke off his deepening gaze in a turn of professional vigilance. He was surprised by a stirring of libido, something that had been absent for so long.

'You must be proud of what you have achieved,' she said. 'Since joining Foston all I hear about are your—'

'His wonders!' exclaimed Dr Sargent, interrupting with an encouraging slap of Dr Bent's drooping shoulders.

'Yes,' said Dr Wang. 'He is what we call a *jin-tou-nao*.'

'What's that?' asked Dr Sargent. 'Sorry, my Chinese is, well—all I can muster is the odd *nihao* or *xiexie*!'

'It means golden brain.'

Dr Sargent chuckled. 'Wow, that's some compliment!'

†

The tour of the hospital reached its final destination, Cedar Block, the unit that had benefited most from Dr Bent's programme of refurbishment, complete with a new albeit modest auditorium. As the dignitaries arrived through the array of electronic security checks and took up their seats, Dr Bent stood at the stylish oak lectern, sorting through his notes and checking his slides. He spotted the government ministers by the behaviour of their entourage rather than anything striking about their personhood. Each minister dressed almost identically in a dark suit and blue tie, contrasting sharply with Dr Bent's gothic dress. As he looked out at them, briefly wondering what they made of him, he doubted their tolerance. Yet each VIP seemed happy enough, picking up and leafing through the courtesy copies of his book placed on their reserved front seats.

Fittingly, the title of his talk was *The New Asylum*. He clicked the slide show icon and indicated that he was ready to speak. The noise levels in the auditorium fell away gradually and he began.

'Long before I came to Foston Hall,' he said, 'I worked in what is best described as an *old* asylum. It was frankly depressing.' He showed slides of a grand-looking Victorian institution. 'Now, in its time, it had extensive, landscaped grounds, a small farm, opportunities for manual labour and so on. Yet reforms drove out these bucolic elements, the visual retreat of trees and fields, and the institution became diminished and underfunded. A place that once had its own orchestra and theatrical programme now lacked anything uplifting. The authorities marked this diminution as progress. This is when I began researching the impact of the environment on mental health.'

Dr Bent stopped at this point and lifted his hand to the slide.

'In that institution, robbed of peaceful, creative asylum, I became depressed. I, the psychiatrist, felt low. Then one day on my rounds, I heard music. I traced it to the end of one of the gloomy corridors and found one of our patients, sitting outside the ward playing his clarinet. He played *beautifully*. This patient was one of our country's great jazz musicians and I was spellbound. I sat down next to him. Right then, I began to ask, who is recovering whom? He was my patient, but he was lifting my mood! This led to my thesis of *the new asylum* and its focus on *mutual recovery*. We all need recovering, not just our patients. We are all struggling with our mental health. We all need to be in positive, uplifting environments. Patients can contribute too. They are not broken, empty vessels. They have resources to support their communities, even here at Foston Hall.'

Dr Bent looked around the auditorium. He sensed that the staff attending were still on his side with all the changes. He clicked through a series of slides outlining the main research findings and his mission to enhance the vistas and facilities available to those deemed too dangerous to themselves or others. He argued that punitively designed high-security hospitals took away much more than the individual freedom of people with diminished capacity.

'So,' he announced, folding his notes and stepping to one side of the lectern. 'It is with great pleasure that I can reveal our latest amenity.' He clicked a remote-control button and, as if by magic, the lectern moved back into the wall and the floor on which Dr Bent stood rose into a decent-sized stage. 'I can now announce,' he said proudly, 'that from the end of this month we will have live music and theatre here at Foston Hall. In addition to welcoming established performers, some events will showcase the creative talents of our staff and patients.'

A final slide went up on the screen of what Jason Hemp called a *tump*, revealing the humane, sculpture-populated space with panoramic views despite the penal fences.

†

Dr Bent appreciated the generous applause at the end of his talk. He looked with some satisfaction at the positive demeanour of the visiting dignitaries. The right-leaning health and justice ministers were more effusive than expected and among the last to retire their clapping hands. Dr Bent felt vindicated in his ambition and the changes he had made to the outdated prison-style hospital. Yvonne Cooper, John Carr and Saif Ali Khan moved around the important guests, animated and roused by the clear success of the project, shepherding the entourage out of the auditorium, courtesy books in hand, for the final drinks reception at the newly designed café. Dr Bent indicated that he would make his way over separately, keen to find out what his colleague, Dr Wang, made of the talk. She had sat quietly at the back of the auditorium. He wondered whether she still thought of him as a *jin-tou-nao*.

Dr Bent's reluctance to join the tour and take an opportunity to connect with Dr Wang was fortuitous in not having to witness what occurred when the group left the auditorium and entered a communal area. Without any warning, one of the most notorious patients at Cedar Block breached the zone, wielding a claw hammer. He ran amok in a direct line for the clearly privileged, suit wearing bodies. The health minister quickly cowed, raising his arms to protect himself, taking a glancing blow from the weapon before the staff piled in and controlled the incident. No one else was injured, but with the minister's collar turning red and his blue tie a deep shade of purple, the alarm sounded and the block went into lockdown. Thankfully, the health minister's courtesy copy of Dr Bent's book had saved him from gross injury. The copy lay like a dead bird on the floor, a deep, lopsided dent in its skin.

By the time Dr Bent reached the scene, desperate to lend his significant expertise, the health minister was already on a stretcher, his head bandaged. His retinue stood aside, letting the medical director through.

'Is the ambulance on its way?' he asked the Cedar Block doctors, seeing that the victim was conscious yet clammy and trembling.

'Air ambulance is on the way.'

'OK, BP?'

'Falling,' one of the junior doctors informed him.

Shit, thought Dr Bent, struggling with the contrast between the calm of the lecture and this post-trauma scene. He noted the spattering of blood on the brand-new grey flooring.

'The patient?' asked Dr Bent.

'In seclusion,' his junior colleague confirmed.

'What did he use?'

'A claw hammer.'

Dr Bent's jaw dropped automatically. He swallowed hard and began to take charge of the transfer, the sound of a helicopter soon filling the air.

†

Jason had begun to nod off with the floppy pen in hand from a morning of editing his invited library talk when the alarm at Cedar Block roused him, sounding loud and repeatedly *beep-boop-beep* across the campus. This was followed soon afterwards by the increasing noise of a helicopter. Intrigued, Jason jumped up and went to the window, watching as it flew in from the south, landing on the far side of the open inner grassland of Foston Hall. The downwash from its rotors buffeted the few, thin trees nearby. Jason stood riveted by the unexpected and unexplained intrusion. He welcomed the diversion and could see quite a commotion, as people emerged from the most secure of the blocks to the north of the campus. Among them, Jason could make out the distinctive figure of Dr Bent walking alongside a stretcher, head down under the slowing rotors. He was clearly anxious, trying to get whoever lay there fed into the back of the aircraft as quickly as possible. Jason watched as Dr Bent and the others carrying the stretcher moved quickly out of the hood of the rotors, keeping their heads low. In seconds, the helicopter prepared for take-off, throttle increasing, then lifting, turning and dipping its nose at Redwood before zooming overhead, the thwop of its rotors dying with the urgency and speed of its flight.

Once the helicopter had left, Jason returned to his bed. At first, he wondered who needed to go to hospital, but soon his mind turned to more pressing and personal matters, ruminating about the coming divorce from Poppy and the ease with which his foundations and family life had disappeared. He struggled with the accumulated estrangement and loss of trust. He had concluded Poppy was the only person standing between himself and the abyss. Without her, there would only be the clinically assigned family led by Dr Bent and Dr Wang to prevent total isolation. These fears were made all the worse in the cabin fever that resulted from prolonged confinement in the *house* in Redwood Block. His anxiety and irritability grew and he slept more during the day, partly to escape the bear pit noises that often broke out. The purposeful timetable of assessments and occupation helped a little, especially visits to other parts of the campus, yet he often succumbed to a deep lassitude. This fatigue won through again and the lids of his eyes began to close. With the auditory trace of the helicopter fading, he leafed through virtual divorce papers in his mind.

37

In the aftermath of the assault on the Health Minister, the *wonders* of Dr Bent came in for harsh, relentless criticism by the authorities and in the press. The media feasted on the incident, gathering a multitude of talking heads to comment endlessly on the state of high-security hospitals and the cost to the public purse of apparently luxurious conditions at Foston Hall. In particular, they focused on the patient David Reeve, who attacked the minister and had previously killed five random strangers in a spree of utter carnage. The story broke that during the recent sweep of renovations, all part of Dr Bent's *new asylum* initiative, one of the builders had left his claw hammer behind in a wall cavity of the toilet facilities at Cedar Block. In an interview after the incident, Reeve informed staff that he found the item during an escape attempt, removing a wall panel secured with the wrong kind of screws. Frustrated by not finding a way out of the building, he replaced the panel and gladly took the hammer, concealed down his trousers and hiding it in the mattress in his room.

Dr Bent had called an emergency meeting of the staff and an immediate audit of security led by Yvonne Cooper, Director of Estates. The incident with the health minister was a significant crisis for the medical director. Although the health minister had been stabilised in hospital, for a while it seemed his life had been in jeopardy. His prominence as a leading politician made the assault press-worthy, a very public matter. Dr Bent had no choice but to introduce new blanket restrictions, including increased random searching at Cedar Block, and field the slew of questions posed to him by reporters over several days. As much as possible, he took radio interviews, where his refined voice carried better than his appearance on television. On radio, his gothic persona was inscrutable in his deep, compelling voice. His piercings did not offend. His clothing did not detract from his expertise. He felt able to account for and defend his *wonders*.

†

Dr Bent looked into the bathroom mirror, inspecting the paleness of his skin with his sharp blue eyes, dabbing the bags under them and tracing a finger over the few spidery veins in the folds of his nose. He roughly graded the yellowness of his teeth and tried to ignore the dark, poorly veneered incisor and the remaining molars full of black amalgam at the rear. He lifted the razor more slowly than usual. Psychomotor retardation, he self-diagnosed. He had spent yet another restless night ruminating on everything. While for now, in the immediate aftermath of the attack on the health minister, he had managed to hold on to his position as medical director, he struggled increasingly to accept what might happen with his *wonders*. It was the threat of losing the tump with its view of the surrounding countryside that most disturbed him. He also feared the dismantling of the new auditorium and performance space at Cedar Block, the swimming pool and even the library. With the damning reports on the incident and the right-leaning, penal approach of the government in charge, such changes loomed. The mining-induced earthquake now seemed a bad omen for the enlightened Foston Hall.

Dr Bent pulled his nose aside for the slowest of shaves. After some time, he completed the task imperfectly before casting the razor into the bin and swopping around the rings on his fingers. He moved slowly back into the lounge of his apartment and picked up one of the newspapers piled up among the books on his black couch. He read the headline "Foston Hall Hotel" and the article which listed the more famous of the hospital's "inmates". It featured an editorially chosen picture of himself in full, gothic regalia with what seemed an arrogantly elevated chin. Taken from below, the medical director appeared superior to the reader. Dr Bent dropped the paper back onto the couch. *Preserve functionality*, he coached himself and set off without pace for his daily rounds of the hospital.

†

On the library table lay several display books as Jason Hemp prepared to give his evening lecture on the mood-busting power of literature. He dressed for the part in his best and only jacket, but disappointingly, the turnout was low. There were only ten members of the general staff, Dr Bent, the librarians, and five patients from the *houses* in Redwood Block. Even so, Jason relished the opportunity to speak, to regain something of his former life. For a while, he could imagine he was back at NEU and the people in front of him, looking up from their chairs, were students at one of his university seminars.

Jason spoke for around thirty minutes, picking up the sample books and reading snippets to illustrate key points. He did not keep still, but moved back and forth, raising a finger ahead of each pertinent comment. Now and again, he lost his way and paused to regain the momentum of his ideas. He spoke in heartfelt ways about novels as the greatest repository of human consciousness. He illustrated how both prose and poetry engaged with our hopes and fears and took us to familiar and unfamiliar mental spaces.

After he closed his talk, Jason asked if any of the small audience had any questions. These were mostly about whether books could help with anger and anxiety. Jason boiled things down and gave concise answers and recommendations, flagging up particular texts now available in the new section of the library. For a moment, he felt unusually exposed and raw when asked about books to help with grief. Swallowing hard, he lifted a rather battered volume from the table and held it up for all to see. It was his own novel: *Desolation*.

Jason was disappointed not to have drawn a question from his champion, the medical director. It was only during the modest refreshments of tea and biscuits provided by the librarians that Dr Bent sidled up and asked his own question quietly and privately. He was looking particularly bedraggled in a poorly ironed long black cotton shirt over his trademark Lycra leggings and standard-issue black shoes. His hair, minus the detachable pigtail, appeared unkempt and uncombed. His chin was poorly shaved, and he gave off a fruitier than usual odour.

'Earlier, you referred to books that help with mild to moderate depression. Which books would you prescribe for *profound* or *severe* depression?' he asked.

†

The JCBs moved in quickly. In a matter of days, they removed the tump that had taken several weeks to install. Dr Bent watched the reversion of the land from the window of his apartment. First, workers removed the abstract sculptures and seating. These now lay in several yellow skips on the main car park, probably destined for a reclamation yard somewhere in Nottinghamshire. Second, the grass was sliced and rolled up for transplanting elsewhere. Third, the topsoil was removed, revealing the bone-coloured aggregates below. These returned to quarry holdings in convoys of trucks, piled high, rumbling the ground like echoes of the mining-induced earthquake. The dismantling of Dr Bent's *wonders* was like a large-scale, gross autopsy. Crestfallen, he witnessed his artificial levitation disappear. Now the patients had no highness, hoist or platform to spy the wider countryside. Foston Hall lost the shoal of land that brought hope to all inside its security fences. The only views available were those from five to six feet off the ground. The human body itself was the only swell and vantage point left in a place without outward-facing windows.

Dr Bent turned his back on the demolition and lay down on the black couch in his apartment. He tried to focus on what remained of his *wonders*, building a psychological scaffold for the coming days and weeks. He closed his eyes and walked virtually through the refurbished visitors centre, new café and staff canteen, and well-stocked library. He viewed the heated swimming pool, the new auditorium and performance space at Cedar Block. Already he hoped that the nascent hospital *ensemble* that Bethany Wall and the music therapists had brought together might perform on the high-tech stage at Cedar in the lead up to Christmas. He had in mind something by Edward Elgar. After all, the great composer had once been bandmaster at Powick Lunatic Asylum in Worcester, something that Dr Bent noted in his book *The New Asylum*. "*Elgar thought to cheer the inmates at Powick through the playing of the asylum band, made up of staff members,*" he wrote. "*They performed quadrilles and polkas, bringing everyone to their dancing feet. What was good then should be good now.*"

Yet, just as easily as Dr Bent firmed up the value of his *wonders*, his mind quickly turned to his blasted, dissolved family. Like the absent spaces of the old coalmine that so recently collapsed and shook Nottinghamshire, Dr Bent's missing family undermined his identity and his trust in anyone, shaking any certainty in the future. Even the excising of the tump reminded him of the removal of his parents and the notion and value of parenthood. It was a trigger, an associated trauma. *No wonder I have avoided having children*, he thought. He suspected that his subconscious had long suppressed any desire to procreate, keeping him *safely* alone and chronically lonely. He also thought long and hard about the abandonment by his siblings and the betrayal of brotherly and sisterly love. He mused what Dr Gluck would make of the viewing mound he had created for the patients. *How would she read this? Perhaps she might interpret it as a maternal bump rather than a tump, a wish fulfilment, a landscaped pregnancy.*

†

Dr Bent doubted the ex-lecturer's claim that books could work on severe depression as effectively as other treatments. To his mind, the research on bibliotherapy looked rather flimsy. He wanted scientific evaluations of active ingredients and mechanisms, not anecdotes. Yet Dr Bent decided to put them to his own personal test for now. Just as Florence Nightingale subjected prayer to scientific evaluation, he pursued the truth of Jason's claims. The removal of the new escarpment that followed the incident with the hammer and the loss of the key feature of his *wonders* left him entertaining ultimate ways of relieving his low mood. If the power of books was to be tested, then his own case offered a challenge.

Alone in his apartment, Dr Bent picked up each of the books that Jason suggested might lift even the most deep-seated melancholy. He unfolded the odd creased corner and read the opening section of the first book to get the gist of it. The plodding knowledge that reading would change little or nothing in his mood seeped in. After all, severe depression made it particularly difficult to focus, to concentrate. Despite this, Dr Bent forced himself to read in a painfully slow way the author's hook. *Nothing*. Dr Bent put the book down and laboured to pick up the next one, with only the slightest inclination to read on. Again, *nothing*. Two more fell subject to his lethargic gaze and dismal reading. The final volume was a collection of poetry instead of prose. He riffled through it, stopping in the middle to read a few lines before his hands and the volume closed inwards like a defensive oyster:

"Away, melancholy,
Away with it, let it go.
Are not the trees green,
The earth as green?
Does not the wind blow,
Fire leap and the river flow?
Away melancholy."

†

It was crisp snow, but only as deep as the warm cheeseburger between Dr Bent's teeth. He sat in the new canteen at Foston Hall, looking out on the whitened campus. With winter moving in, his feelings of aloneness deepened. The dark end of each year brought his mood lower and lower. The incident with the health minister had found its way to prolonged media coverage and a storm of protests about the easy life of criminals in forensic hospitals. This did not feature how the patients at Foston Hall were *people* with mental health problems who needed protection for their own safety as much as for the public. Each patient was someone's father, mother, son, daughter, brother or sister.

With a poor appetite, Dr Bent left half of the cheeseburger and most of the fries on his plate. He badly needed a lift and knew that meant blowing away the cobwebs on his Harley, so he headed back to his accommodation, garbed up in leathers and threw his leg over the motorbike. Despite the light covering of snow, he guessed the roads would be passable. Besides, he embraced the possibility of skidding into oblivion. As the bike edged forward, leaving a patch of clear tarmac behind, the tyres slipped with Dr Bent's keen use of the throttle. He was impatient. He just wanted to blow depression from his head. He knew the wintry air would chill his body despite the leathers and deerskin gloves. If anything, it would invigorate him.

As he raced around the Nottinghamshire countryside, he repeatedly considered crashing the bike at high speed. With hedges blurring and the icy slush and oncoming cars inviting oblivion, he grew tempted to break the safe margin of the tarmac. In the fog of his goggles, he felt lured to the unyielding dark trunks of trees that lined some of the fields. Yet something held him back. As much as he felt compelled to deviate from life, to step out of its torment in one crunching blow, he kept the bike on course to return to Foston Hall. However, the ride had little impact on his mood. Often, he gained verve from the precarious speed, but today he felt as empty as the bike's fuel tank. Back inside his apartment, he sat in silence on the black couch and rearranged the rings on his fingers. Now the plain silver band returned to his left thumb joined by the silver tourmaline ring on the middle finger. The pewter serpent ring moved onto the little finger of his right hand. These tiny acts reassured him. *I am here*, he told himself. *I can still do things. It is all worth it.* With these thoughts, he got back up on his feet and went outside, pen and paper in hand.

38

Finally, after months of abandonment, Poppy visited Foston Hall. Dr Wang had brokered the meeting through the social worker and accompanied Jason to the plush visitors centre to one side of the main reception. He had spent the early morning at the *house* in Redwood Block getting ready, shaving twice with his battery shaver, trimming the fuzz of his sideburns, polishing his teeth, scraping his tongue and dabbing what remained of his hair into some order. He even yanked the age-telling hairs from his nostrils and dressed in his best shirt, trousers and jacket. When he stood in front of the safety mirror in his room, Jason looked at the kind of man who taught at university. He looked fashionably academic. Even though a near-divorced husband, he had the sensation of going on a date, a feeling that he had not experienced in a very long time. The illusion compelled him to do a second tongue check as if the possibility of intimacy lay ahead.

The atmosphere in the little meeting room was understandably tense given the divorce proceedings in full swing. For the first time since his mother's funeral, Jason looked across the table at his wife. She was clearly nervous in the unfamiliar and disconcerting environment of Foston Hall. She had none of her friends with her for support. Jason saw how her face flushed and her lips gathered tightly, expecting adversity. A buff envelope lay in front of her on the table, which Jason assumed held more legal papers for review or signing. Jason was pleased to see that she had made an effort with her appearance. Her dark hair hung nicely trimmed. She had done her nails and lashes. Her pretty, blue dress defined the body he had once known so well, yet now was strange to him.

Dr Wang broke the ice. 'Thank you for coming today,' she said warmly, reaching across to shake Poppy's hand before placing herself alongside Jason, her posture open and accepting. 'I know it is not easy to visit us here at Foston Hall, especially in this weather. There is a lot of stigma attached to the place, but you are very welcome. Coffee?' She pointed to a takeaway tray of three paper-cup coffees in the middle of the table.

'Thank you,' said Poppy.

Dr Wang handed out the drinks, sugar sachets and plastic stirrers. 'Now, as agreed,' the psychologist said, 'I will stay in the room for this first meeting, OK?'

Poppy nodded and looked out of the window at the snow-covered and prisonlike interior of Foston Hall.

Jason breathed deeply, ashamed that his violent behaviour brought such precaution. He had never posed a risk to Poppy, *ever*. His head dropped with the thought that he was officially a risk to others. He looked up again, directly into his wife's eyes. She, however, looked away, unable to accept his gaze, swallowing hard, clearly uncomfortable. As Jason tried not to stare, remaining as calm and relaxed as possible, he hoped to rekindle something with Poppy. Yet he knew that the chances of this were slight. Her abandonment of him for many months had made that clear. Yet it was the hope that was killing him.

'Are you still at Glo-Bright's?' was all he could muster.

'Yes,' she told him, but then fell silent.

Dr Wang encouraged Poppy to share her thoughts, say a little about how she had coped alone in the months since Jason came to Foston Hall.

'It has been the loneliest time of my life,' she admitted.

Jason lowered his head as she said this, imagining her battling on with her new job at the laundry and coming back to an empty home with only Juju to fill the gap once her girlfriends ended their flush of stopovers.

Poppy continued to account for these desperate times and how with the sudden death of Mrs Hemp, Jason's mother, she felt so lost, angry and sad, disorientated even.

'Is that when you decided to pursue a divorce?' asked Jason gently.

'I did not see an alternative,' she told him looking up at him, not deflecting eye contact. 'I still—'

There was hesitation.

Jason suddenly began to hope again. 'You still?'

'I still—'

Jason watched his wife's tears well up. Dr Wang handed her a box of tissues.

In the silence that followed, Jason pictured Poppy in her solicitor's office, dishing up the dirt, assigning blame. He imagined piles of bank, mortgage and pension documents passing between them. He expected to lose any claim to assets they had built together. As he waited for Poppy's silence to break, Jason could only hope in the magic, the power of words: "For better or worse, in sickness and in health, to love and to cherish, till death do us part."

Poppy said no more, clearly struggling to speak, emotional. Dr Wang offered the box of tissues a second time. Jason watched her crying on the other side of the table, her tears falling and darkening the buff envelope under her crumpled face. She looked up at him briefly, questioningly, her mascara smudged in the corners of her eyes. He felt awful. He reviewed the reality of his situation. He had let her down big time. She had been a constant in his life, the one person apart from his mother that he could trust. With an indefinite hospital order, he understood why she wanted a divorce. If he were in her shoes, he would want that too. *Life has to go on.* There was every reason for her to bring yet more legal papers to sign for the divorce.

Now she pushed the envelope into the middle of the table, her hand trembling heavily, and asked to leave. She looked across at Jason as she got to her feet and moved in the same direction as Dr Wang who opened the door to show her through to reception. Jason saw his whole marriage in his wife's dull green eyes, all the good times, the hard knocks and the home they created. He saw Juju by the fire, the big bed where they shared their bodies and the decoration of books. He pictured the mole on the inside of her leg. He saw her angry face when she threw his doorstop of a thesis through the air. He felt her hand on his shoulder when she last served him toast and marmalade. He saw her anguished face when the police took him away in handcuffs. Yet the last image he had as she left the room, comforted by the psychologist, was of Poppy dressed in white, looking up lovingly into his eyes, a single pink confetti horseshoe caught on the tip of her nose. He had kissed it into his mouth and swallowed it down for good luck.

†

The day had started normally for Dr Tim Sargent. In the staff accommodation just outside the secure perimeter fence of Foston Hall, he showered, dressed and finished his standard breakfast of porridge and grapes. He noted little change in the slight crack in the ceiling plaster from the collapse of the old coalmine near Ollerton. The news reports identified it as the biggest of its kind with minor structural damage across Nottinghamshire. That and the major incident on Cedar Block cast a dual, ominous note. Of particular concern to Dr Sargent was the wellbeing of Dr Bent who had clearly suffered with the loss of face from the reversal of the key element of his *wonders*. He had seen the despair on the medical director's face when the JCBs returned to remove the landscaped whaleback that afforded patients and staff a decent view of the surrounding fields.

The mound had been the centrepiece of his dream of a *new asylum*, one that challenged the perception of forensic care. Dr Sargent knew that shame was the enemy at the heart of his colleague's past. Men would rather die than speak about their own shame and emotional pain. He also knew the risk of suicide increased as people either headed towards the pit of depression or came out of it. It was at these points, when people had the energy to do something, *to act*, that the risk increased. Furthermore, the arrival of winter and darker nights could inspire the use of the delete button.

It was with Dr Bent in mind that Dr Sargent set out to work, wearing his tweed jacket and removable tie. As he headed down the main stairwell to the ground floor, he inspected the walls for signs of structural damage from the earthquake before stepping out into the car park.

He knew immediately something was wrong. Dr Bent never left his bike in this part of the staff accommodation area. More than that, he could see a damp envelope marked *Tim*, wilting over the wet fuel tank of the Harley. Inside he found the bike's keys and a short note.

This not working for me anymore. Your turn, Bent.

The note set Dr Sargent into a panic. He quickly shoved it and the keys into his coat pocket before racing around to the adjoining building and up the stairs to his colleague's apartment. He jumped several steps at a time to reach the corridor on the top floor. In less than a minute, breathlessly, he was pounding on his door. When there was no answer, he tried the knob and found the flat curiously unlocked. He burst inside, shouting out repeatedly for Dr Bent, for his friend, checking each of the rooms, expecting to find him doing the longest and final stare in the bathtub, on his bed or couch, amidst copies of his papers and books, an arm lolling to the floor. Yet there was no sign of him.

He raced over to the main reception at Foston Hall and ran into Dr Wang, who had just finished escorting Jason back to Redwood.

She could see the panic in his eyes.

'What's going on?' she asked.

'Have you seen Dr Bent?'

'No, is he OK?'

Dr Sargent stopped to think, sensitive to the predicament. After all, Dr Bent was the medical director of Foston Hall. He did not want to risk a full-on emergency search for his superior that might prove unfounded and humiliating.

'Look,' he explained. 'You probably know, well, it is no secret that Dr Bent suffers from depression.'

'Yes,' said Dr Wang. 'It is common knowledge, right?'

'I guess so, but I am worried about him. Yet I don't want to raise an alarm unnecessarily.'

'Sure, OK, I get you,' answered the psychologist calmly. 'What do you know?'

Dr Sargent quickly explained the sudden gifting of the bike, how he had left it with the keys and note outside *his* accommodation. He pulled the note from his pocket for Dr Wang to read.

'It's a goodbye, right?'

Dr Wang read it, yet was less concrete about the meaning of Dr Bent's gesture. She noted the familiarity with which he signed his name without his title. She had learned that educated Englishmen liked to use their surnames and drop forenames.

'It could be,' she agreed. 'People do that before—'

'Exactly,' managed Dr Sargent finding it hard despite his professional training to retain a calm demeanour. 'They give things away!'

'What should we do?'

'Grab your coat,' Dr Sargent suggested. 'Let's visit the campus and see if he is there first. If we cannot locate him, we will have to raise a general alarm.'

Dr Wang took her winter coat and fur Cossack hat from her

office and they both entered the snowy interior of Foston Hall.

†

Jason sat at the end of his bed, staring out of the window at the whitened campus, seeing Dr Wang, dressed in her long black coat and Cossack hat, moving in haste away from Redwood Block, almost breaking into a run towards the other residential blocks, accompanied by a man he did not recognise. The man wore a tweed jacket and seemed poorly dressed for the weather. The pair occasionally lost their footing in the snow as they progressed, but managed to keep upright. As they approached each of the security gates in the fences subdividing the interior ground of Foston Hall, they looked impatient, repeatedly waving their security cards at the sensor to clear the lock and then pushing through with great urgency. There were no alarms sounding so Jason wondered what had made this couple so rushed in their movements. As they receded to little black sticks in front of Cedar Block, Jason turned back to the buff envelope on his lap.

The day before, security had checked the documents and handed them back to Jason resealed after his short meeting with Poppy in the visiting centre. They had not raised an eyebrow about what lay inside, and he dreaded the correspondence from her solicitor so much that he left the envelope unopened overnight. Now he inspected it, noting the dark yellow frank for Disney and Slater, Solicitors. The famous name threw him. He read his own name and home address on the white label and turned the envelope over. The resealed flap had been box stamped Foston Hall and signed and dated as opened by security. Jason began to unpick the tape, feeling increasingly tense, breathing fast and shallow.

As the seal loosened, Jason anticipated papers dealing with the ownership of the family home, his bank accounts and pension holdings. He expected an aggressive letter from the solicitor demanding all his assets for their client, Poppy. He lifted the top of the stapled bundle of papers, wincing, looking askance as he drew it partway from the envelope. He noted the quality headed paper, then the date, then the opening salvo:

> *Dear Dr Jason Hemp,*
> *Our client: Mrs Poppy Hemp*
> *We are working on behalf of the above client in divorce proceedings. We request that you—*

Jason struggled to read the first paragraph of the cover letter, his eyes flicking back and forth in a panic, trying to identify which of his assets would remain once the lawyers had feasted upon his broken life. He saw the words "property" and "funds", but could not decipher other collocated words and phrases. He felt immediately nauseous, vomiting slightly into his mouth and dropping the envelope to the floor. He got up quickly to spit out the sour and acidic sample of his breakfast into the fixed, partitioned toilet in the corner of his room, flushing it away and refreshing his mouth with a squirt of toothpaste. When he returned to the bed, picked up the envelope and fully drew out the paper-clipped bundle of documents, he found them ripped in two. This scared and puzzled Jason. He had no recollection of tearing the papers in half and suddenly doubted his own mind, one that had him eating cake as a sacrament of revenge, checking scalps in the street, assaulting a student and holding down the squirming head of an undercover police officer on a railway line. He dug inside the envelope and found a small hand-written card. On the front was a silver wedding bell. Inside, Poppy had written to him in glittery ink.

> *Jason,*
> *I made my promises to you and cannot change them now.*

For better or worse, you are my husband. You are not the husband I married, but you are still the one I chose. I will be waiting for you when you come out. I have cancelled the request for a divorce (see enclosed). I will try to visit you when my anxiety allows.

Poppy x

†

On their fraught tour of the hospital, Dr Sargent and Dr Wang had cleared the newly refurbished café and staff canteen and each of the five blocks before crashing through the doors of the library, creating quite a stir, breaking the stately silence. Breathless and agitated, they did not stop to explain their behaviour to the librarians, quickly and methodically checking every corridor of bookshelves. They had half-expected to find him there. It was one of his favourite haunts, but with no sign of him, Dr Sargent and Dr Wang continued their desperate circuit of the grounds. The librarians simply looked at each other and shrugged.

In the head office, the boardroom stood empty and the administration staff had no inkling of the medical director's whereabouts. There was nothing down in his calendar. Similarly, he was not at occupational therapy. The urgency with which they asked Bethany Wall if he were in the building shocked her, causing her to squeeze a ball of clay so tightly that it oozed between her pale fingers. Dr Sargent and Dr Wang did not stay to explain, but quickly raced away, out and through another security gate, waving their ID cards, before taking the long path to the multifaith centre. They caught up with the impeccably attired Reverend Markle, busy adjusting the dog collar of his royal blue clerical shirt in the shared space for prayer, reflection and meditation. He frowned heavily at Dr Sargent's breathless question about Dr Bent.

'No, I haven't seen him. Is he OK?' he asked, looking at Dr Wang's open coat and Cossack hat in hand.

'We don't know,' was all Dr Wang answered as she quickly turned on her heel to follow her colleague, not wishing to delay their search.

Reverend Markle's hand lay frozen on his dog collar as he watched the door to the shared space flap back to stillness.

Dr Sargent and Dr Wang headed for the sports hall. A game of basketball was underway. They interrupted it, urgently beckoning to the staff and asking if they had seen the medical director. None of them had.

'Is he OK?' asked one of the fitness trainers, who did not receive an answer as Dr Sargent and Dr Wang peeled away to continue their search.

The staff members shrugged at each other before restarting the game by dropping the ball between two of the patients.

The fears of Dr Sargent and the psychologist intensified as they approached the nearby annexe to the sports hall with its modest, heated swimming pool. They looked at each other at the entrance, acknowledging the possibility of what they might see. After all, the pool stood empty and unattended at that time of day and it did not take much imagination to picture Dr Bent's floating body like some dark starfish, blasted by pills and alcohol or simply bleeding out. Dr Wang broke the hesitation and led the way, with Dr Sargent staggering forward, psychologically preparing himself for what he might see. He need not have worried. Mercifully, the facility was empty and silent. The water was as still and unmarked as agar jelly in a petri dish.

By now, Dr Sargent and Dr Wang had checked every main facility and as planned, headed for the main reception to raise the alarm.

Yet, as they passed across the snow-covered campus and through two further security checkpoints, they saw a familiar figure through the large window of the café. By the table with the free newspapers, they could see the gothic figure of the medical director, back upright on the faux leather banquette, and, importantly, very much alive. Dr

Sargent and Dr Wang were clearly relieved. They welled up, breathing heavily from the exertion of the search. Sighing deeply, they looked at each other, shaking their heads.

'Shit,' said Dr Sargent, temporarily out of sorts and without his usual self-censoring.

'You can say that again,' Dr Wang concurred.

They both waited until their discombobulation eased, before continuing into the café.

There, Dr Bent was thumbing through a book, a steaming Americano within reach.

He looked up and frowned. 'You both look as if you have seen a ghost.'

'I thought we might,' burst out Tim Sargent angrily, clenched fists on hips, tight-faced. 'How could you expect the gift of the bike to be anything other than a signal of dire intent?' he complained, his voice raised. 'I really thought you had finally decided to head out of the system!'

Dr Bent's mouth opened in apology as he saw Dr Sargent's red face battling to contain his indignation. He also caught Dr Wang's sweaty brow and dishevelled hair. He noted the vexation and real concern in her eyes.

Dr Bent immediately regretted his lack of awareness. At the time, he did not consider his gesture in this way. He took a deep, stalling breath. He avoided his colleagues' eyes, looking up instead at the ceiling. He knew he needed to account for his spontaneous offer of the bike.

'The Harley wasn't helping anymore,' he began. 'I thought you might get more joy out of it than me.'

Dr Bent could see Dr Sargent was unimpressed by this erratic and unexpected generosity. Now Dr Bent suddenly wondered how much his unthinking act had been a kind of rehearsal for the real thing, for the big goodbye. Although he was oddly grateful to see the anxiety his actions inspired, he immediately felt contrite about leaving such an ill-considered note and keys for his colleague. Dr Sargent had been such a good friend after all, and it was understandable that he read more into the offer than Dr Bent intended. Raising a hand to attract the attention of James the barista the now mortified medical director called for drinks for his fellow workers at his expense.

Dr Sargent and Dr Wang finally sat down around the table and slowly the mood lightened. Neither of them wanted to increase their dear colleague's emotional burden.

As the additional coffees arrived, Dr Bent picked up the book lying on the table.

'One of Jason Hemp's mood-busting books,' he explained. 'I am testing it out.'

Then, with his head tilted to one side, surrounded by members of the only "family" he knew, Dr Bent held the book to his nose, like a delicate flower, opened it and took in the *biblichor*, the vanilla scent of lignin from the ageing paper, adhesive and ink. *How fitting that books smell better as they decompose*, he thought. In an instant, he felt a little more hopeful. He flipped through the volume of poetry and found something that seemed to make complete and utter sense. With Dr Wang sitting closer than usual on the banquette, her leg tantalisingly close, he traced the famous lines of poetry with his finger. He thought of reading aloud, yet held back for courtesy.

"They fuck you up, your mum and dad.
They may not mean to, but they do."

After a long sigh, Dr Bent mumbled his own revision of Philip Larkin's words. 'They mean to, and they do.'

It was several seconds before he came out of his thoughts. Then, manufacturing a smile, he closed the book, put it down, rubbed the slight dents in his fingers devoid of rings, and turned to his companions.

'So...'